Richard Parkes

Horse Painter

Provet Publishing

Horse Painter
© Richard Parkes 2006
Published by Provet Limited
ISBN 978-1-905241-01-9
EAN 9781905241019

All rights reserved. No part of this publication may be reproduced, stored in a retrieval system or transmitted, in any form or by any means, electronic, mechanical, photocopying, recording or otherwise, without the written permission of the copyright holder, or in accordance with the provisions of the Copyright Act 1956 (as amended) or under the terms of any licence permitting limited copying issued by the Copyright Licensing Authority, 33-34 Alfred Place, London WC1E 7DP

Any person who commits any unauthorised act in relation to this publication may be liable to criminal prosecution and civil claims for damages.

The CIP catalogue record for this book is available from the British Library.

The main characters and events depicted in this story are entirely fictitious and any similarity to real events or people, alive or dead, is purely coincidental.

Book cover illustration from an original painting by outstanding American artist Carol Ratafia. Visit www.provet.co.uk/ratafia or www.ratafiastudios.com to see more of her work.
The Zulu Girl poem by Roy Campbell reproduced with permission of Jonathan Ball Publishers Jeppestown South Africa.

For full details of all Provet titles please write to :

Provet Limited
Suite 1, The Slade Building
The Square
Gillingham
Dorset
SP8 4AR
United Kingdom

Printed in the United Kingdom

This is for my Heidi

About the Author

Born in South Africa, Richard moved to the United Kingdom in the 1970s to complete a veterinary education at Cambridge. His great affection for both his native and adoptive countries colours the pages of this book.

Richard now lives with his Danish wife, Heidi, in the market-town of Alresford in Hampshire

Acknowledgements

I'd like to thank Mike Davies for some incisive editing, and especially for taking a chance on a new writer.

Thanks also to Sheila Hicks and Clive Chidley: two wonderful friends who did all the hard work, slogging through the first draft. My everlasting gratitude to you both, and hey, guys ...we did it!

I can't forget Olly Kent who paid me the ultimate compliment of saying he finished the final pages sitting on the loo. Reading it, he emphasised!
I miss you, O.

Catherine Venn typed this at quite phenomenal speed and offered masses of enthusiastic encouragement.

Richard Parkes, 2006

1

Plettenberg Bay, Eastern Cape, December 1957

THE alarm clock wouldn't let up. A vibrating, tinny clanging that was horribly persistent, clawing at the boy's dreams. He jerked half-awake and groaned in protest, long arms and legs tangled up all of a muddle like a disorganised stick insect. Matt had certainly been asleep, but not completely, not like he'd be any other morning at this hour. Some awareness of occasion and time had hovered in his sub-conscious and held back the deepest most enveloping sleep that comes in those early hours way before dawn. Fully awake suddenly - and with a start - Matt flicked back the sheet and blanket, and before he really knew it, was on his feet and padding across a cold floor to the yammering machine to silence it. Once Matt had learnt to put the kitchen alarm clock on the other side of the room - on the mantelpiece - he'd never overslept. Nobody would. The loud, cheap clatter from the Zobo demanded attention, and the four or five steps to get across to it and get his finger onto the slide at the back to turn it off meant he simply had to get up. It was necessary. It didn't matter how warm and comfortable his bed was, it was necessary – bloody vital after the last time.

The last time it was also when he had to get up early for fishing and borrowing his mother's travelling clock - the little A-frame one she kept by her bedside - had seemed a good idea at the time. But he'd slept right through the plaintive and sensibly pitched buzzing from that lady's thing until his father, Jake, crashing into his room like a cyclone gone berserk, had grabbed Matt by his pyjama-top and dragged him half-awake and scared wholly witless, out of the bed and onto his feet. 'Get up when the damn thing rings,' was bawled into his face. Hoo boy. Before he could collect his senses his father had been gone, slamming the door behind him leaving Matt on weak, stumbly legs that would hardly work. As he'd turned to switch off the alarm clock his pyjamas had snagged on his leg, warm and wet. He'd pissed himself. Hoo shit; thank God his father hadn't noticed.

But that was then and this was now, and here he was up out of bed, the alarm off, and safe. Matt rubbed hard into his eye sockets with the heels of his hands and then blinked a few times to clear his befuddled senses. He frisked his short blonde crew-cut hair to wake his head up and moved to the window. There he parted the Venetian blinds with thumb and finger and peered out at the night sky. Masses of stars – good. Raising the blinds, he hooked the cord and cranked the brass fitting of the side window, opening it a little way. On tiptoe he hissed down into the darkness 'Piet?'

By way of answer a form uncoiled itself from beside the front door steps and coughed. The rasp and flare of a match-strike was followed by the acrid smell of cheap tobacco wafting up to the window. Piet's nuggety, caramel features appeared in a soft glow as the ghillie sucked on his home-roll siggie, looking up at the window.

'Looks nice, hey?' said Matt, and without waiting for an answer, closed the window and set about lighting the Calor gas lamp next to his bed. Enveloped in the hiss and glow of the gaslight, Matt dragged clothes onto a spare frame that was all bone and tendon, springy as a pullet. He double-tied the shoelaces on his rope-soled shoes and, taking the long lamp handle in hand, opened the door to his bedroom. In the corridor the hiss of the lamp intensified sharply, and as he reached the stairs going down to the kitchen he lifted the handle, careful not to bump the bottom of the gas canister on the treads which would have set the glass rattling. The milk from the old Electrolux fridge in his mother's blue and white carbolic kitchen was ice-cold, cold enough to set his teeth ouch on edge. He made a face, sucking his cheeks in, and then put the glass down on the kitchen table, oblivious to the perfection of a semicircle of pasteurised white sketched over his lip. The two craggy homemade rusks from the old biscuit tin hadn't any such decent defences. Matt wolfed them down and checked his watch. He'd have to hurry. It was all a matter of time now and, as Matt's father had told him God knows how many times, time and tide waits for no man.

There had been a waiting time though, this last week as the south-easter had blown its unremitting hardest, full-force direct at the front windows of the house for four long days. The simple white clap-boarded holiday home with its black eaves was old, experienced and solid, but the gusts and swirls of the seeking wind tore at it nevertheless, making the long panes of glass in from the patio shudder and the corrugated iron roof squeak and groan in protest like a live thing. An annoying, irritating, even unsettling thing after a while, so Matt had disappeared for most of the time into the fishing room in the cellar next to the front door steps. Down there he'd felt safer; more content, and spent hours making up traces and checking his kit over and over again. He'd fixed up an aerial for the radio and had kept up with the weather reports, silently mouthing the weatherman's geographic divisions of the coastline like a mantra, 'Sir Lowry's Pass to Plettenberg Bay and Plettenberg Bay to Port St. Johns.'

With yesterday's radio report that the wind would drop, Matt's preparations had taken on a degree of urgency that brought a wry smile to his mother Hope's face. There were cold sausages in their white fat to be scouted from the fridge, sandwiches to be made, rusks to be bagged and the faded, green canvas haversack with its curled salt-water stains arrived on the kitchen table to be packed. A thermos flask for coffee, milked and sweetened, a plastic water bottle for the Oros, silver foil screws of salt and pepper, and then - as always - the reminder from his mother not to forget the apples and oranges. Matt stuffed two of each into the haversack to please her. He did love his mum, but she was always going on about the vitamins. Matt found it difficult to enthuse about something he couldn't see – or even smell or taste for that matter. He'd had it all about the Holy Trinity in Divinity lessons at school. Father, Son and Holy Ghost. Not to be seen, but important, like all the vitamins, the B and the complex and A and C and all the others, things you were just supposed to take on trust. He'd tucked his little heresy away. Actually, he didn't mind the apples if they were hard and crisp: he enjoyed slices dipped in salt, and peeling a green Granny Smith properly ... difficult, man, but it gave him a chance to show how ace he was with his Swiss Army knife. Getting the apple-skin off in one long coil without breaking it ... not anything like as easy as it looked. He never peeled the oranges though, the stuff in the orange skin burnt the nicks ouch on his fingers - the nicks that came from fishing-line burns when you cast and hadn't dipped the reel first, and salt-water, and hangnails. Instead, he kneaded the fat oranges until they were soft and pulpy, made a hole about sixpence size, and then sucked out all the warm sweet juice. It made his lips smart all right, and tingle, but Jees, nothing like as bad as those nicks on his fingers ... that was really sore if the juice got in.

By the time Matt carefully pulled the front door closed on the latch, Piet, his young coloured ghillie, was already up on the road with the rods, gaff and bags, waiting for their lift to Robberg. As he went past his parent's bedroom window, Matt gave it an involuntary glance. His mother and his father in there, or as Piet called him, Baas Blackjack. Piet also ghillied for an old guy called Jack Ellis up the road and, of course, with Jack Ellis' hair bleached white as chalk he could only be Baas Witjack. Baas Witjack and

Baas Blackjack, the black for Matt's father's shock of hair that fell angled across his brow slanted and straight and just took your eye even if you didn't want it to.

Everyone hated blackjacks, Matt couldn't think of anyone who didn't – those weeds you understand - and blackjacks were terrible weeds, so his mum said. Black seeds on them like exclamation marks with tiny sticky-out spikes on one end that stuck to anything, especially your school socks. Matt made his father one of those in his head, a bad black thing always sticking around and he was glad there was nothing black about him. Not anywhere. His hair, everything; it was from his mum. He didn't want any of his father in him, nothing, niks, and if there had to be, he kept the thought of it distant, as far away as possible. Blackjack - oo gats, imagine if he ever found out about the name, even if it was Piet who had made it up. There'd be consequences his father would say, that was one of his favourite sayings, there'll be consequences, and never nice ones either, his dad's consequences weren't ever nice.

By the time he got up to the road where Piet was standing with the rods Matt could feel the morning chill. Fresh enough for him to rub at his arms furiously through his old blue jersey to try and warm up, but it was pure anticipation of the day that hopped him from one foot to the other. A big drip threatened to come down his nose and no handkerchief, damn it, so he had to sniff really hard - it was the cold, it was still freezing cold and he remembered someone saying something about it always getting colder just before sun-up.

'Cold, hey?' Matt shot at Piet. Piet nodded. More a sideways cock of the head, really; a half-yes, a yes meaning cold for you maybe but not for me and Piet still didn't say anything. Piet was really snoep with words – thrifty, his mum called it. And didn't feel the cold ever it seemed to Matt - or stones either, he could walk barefoot just about anywhere.

They were near the beach, only a three-minute walk down the hill and Matt reckoned that if he couldn't hear the waves from up here the sea must be dead, dead quiet. Man, he could hardly wait, it had to be perfect for fishing. But they had to wait; they had to wait for Gideon, who said he'd pick them up at quarter to four, and with his nose on the go Matt hoped he wouldn't be much longer. Gideon Lidman was an old friend to Matt's family – the Stevens – in fact Matt couldn't remember a time he hadn't known him. He'd tried to call him Sir or Mr. Lidman as his father would have liked, but Gideon had just shaken his head and said no, his first name would do just fine.

Gideon was on time. The yellow lights of his old pick-up, or bakkie as everyone called them, dipped a salute as he braked and then gently skidded to a stop on the gravel on the side of the road. Piet loaded the gear and himself onto the open back whilst Matt wrestled the reluctant passenger door open and then plonked himself down beside the bearded occupant.

'Morning,' he chirped, 'looks great, hey?'

Gideon grunted non-committedly. Matt didn't know whether that was a yes or no. Piet banged on the cab roof to signal he was set and the tackle was secured, and Gideon set off. The bakkie growled through the gears as it slowly picked up speed down the hill.

'Gideon, your one light's wonky.'

'Ja, man, the thing's loose,' came the reply and thereafter the unlikely pair lapsed into silence. Unlike some of the uncomfortable silences at home, this was a companionable one, one that they'd often used before. Matt hadn't had time to learn more than a couple of useful things in life; but one was that old people - men especially, were not at their best first thing in the morning. Gideon was like that, a bit like his old bakkie in fact, he took time warming up. Matt smiled to himself at the thought, but anyway, it suited him fine 'cause he didn't have to think of things to say and could start to look for owls in the headlights. The best spot was as soon as they got off the tar onto the dirt that was Robberg Road; there were usually some there. First they had to go clomp, clomp, clomp over the concrete slabs of the Piesang River Bridge and then up past a whole lot of houses to get out onto the airport road before Gideon could make the turn left onto the gravel. The sound of the tyres on the gravel was always the thing that did it for Matt, the thing that wound him up, got his pulse going, the signal that they were really on their way. Better even than going to the circus. Gideon turned left eventually and Matt soon picked out the outline of an owl just beyond the far reaches of the headlights steadily quartering the verge ahead of them, a wraith-like shadow in the shadows. He pointed. Gideon gave a nod and grunted.

'A good omen.'

Hoo boy, Matt thought, there'll be a story about that for sure.

2

Gideon loved Mythology. Matt called them his stories about the olden days 'cause he just stumbled on that ruddy word every single time. He could see it there in his head – Mythology - simple to see, but before he could get it out, it made a sudden detour around his back teeth and his tongue went big on him. Matt especially liked the story about Adamastor, a sea giant, Gideon said, who lived way out in the ocean and who was cross at being thrown out of Greece ages and ages ago – as bad as being expelled from school, Matt supposed. Grumpy old Adamastor who never forgot or forgave, always out there, always the hell-in, and forever churning and whipping the sea up massively. That's what Gideon said. That's what Gideon said was what made the old Portuguese explorers call it Cape of Storms; the bit round Cape Town anyway, Cabo Tormentosa. He got Gideon to repeat it and did the same to himself over and over until he'd memorised it. Much longer as a word – two words actually, but much easier to remember and especially to say than Mythology. He wanted it for his history project at school on Portugal. It'd look good. He could roll out Cabo Tormentosa on top of his tongue quite nicely after a while.

Once the owl disappeared out of the bakkie headlights it was just another ten minutes on the road and they were very nearly there, speeding along on the last downhill before the Robberg car park. They were going quite fast now – for the bakkie anyway, then it was up the hill going slower and slower, Gideon having to change gear twice to get up the steepest bit near the top. Fourth to third was straight up - easy, but getting from third to second gear meant he had to double-declutch, carefully threading the gear stick down across and down again. He got it into second, but that put the gearbox into a real cadenza with the stick poking out the top vibrating like mad and Matt knew any minute it would jump out. Gideon stuck his hand onto the gear stick to keep it in. Sometimes, when things were more relaxed - not serious like this morning, Gideon even let Matt do the gear changing. But not today, Gideon wasn't thinking of that sort of thing now. He swung the bakkie left in the car park and stopped near the footpath with the sign next door. The sign was a big one: no fires allowed, no dogs allowed, no collecting of bait, all that stuff: now it was just a black blodge in front of them in the dark. Illegible. The bakkie doors squeaked and were banged shut one after the other. Piet jumped off the back and the two youngsters sorted and organised their kit whilst Gideon found two rocks to put behind the back wheels. The handbrake, Matt thought, must be past it. In the same state as the wonky light, but this wasn't the time to be making any smart-alec remarks. Not now, not unless he wanted to get it in the neck. Arching their backs the fishermen ... the man, the boys, slung their knapsacks in place, ready to go. The smell of the bush around them was astonishingly powerful. Battered by the south-easter, the bruised leaves were bleeding their oils, perfuming the air, heady and aromatic, even to Gideon who was used to strong man's medicine like Navy Cut and Dimple Haig. To Matt it was piercingly intense, pungent as incense. He switched his flashlight on and off, on and off, waiting. He wanted to go.

'Ready then?' Gideon asked and without waiting for any reply took the footpath, leading off with purpose. He'd noticed – as had the others – that there were already three other cars in the car park when they'd arrived. Other little groups of ghillies and men who'd be trudging down the path ahead of them. That meant competition on The Ledge for fishing space. Time to go. Matt followed Gideon with Piet bringing up the rear with the rods and gaff bound in a sheaf over his shoulder. The bobbing torchlights were swallowed by the bush instantly and the car park was all silence and darkness again.

Going to Robberg was a big thing for a twelve-year-old fisherman, and after a four day south-easter it was a big thing for a fisherman of any age. Translated from the Afrikaans, Robberg means Seal Mountain, and if it's true that there aren't that many seals on the peninsula any more, it is most certainly still a mountain – a red sandstone mountain half a mile across and three miles long stretching straight out to sea, the entire western arm of Plettenberg Bay. A third of the way out from the base where they'd just left the bakkie, a giant had taken a huge bite out of the top of Robberg. That was Matt's imagination at work, and - thanks to Gideon - he was especially good on giants. He thought that now he could understand their fantastic powers, and he could imagine they did the mad, crazy sort of things that giants do, the impossible things … like taking bites out of mountains. They called this hole in the mountain The Gap – what else? And the crumbs that had fallen from the giant's gargantuan mouthful had crashed down the side of the mountain into the sea as huge, round boulders. Looking down from high up in The Gap almost vertically into the water below and seeing the boulders at that great distance made them rounder and smaller, so people called this place Kanonkoolgat, a sort of Cannonball Alley.

The bush was close around them all the way to The Gap. The only sounds Matt heard were those of his own breathing, of foot striking rock or sliding on gravel and the occasional clinking behind him from Piet's rods on the overhead branches. Gideon walked fast like any lean man but he had walked with the boys lots of times and knew they were easily fit enough. The only time he glanced back was when he heard sole slip on rock – just to check they were okay. They went through The Gap making good time, and then up onto the long climb out on the other side. By the time they reached the top, nearly up to the highest part of Robberg, they were puffing, but here there was a faint breeze. Matt stripped his jersey as this quiet zephyr laced with herb essences brushed over him, as pungent as the coastal bush round the car park, but quite different in a way, sweeter, warm and particular. The bush looked different, too. Here it was flatter and on the sand dunes there were pale lavender-coloured, flat-leafed plants that spread in irregular clumps like jigsaw pieces. You'd never expect to find sand dunes high up like this, but here they were. Walking across the Sahara, which is what his family all called this sandy knoll, Matt saw how his shoes crunched the thin crust of sand formed by the dew, obscurely gratified that he sunk in rather less than old Gideon trudging up ahead of him. The sky was lightening now, a thin easing of the dark on the horizon, a promise of the day ahead but telling them to hurry. Piet slipped past them both, his shuffling catswalk seemingly effortless, going ahead to get the rods ready. It was easier to see to walk at last, and Matt jogged a few strides to get level with Gideon.

'Do you think Cinderella might be there?' he piped.

Gideon grunted. ' I certainly hope not!'

That was the thing about the Point, thought Gideon, you could come out here fishing with it looking sweet and beautiful as God's breath, and if Cinderella was on patrol you'd end up with a cornucopia of bugger all except sunburn and disappointment. The legendary Cinderella: what a ridiculous name for a monster shark the size of a submarine who, if she was there today or any other day, would scare away every living fish for miles.

'You saw her here last time didn't you?'

'We most certainly did.'

He'd come out here with Piet a month back and seen that astonishing fin rear out of the water, impossibly tall with the vast black shadow beneath. They'd both stood in awe gawking as time stopped for the few seconds it took for the fin to slide slowly below the surface again. Piet had hawked up, spat viciously in disgust at the sight and so kissed the day dead.

'Die plek's nou leeg,' he'd pronounced with finality – the place was now empty.

'Bogger all, baas,' he'd said - which needs no translation - and starting packing the rods for home.

'I've never seen her here after the south-easter,' Gideon said - as much to cheer himself up as Matt, and, of course, it was the south-easter they all were counting on one way or another. The pumping gales that had come in straight over the ocean for the last few days would have driven the game fish closer and closer to shore and kept them hungry, the waves and currents making hunting impossible. That was the theory anyway.

They were past the dunes now and back into Indian file again but it was a bit easier to see to walk at last. Gideon picked up the pace and Matt chanted quietly to himself, in time to his footsteps:

> *'A sailor went to sea you see,*
> *to see what he could see,*
> *and all he could see you see,*
> *was a packet of C to C you see.'*

Gideon's decrepit old fishing hat on the salt and pepper head of hair was bobbing up and down in front of him and Matt was starting on the sailor and the sea again when a sudden crashing in the bush right next to him just about gave him a heart attack. As he swung his torch at the sound he knew what it was, a buck breaking away – maybe even a leopard if you believed the rumours. Either way, probably as scared as he was, but he'd seen nothing except empty bush, just felt his heart pounding high up in his chest. A gulp on a dry mouth and then following on again as Gideon led off down the path, and there it was suddenly ... the Point – Rainbows End.

3

There was just enough light to see Whale Rock a little way offshore from the Point; a white blur of water foaming over the top of the sunken reef. They bore to the left to reach the flatter rocks of The Ledge where Piet was busy with the rods, but it was the black sea under a crimson breaking dawn that they all watched intently; the sea and especially the swell. They were an unlikely bunch, this threesome, perched on a slender tongue-tip of Africa with the ocean running deep before them, and the white boy too young perhaps for all this, but Matt's companions were taciturn, watchful people and on that Ledge he could not have been in safer hands.

And the signs were as good as good gets, with time, tide and circumstance all rolled up into one fantastic, tantalising maybe, and as the first true light broke onto a gentle swell sweeping The Ledge, a small forest of rods were ready to test the waters. This was serious business. The Ledge was crowded and Matt had to be careful, especially as his fishing fever was at hot pitch, and that, he knew, meant nasty things like overwinds. He also cast cack-handed, over his left shoulder, always bringing his rod and line close to any other conventional right-hander who might be standing there. This had happened to him once before – not here – but it had resulted in a nasty clash of rods and a fearful tangle of lines ... and the swearing, he hadn't forgotten the swearing. Some hairy-back Dutchman letting fly at him with a torrent of unmentionables: horrible black words most of which he'd never even heard before much less knew the meaning of. He had to force himself to stop and listen to Gideon as he tried to scamper past him on the way down to the water's edge.

'Watch the water, sonny, and don't try and cast too far,'

Gideon growled, then Matt was gone flying from rock to rock like a klipspringer.

They were all spinning now in the half light, casting out metal lures armed with a treble hook, whipping their rods forward and down, each man watching his spinner snaking out over the dark waters, then falling; each man drawing it in below the water's surface, tempting the game fish to strike on the curling, glinting lure. Matt had three casts before he felt the drag on his line and brought the rod up with a sharp pull suddenly feeling the fish fighting the spoon and the adrenaline surge spiking his brain like cocaine. First thing, early like this, it would be elf but it could be bonito and if someone somewhere along the line started with their hoarse, rough shouting you'd know they were into serious business with leervis or yellowtail. These were elf and the slanting early rays of the sun glinted on the twisting dancing fish being landed one after the other by the row of intense fishermen. These runs were always short, lucky if they lasted until just past sun-up, so it was a case of make haste. By the time the run had petered out, Matt had four good size elf and a smaller one in the live-bait bucket anchored in one of the pools. Gideon had seven and Piet three, including a monster of about five pounds.

There was a brief respite as they broke for breakfast, but it was little more than a hurried re-fuelling affair of a cup of coffee and more rusks. Everyone just wanted to get on with it and Piet helped Matt swap his spinner for live bait tackle. The 20lb line was threaded through the heavy pyramid sinker and then tied to a swivel leading onto a thick nylon trace ending in a stubby but wide stainless steel hook. Piet retrieved the small elf from the live bait bucket and Matt tried not to make a face as the ghillie buried the hook deep through the back, the tip emerging just in front of the dorsal fin. Matt's rod was tailored to his size which meant the slender rod shivered and bent alarmingly under the weight of lead and the wriggling elf as Piet made his way to the water's edge. Casting this out required skill, so the ghillie set his feet carefully and then made a long slow swing with the whole contraption. They watched as the bait and sinker arced up and out swinging round each other on a lazy trapeze, the elf's twisting body catching and reflecting the light in blinks of silver. Finally, it fell with a resounding thwack on the shimmering water and was dragged under. Piet spent some time setting the tension and waiting for the pyramid to sink and catch on the sandy bottom. He then freed the line on the reel and fled back and up to the boy waiting behind him.

'Kom _n vis, kom _n vis,' the ghillie muttered, calling the fish in. Piet clicked the reel and, with a quick pull on the line, tested the drag before handing the rod over. Matt freed the line but kept the spool braked with the thumb of his right hand. His left hand cradled the rod, thumb and forefinger gently enveloping the green nylon line. They were after leervis or yellowtail now, but live bait would also tempt scavenging shark and there were plenty of them about here. This technique of fishing is perhaps the most thrilling of all – certainly to Matt. Real grown-up stuff. Leervis have no scales, just a leathery skin covering the streamlined body and a sinuous black lateral line running down each flank like a careless Picasso doodle. They are cunning these leervis, beauty and brains in an express bullet, and catching them with rod and line needs skill and the sort of patience that you'd be pushed to find in a twelve-year-old boy. And patience didn't come easily to Matt either. He was always busy, busy on the rocks; forever reeling in, checking his bait and casting out again, trying somewhere different and it exasperated his father – hugely, for some reason. 'You have to keep the bloody hook in the water to catch something, son', Jake would shout at Matt repeatedly, the bloody hook in that telling everyone within earshot how bloody annoyed he was at having to repeat himself all the bloody time. But Matt did learn about patience eventually - in part because of his father, yes, but mainly because he had to, wanted to ... for leervis. You see, leervis taking live bait isn't your average bank-robber's smash and grab, not a fast-food snack, but a stealing surreptitious feeding by stealth, a fastidious eating habit that suits their elegant looks to a tee somehow. Taking their prey gently in the mouth, they first scale the small fish with rows of fine teeth as they swim and striking now only pulls the bait from the mouth. What the angler needs now is exactly the patience Matt had to learn: the long agonising wait until the bait is swallowed deep into the craw.

Gideon sat on the rocks above the boy so he could keep an eye on him. The line from his heavier rod lay some ten or twelve yards further out in the water than Matt's, and to the left, so their line wouldn't cross. Fumbling in his pocket, he drew out his pipe and packed it one-handed from a pouch, lit it and drew heavily until it was ready to tamp and slow burn. After the coffee the heavy aromatic smoke tasted particularly good and he savoured the moment with the sun now warming the chill from his bones. He had caught at least one leervis every year since his early retirement and he didn't intend this year to be any different. The boy still had to catch his first and Gideon planned to be there for that red-letter day.

Piet had been gone for nearly an hour, disappearing over the Point to the western side with the small rod, a bag of stinking red bait and the live-bait bucket – an awkward shin-barking thing to carry, especially when it was full of sea water and small fish. He'd try Kleinvisvangplek, a spot just around the corner for live bait. Gideon saw Matt suddenly tense over his rod and drop the tip slowly.

'Anything?' he said quickly. Matt didn't turn around, his

intensity focused on the rod and reel.

'I think I had a knock ... Ja, another one' ... a pause, then 'Yep, he's taking it, I've got a run!' Gideon watched as the rod tip gently rose up and down in answer to an unseen force taking the line out into deep water. Taking up slack in his own line he was at the boy's side in a few strides, watching the line empty off the spool at a faster and faster rate. Then it slowed, and then stopped.

'He's gone,' muttered the boy despondently.

Gideon removed the pipe from the side of his mouth, 'No man, wait ... wait, give him a chance.'

The rod bounced again twice, alive again suddenly, and the line under Matt's thumb started to peel off again, but this time at a much slower rate.

'Should I strike, Gideon, should I strike?'

Gideon palmed the boy's shoulder to calm him a little, such was the high trembling excitement in the voice.

'Three runs, Matt, remember what I've told you, three runs.'

The spool slowly crept to a halt again and they both waited in awful suspense.

'Yes, yes,' Matt whispered as his rod was bounced again and the line unwound even further down the spool.

'Okay, Matt, click over, reel in quickly and when he's tight on the line, hit him hard!'

Matt clicked over to lock the spool, started to reel in furiously, and when the line sprang suddenly from the water, the tension scattering droplets along its length, struck as hard as his young body would allow. He repeated this twice – reel down strike up, reel down strike up, and on the third strike kept the rod high. Gideon's hand hovered near the star shaped drag under the reel handle and gave it a rapid quarter anti-clockwise turn as he saw the rod pulled down and the boy give an involuntary half step forward.

'I'm in!' Matt shouted.

'You've got him, Matt, give him line, give him line!'

With the boy leaning hard back on the rod, they watched the nylon slowly peeling off the spool with a tortured, protesting sound. The rod bucked and dipped violently as the fish fought hard somewhere under the water. Finally the spool stopped and the fish was held. Gideon narrowed his eyes against the glare and tried to see where the line cut into the water. He found it and reckoned the fish some twenty or twenty five yards out. They had a good chance if they could tire him out in deep water, and as the boy started to pump and reel in, Gideon told him to stop and just hold the fish. He'd noticed the butt of the rod digging deep into the boy's abdomen, and loosening his own bucket, tied it quickly around the boy's waist. There weren't enough holes so he just threaded it through the buckle and tied it back on itself. With both of them holding the rod, they manoeuvred the butt into the leather cup. Bloody awkward. Just as the boy took the strain again, the rod dipped once more and the fish took more line. Not as long a run as the first, but the boy began to grimace as his thin arms tired.

'Matt, just straighten your arms and hold, boy – just take the strain – don't pull against him, he's too big for you.'

With the secured butt acting as fulcrum and the boy now just leaning back, Gideon could see he was getting the measure of the fight, even if, so far, it was only a stalemate. He reeled his own bait and line in so he wouldn't foul Matt's line. Whatever it was, it was showing real stamina, so probably not a shark unless it was a big one. This could be the day, but there was still plenty to do, and the tricky part was still to come. Two other fishermen nearby also reeled in and sat to watch the battle. The boy was young and that rod so small – a fight to savour. Piet materialised at Matt's elbow with the long gaff in hand. His usually impassive features had been transformed into undisguised glee as he watched Matt do battle.

'Bring him, baasie, bring him!'

Matt flashed a grin at Piet and then started to pump and reel as the fish gave way.

Gideon shouted down at Piet.

'Put that gaff in die water, Piet, otherwise he'll jump when he sees it!'

Gideon had seen many good fish lost at the gaff as desperate, beleaguered fish, seeing the huge hook approach, gave a final convulsive shudder that shed hook from mouth. Then there was the swell that washes across the Ledge from right to left. As each swell passes, the water behind it drops and churns over razor sharp mussel beds below. There wasn't a big swell today but Gideon knew he would have to try and get the boy first to get the fish's nose up so it couldn't plunge and then to bring it the few final yards on the crest of a swell. Unless he could do this, there wasn't the ghost of a chance of landing it. As the fish neared the Ledge its weight would fall more and more on the rod, and if the water fell away, completely so. The light rod wouldn't be up to it and the rocks with their razor-edged armour of mussels would be waiting below for a line stretched close to breaking point. Piet was in position with the gaff hook lying just under the water, peering into the swirling water. There was a flash of silver and he turned and shouted back, his voice charged.

'It's a leerie, it's a big one – a bloody big one!'

Gideon took closer order, shouting at the boy, 'keep it up, keep it up!' and Matt strained at the rod, desperately trying to keep the tip as high as he could. The fish was becoming heavier and heavier but fortune – or perhaps Adamastor - favoured him with a pregnant swell and the rod swung back bringing the leervis to the surface and the waiting gaff. Piet snatched twice, with the second strike bringing the bamboo gaff alive in his hands. Feet wide apart he swiftly manhandled the fish up onto the rocks to a chorus of whoops and cries from everyone. With the weight suddenly off the rod, Matt stumbled back, almost falling over before regaining his feet, which now felt very rubbery indeed. Without taking his eyes off the fish, he clattered the rod down on the rocks with shaky hands and made his way over to see his prize catch.

'Twenty pounds, I reckon.' Gideon said, smiling down at Matt's flushed face. Piet knelt beside the gasping fish, cut its throat and sliced the abdomen to gut it. Matt watched the body quiver and flap, the blood splatter, and the gills stretch for water in desperate reflex as it died.

'Nice and deep, baasie,' commented Piet in satisfaction as he followed the thick nylon trace down the throat to where the hook lay embedded in flesh. Piet disengaged the hook, checked the trace for damage and opened the half-moon lid on top of the live bait bucket lying half submerged in a pool behind him. He took out a streepie, hooked it up and cast out again for Matt before returning to finish the gutting and stow the leervis in a cool spot. Gideon also cast out and made his way over to Matt who made an odd wry face as Gideon sat next to him.

'How do you feel, young fella?' Gideon chuckled as he felt for his pipe. 'Your first leerie.'

Matt seemed too choked for any coherency for a second, a crazy mixture of exhilaration and regret churning inside him. He lifted his rod up just shy of his head and shook it briefly - just once, what he'd done was beating at his brain.

'Hoo boy!' was all he could manage, shaking his head slowly and then a laughing cry of sheer exhilaration bubbled up and out of him and he had to stand. And up it came again like a geyser and up went Matt's rod over his head, square on, brandished and shaken, shaken, shaken. And Gideon couldn't help himself either throwing back his head and joining in as they laughed their mad laughs out at the face of the sea.

4

There were no more days together at Robberg that summer. The weather was awful: capricious in the extreme with no settled spells to plan expeditions to Stilbaai in the west or Tsitsikamma to the east – places they'd talked about fishing together. Matt had contented himself with his favourite early morning spot at Doodval on Beacon Island under the wing of the hotel, and spent the remaining afternoons, as often as not, on the Lookout rocks, fishing off the front. The days slipped seamlessly by and suddenly it was time to take the Penn reels off the rods, grease the nipples and pack them in their boxes in the red tin trunk in the cellar. Something of Matt went in there too. Then the rods threaded into their sleeves to hibernate, the older ones into cloth, the newer ones into plastic, and all of them racked up together on hooks under the cellar roof - a sad old business. Next it was the bait that had to come out of the deep freeze which Piet took, together with a bottle of Old Brown sherry and a pack of provisions that Hope had made up for his family.

'Bye my baasie, next time it's a geelstert, my baasie – a yellowtail for sure!'

Quite a little speech for Piet – so very economical with words usually, but a double dop of sherry, pay, and a bonus from Hope had made him positively expansive. He wrung Matt's little hand, turned on his heels and disappeared out the gate trailing a tuneless whistle of pure contentment.

On his last afternoon Gideon had suggested a walk on Lookout beach down to the Keerbooms river mouth, a spot Matt knew was good for pansy shells. The sea was exceptionally calm, the wave crests little more than soft-serve ice cream curls that slopped and sighed running out in sheets of mirrored glass towards them. And good for walking, too, with the tide well out and the sand flat and hard under their bare feet.

'I wish I could take it with me, Gideon. I hate leaving here, especially when the weather's nice again.'

Gideon looked across at the bare footed boy. So like little urchin Oliver with that look of undisguised hunger and ache for it clear on his face. Open as a fresh canvas.

'And leave nothing for poor us, you mean?' he answered.

'You know what I mean.'

Gideon knew very well what he meant.

They walked a few strides, 'Well, you'll have to carry on with your drawing then, won't you, Matt?' said Gideon, 'or even better - learn to paint; then you'd have something to remind you of all this.'

Matt darted ahead and chased up two seagulls that had been minding their own business and then waited for Gideon to catch up.

'Like that painting in your bedroom? That's of the beach.'

'Yes, this beach actually,' answered Gideon, 'I painted it about five years ago.'

'You painted it?'

Matt stopped, dumbfounded. Gideon smiled with a mock-hurt expression furrowing his brow.

'I'm not just a pretty face, you know!'

Matt made a face to show he was impressed. They walked on in silence for a while, Matt thinking that Gideon didn't have a pretty face either; it was a friendly face, even if a lot of it was hidden underneath his beard. When Gideon smiled his eyes kind of twinkled and went crinkly in the corners with lots of what his mum called laughter lines. But laughters could be so different: the tinkling bell laughter that was his mum's, the rough laughter that came from his dad and his mates when they were braaing and drinking, and Gideon's ... well, it came from deep inside and you couldn't help it, you wanted to laugh straight back at him.

'We'll have a go with the paints next time you come down,' Gideon said. 'You know your mum has shown me some of your pencil sketches – they're good, you have a natural talent there, so you'll have a sort of head start anyway.'

Matt nodded. Natural talent. Gideon said lots of things like that but getting his dad to say something nice and really posh like 'natural talent', well the cows would have to come home first. Back from the Point and Robberg that day, when he'd lifted the sack off the back of the bakkie with Piet and dumped it on the lawn at home, everyone had crowded round while he slit the string at the top. Just as he slid the leervis out of the hessian sack his dad had walked up. 'Managed to get one at last, I see,' he'd said and then nudged it with the toe of his shoe, quite hard, like it was a dog poo on the lawn or something. Jees! It had spoiled everything forever.

Something caught his eye and Matt pointed out at the waves, 'look – porpoises!' He ran off to stand ankle deep in the surf, hands cupped either side of his face to sharpen his vision, glorying at the balletic shapes in their twos and threes effortlessly surfing the first line of breakers.

Gideon watched the boy standing in the shallows, reflecting that he would miss Matt's company a great deal – and Hope's too of course – but that last was a minefield that needed to be skipped over very quickly ... as ever. Picking at scabs – a bad idea.

It had taken quite a while to get under the boy's quiet reserve, but now that he was trusted (he supposed – and he supposed correctly) Matt had opened up, sometimes even become quite chatty, and full of quirky, original observations that frequently had him chuckling. And all with a complete lack of any side that appealed to him ... greatly, if he was honest. Not that Matt was any sort of perfect miniature man; far from it. The boy was all twelve-year-old wickedness in all important respects including the ability to deliver a particularly evil cushion creeper ('silent but violent, hey Gideon?'), and (once he'd swallowed enough air) his pièce de résistance, a wonderfully resonating 'Stereophonic Radiogram' baritone talking burp. Even those he'd miss, Gideon decided; even the body gas, but being without company wasn't going to be too difficult either. He was a solitary rather than a lonely man – an art he was practised in – and there were distractions: the two horses he had in training in Port Elizabeth which he travelled to see running whenever he could, and the yearly winter visit to the Highveld to take advantage of the crisp, high and dry martini climate and see his sister and husband in Witkoppen on the outskirts of Johannesburg. This gave him an excuse to visit the Stevens. He usually took Matt off to the Zoo. But last time he'd taken him to the War Museum where Matt had spent most of the time in the tiny submarine, climbing down the conning tower into the unbelievably cramped quarters. Gideon had been reminded of his long-held opinion about submariners – a completely different breed.

Except for not finding any pansy shells, their beach walk to the river mouth was perfect, or would have been if it wasn't for meeting Jack Ellis and his plodding labrador on the way back. Matt had Mr. Ellis mentally pegged as old Witjack, Piet's alternate employer.

'How's the fishing been?' Jack Ellis started straight in with his horrible singsong voice. 'I hear you were out at the Point with this young fella after the south-easter.'

Matt knew Gideon hated both sight and sound of Mr. Ellis beyond reason: an ou witkop skinnerbek he'd called him once, a terrible gossip; something Gideon said was an unforgivable vice in a man. Matt could see Gideon's eyebrows bunch in irritation but before he could reply, Mr. Ellis was off again in his piping whine that was all at odds with six foot two of string bean and a white topknot.

'A big garrick, they tell me – twenty-five pounds. Hell of a thing for a youngster!' He patted Matt on the head like a puppy.

Oo gats, two big mistakes by Mr. Ellis in one sentence, thought Matt. It was only people from Natal who called leervis, garrick, and as with Mr. Ellis they weren't liked much. Of course, neither were the Vaalies who flooded down on holiday from Jo'burg in December every year; but they didn't pretend they could fish and had pots of money they cheerfully spent like water which meant tolerance over Christmas while the beaches heaved and the locals sat Kings in their Counting Houses counting out their Money. The Banana Boys from Natal were plain foreign trash. Even the rich ones, the sugar cane farmers, were tight with money and slated roundly in every high street shop all the way down to Monks. They called leervis, garrick, they called elf, shad, and they fished with antiquated centre-pin coffee grinders, casting sideways of all things, with a ridiculous sort of underarm heave.

Gideon shook his head and sighed.

'Eighteen pounds, Ellis. Plenty big enough.'

That was the other mistake, thought Matt.

'If you say so, Gideon. If you say so.'

Gideon stuck his hands in his pockets and looked at his feet. After a couple of uncomfortable seconds Jack Ellis took the hint, offered an unconvincing, 'well, it'll be cheerio, then', and called to his dog who was trying to complete a wholly inelegant crap on the sand. Ellis stumped off and Gideon scowled at his back and the world in general muttering, 'everyone's nose in everyone else's business as per bloody usual!'

'You going to pick up that turd, Ellis?' Gideon shouted after him and then shook his head, sighing in weary resignation now.

'Bloody incestuous, this place; and exaggerating all hell out of it as usual.'

Matt though that incestuous meant doing it with your sister so he didn't understand that bit. But the rest he did.

'But that's fishing stories, isn't it, Gideon, exaggerwhatevering? Making things up. It's allowed if someone else does it, isn't it?' The word was as difficult as Mythology.

As they walked up towards the Lookout rocks Gideon laughed, acknowledging Matt's point with a wave, his usual humour restored.

'You wouldn't even mind horrid old Ellis around all day if you could stay on here, would you, Matt?'

Matt nodded. No, he really wouldn't.

Mind you, thought Gideon, at least the wretched Ellis had shown some interest, some enthusiasm, about Matt's leervis. He couldn't for the life of him work Jake Stevens out. Was he being crass on the day or was he just plain insensitive? The comment, managed to get one at last, I see, and the dismissive tone: all so unnecessary and … unpleasant. He'd noticed that Matt had never talked about the day or his fish since, and if he himself could still taste the sourness of Jake's sauce then hard to imagine what the boy must feel. What Gideon took as respect – and sadly, probably fear, too, he realised – was apparent in the distance he could see that the boy put between himself and his father: the distance of a speak only if you're spoken to dutiful silence, and the other distance, the one you measure in inches.

Gideon was right about the fear, but he was wrong about the respect. Matt didn't respect his father; he loathed him. Loathed him bitterly and instinctively and hated himself for doing it, too. To his knowledge he'd only really upset his mother once; and that was when he'd said it out loud.

'I hate him!'

Matt couldn't even remember what for now, but his mother's response had been shocked and instantaneous.

'Don't ever speak about your father like that. It's jolly well ... unnatural. You're not to, Matt, not ever, ever, ever again!'

Unnatural was bad, then. Very, very bad. The worst. A crime if his mother's red cheeks and tight lips had been anything to go by, so Matt had kept it all to himself as his black secret ever since. He'd tried wishing it away, praying it away, even writing it on a bit of paper and blowing it up in a home-made bottle bomb, and sometimes it almost went away, and just then his dad would go and do something ... like his toe with the leervis.

5

'How much further, mum?' Matt asked from the back of the car, folding the page corner of his Jock of the Bushveld and putting the book down. He meant to Colesburg, their usual overnight stop on the way back to Jo'burg. Matt was bored stiff by all the scorching miles they'd travelled through the Karoo for what seemed like all day.

Hope turned her head a little, looking at Jake.

'What do you think, darling, about another hour?'

Jake nodded and Matt subsided back into his seat, watching as his mother trailed her hand across the top of the front seat resting her fingers lightly on her husband's shoulder.

Matt looked away out of the window. Not that anything was very different out there, he thought gloomily: the same flatter than flat scrubland, occasional kopjies with their sawn-off tops dotted around, and every now and again the inevitable uitspan next to the road - Roads Department picnic spots, all virtually identical with their three or four sad pepper trees, lousy concrete bench and table, and a 44 gallon drum attached to a pole with VULLIS – RUBBISH painted in large stencilled letters on the side.

'You still reading that book?'

His father was speaking to him.

'Yup, the bit about the baboon on the pole. You know, at the store when the chain's too short and Jock gets him.'

His dad had been in quite a good mood all day, but hadn't had to keep order in the back of the car for once. Matt's older brothers – his very much older brothers, Sam and Teddy - were staying on in Plett for a few more days. They'd usually be in the thick of things by now, bored stiff like he was and seeing who could give the best lame-arm punches, or in a tickling fight with snorts and grappling and giggles and misdirected elbows and knees that always ended up in Matt's direction - but he still missed them.

'You know how they used to catch the baboons on your mother's farm?' Jake's eyes searched for Matt in the rear-view mirror.

'No?'

Hope slid her hand off Jake's shoulder and clasped it firmly in her lap. Why did she have the feeling something not very nice was coming? Experience, that's why – and that note in his voice she hated.

'Well,' he started with relish, 'first they used to get this big pumpkin, O.K.? And cut a hole in the top – you know, where the stem comes out – just big enough for a baboon to get his hand in … juust big enough. Then they'd scrape out some of the insides, put some comb honey in, and stick the whole thing in the mielie field.' Jake gave a cackle … ' and along comes old Bogom baboon and thinks it's Christmas. First it's the finger in licking away and then it's in with the whole hand to grab the comb which is when the farmer arrives and all hell breaks loose.'

Jake beat on the steering wheel in delight. 'The baboon's too mean and thick to let go of the comb, see? So he's off, dragging this big pumpkin along which gives the farmer time for an easy gut-shot.'

'My father did no such thing!' Hope protested.

Jake waved her words away. 'And you know what they do when they're gut-shot? Well, I'll tell you. The dumb bastards get knocked over off course, POW!!' Jake made a rolling gesture with his hand, 'then up they get, hand out of the bloody pumpkin at last and start looking for the hole.' Jake looked down with a 'duh' expression, scrabbling with his finger where his belly button would be. 'And pull their derms out!! Looking for this damn thing that's hit them. How dumb is that? Pulling their guts out of the hole, looking for the bloody bullet.'

'Hahaaa!'

One last blasting guffaw and another beat on the steering wheel while these images of poor Bogom settled like unwelcome guests. Matt looked as though he'd been eating lemons and his mother's eyes were shut tight, her lips pursed in disgust.

'There's another way you can get rid of the buggers, too.'

O'miGod: fascination loomed and he couldn't help it, Matt was all ears.

'You catch one of them in one of those big leopard traps. I saw it once, down at Boven, Christ it was funny. The blokes down there got him - this baboon, in this cage-trap, see, and chucked a whole lot of white paint over him 'til he was white, white. I mean white all over, top to toe. Then they wait until the whatchacallit, the troop, comes back in the afternoon and let him go.'

Jake hooted with laughter, hardly able to go on.

'Man oh man – haha - you gotta see it. The baboon pisses off quick, fssst … like shit off a shovel, and these other baboons see this white thing coming, I mean they shit themselves, this thing coming like a ghost, straight at them, galloping full bore.'

'PANDE - BLOODY - MONIUM!' Jake gave two guttural bogom bogom barks.

'And the whole troop is off, high-tailing it, scared shitless, which only makes old whitey go even faster trying to catch up. So they go faster, so whitey's into overdrive. Man, those baboons they never came back!' Jake was wiping away tears of laughter.

'They're probably still running away from the poor bugger!'

Hope seethed inside; for God's sake, her father was the last person who'd be – what did he call it? – gut shooting baboons – ever! Those stories sounded rubbish, anyway; or perhaps Herman Charles Bosman, but she did know exactly where Jake's contempt for baboons came from, oh yes.

That weekend about eight months after their marriage when they were down visiting on her dad's farm in Thaba Nchu, Jake would just not leave Cousin alone. There was a spooky – almost macabre – intensity in his fascination with the farm's tame baboon. Slow and old by then – or seemingly, Cousin had been found years before as a pathetic little bundle attached to his mother's still warm carcass – dead from nobody knew what – and Hope had raised him more or less by herself, complete with nappies and a clinging presence that would not tolerate her out of his sight, even for a split second. What had astonished her – even more than that overwhelming dependence – was the mite's constant state of alertness. Cousin's nervous system was, from the beginning, wired spectacularly. The darting eyes, the jittery hands, the chattering teeth and the constant nervous tic that made him look as if he was getting little electric shocks from somewhere. Someone explained to her that it was Nature's way of keeping him 'on the ball', ready for anything, for any eventuality; but Hope preferred to believe that Cousin saw the world quite differently and she'd spent hours looking into those cool, fathomless eyes wondering just what went on inside.

Jake treated Cousin like an imbecile toy, but there were there, elements of a teasing cruelty – throwing windfall guavas at him in the orchard – 'hey, can't you catch bogom?' – subtle little slights and tricks that racked up the ante day by day and bothered Hope unaccountably. It all came to a head on a weekend fishing expedition down to the wide river that lay stretched like a lazy brown dog across the furthermost of her father's acres. Before lunch, the men fished the muddied waters for what was there; barbel and carp mostly, casting their baits over towards the reed banks near the opposite bank where yellow carp fins could be seen rippling the surface.

Cousin was with them, sitting immobile like a stone Anubis on the turf mound above the tartan picnic-blankets spread out on the river bank, and as Hope and her mother started to set out the plates of meats, salads and the ginger beer for lunch, there was a burst of laughter from below them. She'd looked up to see her father and Jake chatting, her father making a slithering action with his one hand, obviously a description of some sort. She'd thought they'd been talking about fish getting away or something, but as it turned out later, they'd been talking about Cousin's one great fear in life – snakes. In hindsight, what would happen next was all too predictable; especially when Jake hooked an eel out of the river early in the afternoon.

'Come Cousin,' Jake had called wheedlingly holding out a hand and Cousin had come ... slowly and trustingly, lolloping along with his awkward Simian swing his hand comfortably in Jake's, the pair of them walking towards where Jake's eel lay dying in the long grass. As Cousin's left foot curled onto the writhing eel he simply elevated – in a blink, like a rocket, bounding up level with Jake's shoulder and with a ferocious WAAAUUGH bark pushed off with a huge shove, his bowels exploding in a liquid shower everywhere.

'The biter bit ... covered in ... Ooh, look at you, man!' shouted her father, just about beside himself with laughter; and it was funny; shit all over the place; all over Jake's shirt, all over his face, in his hair, everywhere, and her husband caught standing there locked into immobility like Lot's wife. The trouble was that Jake didn't think it was funny at all, and stank just too terribly – even after he'd washed up in the river. To compound the error, and standing oh so heavily on his dignity, Jake then insisted on walking the three miles home alone like a overlarge disgraced schoolboy, with nobody feeling the slightest bit sorry for him for it either, while Cousin got to ride home in the dickey seat of the

Chev Imp. His look as he lorded it past Jake was priceless. A swivelling, knowing, penetrating stare and a baring of his teeth at Jake for an instant that only Hope saw. Threat or mocking smile – it didn't matter; either would have done perfectly well.

She opened her eyes as she heard the click, click, click of the indicator. Jake turning the car off the main road into Colesburg. All Hope could think of was lumpy Maltabella porridge, which was what they'd probably get at the Motel for breakfast tomorrow, followed by plastic fried eggs and the too awful boerewors, but if she was truthful, what depressed her really was that she was remembering something else. It was that weekend with Cousin she'd had the first, same sort of thought she'd vilified Matt for. Not quite the I hate him that he'd burst out with, but something very similar. A feeling of distaste she was extremely reluctant to put a name to, and, of course, when Matt had come out with it – put a name to it – it had struck her to the bone. Too horribly near the truth for words – except for the awful, instinctive ones she'd flung back at him, of course; her pathetic blind defence that had upset and wronged him dreadfully. And fleeting though it was at the time – what had happened that weekend on the farm, was, at the time, a blow that had shaken the foundations of everything good she believed of her young marriage … and all because of a baboon? Ridiculous, she knew, and phrases like 'a sense of proportion' and 'overexaggeration' had often come to mind since over this … and other things; but, heavens, she scolded herself, she'd be home tomorrow evening and things would be O.K., surely – they were bound to be.

Home was in Illovo, one of the posher suburbs on the northern side of Johannesburg. Late the following afternoon, Jake turned the black Chev through open wooden gates and up past the tennis court towards the house which lay at the far side of the two acre property. Hillcrest had been built in Cape Dutch style but somewhere along the line the architect had got it wrong. The elements were there, all right: the white walls, the gables, the swirls and all the rest, but the proportions were off, it just didn't work, and – this being the Transvaal – it was in the wrong place, anyway. As Jake slowed the Chev a grizzled old black dog pulled himself to his feet out of the shade of a large jacaranda tree that dominated the back lawn to the house and made it into a stiff canter towards them. As soon as they'd stopped Matt was out of the car in a flash, slapping at his knees.

'C'mon Wiggs, c'mon!'

Old Wiggie threw himself at Matt's delighted face covering it with licks and making the crooning sounds of welcome that could only be the Staffie blood in him. Elias and Torrance, the two Shona houseboys, arrived in an enthusiastic rush. Neat in their work uniforms of white with red piping they started to unpack the car and lug the suitcases into the house while Wiggie sniffed and circled the adult's ankles making his more circumspect hellos. Jake kicked at him ineffectually, 'Bugger off dog,' he muttered looking over at the noise of the kitchen door gauze screen slamming shut. 'Here's Maggs,' he said, touching Hope's shoulder and pointing at the formidable Mrs. Maggie Mabe, their Basuto quartermaster coming across the lawn like a rolling black blancmange. Matt darted round the car, fossicking in the boot for the two big coke bottles he'd filled with seawater for her. He met her halfway holding up the two bottles like trophies.

'See, I didn't forget, Maggs, and there's some sand in the bottom from Middle beach!'

Maggie beamed. 'Ah, baas Mattie, my muti!'

The two bottles disappeared into the pale capacious inner depths of her hands and Matt was enveloped in a bear hug, bottles and all, the blue uniform dress straining at the seams and Matt lost for a second in Maggie's India rubber expanses. Even bent over him, she was enormous, a towering black colossus – and lovely, one of Matt's constants in life: a tolerant and caring ever-present whom he thought of as much a part of his family as any one else. Maggie must have Bushman blood in her somewhere – it was said. How else to explain the enormous bottom which jutted out behind her like a high Victorian bustle? And because it sounded so much fun, it annoyed Matt that he couldn't remember what his mother said he'd done when he was much younger; that he'd ride around behind Maggie with his hands on her shoulders and his feet balanced on the top of her bottom, 'like a Liberty horse rider at the circus, Matt, darling' his mum had said – which sounded good until he'd been to Boswell's circus and seen that the riders were girls in ballet skirts who jumped through hoops as the horses went round and round. But he had had a thought.

'You know you said about me and Maggie, Mum, when I was little, like a circus rider on those horses? ...They're girls, Mum. Couldn't I have been Hannibal on his elephant, instead, going over the Alps?'

Hope had raised her eyebrows, thinking that it was all very well for Matt to be the heroic Hannibal, but that Maggie wouldn't necessarily be pleased to be his elephant ... but there again, African kings and queens did call themselves she-elephants and great-bulls and that sort of thing: and weight – or fat really, to them was beauty, so perhaps Maggie wouldn't mind after all. Perhaps she'd even take it as a superb compliment. After some deep thought Hope decided not to risk it, and so they'd compromised. Matt could be Hannibal but he wasn't to mention the elephant bit to Maggie.

Hope and Maggie walked off towards the kitchen door, already in deep discussion about dinner, and with Matt off somewhere in the garden, Jake strode into the lounge to fix himself a whisky. He was on his second glass standing out on the back veranda and stretching the journey out of his back when Hope arrived and plonked herself down on the rusbank with an exhausted sigh.

'Why on earth should travelling make you so tired?' she demanded and lifted a hand to train a stray lock of hair back in place.

Jake looked at her without reply. Stretched out like that, and with the late afternoon gilding her hair, there was no denying – tired or not – that his wife was still a very good-looking woman. Beautiful even. A slim body that had hardly been bothered by bearing him three children and the fine, crafted features that had made him determined to own her the minute he first saw her. She'd reminded him of the most perfect porcelain doll in those days, and, for a while at least, he'd been almost unwilling to possess her in the way his hot blood had demanded. Not that that was any problem these days, Jake thought to himself and with a twist of a smile put his head back and drained the glass.

Matt appeared round the corner of the house running at full speed with his arms trailing behind in a Vee making aeroplane engine noises. Hope smiled having seen what was in his one hand.

'Air lifting greens for his budgies,' she commented, turning her head, but it was to empty space, Jake had gone inside.

Matt was nuts about animals, and – having first checked out all his secret places in the garden – he was now on a private mercy mission from the vegetable garden to the aviary. The secret place list, however, was a big problem to Matt and he was still thinking about it as he landed his plane next to the aviary. Which one was going to take over as favourite now that the slow-combustion room was off the list? It used to be easily his best; dark, warm and comfortable with all the coal piled up next to a pot-bellied stove and a tiny wooden bench to sit on. That was before the end of last term when he'd come home from school on his bike to find Elias and Torrance lunging furiously with long garden rakes at something in there. It went on for quite a while, the two of them hissing and grunting Ha! sst! Ha and striking some more and then darting back in alarm, and then going in again, eventually pulling out two writhing rinkhals on the end of their rakes and shaking the horrible things off onto the lawn. Matt didn't go close 'cause he knew those spitting snakes could play dead and then just have you; at least not until Elias had fetched a spade and chopped their heads off.

With his budgies seen to and chattering happily over their spinach, Matt couldn't think of anything else to do. Wiggie wouldn't play for very long either, these days. At a bit of a loss, he ambled onto the stoep.

'There are two lutino babies, Mum.'

'Are there, sweetie?' Hope pulled herself up; she'd been miles away. 'Your father's inside so you wouldn't be an angel and get me a glass of sherry would you?' and with a skip Matt was off. This getting of drinks for the adults was a little ritual he enjoyed and a minute later he was back holding an over-full amber glass with two hands, walking as if he was on a high wire – carefully, so very carefully. Hope's heart went out to her boy. He looked too adorable, step after slow step, concentrating madly. And then the brilliant clear smile before turning saying, 'I'm getting a sparkling orange, Mum, is there any biltong?'

She nodded and relaxed, sipped at her sherry and felt that, yes, now that she was home again, she was sure to feel better soon – or any minute she would. What else should she feel, for heaven's sake, surrounded by everything that was comfortable and familiar once again, and life just that much easier these days? Teddy and Sam off at boarding school, Matt esconced in Prep and Jake, God

... barely visible these days, busy enjoying meteoric promotion in that good, if unspectacular accounting firm of his. She ticked off her assets one by one. Jake's social life, too, had that satisfied look about it. Memberships of any number of clubs: Rand, the Country Club, Inanda and Royal, and all of them providing him with a steady circle of like-minded business and golfing 'chommies', as he called them. Four clubs; a good hand he'd joked; and as if he'd never tire of telling her, it was all very good and all very necessary for business, too. But what that also meant was that he arrived home late more and more often, and that he golfed virtually every Saturday and Sunday – and mid-week, too, if he could wangle it. Hope supposed it was right – perhaps the golfing and the business and the nineteenth hole – plening of liquidity there – was his right – something just plain necessary because their Northern suburbs life and the private schooling demanded it. These men's pleasures his due – all worthwhile? She made a face, unconvinced. Despite all the assets, she was still desperately unconvinced.

Thinking back; it had all been so different when the kids really were still kids, when he'd spend hours playing cricket or footers with Teddy and Sam on the weekend and usually be home early on weekday evenings, too; spending an hour – or even a few minutes – out here on this lawn, here right in front of her with the boys. These days, she reflected, Jake hardly ever saw Matt. No messing around on the lawn any more, no more chipping a football back and forth, no French cricket, no shouting 'let me, Dad, let me', and grabbing at Jake's Ronson to light his cigarette for him. None of that. All that was left was this quiet, empty and somehow this evening, rather cheerless garden. They all suffered from his absence in a way that was difficult to define and not the sort of absence that made a heart grow fonder either. An estrangement? – too strong. A distancing? – far too corny; but it all amounted to the same thing anyway, and whatever you called it, Hope decided, it still bloody well hurt. It had pushed her away, everyone apart, and realising it saddened her so awfully inside.

The holiday had helped a bit, sure. But even there, Jake fished less and golfed more; Sam and Teddy old enough now to be forever partying and chasing girls, and her dear Matt? Out somewhere fishing, always fishing! Her role of cook and homebody was to some extent the same, whether they were here at home or down in Plett didn't matter. A constant repetition of providing large meals for hungry men who took it all for granted, she supposed, and who then promptly disappeared again until the next meal. Not very edifying to be plain old cook and bottle-washer, was it? Matt even took packed lunches, for heaven's sake, and was then often as not away for the whole day! There was a time long ago, she knew, when she would have been thrilled – ecstatic even – just to be free of her kids for one whole day. Too much dependence in those days, and now too little somehow. Edifying or not, it certainly had given her more time for herself alone, and somewhat guiltily she had gone up to the library behind their holiday home in Plett, taken out her cards and brought back an armful of books to read. Quite delicious for the first week, but her living, she soon realised, couldn't become entirely vicarious, and she found herself at a complete loss as to what to do about it – or even who to speak to about it! Her dear friend Doris Cleaver, also down from Johannesburg (as she was every year over Christmas) was as keen as ever to make her into a bridge player, but Hope blanched at the thought of chasing cards in the company of a coven of women. They were fiercely hierarchical, she'd heard – those iced tea shrewd old clever, knew-they-were-clever women. Hope reckoned she'd just always end up being dummy, but she did envy their astonishing self-assurance, every single one of them. The aplomb, the confidence: astonishing; she'd never compete …

wouldn't – couldn't, and anyway, having had men around for all of her life hadn't exactly left her with a taste for extended bouts of female company ... just not her style, sadly – it would have been such an uncomplicated solution, and Doris was such a dear. Hope felt churlish, old-fashioned, so childishly ungrateful for this newfound leisure, wishing fervently that she could find it within her to enjoy it more. The consololation that she'd relied on, that once the holidays were over and she was back home would somehow make things all right was a nonsense. It was the same problem, just wearing a different coat. She could scarcely credit it and smiled to herself, a wry little face, thinking how terribly spoilt she must be. How could she possibly feel sorry for herself, annoyed with herself and ungrateful all at the same time?

A great gusting sigh helped Hope drag herself upright on the rusbank. She should go in. She paused and looked down at hands placed directly on her knees waiting to push her up onto her feet. She stared and spoke to them.

'Your're just too bloody idle,' she said, and the wayward thought that she'd better find something useful to do or else the Devil would soon find work for them annoyed her intensely. She had recognised herself parroting one of Jake's horrid little sayings.

6

Jake's early morning routine was as stereotyped and Spartan as the man, and today's ritual no different. He peed vigorously, pulled the chain ... vigorously and then shaved whilst he ran his habitual cold bath, scraping away at the black stubble under the shaving soap. As he leant forward towards the shaving mirror to do his upper lip, a lick of coal black hair fell forward over his brow. He paused to flick it back. At thirty-seven years of age, his thick straight hair had hardly a speck of grey, and – bar the widow's peak – there was no hint of recession along the craggy shoreline of his brow. He took pride in his ebony mane beneath which heavy, arched eyebrows sat on guard like two angry black caterpillars.

The cold bath was always quick, accompanied by a slapping soaping of an unusually long upper body, a lot of noisy plunging under the water and an equally energetic drying session with a huge bath towel easily the size of a small republic. Invigorated – as was intended, and reminded of a time when there was no such thing as hot water for baths – as was intended, this was his hair-shirt, after all – Jake hurried to the bedroom, his towel wrapped round him like a cape. Taking one from his stable of dark suits in the walk-in cupboard, he dressed quickly as always, but with care and, taking a last look in the bedroom mirror, strode off with military intent towards the dining room. Jake's walk said it all, his elbows just shy of his sides, an energetic bustle and the bobble of his chin stuck out aggressively like the beak on a plough. Even the air in the corridor parted hurriedly to let him through.

'Thanks, Maggie,' he muttered and lowered himself into the carver as the large, black and bountiful Mrs. Mabe brought him his two boiled eggs and a slice of toast – a slice that had to be thin, cold and hard. Jake buttered the bent slice and turned out the boiled eggs on top of the burnt offering with a teaspoon. Taking the knife and fork he cut into the eggs and worked the soft yolk into the toast before piercing the mixture and gathering a first mouthful onto the fork.

As he finished chasing round the edge of the plate for morsels, Maggie served his coffee, piping hot, with sugar bowl and a small jug of heated milk. The Rand Daily Mail appeared at his elbow, and as Jake opened this with a crack and a flourish, Maggie deftly removed the plate and silently went out to the kitchen. Jake placed the paper in front of him, dribbled milk into the cup and sugared the coffee with two spoons, turning his attention to the headlines as he started stirring. Only if the news was very good – or very bad – did the stirring stop momentarily. There were his stock prices to check and the business page headlines before the paper went back into his briefcase for a closer read at the office.

Maggie stood in the kitchen in front of the sink washing egg off the plate. If she had seen the Bass's breakfast once, she had seen it a thousand times – always the same, except that the Bass liked to have his fried eggs, bacon and banana on Fridays and his flat kippers on Sunday that made the rubbish stink. This was all she saw of him week in and week out because Elias served dinner, and it was always the same two muttered words as he sat down each and every morning. She had worked for the Madam's family for years before this bveni as Elias called him, this baboon man with the long body and short legs had come to claim them both and take them from the farm in Thaba Nchu to Jo'burg. He had talked to her often, in those early days, and made her Madam happy, too. There were the young children then, and she had seen the Baas laugh with the young baasies when they played together after his work. There was nothing now, she thought. She turned the plate into the draining rack with a scowl – and the little baasie, baas

Matt, hau! Her useless scowl loosened to fall into a small sorrowing shake of her head – hau, hau, that boy, he was sad with his father.

Jake left very early in the Chev to avoid traffic and frustration and swept up through Illovo, Rivonia and Parktown with only the odd red robot to slow him down en route to the office, enjoying – as some people do – the feeling of moral superiority in that he was out and about well before most people were even awake. This smug, powered-up, look-down-your nose feeling was bolstered even further when the staff, arriving at eight o'clock, invariably found him already hard at work. His secretary, Carol, brought him coffee at nine o'clock, by which time she had sorted his post into that she could deal with, that she couldn't, and the obviously personal letters. With the holiday there was a mountain of mail which she put on his desk with an apologetic smile.

'Morning, Sir. Sorry, Sir!' Carol was still young.

Jake leaned back in his chair and smiled at her.

'Morning, Carol.' He gestured at the pile. 'That's what I get for lazing at the sea, I suppose.'

Her smile stayed, hoisted by the arch of disbelieving eyebrows. Carol had never seen anyone less lazy in her life. She fancied him awfully in a hero-worship sort of way.

Jake took his first sip of his coffee, thinking how rejuvenated and refreshed he felt by his break; just mustard for the office. Clattering his cup into the saucer he bent to his work and his correspondence with a will. His best work was always in the mornings, he had found; and so always worked until one o'clock in the afternoon before breaking for lunch, a meal he preferred to take alone in his office. By long tradition, one of the caterers, usually Mrs. Solomons, would bring something up from the staff canteen, with tea to follow from the ubiquitous caterer's steel pot.

He was engrossed in his work when Mrs. Solomons knocked

quietly and, without waiting for a reply, opened his door and bullied her trolley in. Jake looked up.

'Goodness, is it that time already – and how's my favourite lady, then?'

'You'd better not let Carol hear that, Mr. Stevens,' clucked Mrs. Solomons who was very like an old hen, and pleased at Jake's remark, smiling broadly, 'and how was your holiday?'

Jake stretched, happy to switch off his mind.

'Oh, plenty of golf for me and sun and fishing for the rest as usual,' he replied rather blandly and not really listening very hard as Mrs Solomons set out his tray blathering on about how ever since her Ikey had died she never bothered with holidays anymore.

'Well, I'll leave you to it, Sir, but don't let your food get cold now.'

Ruth Solomons' motherly attitude towards her employer was appropriate considering the age difference, but there was more to it than that. She had lost six of her European relatives in what they called the Holocaust and considered the fact that Jake had gone north to fight the Germans more than admirable. Admirable was her favourite word. There were plenty of others, she knew, who had remained in the Union for the duration to further their careers, or been in 'strategically important' jobs (less than admirable, of course), but her Mr. Stevens, as she thought of him, had risked and given four years of his life up there and done a great deal more, she knew, than all her home-grown bitterness and hate could achieve.

She saw Mercedes Benz cars more and more often on the streets of Johannesburg these days and it was a source of comfort to her that none of the firm's partners drove anything but English or American cars. Her Mr. Stevens had come back a Captain, with a decoration, and it was only right they quickly made him up to partner in the firm that had been her life. No doubt she would have been less pleased to know that Jake was a paid-up member of a Club that had steadfastly refused to admit blacks, Jews or women since inception, and it was perhaps fortuitous that the misogyny and bigotry entrenched in the Rand Club were so well beyond Ruth Solomons' ambit.

With much of the catching up to do under his belt, Jake's lunch was leisurely, with time for a second look at the paper before strolling down the corridor to what was then called the partners' room and would be called a conference room today. Carol had given him notice of the meeting and he entered the room to be met by a buzz of conversation amongst the other senior men already gathered there. There were a few handshakes, backslaps and some good-natured bantering as the men welcomed one another after the break, although the work ethic nevertheless always demanded an arrangement to stagger the leave, ensuring that there was always at least one partner in the office over the Christmas period – one of Jake's refinements. Finally they sat and worked through a short agenda of business matters: new account briefings, staff appointments, resignations and the like before the most senior partner and firm founder, the cheerful, rotund Bob Wilkens called them to order.

'Chaps, you all know, or most of you know, that my elder brother Ted who started this firm with me back in thirty seven has been retired to his Norfolk family home for some four or five years now. Well, he has invited me and Jake, and our families, across to the U.K. for the month of June – and I must say I'm very inclined to accept.'

He waved a hand in Jake's general direction and continued.

'Jake, as you know, has been my right hand in getting the accounting measures for the Brathrow Steel subsidiary in this country organised. He'll be taking further instruction from the parent company in London while we're there so it won't be all pleasure, I assure you. We will be away for about a month, as I say, but I am sure you,' Bob gave a small bow, 'my very, very capable colleagues can cope while we are abroad.'

The announcement was greeted with a smattering of sycophantic applause: Bob beamed, which he was good at, and well-wishers indulging in some gentle banter surrounded Jake. There were a few well camouflaged, covetous darts and glances. Jake noted them – but didn't care, coming as they did from blokes already floundering in his wake.

Bob, expat and devout Anglophile, spent at least a month in England on holiday every other year, but his briefing to Jake early that morning had come as a great surprise. Jake's first thought had been what this would do for his career – he hoped much – and then how delighted Hope would be. She had seemed so distracted lately, and this would do her a 'power of good', as he thought of it. His thoughts had also lingered on the airmail letter he'd had in his post that morning amongst his personal mail, post-marked Stock – Essex. The realisation that he'd be able to see Ashleigh again had his head seething with images he'd thought were all safely packed away.

Drinks came out of the large and well-stocked cabinet at the back of the room – kept there for just such occasions – and with Bob in expansive mood, any thought of further work in the late afternoon disappeared. By the time they filed out of the offices, Jake was enveloped in the rosy glow of a contentment lit with agreeable intoxication. Sitting in the Chev, and after organising his briefcases and paraphernalia, he took time to light a cigarette before twisting the ignition, firing the engine and swinging out of the car park to head home. Anxious to tell Hope his good news, he would give the Club a miss tonight. The trip home was made beautiful by a scorched, red Highveld sunset and it was a pleasant-humoured Jake that arrived on his doorstep, briefly ruffling

Matt's hair.

'Son, fix me a whisky and water on the stoep. Where's your mother?'

'Here somewhere, Dad.'

'Hope!' he called, 'where are you, for heaven's sake?'

He found her coming through the house and picked her up – hands encircling her waist – swinging her round.

'Guess what, Hope? We're off to England in June!'

Hope gasped, her hands going to Jake's shoulders as he twirled her round.

'What do your mean? When, why?'

He set her down, bending both knees, cackling almost.

'June, I said, doll, June. Jees, can you believe it? With old Bob and Thelma on a business trip for the firm. All paid for, too. I've just got to tie up some loose ends with Brathrow Steel's head office in London and the rest of the time is ours – do what we bloody well like. A whole month!'

'A month!' Hope stopped dead still, 'Jake, we can't just leave Matt for a month!'

Jake bridled, eyes narrowing in resentment.

'Ag, we can work something out for him … with family, friends … something. Sure we can.'

He waved a hand in a dismissive gesture, 'anyway, let's have a drink to celebrate.'

Hope could see that Jake had been celebrating quite hard already and knew also there was no stopping him in the full flow of one of his enthusiasms. She'd say nothing until later when the torrent had slowed a little, but didn't relish the prospect one bit.

Out on the veranda, the source of her concern appeared with his father's drink and a hopeful expression.

Jake grabbed his whisky, 'go get one for your mother, son.' He turned to Hope.

'What are you having, doll?'

'Just a sherry please, Matt,' she said slowly and turned an uncharacteristic tight little smile onto her husband. She hoped it would hide her rapidly escalating concern, only half listening as Jake went on about flight dates, suggesting things they might do, and with what people and where, and even relatives they might see. Matt appeared with her sherry and Hope took a large swallow. She'd better wait until after dinner, she thought, wishing she could wait forever, but her niggling concerns about Matt's quietness, his being so very solitary, crowded into her mind and had set all the alarm bells ringing. He's the one who's going to pay for this trip, she thought desperately. When she had premonitions like this, Hope knew she was seldom wrong. It was what her mother used to say, she was fey, had foresight – something she'd be quite happy doing without sometimes – so she'd have to say something sooner or later, but explaining it to Jake would make her sound so unbelievably pathetic – she knew it. She took another large swallow.

Jake watched her picking through dinner absent-mindedly, his irritation growing minute by minute. When Elias had cleared the dessert plates and disappeared to the kitchen he took up his cudgels.

'For God's sake, Hope, here you are with the offer of a lifetime and all you can do is whine about missing the boy!'

Hope shook her head and put up a protesting hand to stop him.

'No, Jake, sorry, it's not me missing Matt – although I'm sure I would – it's about Matt being without us. I don't think it's good for him at the moment ... I'm so worried about him – he's so' – Hope searched her mind frantically for the right word – 'remote in a funny sort of way.'

Jake glared at her, digesting what she'd said and then dismissing it. He wiped his mouth and flung the linen serviette down on the table in a gesture of intense annoyance.

'You'll make him into a bloody namby-pamby with all your damn cosseting, Hope, and why all this sudden concern for Matt when the other boys are doing just fine without any of this? He'll end up a Mummy's boy, you know, and all your fault, Hope, your own bloody fault. Your own homegrown fucking little sissy. Is that what you want?'

Hope put her hands to her face, feeling hot tears springing suddenly from her eyes. She ran from the dining room taking refuge in the corridor bathroom where she sat on the edge of the bath letting the unwelcome wave of emotion wash over her. 'God, I'm being useless,' she muttered to herself, leant over to run some cold water into the basin and splashed some onto her face and swollen, red eyes. Her hands were shaking, and seeing that sent another shudder through a trembling frame. She effected her running repairs, nevertheless, and combed and touched at her hair carefully, taking time. Then, taking a deep, deep breath she walked upright into the living room where Jake was busy with a small brandy snifter.

'All right, then?' He enquired gruffly.

'Yes, yes,' she replied. 'I really don't know what got into me. I'm so sorry ... and everything you say is true, it's a wonderful opportunity ... and we must go, but I just wish I didn't fear it all so much for Matt's sake! I can't even make it plain to myself, much less to you, but he's drifting away from me – and from you, and seems vulnerable ... but vulnerable to what, I don't really know!'

Hope's desperation was evident in the loose exaggerated hand movements and the way her voice rose, cracked and then fell away, but enough there to persuade even a riled Jake to adopt a more conciliatory tone.

'Don't worry, darling, he'll be fine.'

He'd made a gesture but Jake's flat blanket cover of 'it'll be fine, or he'll be fine' did nothing to rid her of the intense sense of unease and a feeling that now something awful for Matt was out there waiting for him.

In bed that night Jake turned to switch off his sidelight, punched his pillow, crashed into it and then lay still as death with his back to her instantly fast asleep. How could he do that, she wondered? Her mind was still going round and round in circles, but huge relief flooded her because this was when it usually happened, when he'd had too much to drink, like now and when he called her 'doll'. Things he did she tried to blank from her mind. She'd got away with it this time.

But she hadn't at all. Hope half woke sometime deep into the night, feeling his heavy weight straddling her high across the back of her legs. He sat there doing something with himself. The old fear gripped her and instinct screamed at her to get away, but there was no getting away. He leant forward, gripped her hair and pushed her head hard down into the pillow stifling the No, no! terror cry and the high scream of pain that followed.

Hope lay turned carefully away, both hands tucked between her legs near where she was torn and sore. Her eyes were fixed, sightless as stone, gazing into the dark. She stayed like this through the hours, not awake and not asleep, desolate beyond tears, numbed through and through. In her twilight trance Hope's mind drifted to the farm where Jake had first come to court her, or lay siege to her more like. Not that she'd been unwilling, sadly; absolutely in awe as she was then of his dark brooding looks and thrilled by a powerful aura that, in spite of an obvious restraint, had still reeked of danger. She had brushed away the forewarning –

he was simply too exciting – and so very ambitious. Only later had she understood that their ideas of success and happiness were poles apart. He, driven by success and the will and want to win, and she by her Thaba Nchu family values – values like kindness and honesty mixed happily with the laughter that seemed in such short supply these days, values that, when she mentioned them, Jake scornfully dismissed as her picket fence philosophies. She found no answers and no understanding of Jake's hot breath uttering evil whisperings into her neck as he did it to her, submerging her in a sea of pain. They haunted her, those words, until exhausted finally, she fell into a shallow troubled sleep near dawn. Her last thought was why 'ash', why had he kept saying 'ash?'

7

It was settled then. Matt was to stay with his Uncle Frank and Aunt Edith, Jake's sister and brother-in-law, while they were abroad.

Hope had reservations about her husband's shrewish older sister, a thin dark little woman starched upright by the bad smell that evidently hovered just under her nose; but they lived so nearby, in fact only a few streets away in Boundary Road so Matt could still cycle to and from school everyday and not disrupt anyone's routine too much. As far as Jake was concerned, the boy would just have to be fed and watered and checked to see his homework had been done, and he said as much to Hope in straight no-nonsense terms. She didn't think it was as simple as that at all, not for a minute, but Frank and Edith did have a boy at the same prep school – Pridwin – one year ahead of Matt, so perhaps the acquaintanceship between the two could ripen into friendship. She could hope anyway. It only remained to tell Matt about their plans and arrangements, but Hope's conscience gnawed at her so much that she fretted and procrastinated endlessly.

Matt had been ferreting around in Jake's chest of drawers and had come across the badges his father had collected in North Africa during the war, all packed away in cotton wool inside an old red cigarette tin. There were cap badges and flashes, even Jake's old dog tag.

'Wow, look at these, Mum, where are they from?'

Hope looked down from her dressing table chair to her son on the floor.

'I think your Dad collected them from the different regiments when he was up fighting Rommel in the desert during the war.'

'Who was Rommell?' quizzed Matt with a screwed up face,

peering up at his mother as if he had trouble seeing.

'He was a famous German general and he was so clever at fighting they called him the desert fox.'

'What's all the writing on this one, Mum' Matt gave her a small silver badge whilst he continued to look through the others. What tiny writing, thought Hope, getting up from her chair.

'Let me find the magnifying glass, I'll be back in a tick.'

She found the glass with the stamp collection in the roll-top desk and bore it back to the bedroom.

'Let's see,' she brought the badge into focus. 'It's a badge from the Rifle Brigade, with their battle honours – those are battles they fought well in, I suppose, imprinted … well just about anywhere they could find room on this cross in the middle of the badge.' She pointed out the small cross to Matt. 'It's called a Maltese cross … and there are more of their honours on this wreath surrounding it. The crown on top,' she pointed again with her finger, 'means that it's probably a British regiment, but we might be able to tell for sure from some of the honours, 'cause they're often place names as well. You know all about Napoleon from history at school, don't you?'

'Well, a bit,' Matt conceded.

'He was defeated by Wellington at Waterloo, wasn't he? Now if you look through the magnifying glass you can see Waterloo written just under the crown. See it?' Matt nodded enthusiastically. 'Wow, Mum,' he paused, 'so the Rifle Brigade fought at Waterloo and then with Dad?'

'It would appear so,' Hope replied, rather pleased with her detective work and humoured by the thought of a rag-tag bunch of Waterloo veterans turning up to give Jake and the Eighth Army a hand. Matt's attention turned to one of the other of the regimental badges while Hope turned some of the others idly in her hand, finding one in the shape of a Maltese cross rather than embossed with it, with a bar above bearing the motto Steadfast and True. She had difficulty reading the circular lettering within the cross and picked up the magnifying glass to help. Royal British Nursing Association. Well, well, wondered Hope. She hadn't quizzed Jake about what he did for female company during the four years up north – hadn't wanted or dared to – thinking that what the eye didn't see, or in her case the ear didn't hear, the heart couldn't feel; but four years, even with leave thrown in, was a long time to be apart, and she herself hadn't been entirely without blame in that department either. She blushed at the thought even now, knowing also she'd lingered a little longer there than she should have and certainly longer than it was safe to. Turning the badge over she could faintly distinguish a name scratched into the metal: A.Hall, and who on earth were you, Miss A. Hall? she puzzled to herself. Dismissing the thought, and the other one that still made her ache inside, she tossed the badge back into the tin, left Matt to his imaginings and went to organise afternoon tea. She still hadn't spoken to Matt about the overseas trip, as if procrastination could somehow wash her explanations into a more acceptable light. Mentally she tried to work up her resolution and as the kettle started to whistle suddenly determined to do it – straight after tea.

Matt listened to her explanations about the trip with an absolutely blank facial expression, his eyes never leaving hers, his body abnormally quiet and still. Hands that would usually have been pulling and tugging at something on his frame were motionless at his side for once, and the strange sight made Hope nervous enough to babble on until abruptly, she ran out of words. There was a silence between them for three or four seconds that, to Hope, seemed ages, then the boy's eyes slid away. He whirled around suddenly and slipped away soft on bare-foot quiet as you like, and was gone out onto the stoep and into the garden. Hope rose quickly and took two or three steps after him hand half raised before letting it flop hopelessly against her skirt. She heard the gauze screen door bang at the back of the house a few minutes later and found him in his room, fossicking around in the box seat under the window where he kept all his toys and Eagle comics.

'Ma-aat,' she called tentatively – long on the vowel, poking her head around his door, 'are you alright?'

'Sure, Mum,' Matt answered, his voice muffled and head buried deep in the muddle, 'I'm just looking for my football.'

'You polished it yesterday, so it must be in there somewhere,' Hope offered. Grateful for the diversion and thankful that she appeared to have got off the hook, she became over-talkative, over-helpful, offering to go to the playroom cupboards to see if it was perhaps there.

'Don't worry, Mum, it's here I think,' and with a groan and a tug, Matt produced the shiny ball, scampered past her and went out into the back garden to kick it against the garage wall. Hope watched from inside the house – it was also where he practiced his tennis, beating ball, large or small, against the whitewashed surface for hours. She was perplexed, why had she got off so easily? She'd expected anything except this. She made a hmph in her throat and turned away, but a closer look might have shown a savage concentration in the boy's narrowed eyes as time and time again the slight figure attacked the returning ball, smashing it back at an indifferent wall just as hard as a little body would allow.

The intervening weeks slid by uneventfully, and Hope was caught up in the endless preparations of papers, passports, clothes and packing – with little spare time to attend to Matt or Jake especially well. In any event, Matt didn't seem to mind the idea of the trip, or else he hid it very well, and Hope reported back to her husband rather thankfully that he had been right all along. She'd been making mountains out of molehills after all. There was just the one small thing: she noticed that Matt, whilst affectionate enough, no longer brought the mohair blanket to cuddle up beside her during evening drinks on the stoep. He'd taken to sitting, as he now sat, on his hands on the rusbank, rocking gently back and forth, looking serenely out into the garden.

'Matt, do you want to bring your blanket over and sit next to your old Mum?'

He coloured slightly and shook his head.

'Naa, it's okay, Mum.'

She thought it was probably just the boy growing up, but she would miss it, she acknowledged to herself silently. Her last little boy – not such a little boy anymore. More was the pity.

They were to fly on Monday, 25th May so the parents took Matt and his little suitcase over to Frank and Edith on the afternoon of the 24th, Whit Sunday – Empire Day. Edith took Hope and Matt off to settle him in his room and pack his clothes from the suitcase into the pine chest of drawers while Frank and Jake went to 'inspect the contents of the whisky decanter' – as Frank put it. After desultory chatter that by content excluded the boy, Jake banged his glass down on the table, rose to his feet and announced that it was time to go.

'One for the road, Jake?' Frank asked half-heartedly. Please stay for another drink – Matt begged his father silently.

'Thanks, Frank, but no – we've still got packing to finish.' Fear of the separation, now here, drained Matt's body and he could hardly put a weak little leg forward and raise a hand to meet his father's halfway in a formal handshake.

'Goodbye, my boy,' grated Jake, 'be good and behave yourself, you hear?' Matt nodded, unable to produce a word. Hope swept him up in her arms and he breathed in her wonderful scents as she hugged him close.

'Bye, my darling, we'll be back before you know it, you'll see.'

The sense of loss and betrayal as the black Chev pulled away over-powered him. His throat closed in a spasm and tears boiled at his eyes, threatening to break over in a torrent. He clenched his fists at his sides, willing himself not to allow it, and tucked his head down so no one could see the torment in his face. Unable to resist any more and desperate to avoid the shame he suddenly ran away down the drive in the opposite direction to the departing car. Frank and Edith turned at the noise of leather on gravel to see the flying figure disappearing into the trees near the bottom of the entrance drive. Edith started after him but Frank laid a quick restraining hand on her arm.

'Give the little bugger some time, he's gone to have a little weep, I expect.'

Frank aimed himself towards house and whisky decanter. 'Let's have another snort, darling, he'll be back soon enough when he gets cold and peckish ... God protect me from children, especially your brother's bloody sprogs.'

Bald and freckle-headed, Edith's husband was years older. An ex-Royal Air Force bomber pilot – and never one to let you forget it, Frank sported his over-large, nicotine-stained moustache like a badge, two long orange handlebars steering him as he blustered and bullied his way through life like an irascible Churchillian bulldog. The civvies uniform carefully asserted his beloved Battle of Britain time-warp: the archetypal blazer, the cavalry twill slacks, the polished brogues and ties full of slanted, rainbow colours that boggled the eye and defied imagination. A walking caricature of the type, full of piss and vinegar and spouting wah wah clichés, Frank was vain and intolerant to a fault. Even Jake reckoned him tight and mean as chicken shit, a miserly bent not entirely explained by the fact that he was perpetually strapped for cash either – it derived rather, from a thin spare spirit soured even further by a lifetime of under-achievement and attention to the bottle. Firebombing Dresden had been the high point in his life, the remainder of which seemed to have been devoted to fighting a rearguard action against crumbling values in this colonial backwater. He didn't understand the fifties at all, and children, especially other people's, were not on any of Frank's preferred menus either. He'd undoubtedly been one himself once but it was very long ago and neither hint nor soft remembrance of this former life remained in even the furthest reaches of Frank's recall. No sympathetic chords sounded here. Children, as he saw them and the old saw proclaimed, were to be seen and not heard, and the less of the former he had to endure as well, the happier Frank suspected he'd be. His stepson, Denis with one n, would at least be some sort of foil for the Stevens' sprog. With any luck, he thought as he unstoppered the whisky decanter, the two brats would keep one another amused.

He took a good slug of Scotch.

And out of his bloody hair completely if he had any.

Matt had run into the stand of blue gums at the bottom of the drive, picked up the nearest fallen dead branch he could lay hands on and smashed it onto one of the tree trunks. It shattered extravagantly, springing out of his grasp and sending bolts of excruciating pain shooting up his arms. He looked down to his hands to see slivers of wood piercing both palms, small ribbons of skin hanging loose and blood beginning to run in bright red rivulets down the creases of his skin. The tears ran easily now emptying him from inside. All that remained in the pit of him was disillusion and hurt that his parents would leave him like this.

Hope had misread her child. There hadn't been a peep of complaint about their overseas trip because Matt, dutiful child that he was, had always tried to please – if not his father, then certainly his adored mother. He knew he just had to accept it – they were going – there was no changing that and hell would freeze over before he'd complain about it, anyway. If he did, all he'd get in return when he heard about it was one of his father's lectures telling him to 'stop whining' – or 'not to be a wimp' or Dad's favourite, 'for God's sake, pull yourself together, boy!' Awful blasts of cold venom delivered with such withering scorn that they shocked. Shocked so much that Matt never whined, always pulled himself together and tried desperately hard never to be a wimp. This is how Matt arrived at being 'dutiful' and 'well-behaved', and this was how Jake reckoned he'd be the making of the boy, making him tough enough, someone a bit hard, things Jake knew you'd need to be in life if you wanted to get on and get to be a real man. That others might call it something quite different, turning the boy into a cold insensitive bastard like he was, perhaps, didn't occur.

It was the first time Matt had ever been away from home without them in his life and he felt abandoned – a spare part, in the way, and now shunted out of it, unwanted even. This was an overreaction, of course, but what had made it seem that way – made it worse, magnified it out of all proportion in fact, was the way they had looked forward to it so much – being without him, that is. It was an exclusive party he hadn't been invited to, and he had heard them telling all their friends time and time again how great the overseas trip would be – the fun they'd have, and again – all without him. Matt was no spoilsport so the open enthusiasm so plainly on view might just as well have torn his tongue out. He'd say nothing by choice. He'd say nothing because he'd seen his dad spoiling things for other people like his mum and for himself with the leervis that day. Mum called it pouring cold water on people's ideas, but dad's cold water came out of his mouth – not from a jug or anything – from his mouth, and it could freeze you just like that. In a second. Perhaps he swallowed all that cold water when he had those freezing baths every morning.

No, Matt decided he'd keep stumm. He'd never be a spoilsport like his dad. Not now and not ever.

As the one pain inside abated a little, the other – from his hands – sharpened and burned. Reluctantly, very reluctantly, dragging heels and heart, Matt turned back to the house. Edith, Frank's true acolyte in these matters, tut-tutted when she saw the damage and shepherded him into the bathroom, her pinched face frowning in disapproval, the smell under her nose even stronger.

'How on earth did you do this child – heaven's sakes – your parents aren't even out of the country, and here you are in some sort of scrape already!'

Matt maintained a studied silence in the face of his aunt's censure. In spite of herself Edith was surprised to see little or no reaction when he snipped off the snags of skin, or even to the iodine when she dabbed it onto his shredded hands, and Edith knew it must have hurt like the very devil. There was something of his father in this little shit after all.

'Just like your father, you are, no sense, no feeling,' she muttered, glancing at Matt, hardly noticing the empty eyes. Cleaned up, she saw that, thank goodness, there was only the one cut on the side of one hand that might need an Elastoplast. She peeled the backing off one and stuck it on like a great birthday present.

Packing everything away into the bathroom cupboard Edith closed the little door with a snap. She poked Matt in the back with a stiff finger.

'Now you buzz off to the kitchen. There's a sandwich and a glass of milk for your supper, and then it's bed, d'you hear?'

Matt drifted off down the corridor towards the kitchen and supper with the sharp clack of Edith's heels echoing away down the corridor.

He didn't think this was going to be a nice place.

8

Right on schedule, Jake and Hope arrived in London on Tuesday, 26th May, and were instantly plunged into a whirl of business and social activity. Accommodation had been arranged at the Goring Hotel in Belgravia where the two Wilkens families reunited. Bob, his brother Ted from Norfolk and their respective wives were lodged in adjoining suites in the hotel, and Jake and Hope in a room near the head of the stairs on the first floor. Hope barely had time to unpack her two suitcases before it was time to freshen up for lunch in the hotel dining room. The flight had been tiring, so much so that after lunch everyone agreed on the wisdom of an afternoon zizz before their evening dinner dance at Quaglino's. Hope was in a state when she discovered her evening dress was badly travel-creased but the staff at the Goring made light of getting it pressed before six o'clock. She knew how much emphasis Jake always put on appearance.

Wednesday, the following day, was an important one. They were invited to dinner with the Cunninghams at Claridges. John Cunningham was the grande fromage at Brathrow Steel U.K., managing director of the company who were setting up a subsidiary company in Johannesburg – in the market for accounting and financial advice and, as Bob Wilkens had confidentially advised Jake, local directors too. This added incentive had put Jake much on his mettle – and Hope too, hanging as she did during dinner on the senior man's every word as he expounded on the virtues and intricacies of fishing the chalk waters of the Test, hunting in the West Country – and ungrateful children. Hope was an excellent listener. She had also taken particular care at the hairdresser that morning and dressed to look her absolute best. Hope's looks had drawn comparisons to Grace

Kelly all her adult life and there were indeed similarities in the blonde good looks and fine boned classic features. Making the very best of her attributes she looked every inch the princess herself with her lustrous fair hair, pale gold full-length silk dress and a short matching jacket, close-cut and covered with thousands of tiny shimmering beads. A choker of fine pearls circled her throat and was matched by drops from delicately scrolled seashell ears. Even the gold shoes were exquisite; discreetly beaded in sunburst lines to the toe and swagged back to the heel. Hope had been secretly pleased at the looks she drew as they took their seats at the table. The food was ambrosial, and the atmosphere and music heavenly – a swing band with a bursting brass section squeezing out real toe-tapping American dance hits. The bottles of Tattinger kept arriving in steady succession and a cheerful, spirited chatter flowed around the table as freely as the champagne. Hope was surprised to find John Cunningham an excellent dancer. He was a tall man with a slight curl in steel-grey hair allowed to wander a fraction over the collar of his elegant tailcoat. Patrician features and a languid English drawl made for a distinguished picture. Less welcome to Hope was the press of his body on hers as they danced; not overt, but just one notch closer than she could feel comfortable with. She was experienced enough to pretend to twist her ankle slightly and so escape quite gracefully and without giving offence. Jake looked dashing, Hope admitted to herself, even if the tanned face hinted at colonial origins and the accent confirmed it. He was wasted on the dowdy Jane Cunningham, she thought, but as the lady in question departed for the powder room, Jake turned in his chair and fixed his eyes on Hope, giving her an exaggerated wink followed by a wide smile. She was pleased as he brought his chair a little closer to hers, but pulling Hope's head gently onto his shoulder, Jake talked straight past her to the older man.

'You'll come down to the Kruger with us when you come out to South Africa, John.' It was statement more than question.

Cunningham leant back in his chair. 'The Kruger Park – delighted to, dear boy, delighted to.' The syrupy vowels oozed content. 'We've heard so much about it from Bob and Thelma. It seems they get down there whenever they can. Closest I've been to the wild is reading old Fitzgerald dont'cha know.' He leant forward conspiratorially. 'But we must talk a little business next week, I fear. I don't know quite how you are fixed, Jake, but what say Monday at the offices at nine o'clock – would that suit? And then a spot of lunch perhaps?'

Jake accepted, singing inside, only too happy to accede. He took a large Havanna from a waiter who had appeared with two large balloon glasses, a decanter of brandy and a bottle of Armagnac.

'Anything for you, my dear?' John inquired of Hope solicitously.

'No thanks, just some more coffee for me, John,' Hope replied, taking her head from Jake's shoulder, 'and I think I'll go and see how Jane is getting on in the ladies room while you men talk shop.'

John watched Hope's derriere sashay across the floor with an appreciative eye and sighed. 'Damn fine looking woman you've got there.' He poked his cigar at Jake. 'You're a lucky chap!'

'You're right there, man,' answered Jake, pleased that Hope had made such a good impression.

'Bob tells me you did your bit in the war, Jake – in the desert was it?'

So they had been discussing him! Jake thought, prickling through and through. He kept it inside forcing an even reply.

'Ja, I was commissioned in the Sixth Armoured Division. The desert first, as you say, and chasing old Kesselring all the way up the boot of Italy, right the way to the top. I caught a packet and was invalided back home early in March, but the Division's last attack, as part of the Eighth Army, of course, was in early April of forty-five I think, between Faenza and Lake Comacchio. The krauts surrendered about three weeks later.'

John guffawed suddenly. 'I had a kraut surrender to me once. Our troops were moving across Germany at great speed towards the end – the same sort of time your chaps were launching your attack in Italy I wouldn't wonder. Anyway, one of our flying columns had more or less bypassed this little hamlet – going lickety split you see – when suddenly up pops this SS Major-chappie wanting to surrender his unit. Well, our fellows were in too much of a hurry, of course, so they just left one of the corporals behind to march the whole lot back to HQ where I obliged him on the spot. Never seen anyone more relieved in my life! The buggers were terrified of surrendering to the Russians – thought they'd be shot out of hand, and were probably right about that, too. Funniest thing was, Jake, that the Major turned out to have been on my Oxford staircase back in thirty-eight. A pompous shit with a most impossible name, Schwartz something or other as I recall but, of course, we all just called him Fritz and stuck any letters we got addressed "To the Occupier" under his door.'

Laughter from the two men was swallowed up in the music.

'I've still got his dagger and hanger in a drawer somewhere at home,' John continued, 'Meine Ehre Heisst Treue – My Honour is Loyalty. That was their motto – it's inscribed on the blade. Funny thing – the SS couldn't have a motto including the word "God" because Christianity derived from the Jewish faith! You know that, Jake, hmmn? Quite unbelievable really.'

John Cunningham drew on his cigar reflectively, his mind still in Germany. His eyes narrowed in the smoke and then focused on

Jake sharply. 'Mind you,' he poked his cigar again, 'they've got all their bloody arrogance back in full measure these three days. Damn starchy little official at the German border gave me the devil of a time filling in forms last year. Kept asking me when I'd last been in Germany and in what capacity and what was the purpose of the visit and so on and so forth – blah diblah diblah. In the end I got absolutely fed up – told him I was coming on holiday and that the last time I'd been to Germany was 1945 and in the capacity of conqueror!'

More laughter greeted Hope and Jane as they rejoined the men bringing what was by Jake's reckoning a very successful evening to a close.

Hope took off her shoes in the taxi with a grateful sigh of relief. 'God, my feet are killing me!'

'How's the ankle?' Jake asked.

'Oh fine, it was just a ploy ... Dear John,' Hope's voice faltered for a second.

'Dear John dances a little close for comfort, I'm afraid.'

Jake leaned forward – concerned. 'Christ, I hope you didn't say anything!'

'No, no, don't worry yourself.' Hope answered. 'I didn't slight him or anything.'

Jake gave her a suspicious glance – almost as it if had been her fault, Hope thought, and then leaned back into his seat, relieved.

The taxi accelerated away from the traffic lights with Hope wishing that he could find it in him to consider her feelings just for once.

The following day saw Jake on the train to Chelmsford in Essex, travelling northeast out of London. He'd told Hope that he was going to look up an old friend, an officer friend who had married an English girl after the war and subsequently emigrated to live in England. Hope seemed only slightly disappointed not to be going with him, but was expecting her friend Margaret up from Ludlow in Shropshire for the weekend. No doubt, Jake thought, it hadn't been too difficult for her to persuade herself to be content to have him out of the way while the two of them caught up on old times, not to mention the indulgence of London shopping to look forward to with an allowance Jake made sure was overly generous.

As Jake bumped along in what, to his mind, was an absolutely filthy train towards Chelmsford, he wondered how the intervening years had treated Ashleigh. They had met in the hospital compound outside Cairo and it had been unforgettable, not least because he'd only just come in the previous night as a stretcher case and so riddled with paralysing diphtheria toxins that he could hardly lift a hand or swallow. What he'd thought of a few days earlier as just a desert sore throat and feeling of being vaguely unwell had rapidly progressed into a creeping paralysis that was terrifying. He'd woken early the following morning to the sound of his mosquito net being pulled aside – God, he'd never forgotten the sound – and there standing smiling at him on either side of the bed were the nurse and the orderly. And fuck, that was it wasn't it? That first sight of them both and their looks across the bed at one another, that ricochet of complicit smiles, conspirators in something he, most extraordinarily and sick as he was, felt instantly part of. And he'd been so sick, so very, very sick and so bloody helpless which had only made it easier. For all of them really. One minute an independent soldier out in the blue, and the next landed powerless in a hospital bed, weak as dishwater and putty in the hands of Peter Pan and Wendy gone to war! Those days had changed him. Days of being fed, watered, bathed and turned in his bed by the twins: whispered to, cajoled, shaved and slowly nursed back to health. It took three weeks of lying prone.

Three long frustrating weeks of fruit and oranges dipped in Pinky – permanganate of potash – and drinking purple chlorinated tea, swishing away the huge bloated flies that were everywhere all over everything all the time. Clouds of mosquitoes came at night, crickets plopped and mantises and locusts hung in the mosquito netting. It was only the armies of ants that could be kept at bay by standing the bed legs in pots of Lysol.

Convalescence made up for everything. It had to be a long, slow one to prevent cardiac complications, but Cairo was only an hour and a half away and he'd gone in with the twins in the back of a lorry. If nurse, officer and orderly together made for an unusual sight, it hadn't really mattered as they were swallowed up instantly in a seething mass of people jamming the city and its streets. The clothes were too fantastic: turbans, caps and a thousand bobbing fez. Suits, uniforms and striped galabeahs jostled for space in a mix of cars, lorries, camels and carts pulled by oxen or scrawny donkeys. They haggled for bright semi-precious stones in the Al Muski bazaar and drank gritty, black coffee served in tiny glasses, and later did the sights, too, of course; the pyramids and the sphinx. Ashleigh and Ashton had been saving up money and leave to go down to Luxor by train with him on a Cook's tour and a fortnight later they were in their grand hotel fronting onto the Nile. The high ceilings, cool lemon drinks and whirling fans made it a wonderful refuge from a sea of desert heat. That first night they went out with men and donkeys under a full moon to the Temple of Karnak and walked hand in hand in silent awe under the seated stone figures of pharaohs. Taking their hands – the same familiar ones that had nursed him over the days, nights and weeks – seemed as natural to Jake as anything could. Later, as he lay falling into sleep with a slow fan turning high above his hotel bed the two of them had slipped into his room and come to stand on either side of the bed. Just as they'd done in the hospital. And he knew then they'd be smiling those same smiles, and that it had all been planned this way from the start. They stripped where they stood, clothes falling at their feet, two slim, beautiful reeds silvered in the moonlight. A heartbeat pause and then they were in his bed beside him, hands reaching for him and claiming him.

At Chelmsford station he organised himself a taxi and gave instruction to the surly driver – an address in Stock. It was a short trip out of the city and then down a road cutting through Galleywood Common before they approached and entered the little village. The taxi turned left immediately down the side of a tiny cricket field where Jake could see a portly groundsman rolling the square with slow, measured tread. They wiggled through several leafy lanes at the back of the village to find the address, which turned out to be a quaint little cottage at the bottom of a single track. Jake clambered out, paid off the taxi and with his senses agog and aware of a shortness of breath, turned to walk up the gravel path. The door of the cottage flew open with a shriek. Ashleigh launched herself at him, kissing him hard, full on the lips.

'Bloody criminal! You look so disgustingly healthy, Jake. God, it's good to see you again!'

She grabbed his unprotesting arm and hugging it to her, waltzed him into the cottage, taking his coat and hanging it before turning and hugging him again fiercely.

'Come through, come through – I thought tea but then reckoned scotch would probably be more it.'

Jake watched as she put ice in a glass and poured him a drink. Dress apart, she didn't appear to have changed at all. The same sylph-like figure, the crackling energy and bright eyes that flashed, taking such obvious, wonderful delight in the simple fact that he was there.

'You haven't changed a bit.'

'Flatterer!' Ashleigh answered. She was wearing dark green, fine-striped corduroy slacks over her slim legs, a pretty navy blue blouse and patch-worked open waistcoat with gold buttons. So different, Jake thought as he took his drink.

'Well, the hair style, I suppose, and the clothes, I never saw you out of uniform, remember.'

Ashleigh threw back her head of dark hair and laughed.

'You bloody well did! Stark naked for the best part of a week in Luxor if you remember, don't tell me you've forgotten!'

Their eyes locked as Jake slowly shook his head, a smile tugging at his lips.

'No, I've never forgotten any of it.'

'Pleased to hear it. Gawd, no drink yet, what am I doing?'

She turned to the sideboard drinks tray.

'G and T for me. That rhymes, ee, how pathetic. I must be nervous or something. By the way, we're going out to a pub for dinner ... okay? I can't bear the idea of cooking while you're here.'

Nervous, my arse, thought Jake.

'Sounds great,' he replied, 'but can I have a bath before we go? That train trip has made me feel uiters vuil, very grimy.'

'Our infamous British Rail,' Ashleigh grimaced, took a sip and looked at her glass appreciatively.

'That's soo much better. Yes, the trains, they're an appalling advert for the country aren't they? But you're here and that's the main thing. And the bath's easily fixed, but later, let me fix your drink first. Bird and one wing and all that crap.'

Jake got his freshened glass with a 'cheers ... Captain,'

'Yes, and cheers, nurse, and God, that seems so long ago now, you know; the war and Italy and all that. I lost some bloody good mates up there. Still,' he shrugged his shoulders, 'if it hadn't been for the war, I never would have met you, now would I?'

So it went on and so instantly at ease with one another were they that the years just fell away, both of them lounging back in comfortable settees drinking and chatting about anything and everything that came to mind. And that, of course, included Ashton.

'Where is Ash, by the way?'

'Down in London making a fortune as usual. He knows you're here, of course, and can't wait to see you, I mean he's frantic to, but the house he's doing at the moment has got to be finished by the end of next week.'

'This decorating thing you wrote to me about?'

'Yes, and this decorating thing, as you call it, is making my brother a small fortune, Jake. I mean he's so brilliant at it, it's wicked.'

'So he's in London most of the time?'

'Practically all the time, these days.'

'And that's okay with you? I mean you guys were sort of inseparable.'

Ashleigh made round eyes and waved her glass.

'Be a darling and get me a drink. No, I'm not as stuck in Stock as you might stink – sorry, had to do the little alliteration there, I mean as you might think. I get down to London often enough and see plenty of him; shit, I think I'm there far too often sometimes, but it's where I do most of my private nursing and I need my regular theatre fix every now and again as well. But you know, if Ash goes on at this rate we can all retire soon. Put up our feet and vegetate. Go nowhere. Watch the grass grow. I've got a stake in the business, you know. Not that I do any of the work – he does all that.'

Ashleigh smiled before adding, 'I suppose that makes me what you might call his sleeping partner.' She laughed.

'But you'd know all about that, Jake.'

Somewhere in the distance a church bell tolled.

Ashleigh pointed at the sound. 'That's what I'd like, Jake. Country life on the small scale with a dash of London for colour,' she took her drink with a laugh, 'and you here preferably to look after me, speaking of which – the looking after – I'm having a sip of this and going to run your bath for you.'

Jake was luxuriating in a deep, sudsy bath which was something of a novelty when, after a small knock on the door, Ashleigh appeared from around it, whisky glass in hand.

'I thought you might need another refill and a back scrub.'

Jake sat up to take the glass and she knelt behind him, slowly soaping his back and then rinsing it down with a soft sponge. Looking at his back brought urgent memories flooding back. She softly kissed the side of his neck and murmured, 'you don't mind this, do you?'

Jake leant back and sought her mouth.

'Wait!' she said. She stood up, quickly slipped out of her clothes, and stepped into the bath sitting down opposite him between his legs. Her hands glided down the inside of his legs and she gave a soft moan of acknowledgement as she found him.

'Holy Maroni, Ashleigh's got her pony.'

They laughed about it later, because getting from bath to bed had been a complicated but extremely urgent obstacle course. Towels, water, kissing, grappling, grabbing, tripping over shoes and clothes 'and you slamming poor pony against the basin, Jake!' squeaked Ashleigh squeezing her nose and trying to keep the giggles in.

'What's with the pony?' Jake asked, infected by the giggling.

'Something to ride, you idiot.'

'A cocky jockey.'

Ashleigh wasn't winning with the giggles. 'Didn't it hurt? I mean ... Boingg – poor pony!'

'He didn't feel a thing at the time, I can promise you.'

'Like water off a fuck's back, you mean? And lucky you went straight through the door.'

'Jeez, Ashleigh, you're something else. Come here.'

'No, wait – don't you want to know why?' Ashleigh made buck-teeth and Chinese eyes with her fingers, Confucius say man with elexion go sideway fro door going to Bangkok!'

The second time was better, less urgent, and they slept for a dreamless hour afterwards, entwined and sated. They rose easy and languid and took another slow bath together, chatting as they dressed and then set out for their evening meal in Ashleigh's old Morgan.

Jake thought the car an apt reflection of her personality and enjoyed the animal growl of the engine and the rapid acceleration as they pulled away from the cottage. The suspension wasn't the best for bumpy lanes perhaps, but the wind in his hair as they bowled along was wildly exhilarating, the countryside slashing past in a green blur. He caught the mixed scents of mown grass and diesel as they hustled past a farm tractor working the hedgerow.

'There it is,' Ashleigh shouted over the roar of the engine about ten minutes later as they approached a thatched pub perched on the side of a triangular green. She changed down into third gear, double declutched into second and with a flick of the steering wheel, pulled into the pub car park.

'Some car you've got there, Ashleigh.' Jake commented as he extracted himself inexpertly from the passenger seat. She smiled as she took off her headscarf.

'It's not a car, Jake, it's my child ... one of my small pleasures to keep me sane in this boring old world.' She laughed, shaking her head, mahogany hair bouncing gently on her shoulders. They had to duck to get through a diminutive front door under the thatch leading to a cosy, enticing interior. Ashleigh chose a discreet table in a nook beside a small fire in the annexe whilst Jake made his way to the bar to order drinks and ask for a menu. On his return he found Ashleigh gazing wistfully into the coals.

'Do you know, they always have a fire here, or nearly always. I love this little place – adore it – and it's so nice to get away for a change.' She paused and then added a little disparagingly, 'away from the village that is.' At the sight of Jake's questioning look she continued, 'well, I value my anonymity, darling, and that's a commodity in short supply in the village. The professional bloody busybodies, the Hatchet Annies, are forever trying to poke their noses into other people's business – mine especially.' Jake was rather amused and prodded gently, 'Are they really that bad?'

'You have no idea!' Ashleigh took a hefty swig of her gin and tonic and then fumbled in her bag for cigarettes and lighter whilst she sorted her thoughts into a more congruous answer. She lit a cigarette, returned the lighter to the bag with a flourish and then fixed her gaze on Jake, picking a shred of tobacco from her lip.

'You see, Jake, I don't fit into other people's perception of what constitutes a normal life round here. I don't work in the village, I don't shop in the village – for anything whatsoever – and I don't belong to any societies, clubs or churches. I just keep myself to myself. If I was of an age, had a hooked nose, a broomstick and a familiar, I'm sure they'd have drowned me in the nearest river as a witch long ago! Or would have done a few centuries ago. It's a village of peeping windows.'

'And so?'

'Well, I just put it about when I arrived all those years ago that I was a private nurse who worked long and peculiar hours, but they'd still be delighted if they could winkle some tasty bit of smut or gossip out of me to give their humdrum lives an ounce of spice.'

'What do you do with your life, Ashleigh?' Jake was intrigued. 'Your letters give precious little clue really – apart from news that you've holidayed in Patmos or wherever.'

Ashleigh nodded. 'Oh yes, I travel abroad a good deal, that's true – Italy especially. Fortunately, private nursing pays reasonably well, and I'm single which helps – but you're not trying to wheedle information out of me that the village gossips would give their eye teeth for, are you, Jake?' A smile came to draw the sting from the mocking accusation. Jake waved his hand as a hasty disclaimer. 'No – no way, I really didn't mean to pry.'

'But you would still like to know, I bet' Ashleigh kept her amused smile for a second and then sighed.

'You'll be gone soon, so I don't suppose there's any harm in telling you … some of it anyway. You see I decided very early on – when I was about seventeen in fact – that I never wanted kids, or to be more accurate, I wasn't any good with children – young children anyway. Not enough patience, and no maternal instincts whatsoever. Give me a baby to hold and what happens? It starts bawling its head off, every single time. And that was another thing, I couldn't seem to hold them properly either, not naturally or comfortably like other women do … Christ, I felt guilty about it for years. After all, having children is what women do, Jake, caring for them is what they're good at, our deadly common destiny, but I seem to have missed the boat when they handed out this particular thing – what do you call it? This natural ability. Dad always told me to stick to what I'm good at, and it was sound advice. So … no children for me I'm afraid – it wouldn't be fair on them, and it wouldn't be fair on me.'

Ashleigh paused to draw on her cigarette, upright in her chair now and, Jake could see, a little on the defensive.

'And marriage is to have children, right? So little point in that exercise either, not to mention my parents' well-documented 100-year war, which thoroughly disabused me of the whole institution anyway. Mind you,' her eyes softened, 'I can understand the companionship element of marriage all too well, and I envy it enormously, hugely, in some of the couples I see, ones that have that contentment in each other. But I'm a solitary soul by nature, Jake; probably a bit whacky too, so marriage isn't for me – most definitely not, I'd be a disaster.

And that means there are "rules",' Ashleigh made inverted commas with her fingers, 'rules I've made up for myself here. No local contacts for instance, so I don't have any stray men sniffing around to see if I am on heat at last, and several sort of compartments in my life that are all pretty well exclusive – separate from one another. I suppose I should really live in London, or some other big city somewhere, but the cottage has taken me years to get just to my liking, and I adore my garden too. It's my own little fort – too little for a castle see – my stronghold if you like, and I simply love it to bits.'

'Am I one of your compartments then?' Jake asked softly.

'Yes, you are – sort of,' Ashleigh chortled, 'more like in one though – in a big, important, luxurious compartment – like the ones British Rail certainly don't have!'

Jake barked a laugh as the publican appeared at their table to take orders. Jake reckoned he'd try the native oysters on offer and Ashleigh opted for a smoked salmon concoction with capers.

'These native oysters – they're black or something are they?' Jake teased.

'You know I can understand why we gave all our colonies back sometimes. You can be such a pig, Jake Stevens! The only thing black about them is the Guinness you should wash them down with.'

'No man, white wine surely?'

Ashleigh shrugged her shoulders. 'It's optional, but a Chablis should suit us both.'

The publican disappeared with their order and Jake nodded his thanks with a confession that he hadn't been able to make head or tail of the continental wine list up at the bar. A waiter arrived with the wine. The young man poured with exaggerated care. Smiling her thanks as he left, Ashleigh sat back and perused Jake over the rim of her glass.

'Does that all sound too awful Jake? I mean about the way I live? I'm sure I must sound like some awful, cold, heartless bitch. It's not too bad if I think it to myself – but I've never said it out loud before – Christ, it sounds quite dreadful!'

Jake saw that the question, although it was extravagantly put, was meant in all earnest. Calling a spade a spade hadn't even been a problem to him, but this obviously worried her: typical woman, he thought. Jake toyed in the basin of one of his oysters with the little fork for a lengthy second before answering.

'No one could classify you as cold, my sweet, but I don't think you meant your bedroom manners did you? No, in answer to you, I don't think you're cold. Single minded – perhaps, uncompromising, definitely. You have your boundaries, your "rules" as you call them, but sticking to them gives you a great freedom, doesn't it? I envy it in a way.'

Leaning back he pondered the inside of his wine glass momentarily and continued,

'I don't suppose for a minute that I could make a success of that type of life, but you obviously can. I admire it. It's ballsy, and I like that. England is full of eccentrics anyway, isn't it? You're probably just one of its more interesting types.'

Ashleigh bridled coquettishly at the oblique compliment. 'Thanks, Prince Charming.'

Jake shook his head, 'Christ, I didn't mean to mock you, not for a second, and I'm flattered you telling me about your life – I really am. You might call yourself strange and a bit different, Ashleigh, but you're about the most fascinating woman I've ever met, and that's by a long chalk.'

Few people can resist flattery, even if it is ladled on with a trowel, and with two glasses of Chablis under the belt, Ashleigh had little inclination to either. She giggled and leant forward with a stage whisper. 'I know oysters have aphrodisiac qualities, but do you think we have time for a main course before we go home, I'm famished!'

The publican reappeared and she ordered a Chateau Haut Brion which they appreciated in slow, reflective sips.

'Life's too short to drink shabby wine. Do you drink much red wine in Africa, Jake?'

He raised his eyes from the menu. 'Uhm, well yes, we have some excellent wines of our own, and a lot of them are made from the same grape as this if I'm not mistaken – the cabernet sauvignon. They certainly don't taste a bit like this though.'

'How so?'

'This gives you that fumey bite at the back of the throat which our chaps, nice as they are, don't really. Ours are more a sort of all-over taste.'

She nodded. 'I'm simply mad about clarets, and as the price will tell you, this is one of the very best. It's a first growth and there are only about four or five of them. Latour, Lafite, this one Haut Brion, Margeaux and … oh dear, it's on the tip of my tongue,' she hesitated and then remembered, 'Rothschild, that's it – Mouton Rothschild, the pretender. A second growth but every bit as good as the others.'

Ashleigh seized her glass and took an energetic, slopping swig.

'Bloody Americans!'

'What?'

'No, I'm going off at a tangent here. Sorry. It's the name – nothing to do with the wine – the Mouton – except that I just happened to have finished nursing a very difficult American in London – first cousin to a Rothschild as he keeps telling me. Rich as Croesus and absolute hell on wheels. Conceited and contemptuous. A one hundred percent genuine, dyed in the wool, foreign old fart.'

'You don't like any Americans then?' This was so amusing.

'Generalisations are like comparisons, Jake, they're odious: but, yes, we're like the rest of the world – we detest the Yanks – in the cordial English sort of way, of course.'

'You're talking in circles. That's a contradiction.'

'I'm allowed to, I'm an eccentric, remember? But we don't hate them. It's the same sort of feeling you get when your rich sister-in-law's spoilt brat tears around your house all day screaming his head off and ends up by kicking your favourite cat. I mean the way they dress for a start, Jake, beyond belief! Why get tarted up in all those frightful checks and loud colours when all it does is draw attention to their appalling taste? Old fuddy-duddy, the one remove from a Rothschild, looks like a lecherous old turkey with highlights when he goes out – right down to his disgusting neck wattle. Why advertise you're an American? Ye Gods, if it were me, I'd hide under the nearest stone. And the arrogance, Jake, all that overbearing arrogance – about what may I ask? Material sophistication masquerading as intelligence – that's what!'

'So, prejudice isn't a South African preserve then?'

'Quite so,' Ashleigh laughed, 'clever that. Yes, we have all the vices, too – xenophobia, and envy – so the Yanks will tell you, except that we don't spell it out in our legislation like you do in South Africa – we are in the majority here – that's the difference.'

They'd decided on a chateaubriand to complement the wine,

ordered a second bottle of the Haut Brion and fell to desultory chatter about plans for the rest of the week.

'I can't believe I've got you here at last, and for the whole weekend as well,' exclaimed Ashleigh for the umpteenth time. 'Lucky me! Mind you it's as well you came by taxi. A strange car at the cottage for the best part of a week would raise a gale of whispers.'

'How far are we away from Stock?' Jake inquired.

'About ten miles or so, but most of them are far too tight-fisted to pay for gourmet food like this. Marcel – he's the chef here – tells me it's mainly wealthy businessmen with expense accounts that frequent the place – and women with extravagant lovers of course!'

She beamed and Jake chuckled, stretching contentedly. The chateaubriand arrived with due ceremony from publican and waiter as they shepherded the plates and silver platters to the table in orderly succession. It was served expertly, with the minimum of fuss and clatter, and they tucked in with relish whilst their glasses were charged.

Ashleigh wanted to know all about the business side of Jake's trip. 'If it comes off ... this directorship,' Jake commented between mouthfuls, 'I'll be in England at least two or three times a year, or so Bob Wilkens, my senior partner, says. How would that suit you?' he asked. 'Will I be allowed to get into a different compartment?'

Ashleigh hurried to finish her mouthful. 'If this afternoon's performance is anything to go by, you can get into as many compartments as you wish, my love. You can take over the whole bloody train if you like.' She waved her fork around. 'At this rate, I'll hardly be able to walk by the end of the week!' Ashleigh's artless turn of phrase brought a pleasant tug of pleasure to Jake's loins. Ashleigh held his gaze, a mischievous smile playing on her mouth. Complimenting a man's libido always worked such a treat. Not so artless after all.

They were interrupted by the bustling arrival of a large, white aproned, busy man at Ashleigh's side.

'Ah, mademoiselle, 'ow wonderful to have you back.' He turned to Jake. 'Monsieur – pardon – I am Marcel, zis lady, 'ow do you say? A true gourmet – she travels you understand, to cook for 'er – vraiment, mon grand plaisir.' The expressive hands parted and offered like butterfly wings. 'Now what for dessert? Crème Brulee I zink, and some Armagnac I zink. I must prepare.' He planted a noisy kiss on each of Ashleigh's cheeks and hurried away in a duck's walk towards the kitchen, arms flailing. Ashleigh was in a fit of giggles, eyes shining with wicked delight.

'Marcel's a real sweetie, Jake, and cooks like a dream, but I'm told he's hell, absolute hell in the kitchen. Wonderful entertainment for the patrons too – providing they behave. They threw out a German couple last year because they had the temerity to ask for salt and pepper can you believe – quelle bloody horreur!'

Their evening wound down gently and Jake drove the Morgan very sedately home with Ashleigh's head resting easily and contentedly on his shoulder.

The following day they motored up to Cambridge and spent the day as tourists. King's College Chapel (a great definition of understatement), the Backs, and at Ashleigh's insistence, the Fitzwilliam Museum, to seek out the Stubbs portrait of a horse called Gimcrack. Jake peered over her shoulder at the painting with indifference.

'Looks like a jockey on a pony.'

Ashleigh laughed, 'that's just the point. I came to see it because they trumpet it as one of the museum's treasures. Being a Stubbs, that is, and that's exactly what I thought – terribly disappointing with this Pratt up on what is little more than a pony. And that really was his name, John Pratt. But when I read up about him ... Gimcrack, he was tiny, fifteen something, but could beat the pants off anything else. My type of horse exactly and just the opposite of that monster Phar Lap that's the Australian idea of a hero. A huge horse with the heart the size of a poodle. Sixteen pounds. You can just imagine them weighing it can't you!'

'Your slip's showing again,' Jake warned her.

Ashleigh wrinkled her nose, 'yes, but it's fun isn't it?'

Jake commented on her intimate knowledge of the place.

'Oh, Ash was at Queen's and he'd ask me up for the May Ball every year – usually as a partner for one of his spotty friends – but it's a magical place, Jake. After the first time, I used to come up here whenever I could – to escape – because it has so little to do with the real world, and I liked that – more than you can believe – more than was healthy, quite possibly. It's really difficult to explain to anyone who hasn't lived the life here, and yes, the architecture is beautiful, and yes, the colleges are stuffed with history, but it's the atmosphere that is so extraordinary, rarified almost. And being young helps enormously, it's probably essential in fact, and the minute you leave it's gone – quicksilver in the hand. I come back to relive a past, my crock of memories.'

They were walking and she took Jake's hand, giving his sleeve a quick rub with her other hand. 'They just need a little shine now and again to keep the lustre from fading, you see?' Jake's expression was quizzical, an invitation to go on.

'I met people from all over the country – all over the world too; some fabulously rich and unbelievably spoiled and others poor as church mice. The meek, the mild, the vain, the eccentric: sporty people, booky people, radicals, the lot. Cambridge caters for every class and category of person you could imagine, Jake, and some you couldn't – some that would appal you, frankly. Ash – in one of his more lucid moments, called it a three year mind fuck.' She giggled. 'It's a crude description, but it's still probably the best I've heard.'

'No boyfriends?' asked Jake.

'Interesting you should ask that.' Ashleigh commented, 'It was a curiously sexless sort of place at the time,' she waved a finger round, 'masses of cerebral shenanigans steeped in alcohol for the most part, and for me and Ash the sex was – well you know how it was.'

Jake didn't know how it was. Not exactly. And he would have very much liked to have known. But this surely wasn't the time to ask.

On the Saturday morning, back in Stock, Ashleigh was already up and dressed in one of her multi-coloured outfits – red slacks and green silk shirt – when she woke him with tea. She looked incredibly fresh and vibrant and he caught a waft of something citrusy as she leant to brush his forehead with a kiss.

'I'm off to do some shopping in Chelmsford which would only bore you to tears. You have a lie in. I should be back before ten – so if you can think of something nice to surprise me with – I'll promise you a proper English cooked breakfast in return.'

He heard the Morgan roar away and sat on the bed to drink his tea. Jake smiled to himself. A lie in – fuck, that was an indulgence he'd never granted himself – ever, a criminal waste of time by his reckoning. He shaved, had one of his morning cold baths, dressed, and then went into the living room with a cup of coffee and a cigarette. It was the first time he had actually taken time to look around properly and he wasn't surprised Ashleigh was wed to the place. Her main pictures reflected an eclectic (a new word he'd learned) taste, with Southern European scenes – Italian ones, he reckoned, especially predominating. The largest, an oil painting some three by four foot wide, stretched wide, almost too big, over the fireplace. A distant Mediterranean blue sea and close to, a veranda drenched with sun set with a heavy, crude table laden with local fare. Curled fish looking like small mullet blackened on some invisible stove, bowls of shiny olives steeped in oil, salads rich with feta, soft tomatoes and red onions. A dark wine bottle and glass lay to one side beside the single plate and fork. There were many other paintings, but this large central picture dictated the atmosphere of the room. Flanking the picture, hung one on either side of the chimneybreast, were immense, roughly thrown plates, decorated in swirls of blue on white. Necklaces of dolphins encircling a central seahorse on each extended the maritime character wonderfully well. Portions of the three remaining walls in the living room were draped with heavy linens in opulent gypsy colours, suspended from gleaming brass rails fixed flush with the ceiling. Jake nodded to himself: whether it was clothes or furnishings ... or life, Ashleigh wasn't afraid of colour. The remainder of the wall space was host to a mass of smaller pictures that jostled for elbowroom. Oils, pastels, watercolours and pen and ink sketches – they were all there. The chairs and sofas were all large and comfortable, the more decrepit of these covered with throws and cushions in primary colour combinations rich to the eye. Most of the cottage was deep pile carpeted wall to wall in a plain oatmeal colour with Persian and oriental rugs overlaying almost all the available floor space. The only illuminations were from the many lamps perched on various side tables, an antique desktop, and a baby grand piano. The piano top was covered with a vast array of picture frames – some of them silver displaying what Jake presumed were family photographs. He peered at one of a kid on a woolly pony. That would be her niece, her elder brother Giles' sprog. He couldn't remember her name now, but left fatherless, evidently, when the silly bugger had got himself shot two days before Armistice. Ashleigh had been all tearful about it yesterday when they were talking about the war. Jake stood straight and stretched his back, remembering her saying that the wife had subsequently married into an Irish family, so that was all right then. His gaze lifted to a glass vase of blue irises behind the frames at the back of the piano that complemented a room exuding pure sanctuary and ease. He envied her this place. In the kitchen, the carpets gave way to quarry tiles. Small squares of turquoise tile laid obliquely at the junction of each square of four of terra cotta gave vivid counterpoint and took the eye forward to the pine dressers and pine surfaces all crammed with the paraphernalia of cooking. There were delightful personal touches with postcards, mostly Italian and Greek he noted, pasted randomly where space could be found; small pictures, shelves for old and new recipe books, and a melange of crockery of indeterminate origin arranged in seemingly haphazard fashion – a haphazardness, he realised suddenly that was a skilful contrivance. There were books and magazines everywhere in the cottage. Jake supposed that a solitary life encouraged reading – something he did very little of, except for accounts and the daily paper of course. He was idly paging through Country Life in the kitchen when he heard the Morgan pull in and then Ashleigh's voice from the hall.

'Don't tell me you've taken up reading at long last?'

Jake's distinct lack of literary and artistic inclination had long been a source of amusement to Ashleigh, but she took it as a failing of a colonial upbringing rather than any shortfall of his own. Indeed, he indulged her interests without any hint of condescension, and that she found civilised in itself.

'Have you thought up any nice surprise for me yet?'

The last three words were delivered in a crescendo squeal as Jake lifted her up by the waist and plonked her, giggling, onto the pine table. He stood close and she hooked her heels around his calves, leaning back on the flat of her hands.

'I think I've found a novel use for your kitchen table. It's at a very interesting height!'

'Watch out for the eggs, Jake, they're behind me in that shopping bag.'

Ashleigh couldn't stop giggling.

'Scrambled eggs,' he was laughing too now, 'we'll have scrambled eggs.'

9

Jake had plenty to think about on the afternoon train from Chelmsford back to Liverpool Street early on Monday morning. There had been no tearful farewells today as there had been in Egypt all those years back. This time she'd just kissed him hard on the lips, given him a fierce hug and made him promise to land the appointment he'd told her about over dinner – 'Just get it, you hear?'

That was tomorrow's business, and – no – he thought, he needed no pushing, no incentive.

'Damn, damn – I'm so ready for this,' he muttered to himself and rubbed his hands, frisking them energetically. The old lady sitting opposite him in the carriage looked at him suspiciously, disapprovingly, marking him as a foreigner.

Ashleigh was really quite remarkable. He supposed, musing to himself, that his life, in its own way, was also quite compartmentalised. A bit like hers, in spite of what he'd said! He had his work, which now promised fresher, greener pastures; his liaison with her which was gloriously unencumbered, his clubs and his golf at home (those two belonged together and fed off one another) and his family life with Hope and the boys who – young Matt apart – would be out living their own life soon enough.

He reflected that he had only really wanted the two children, but it was Hope who had insisted on the third. She'd even had the nerve to threaten to adopt a child unless he would give her one, and so, he remembered sourly, he had had to give in. His mind went back to the standing argument they had about Matt last year before the holiday. All that nonsense from Hope about him neglecting the boy. What rubbish, and hadn't he gone on to remind her that having him had been her idea all along? Not something he wanted then ... or now for that matter. The raised voices late at night after a party, and fuelled by alcohol, had woken the boy who had come to stand at the open door to their bedroom listening to the row until finally they had seen him. Jake had never been certain how much the boy had heard or even understood, but he didn't care, frankly, and hadn't given it another thought until now.

Continuing his mental inventory, there was also the wear and tear that the bearing and birth of three children had exacted on Hope's body – not a great deal he granted, but there was still some measure of contrast with Ashleigh. Fresh images of her lean belly flashed through his mind and he shifted in the seat as the thoughts took hold. And he wondered how he would find things with Hope after the exhilaration and excitement of being so charged and alive these last few days. Sex with Hope happened about once every three or four weeks these days – even less frequently if there were undue pressures on either of them. There was that rule between the two of them that either could say no without giving offence, so sometimes these intervals between sex lasted up to six or eight weeks. And, of course, rules were there to be broken, but there was little doubt that his desire for sex these days, at home anyway, was considerably less; sometimes even done as a duty. He assumed that was just what marriage was, and wouldn't constant repetition of the same thing make anyone bored? Of course it would. What was the name of the play he'd read about in the papers over the weekend? The Mousetrap, that was it, the something thousandth performance. How did the actors do it? Day after day, night after night, the same actions, the same words, the same inflections even. It would drive him crazy. Jake shook his head with a dismissive grunt which earned another frown of disapproval from Mother Grundy sitting opposite.

He knew that to some extent, his sexual drive had been redirected into a striving for success at work. He craved success, just as he used to crave sex, urgently, constantly. Then a weekend like this when all the stirred sexual embers burst into flame, searing his senses. Perhaps, Jake thought, he could now quite possibly have the best of both worlds: a conventional family life in South Africa and an exhilarating mistress in England, one whom he knew wouldn't be making any ludicrous demands on him either. He had no intention of ever trying to break up his marriage. To begin with, it was a form of social suicide as far as he was concerned, as witnessed by his sister Edith who had divorced a philanderer only to compound her error by marrying that dreadful man Frank. When last were those two invited anywhere for dinner for Christ's sake? And this while the philanderer married his pretty young thing and took her off to a new life in another city. There would be none of that, just some adjustments to fit in with the changes in his life, but he knew that a director's chair in London would make all the difference.

He phoned from the station, so Hope and her friend Margaret were waiting for him in the lounge at the Goring.

'Darling, did you have a wonderful time?' Hope asked cheerfully as she bounced up from her chair, taking the peck on the cheek. 'I can't wait to show you the new dresses we bought – you won't have that fashion leper as a wife any longer! You remember Margie.' Jake greeted Margaret, sat and listened to the prattle about their shopping expeditions wondering briefly how much it was going to cost him. The enthusiasm suggested to him more than he'd allowed. Worth it – worth every penny of it. Business or pleasure, Jake's moral sense spoke to him only of expedience. The small voice of conscience lay deep inside him well coated with lacquered layers of indifference, and it was a very small voice beyond hearing.

He ordered a scotch for himself, refills for the girls, and asked about dinner plans. Hope smiled brightly at him in answer. 'We thought just dinner in the hotel tonight, darling. You've got that important business meeting first thing tomorrow and you'll want to be fresh, no doubt.'

Jake was grateful for the consideration as they moved through to eat, and that the girls could provide most of the chatter amongst the normal clamour of a busy hotel dining room. Hope inquired in interested fashion about his weekend with his friend. Jake started to recite the long list of banalities he'd prepared, and as soon as he saw her starting to lose interest, judged it safe to switch to another subject.

His alarm clock sounded just as the telephone rang with the desk clerk giving him his promised early morning call. He acknowledged the call and asked the clerk to arrange a taxi to pick him up at eight o'clock sharp. He took an early breakfast alone in a deserted dining room with a sleepy waiter and then spent half an hour combing the morning papers for snippets of business, political and sports news. He wanted to be able to make informed small talk both at the meeting and the lunch afterwards. The taxi was on time and so was he, arriving at Brathrow Steel offices at a quarter to nine. The huge, spanking-new granite building shouted money, confirming the exhaustive research Jake had done on the company. Great wealth here. The secretary was expecting him, giving him a pleasant smile, a seat and a promise of a cup of coffee to follow. Before it had time to materialise, John Cunningham arrived – glided in, really – greeted Jake in his habitual smooth manner, and steered him down a corridor to his capacious office. In spite of the genial manner, John Cunningham's suave exterior concealed a sharp mind, and after their coffee had arrived, he grilled Jake at length about his involvement with other steel companies in Johannesburg. Jake's concise and pithy answers seemed to please him, and at length he slapped the flat of his hand on his desk in approval. 'Capital, Jake, absolutely capital: it's just as Bob told me, old chap, you have all the local contacts we will be looking for. I'm delighted you've worked so closely with Baldwins in Langlaagte. We'll need the self same structures and contacts they have in place when we start to set up.'

'There will be no conflict of interest, I hope?' ventured Jake.

'No, no: heavens no,' he was assured genially. 'Bob will just put one of your other partners onto their books and you will be assigned to ours. But I want you in as one of the directors Jake – financial director. We're putting a lot of money into this venture, and I want someone with a trustworthy accounting eye in place overseeing it. The two others, managing director and operations director, will be Seymour and Evans, two of my young Turks coming from head office here. You'll meet them at lunch. Speaking of which, I think it's time to go.' Jake glanced at the hands of his slim Bezzieme watch and was surprised to see it was twelve thirty already. He'd been closeted with John Cunningham for over three hours.

Dickie Seymour and Gareth Evans were chalk and cheese: the one a Londoner with a plumy, upper class drawl, and the other a Welshman with the lilting, singsong accent of the valleys. They wanted to know all about Africa and quizzed him endlessly about life on the southern continent. Over coffee and brandy, conversation fell to cricket and rugby, and Jake realised that both men were sport fanatics. 'You'll both get along fine,' he chuckled, 'South Africans are all sports mad. Do either of you play golf by the way?' Both were keen hackers, they said, and Jake proceeded to outline the charms and allurements of Royal Johannesburg and the Country Club in Auckland Park. Talking about home, his clubs, batting on his own turf, as it were, was such a pleasure and he could quite easily have got carried away, but Jake wasn't even tempted. Instead, he just sketched the picture lightly leaving John free to continue to hold court. This was Cunningham's show, the Cunningham business, his appointments. Jake had got his foot in the door, and that was enough, quite enough – for now.

It was after four when they rose from the table in a great cloud of bonhomie and cigar smoke. John Cunningham walked him the few steps to his taxi and clapped him on the back with one hand, shaking his hand enthusiastically with the other.

'Welcome on board, Jake – if you'll excuse the pun!' He roared at his own joke. 'I'll get Jane to give … aaah,' he searched momentarily for her name, 'your Hope a ring. We'll have you both down to our place in the country for a weekend before you leave.'

Jake took the steps at the hotel up to their first floor room, two at a time. He burst through the door to find Hope at the small desk writing postcards.

'Success, success,' he crowed, and Hope put down her pen, looking up at him, mixed emotions showing in her blue eyes.

'I'm so pleased for you, Jake,' she said, and that was the truth. She was pleased – for him.

10

The postcard that Hope had been writing arrived in Matt's hand eleven days later, one of a collection of English postcards from his mother with their strange stamps and shiny pictures of Piccadilly Circus, Trafalgar Square, Buckingham Palace and Big Ben. He liked the Beefeaters; they looked as if they ate lots of meat. He had peered into the pictures and re-read his mother's schoolgirl handwriting hundreds of times, as if doing so could somehow bring her closer. There was nothing from his father.

After one utterly miserable week with Edith and Frank, Matt had summoned up all his courage and late one afternoon ran away back home, albeit on his bicycle. To his huge relief he had found Maggie in her room next to the garage, lying on a bed stood high up on bricks so the tokoloshe couldn't hide under it.

'Baas Matt, what are you doing here?' Her ample black face creased into a look of concern and the bed swayed as she propped herself on one elbow.

'I hate those people, Maggs,' Matt answered as he attached himself to her like a limpet, 'I'm never going there again. I'll stay here with you until Mum and Dad get back. I've brought all my homework.'

Maggie opened up the back door to the kitchen in the house, made tea with her own milk, and found some rusks for Matt at the back of the cupboard. Making sure he was occupied, she waddled off to the telephone on the other side of the house and phoned Edith on the number Hope had written down for her on the pad. Returning to the kitchen, she eased her colossal frame into a protesting bentwood chair and leant forward towards the boy.

'Baas Matt, you can't stay here. I've got no food ...' she turned her hands over in helpless expression, 'there's no food for you or anything.'

Matt stopped in mid bite and put down the rusk quickly. 'I'll just eat bread and jam like you Maggs ... and pap, it's fine. I'll ride to school from here.' He'd done his logistics.

They both turned as they heard the car speeding up the drive and then braking violently. There was a loud bang of a car door and suddenly Edith was in the kitchen. Her voice shook with rage as she shouted at Matt.

'Christ, I've been worried out of my skin about you, you ungrateful little shit!'

Matt got up and backed away. He'd never heard her swear before and she was close enough for him to catch the sour stench of alcohol on her breath. She moved swiftly towards him and scruffed him aggressively, her nails raking his neck. For a scrawny woman she possessed surprising strength. Matt ducked down under the assault and struck out reflexly, defensively, with a blow that caught her in the lower abdomen, driving breath from her body. Edith screeched with fury and started slapping the boy around the back of his head. She hadn't let go of his scruff. Maggie moved out of her chair with a single heave and enveloped the two struggling bodies in her immense arms. 'No Madam, no Madam.' Edith suddenly came to her senses and released the boy. He staggered back and, unknowingly, fixed his aunt with a look of such loathing and fear, that it was palpable, even in that charged atmosphere.

'Get into the car!' There was nowhere else to run to. The dread realisation dawned on Matt that he would have to go back with his aunt to that house. Hoo shit, to the others there too. His heart shrivelled.

'Get into the bloody car, I said!'

Defeated, Matt walked over to the green Austin A40 and climbed in without even a backward glance at Maggie who was standing with her hands, almost in prayer, the fingertips tapping against one another lightly. 'Hau, hau,' the black lips whispered in concern as Matt's aunt slammed the door, started the car, engaged the gears roughly and sped away. There was more to come. Frank came visiting that same evening as Matt was doing homework in his room. As Matt heard the heavy footsteps outside the door he quickly put down his pencil on his homework book and slid off his chair on the far side, instinctively putting it between himself and the man who stood at the door wagging his finger at him ominously.

'Any more trouble from you, you little squirt, and I'll give you the hiding of a lifetime. Hear me?'

Matt just looked at him saying nothing. He had learnt the value of silence in deflecting anger.

'DO YOU HEAR ME?' The older man shouted at him, his boozer's nose now puce and the corded veins prominent on his forehead. Matt nodded twice, convulsively. Frank glowered at him and then sneered unpleasantly.

'Cat got your tongue has it?'

He turned and stomped from the room leaving the boy with an unpleasant feeling of nausea creeping into the pit of his stomach, and a sapping weakness of limb that only served to underscore his impotence. The following day, Denis arrived at the bottom of the garden where Matt was playing with his dinky toys, having painstakingly constructed an intricate series of roads and garages in the sand pile he'd found there. 'They've said I've got to come and play with you,' the Billy Bunter boy announced in an infinitely bored voice. Denis usually ignored Matt completely, but was now obviously acting under extreme coercion from his parents. He knelt down and started running one of the cars furiously up and down the little dirt roads making loud revving noises and then squealing noises as he rounded a corner. A wheel came off. Matt stood up and spoke at the older boy.

'You'll break it!'

Denis ignored this, continuing even more vigorously for a few seconds before standing up and hurling the little car into the trees.

'See if it can fly,' he mocked and then started kicking the sand tableau to pieces.

When he had finished he turned and jeered, 'See, I've played with you then,' and walked off towards the house, his disdain apparent in every swing of the contemptuous swagger.

For the last week of his stay, Matt was more or less invisible in the house, turning up promptly for meals, but spending most of his time reading or studying in his room. He never found the MG dinky in the trees, but the remainder of his collection was packed away safely in his suitcase, waiting, like he was, to go home. His begrudging hosts were persuaded that he had learnt his lesson and was behaving properly at last. He supposed they never found out about the dribble of spit that went into the whisky and gin decanters on the sideboard when no one was looking, or that Denis' peanut butter jar received the same treatment, or even that he was responsible for the hysteria that erupted when Edith found an aggressive red-lipped herald snake coiled up in her bath one morning.

Spit and snake apart, the most enjoyable part of Matt's whole time spent with his aunt and uncle was packing his suitcase to go home. It was lying open on his bed when his Aunt Edith walked in.

'Your mother and father aren't due home until the end of the week, you know.' She moved around the room straightening things with small birdlike movements. A water-wagtail woman.

'I think it's best if we don't speak to your mother or father about this running away thing, Matt. Your father would be furious of course, and your mother – well I dare say she's had a wonderful holiday, and I don't think we should be spoiling it for her just because you've been a naughty boy, now should we?' Matt thought of the spit in the Gin decanter and nodded. 'Good, that's settled then. You know it hasn't been easy having someone extra in the house for all this time. Extra food, extra washing, extra ironing ... expense, you know, lots of expense.' Matt could hear that it was the expense that burned his Aunt Edith the most.

She busied herself around the bed, plumping the pillow.

'Your parents wouldn't want you to seem ungrateful I'm sure, for all we've done for you I mean.'

She stood arms akimbo directly in front of him to ensure he took her meaning. 'So you keep your mouth shut, young man, and Frank and I won't say anything about your escapade either.' She pursed her lips at him and then returned to the bed, straightening the corners once again. 'I've spoken to Maggie about it and she agrees. No purpose to be served, none at all.' Edith waited. 'So that's all settled then?' Matt thought of the red-lipped herald and nodded again.

Matt went over and sat on the bed when his aunt had gone, hugging his arms, intent on his own thoughts. She'd got it all wrong, he thought. He had never had the slightest intention of speaking about his time in this house to anyone, least of all his parents. They'd treated him horribly. He had none of the big words to describe this feeling – one that he was deeply ashamed of, but no, his parents would most certainly hear nothing of this from him, not ever. Shame was secret, and after all, they had been the ones that had put him in this hellhole place with these terrible people, people he feared so much, too. He was an expendable, something to be cast aside whilst they'd flown off to the other side of the world. He was in turmoil; he'd been so bitterly angry with his mother and father, but now he couldn't wait to see them again.

'It's not the end of the week,' he muttered to himself, 'they're coming on Thursday.' It was three more sleeps, just three more sleeps.

To his astonishment, it was his father who picked him up to take him home. He'd expected his mother and was a bit disappointed – but only a bit; nothing could extinguish his inward delight at escaping from this place. He knew he'd have to go up and say 'thank you for having me', perhaps even endure a Judas hug and a handshake, or have his hair ruffled which he hated; but that also didn't matter just now, just as long as he could leave and go home.

Jake sat with Frank and Edith on the stoep and regaled them with his sanitised travel stories over a cup of tea. He cast his head over his shoulder at the silent little statue that was his son.

'You can say thank you, boy, and then go and put your stuff in the car.' Matt did as he was told and sat on the front seat of the car, waiting for his father. After what seemed an age, Jake appeared at the front door, taking his leave with a hearty handshake for Frank and a kiss on the cheek for his sister. Matt watched him stride across the lawn in his usual brisk fashion, open the door and slide into the Chev's driving seat.

'Your mother's at home and is dying to see you. How have things been at school?'

11

Things at school, as Jake put it, had been going very well. Perversely, Matt's solitary life in his room in the afternoons and evenings had led to a surge in his academic prowess, his sporting endeavours prospering too; both, in their way, paradox heirs to the same encounter. The slings and arrows from the obtuse Frank and the grim, unforgiving Edith had 'toughened him up no end' as his father would have put it. Innocence was forfeit to the armour that the boy now donned: if things were difficult, he could shrug off more; and he was apparently less sensitive, at least on the surface. What emotions did lurk there were hidden. His teachers rated him more competent at just about everything that 'mattered' at school, but he was also quieter, more considered with his actions – laconic even at times, and wary: Matt watched life out of the corners of his eyes.

School, while his parents had been away, had become less deserving as the traditional butt of schoolboy scorn. Now it was more of a haven – a refuge from Frank and Edith, and in 'doing well', Matt found something he rather liked. He enjoyed the feeling, and they gave out carrot rewards for performance too. In consequence, by the end of the year his prospects were very rosy indeed. Jake quizzed him as they walked across the lawn to the car on their way to prize giving, when all the posts for the next year, Matt's final year at prep, would be announced. 'What do you think you might get?'

Matt shot his answer straight back: 'head of house, captain of cricket and to run the library.'

His father's two black caterpillars went into action, arching their backs extravagantly above his eyes as Jake put a heavy curb on Matt's expectations.

'Well, don't be too surprised if you don't get any of them!'

Jake snorted, signalling his obvious disbelief; but Matt's prophecy hadn't been intentionally boastful – he was just trying to be factual – and he was pretty accurate.

With the exception of the library appointment, the remainder were confirmed that same afternoon. Hope was ecstatic as they met up afterwards on the school lawns, giving her son a heartfelt hug and patting him repeatedly on the back.

'That's enough now, Hope!' Jake pulled her arm away. 'He's not a baby any more.'

He shook hands with Matt briefly. 'Now let's see what you can do with it, my boy ... but well done anyway.' His father's approval was conditional, as always, it seemed. Matt saw that the compliment was given as an afterthought, almost grudgingly. He cared, however, a little less than he might have before.

His cricket year turned out to be an unexceptional one, but not because of any failing on Matt's part as captain – he was merely one good player of three, surrounded by mediocre ones. The highpoint was a visit to the school by the great English cricket writer, E. W. Swanton, who addressed the first and second elevens, leaving Matt with one of his books and a flyleaf signature under a personal note. His favouritest thing, almost ... after the fishing book. Matt's house leadership was more than successful with creditable results both in the classroom and on the sports fields. The four houses at Pridwin were whimsically named after knights of the round table: Bedevere, Galahad, Lancelot and Tristram, and represented by large shields in yellow, red, blue and green, arranged behind the stage in the assembly hall. These were rotated according to each house's performance throughout the year and Matt's house, Bedevere, managed consistently to be in either first or second place – something he'd naturally have expected, Jake had commented to Matt. It was a bland, truly joyless remark.

By year's end, Matt's thoughts had begun to turn to Plettenberg Bay and the summer holiday ahead. He didn't expect to be spending much time with his two older brothers – they'd be after girls again, no doubt. His main concern hovered around the likelihood of persuading his mother and father that his few extra inches warranted a bigger rod and a Penn 49 reel.

Having wheedled the promise of a new rod and reel out of his parents in lieu of a Christmas and birthday present, Matt wasted no time on arrival in Plett in getting up to the Crawford-Brunt's fishing shop and picking a new rod; one with dark red and green bindings. He was aching to try it out, and found that the new tackle and his few extra pounds in weight and inches in height had given him yards and yards extra on his cast. Piet became more of a fishing companion as Matt's improved abilities with rod and reel bred an independence of its own. The two youngsters still sought out Gideon's advice and company, and more often than not, would end up at the older man's modest cottage near the old timber shed after a day's fishing. The ancient cottage was very worn, with the paint on the window frames blistered and cracked, but the thick, whitewashed walls and enveloping trees lent a contented air to the spot. A long, narrow veranda fronted the cottage, and on the second Monday of the holiday, Gideon was watering some of the hundreds of pot plants that lived there when he saw the two boys making their way along the path up to the gate in the picket fence.

'Catch anything?' he shouted down to them cheerfully.

Matt half waved his rod by way of answer as he fiddled with the rusty bolt on the gate. The bolt finally gave way and the gate sagged in exhausted fashion, evoking a couple of annoyed shoves from Matt before the two of them could slip through. Piet disappeared around the back of the cottage giving Gideon a wave and brief greeting as he went. Matt parked the rods against the front of the corrugated iron roof over the veranda and smiled up a Gideon.

'I must fix that gate for you. It drives me crackers every time we come, and I always forget to do something about it. Can you lend me a screwdriver and I'll see if Piet and I can lift it up a bit?'

Gideon disappeared into the house for a minute and then reappeared with a doubtful looking screwdriver which he offered.

'You have a go and I'll make some tea and see if there are any biscuits left.'

The boys were still tackling the gate when Gideon put their mugs of tea down on the low table in front of the rusbank. He went back for the biscuits, watched for a moment, and then called down to them.

'Come on up before it gets cold.'

Matt's expression radiated self-satisfaction as he took the last step up onto the stoep. 'It's fixed – the wood's a bit rotten so we've put in two bigger screws in the top hinge onto the post – Piet's had them in the fishing bag all last week ready for the job!'

Gideon sat back in the rusbank with his sandy legs stretched before, nursing the mug of tea in knotty, weather-beaten hands.

'Thanks, young man! What's Piet doing round the back?'

'Oh, we got a couple of elf for you early this morning in the surf.' Matt replied. 'The fridge at home is full, so we thought you might like them ... not being a fisherman yourself!' Matt chuckled mischievously, sat down and started a stretch. 'No, he's just cleaning them on the slab outside the kitchen, I think.' He finished pulling satisfaction from the stretch and then collapsed his shoulders.

'Gideon, there's not much going on at Robberg at the mo: can't we try somewhere else just for a change?'

Gideon looked out over the stoep palisade and scratched his wiry salt and pepper beard pensively with the stem of his pipe.

'Somewhere else ... somewhere new perhaps,' he said slowly and then straightened suddenly with a thought. 'I'll tell you what; I'll try and get the keys for us to go to Stilbaai. It's a bit further down the west coast, on the other side of Robberg, but to get to the place we have to go through private property, which is why we'll need the keys you see. The fishing can be good, but even if it isn't, the place is quite spectacular.'

The sparkle in Matt's eyes signalled his enthusiasm for Gideon's idea and the two fell to discussion on days and times. When their tea was finished they moved through the front door and into the cottage living room – and Gideon to the telephone on the oak roll top desk. Matt's eyes, as always, roved around the room that he loved so much. It was an Aladdin's cave, stuffed in careless, casual fashion with all the mementoes and keepsakes of a rich life. By now Matt knew the story behind each and every one. The yellowwood floorboards reflected a honeyed light through the room, softening the white of the pitted plaster, the width of the boards reflecting their immense age, sawn in a day when these huge trees still grew in abundance. Some sections of plaster were missing, showing whitened stone edges through, the whole giving an informal, timeworn and relaxed character much in keeping with the owner. A hearth had been let into the stone at calf height, home to a scrolled grate guarded on either side by staunch, Empire-style brass firedogs. A large sofa faced the fireplace and lay back to back with its pair, separated only by a thin refectory table of a matched height. The high polish of the table reflected lights cast from the nacre of exotic shells collected from East African shores. Scattered amongst these were corals, millefiore glass, silver picture frames holding ancient, browned photographs, writing impedimenta, stray antique fly fishing reels, and two impossibly long, sheathed bayonets. A lengthy chaise longue, parked under the side window, was covered with a colossal tiger skin complete with stuffed head and glass eyes that glared angrily across the room from the top of the single arm. Two leopard skins enveloped one sofa and a faded Newmarket blanket the other where Matt now sat – and then sprawled comfortably, looking up at the walls. His eyes fell on a faded, framed document that Matt knew was Gideon's officer's commission. Above this, on a wooden ox yoke, hung a dozen brass bells with leather thongs. Apart from a milk churn at the door that served as a walking stick repository, the bells were all that remained of the Lidman Jersey herd and Gideon's parents' farming days in Central Africa. The wall above the desk, where Gideon sat with his head bent to the telephone, swarmed with paintings and photographs of family, of favourite horses, and dogs, and polo matches. The other walls held a hotchpotch of pen and ink sketches of coal driven naval cruisers and destroyers of another era; and landscape oils, now so old and begrimed that the subject matter was often all but lost. The naval theme was continued by a battered ship's lantern perched on a bosun's chair in one corner; and a brass and leather telescope, mounted on a tripod, that gazed out of the corner window through a gap in the trees onto the Lookout rocks. The only slightly more novel addition that Matt had noted recently, was the appearance of several tightly woven red and green mohair carpets and runners of African design, which looked remarkably good on the gleaming floors. Gideon had grumbled about his cold feet in the winter and these were evidently designed to fix the problem. Matt's daydream was interrupted by Gideon thumping down the receiver and enthusiastically swinging his chair around.

'That's organised then.'

Gideon fished in a pocket for his companion pipe and gestured at Matt with it before starting an energetic packing of the bowl with his Navy Cut.

'But only next week I'm afraid. Those people up there are very

Manyana about life.

And if you've nothing better to do in the meantime, what about coming up to P.E. with me tomorrow to see my horses run?'

He lit the pipe. 'We can take in a movie if you like.'

The day before the Stilbaai expedition Gideon went to collect the keys from the agent and Piet was out early at low tide collecting bait, returning from the rocks in the early afternoon with a good haul. Red-bait, looking for all the world like a macabre collection of black nipples with orange-red flesh surround, spindly mussel worm, and a small, unlucky octopus. There was still mackerel to be bought from the fishing boats and Matt had spied them from the Stevens' balcony just after three o'clock. Jake and Hope's holiday home was perched on the side of the hill overlooking Middle beach, high above the old Timber shed and Gideon's cottage which lay almost side by side behind the dunes, cloistered in the sanctuary of the indigenous wood. The balcony that fronted the house, like a rude nose, made amends for the insult by providing a spectacular view of Middle beach, with Beacon Island and the Lookout rocks flanked on either side; and it was from this vantage point and through his father's binoculars that Matt spotted the boats way out to sea. As they neared landfall on Middle beach, Matt marked the cloud of seagulls swirling above and behind the four boats, and as they hove-to about three hundred yards out to complete the cleaning of the fish, he saw that they sat heavy in the water. A good catch, then. He called to Piet and they hurried off barefoot down the path to look for their mackerel and see what else had been caught. A small, enthusiastic crowd was, as usual, gathered round the wooden, clinker-built boats beached on the sand. Coloured fishermen, in pairs, struggled up the beach, line astern, with long oars strung between them, threaded with huge kob. The giant fish swayed gently, mouths agape, tails gently brushing the sand, the faint, pink iridescence on their flanks now almost extinct. There were some red fish in the boats and Piet pointed out a small red steenbras to Matt. 'That one for your Ma.'

Hope had asked the boys to look out for something special she could use for an upcoming dinner, and at about eight pounds this would be ideal. Small red steenbras flesh was sweet and succulent and Piet had to bargain earnestly to secure it at a sensible price.

Coming up the back way to the kitchen with the fish, Matt heard the sound of his brothers' loud voices coming from the sitting room. Obviously back from chasing girls in Cape St. Francis he thought, as he pushed open the fly screen door, letting it bang shut behind him and hefting the steenbras and half dozen mackerel onto the kitchen table.

'Is that you, Matt?' Hope called, 'your brothers are here!'

Matt quickly rinsed his hands under the tap, and wiping them on the back of his shorts, hurried through to the sitting room. The handshakes and backslaps were followed by the inevitable banter and teasing from the two older brothers.

'Caught any fish with the fancy new rod yet?'

'Plenty!' Matt answered, 'caught any girls with the shitty old car yet?'

'Language, Matt!' Hope warned, but in spite of the objection, Hope watched the interaction between them with a small smile playing on her face. It was rare for the three brothers to be together and she enjoyed the moment: Matt, she saw, nowadays gave as good as he got. His two brothers were as like as peas in a pod. They took after their father, both having the same straight, black hair swept back from a prominent widow's peak. Angular faces in sharp planes that cracked into easy smiles surmounted lanky, spare bodies that were never still for a second.

They heard Jake's Chev pull up outside the house and within

the minute he was opening the front door looking eagerly for his two boys. Sam and Teddy fussed him, taking his golf clubs and pouring him a whisky from the drinks table. The men's talk that followed out on the balcony all but excluded Hope and Matt. When he caught her concerned look at him (concern for him really), Matt made wide, mock-astonished eyes at his mother followed with a small shrug and rueful smile – his signal not to worry, telling her he wasn't. Nevertheless, he wasn't slow to slip away to pack kit for the morning. Half an hour later the two brothers ducked their heads through the fishing room door to say cheers.

'See you, boet!' they chorused, a 'stywe lyne – tight lines!' from Teddy and they were gone. He heard the engine of the Wolseley catch and then roar away as his two brothers started back for St. Francis.

Getting to Stilbaai the next day took some time. There were two sets of farm gates that had to be opened and then shut behind Gideon's bakkie as they wended their way across dry and dusty lands, following little more than dirt tracks towards the sea. The climb on foot down to Stilbaai was steep and treacherous. Part of the descent involved traversing large areas where loose, round rocks lay packed against the precipitous slope. The free, cobblestone sized rocks often gave way underfoot making them progress, as often as not, by means of strange slides of six inches or more downwards while trying at the same time to keep balance. With rucksacks and rods this was awkward, and a steadying hand put down was usually rewarded with a resentful nip from the shifting milling stones as they grumbled and complained at the disturbance. The striking feature of Stilbaai, its isolation apart, was in the number of rocky shelves that threw themselves out into the sea, giving wonderful access to deep water. Halfway down, after shrugging off his rucksack and lighting his pipe, Gideon sat on a rocky shelf and watched the waters pounding the coastline hundreds of feet below. At length he removed the briar.

'What do you think of the water, Matt?'

Matt, crouched beside him, had expected the question and had also been observing keenly.

'Too early to tell about the swell. I'll watch for a while.'

Gideon grunted in satisfaction at the reply. He knew of too many good fisherman who had been washed off rocks and killed hereabouts; or simply disappeared and never been seen again. He loved the sea, lived at the sea, he had even gone to war at sea, but she was a mistress he remained very wary of. He waited with interest.

At length, a massive swell crowding in behind the others smashed onto the rocks obscuring them totally and throwing up mountainous clouds of white spray.

'No chance.' Said Matt, shaking his head ruefully.

'Not if something like that catches you there isn't,' Gideon agreed.

As they made to turn back, two great black winged shadows slipped over the edge of their vision to the right and below.

'Black eagles!' whispered Gideon.

The shadows glided past below in silent half echelon, quartering the ground beneath them where rock met bush. Cut into nape and neck of the great birds flashed the tell-tale white arrowheads of identity, the reason for their formation instantly clear as other smaller, moving shapes mottled the ground; scores of sun-bathing dassies, rock hyrax, fleeing for life and cover. The lead bird, flying to seaward was acting as decoy, flushing the prey. The second bird dropped onto a scampering dassie, snatching it up with only what appeared to be the slightest change in trajectory. There was a faint cry and they were gone, disappearing as they had come, like wraiths.

Matt exhaled, made aware that he had been holding his breath for too long.

The pull up and out of the bay was exhausting. For every step forward on the loose stones on that steep face they almost seemed to slide back two. It was heavy going and it took a good spell before they reached the bakkie at the top.

Hope invited Gideon in for a drink when he brought the two tired boys home. Jake was still out at the country club – on the nineteenth hole again no doubt, thought Hope, with a measure of irritation as they all went out onto the balcony. They sat around the friendly light of a single candle in a glass, and under a brilliant diamond studded southern sky. Hope turned to her son.

'Matt, please see that Piet has a good dop of sherry, poppet; and a packet of mielie-meal next to the kitchen scale on the table ... that's for him too, and some oranges from that big pocket.' Her voice rose to reach her son as he went further and further away towards the kitchen, hurrying to obey the instruction before it was half given.

'You had a good day I gather.' Hope looked into Gideon's sun-washed blue eyes.

'The eagles', yes.'

He told her more. About the eagles yearly migration from the lofty basalt mountains of Basutoland, soaring down on high air currents, gliding hundreds of miles with hardly a beat of a wing. 'Although I suppose I should call it Lesotho, these days,' he added with a smile.

'What a wonderful thing for Matt, to see them hunting on the wing like that.'

'I enjoy having the boy with me.' Gideon answered simply.

'Well, it's as well you do, because it appears Jake has little time for him these days.' Hope's voice was laced with asperity and her hand shook slightly as she put her glass down.

'Is everything all right, Hope?' Gideon's even voice was tinged with concern and he lent forward to take her fingers lightly in his. She brushed away a tendril of wayward blonde hair with her free hand and gripped his fingers with the other.

'Sometimes I wish things could have worked out differently – that's all.' They heard Matt's footsteps coming across the sitting room and Gideon stood up to go. He knew Jake would be home soon, and was somehow always a little uncomfortable in his presence these days.

Driving home down the hill, Gideon was thinking of his horses. The breeze on his arm bent out of the bakkie window reminded him that there would be other horses out in the bay if the wind got up any more tonight. White horses. Bribing young Matt with a movie ticket had been a bit of a subterfuge to get him up to P.E. with him last week; but well worth it, he mused; if only to see the boy's face on the gallops when pairs of Thoroughbreds came thundering out of the early morning mist and flashed by. There had followed a long discussion in the bakkie on the way back home. Matt wanted to know just how Gideon went about choosing a racehorse to buy and send into training. Whilst he had gone on and on about blood lines, prepotency, nicks and conformation, the boy had sat there listening with one ear and nodding occasionally, sketching on the back of an envelope he'd found in the cubby-hole. An astonishingly good drawing, too. Two stretching racing Thoroughbreds vying for advantage, both jockeys going for all that it was worth in a frenzy of fluid action. He realised guiltily that he'd never bought the paints and artists materials he'd promised Matt. It was something he should remedy.

12

The next forty-eight hours proved to be the watershed in all their lives, the time when the fabric of the Stevens family began to tear irreparably. Jake had arrived home very late and much the worse for drink. His false, jokey bonhomie, designed to paper over any cracks, fell flat, stilled by Hope's cool demeanour and soon turned to truculence. And finally to rage, which is when he struck her full across the face. The force of the flat of his hand spun her round, and as she lay stunned on the floor with her back to him, he had raged.

'You stupid cow – what I do with my time is my affair; if I want to stay late at the golf club – I bloody well will. It's not your right to fucking-well interfere with me, do you hear?' He raised his voice another notch, the spittle flying.

'DO YOU FUCKING HEAR!!?'

The sight of his wife dragging herself round and holding her ashen face in one hand seemed only to enrage him further.

'And another thing, your precious bloody son is going to St. Andrew's next year. I'm not having him tied to your bloody apron strings any longer. It's time he learnt to cope in this life and not be fed with a damn silver spoon all the time. I'm sick to death of both of you.' He paused to walk to the drinks table, slop some whisky in a tumbler, drain it, and then refill it. Hope's fearful eyes followed him.

'You live the life of Riley here, all of you, and all I get is rank ingratitude; complaints from you and sullen compliance from the boy. Thank God for Sam and Teddy – I can at least talk to them without feeling I'm doing something wrong all the fucking time. You all get on my wick here – no wonder I don't want to spend time at home!' His tirade spent, Jake slammed down his glass on the drinks table and marched off down the corridor.

Above the singing in her ears, Hope could vaguely hear him in the spare bedroom, crashing about, slamming cupboard doors. He had never struck her before, and so hard! She ran her tongue gingerly around the gum on the side of her mouth, tasting metal and salty blood and wincing as she came to the split inside the cheek where it had been driven onto her teeth. Hope was shocked to the core. She pulled herself onto the chair beside the fireplace and put a trembling hand to her throbbing face. She blinked as tears filled her eyes, realising that all her worst nightmares had come true. Surely never this. She had heard about men that beat their wives, but had never thought to be one of the victims, never. He had changed so much, especially since coming back from England, and the directorship, the new appointment he was so proud of. Cockier, harder; and there was the indifference; she could stand all that – but this? Suddenly she feared for herself for the very first time in her life. A lance of terror pierced her. Eyes closed, she bent double in the chair and moaned, the wound seizing her breath, making a mockery of her name.

Jake was wrong about one thing: he wouldn't always be able to talk to Sam and Teddy. At nine o'clock the following morning, Warrant Officer Gerber took the four steps up to the Stevens' front door. They were slow and very unwilling steps. He knocked briskly on the door and waited, looking out at the bay – seeing little and with an expression of extreme distaste stitched across his face, thinking that this part of the job was something he'd never get used to. Jake answered the door as the policeman composed his features into a bland mask.

'Mr. Stevens, Sir?'

'Yes.'

'Mr. Stevens, can I come in please. It's about your boys, I'm afraid. It's not good news, Sir.'

In his heavily accented, guttural English; but kindly and apologetically, the Afrikaaner police officer gave Jake the news that both of his sons had been killed instantly in a head-on collision with a truck just outside Cape St. Francis.

'Their car was completely wrecked, I'm sorry, Sir. No one's fault either, the truck's front tyre exploded and pulled it across onto the other side of the road. He's dead too, the driver of the truck. I know the family from Knysna.' The fractured explanation droned on but nothing could touch or ease the devastation that the policeman's news had brought. It was news that engendered a desolation so profound that it hung like a malevolent, cloaked curse over the house, an oppressive pall that drew the guts from them all. They retreated into silences, each to their own, none knowing how to give comfort to themselves, much less to others. Neither was there any prospect of solace for a family that had once been a rounded whole and was now only part – a much smaller thing – incomplete. Both Jake and Hope knew it was a mortal blow. Things could never be the same again. All those expectations of life, of careers, of marriages, children and grandchildren; the sharing of major successes and the commiseration over minor failures: they were all gone, wiped out in a crumpled black wreck on the N2. The void was too terrible.

On a dismal grey morning two days later, with Jake at the wheel of the Chev, what remained of the shattered family crept out of the village en route to the Port Elizabeth Crematorium. There was a little small talk, but it soon lapsed into silence as mile after bleak mile unfolded.

'Somewhere here,' muttered Jake as they saw the signs for Cape St. Francis. As he said the words they were overtaken by two hearses hurtling past them with coffins swaying in the back. Hope gasped and clasped the choke of her black dress. Jake snatched off his hat and burst out. 'The boys, there go my boys!' Matt looked over the back of the seat in wide-eyed horror as the hearses sped away in front of them and then eventually sank back into his seat as the tension of that awful moment evaporated slowly. In the crematorium chapel, he hardly heard a word of the prayers and short eulogy; his eyes were fixed on the two coffins holding his brothers. As the machinery whined and the rollers started to move the coffins towards the velvet curtain, the concept of never seeing them again was made devastatingly real. He lowered his head and wept. Hope's hand crept over his shaking shoulders as she watched her sons disappear from her life and ken. She bent her head also and wept with him.

'Do you want to go back to Johannesburg now, Hope?' Jake had posed the question as they sat at home that evening, uncomfortable as strangers. 'I could certainly do with the time at the office before I fly to London.'

Hope had cast her head down for a brief moment and then shaken it slowly.

'No, I think it's better if you go up by yourself. I want to stay here with Matt for a while. I can't go back just now. I'm sorry, I just can't.' There was a finality in her tone that, for once, brooked no argument, and Jake had agreed readily enough, anyway. He wanted to be away from there.

With Jake gone, Hope seemed to drift around the house with a preference for her own company. Well-meaning friends and acquaintances who had called to offer condolences had been turned away at the door with polite assurances that, yes, she was managing and thanks very much for the concern. She had been out just the once, to Knysna to see Mrs. Marais, wife of the truck driver who had been killed in the accident. She looked so pale and exhausted when she returned that Matt hadn't dared ask about it.

She encouraged him to get out with Piet, and perhaps to see Gideon if he felt like it. Matt was initially reluctant to leave his mother alone but soon saw that it was what she wanted. As the first week passed he more often found his mother down at Gideon's cottage in the afternoon when they came back from the rocks. Usually she would be in the garden tending some of his plants, or weeding, or on the stoep curled up in a large squashy chair reading a book.

'Won't you come out with us Mum?' he had pleaded one afternoon as they walked back up the hill back to the house. 'You always used to, and we can ghillie for you, no problem.' Hope was touched by his concern and smiled at him fondly.

'Okay, I'll tell you what, I don't feel much like clambering over rocks at present, so why don't we go down to Keerbooms, on the other side of the river mouth, and fish off the beach? I can do a picnic lunch for us and we can make a day of it.'

Their day was a great success. Matt was delighted to see his mother on the beach, rod in hand once more. 'How long since you last fished, Mum – a year?' Hope nodded; she had forgotten how wonderful it was getting down to the beach. The simple things, watching the ebb and flow of the water and the groups of little sandplovers on their clockwork legs, scurrying back and forth so earnestly.

'Look Mum, oystercatchers!'

Hope turned her head to watch the pair of black-bodied birds flying low, just over the breakers, their red beaks aimed unerringly towards the river mouth. The boys had collected bait there at low tide, pumping mud prawns with an old tin, using a wire hanger for pencil bait and digging furiously for blood worm in a race against the impossibly long creatures as they tried to escape, drawing themselves ever deeper into the estuary sands. These were all tasty baits and they were hoping for some grunter during the day on the smaller rods. Matt was concern itself, hardly allowing his mother to cast or bait a hook all day; a day that was thankfully wind-free so the picnic lunch wasn't plagued by swirling sand. Gideon had brought some potatoes and onions which he baked in foil in their skins on a small fire – sweet and delicious with their cold meats and freshly baked bread. In spite of the good weather and prime baits, there were only two fish to be had. As they decamped in the afternoon and turned for home, Matt apologised to his mother.

'Sorry we didn't catch Mum.'

'No, Matt, it was a wonderful day! Just to be out here was tonic enough!'

He wasn't entirely convinced, but his mother did seem happier in a way for the first time for ages so he tried to take comment at face value. Even small profits were welcome just now.

Back at the cottage, Gideon cleared the few leaves out of the small brick fireplace at the end of the veranda, laid and lit the fire. There was time for a sundowner whilst the rooikrans wood burnt down to the coals, ready for the pot. Piet had taken the rods and haversacks up to the house and would then, no doubt, head for home. He took the two small sand steenbras and Gideon had poured him a stiff tot at the cottage to ease his step up the hill. Gideon sat chopping vegetables and herbs at the table for the pot while Hope and Matt sat watching him work.

'You're sure it's all right for us to stay for supper, Gideon?' Hope asked. He chuckled. 'It's no fun cooking for yourself, Hope. This gives me great sense of purpose if you must know. What's more, you haven't ever really had curry unless you've tried one of my specials – some really unique spices I promise. The trouble is, this all takes about three hours, so we won't eat before nine o'clock.' He gestured at Matt with the small knife. 'Tell you what, Matt, go into the kitchen and you'll find some biltong in the middle cupboard, and bring the wooden plane you'll find there too.' The legs of the chair scraped as the boy stood up and he disappeared with a faint whistle of some tune.

'I see he's taken to looking after his mother.' Gideon started to fill the pot with his chopped vegetables, herbs, spices, lamb knuckles and stock. Hope smiled. 'Yes, it's adorable really – he's quite the little man now that Jake's away.' Her smile became rueful, 'I can't say it comes amiss either, I'm still feeling very fragile, and I can't thank you enough either for all your help. Your cottage is a little haven for us both just now.'

Gideon took up the pepper grinder and started to mill pepper into the pot. 'So it's boarding school now for him, is it?' Hope looked down at her hands and gave a shrug of both shoulders. 'Jake insists.' She paused, 'I wanted him at home – perhaps as a weekly boarder at St. Johns if such a thing exists – but Jake …' She left the sentence unfinished. Matt arrived back from the kitchen and Gideon showed him how to shave off slivers of biltong with the old plane turned over, tucked into his abdomen and the stick of biltong drawn towards him over the blade. The air was soon filled with mouth-watering aromas of spices and curry as the pot came into a slow bubbling boil and by the time it was ready to eat they were all famished. After the meal Gideon asked Hope: 'When will you return to the big city?'

'We'll go back next week,' she answered with a sigh. 'I've still got to buy school clothes for Matt, and shoes, and sew all his labels. He's also got to have a large trunk for kit and tuck, and God knows what.'

Gideon looked over at Matt who was trying to suck the marrow out of the bones without making too disgusting a noise. 'What do think of all this, lad?' Matt stopped sucking his fingers for a moment to consider, and then passed what he took to be apt comment 'I've got a few friends from prep coming down with me, so I suppose it will be all right ... but I'd have rather stayed with Mum and gone to a school nearby.'

Gideon noted that he didn't include his father in this, just as he had noted the heavy bruise that had appeared on Hope's cheek, and just as he had noted her increasingly distracted air, ever since the family had arrived on holiday. The tragedy surrounding the loss of her two eldest sons had overshadowed everything else of course, but he was now reacquainted with his earlier unease.

13

They only stayed on another few days as Hope had organised a lift back to Johannesburg with Doris – the bridge player – her long-time friend, who was pleased to have travelling companions for the trip back up to the Transvaal. It turned out to be quite a change from the usual two-day trip with overnight stop at Colesburg. Doris picked them up at three o'clock in the morning and then drove the big, black Buick at murderous pace straight through to Johannesburg. Their only stops were for petrol and toilets, and as Hope had offered to do sandwiches, they could all picnic in quite grand fashion in the car whilst the big Buick continued to devour the miles beneath them. Matt was pleasantly surprised at how chatty his mum became, he even heard her laugh for the first time since forever. He recognised Doris as somebody quite glamorous. Something to do with her and everything about her being so smart; the big diamond ring, that long cigarette holder and a talent for looking relaxed and slightly languid. Matt liked her instinctively.

The days passed in a blur of organisation, shopping for school clothes, and packing; and before he knew it, Matt was on the platform at Johannesburg station next to a hissing steam train bidding his mother farewell, giving her a big hug and feeling an unwelcome lump in his throat. It was horrible, the waiting, and everyone was so uneasy. His mum kept saying what a wonderful time he'd have, that he'd be bound to make wonderful friends, everything was going to be wonderful, wonderful, wonderful. She was talking too fast, straightening his clothes and trying repeatedly, and rather unsuccessfully – annoyingly – to get the hair on the crown of his head to lie flat. She only talked and fussed like that when something was wrong. He knew that.

At last it was time to board. His father pumped him by the hand briefly with his iron grip. 'You know what I expect of you, my boy, now have a good trip.' The carriages bumped and rattled briefly and the train started to pull away. He could see his mum dabbing at the corners of her eyes with a little handkerchief and the lump in his throat grew. He tried to swallow, waved at her and mouthed the words, 'bye, Mum ... bye.' He couldn't see his father anywhere.

There were three other boys from Pridwin on the train so at least he knew someone. The dark-haired boy sitting next to him was from The Ridge – he introduced himself as Paul Rennat and he was much more friendly than the others – easy to talk to, and he also kept budgies at home. The train trip took two days and was a bit of an adventure at first. It was his first train ride, but there were two of them, and that made Matt and Paul brave enough to explore. They thought the toilets were hysterical, with handles to steady you when the carriage lurched, and a foot pedal that opened a plate and disgorged the contents onto the track.

Paul said, 'and so you're out on a Sunday walk with your Gran, and you're walking along the railway track when all of a sudden Gran says "what's that on the track?"' They broke into shrill hysterics. The sound of someone knocking on the door stilled them and they unlocked the door to make way for another boy needing the loo. Back in their compartment, Matt shared some of his fly biscuits with Paul and they went through all the things that might possibly happen if they were brave enough to pull the emergency cord. The written threat of the stiff fines next to the cord in its important little red nest made it much more tempting somehow. The puffing billy engine worked on, constantly generating the smuts and cinders that crept insidiously, and everlastingly it seemed, into every seam of every compartment. By the time the boys reached Grahamstown in the far away

Eastern Cape on the second day, they all looked and felt dirty, sticky and grimy and were heartily sick of travelling.

There were several premier, private schools distant from Johannesburg that Jake had as options for Matt, all closely modelled on the English public school system. Michaelhouse and Hilton in Natal, Bishops in the Western Cape and Jake's choice, St Andrews, a school set in solid buildings, some of stone, some brick and some white plaster, that lay perched on the north western side of this little settler town. With Cathedral and Bishop, Grahamstown could boast of being a city, but no one – even today, really believes that. Too small, too parochial – but an education mecca nevertheless, with many good schools and Rhodes University, the gate of which looks benevolently down the long High Street onto the spire of the great Cathedral of Saint Michael and Saint George.

There is a glorious but sometimes painful history of settler families carried all the way from England to this remote outpost of Empire. Brought here in 1820 by Lord Charles Somerset, Governor of the Cape Colony, the settlers were designed to act as a bulwark between the Dutch trekboers coming from the western Cape and the Xhosa tribes migrating south westwards. By the time they arrived, four Kaffir wars had already been fought, and five more were to follow. Frontier town became garrison town. Many were allocated farms of 100 acres in the district. More than enough acreage in England, but woefully inadequate in the harsh, arid sourveld of the eastern Cape, cast in innocent as they were amongst hostile natives adept at stock theft and surreptitious murder. Many failed to prosper, abandoned their farms and came to live in Grahamstown, taking up trades such as masonry, carpentry and brick laying. Destitute, they were granted small parcels of land in the southern part of town around Artificers Square, where even today, the same quaint terraced houses built by those English yeomen remind one instantly of England.

Matt was placed in Upper House and suddenly thrown in amongst boys he had never seen before, but much to his delight and relief (as he'd found out on the train) – so was Paul. A Garibaldi biscuit beginning. Far too young to notice the sublime architecture or to appreciate the shading oaks, Matt found the new surroundings rather strange and intimidating, so too the seniors, especially the prefects who were huge, quite as big as his brothers had been. Some rub of Hope's prescience put him in awe of them and not a little fearful. Most of the new boys in Upper came from St. Andrews Prep, just around the corner, and many were from Albany district farming families, often descendants of those 1820 settlers for whose sons' benefit, John Armstrong, first Anglican Bishop of Grahamstown, had founded the school in 1855. These local boys arrived as a cabal, at ease amongst themselves – often even related – and had little use for outsiders, as Matt was to discover.

His new 'home' in the new boys dormitory was a contraption designed and built in the school workshops, which consisted of an oblong chipboard base to support a mattress, a clothes rail mounted in a cupboard built onto the foot board, and two drawers that opened sideways from beneath its Heath Robinson length. Very different to his comfortable bed at home, a home which now seemed as unreachable as any distant planet. The sick bay was just four steps away next-door, lair to a crotchety matron who dispensed Friar's Balsalm for anything above the waist, Castor oil for anything below and a deaf ear with both. It didn't seem a very friendly place – crude, dirty and certainly not private with loud, shouting boys trying to hang towels on their morning glory pricks and painful pink cracks between the toes from the athletes foot that everyone seemed to have at one time or another. The food was dreadful: scrambled eggs made from powder and thick, black pieces of liver that bounced like India rubber. Just learning the ropes – what to do, and when, and where, took the best part of a fortnight and a mistake was inevitable sooner or later. The shake of Paul's hand and urgent voice had woken him from a night of busy dreams.

'Quick, you gonna be late!'

He'd hurried as best he could, dragging his clothes on, stumbling down the stairs with his shoelaces untied and trying to comb his hair with his fingers. An hour later, just as he'd convinced himself that he'd managed to slip through, he felt the disabusing tap on his shoulder. It was from one of the monitors.

'You're up.'

His failing was that in his haste, he'd forgotten to make his bed. His heart lurched and he felt sick in his stomach. None of this was made any better by the glinting meanness in the eyes of the monitor who plainly enjoyed the moment. A day of dread anticipation culminated in his timorous appearance in the housemaster's study the following morning. The wheezy old man with the leather patches on the elbows of his coat squeezed out his cigarette in an ashtray full of butts and barked name and sentence as he reached for the cane.

'Stevens – four.'

Nearing retirement and weakened by emphysema, housemaster Mr. Phillip Windgold was saving his dwindling breath for the thrashing, which he now delivered with a clinical efficiency. It hurt like hell – bloody sore, worse than he'd expected, and to cap it all, Matt then had to walk through all the other boys hanging about round the corner, there to watch the fun. It was a spectacle sanctioned on the *pour encourager les autres* precept, but it was one that had rather more in common with the thumbing down, bloodthirsty instincts of a corrupted Roman mob. He walked with as much dignity as he could muster, which wasn't a great deal, and then bumped into Paul who had been anxiously waiting for him in the corridor upstairs.

'You okay ... was it sore?'

Matt's Protestant core shuffled forward and dragged the insult under cover.

'Naa.'

Paul could see from tight lips and the white face that it'd been really bad; but what could you do?

If Matt, in a misguided moment thought that this caning, or similar, was the worst that could happen, he was much mistaken. If anything it was only a taste of what was in store. Fagging was one of the not so quaint customs inherited from the English public school system, one that amounted to little more than institutionalised slavery. Each prefect in the house was assigned two new boys as fags who were made subject to his beck and call, to his every whim. Making beds, shining shoes, blackening rugby boots in winter and whitening cricket boots in summer, hand washing socks and disgusting jock straps, running errands and messages, cleaning takkies – a thousand scurrying duties. As in medieval times, overlords here tended to the benign or the despotic. Matt's was the latter. Snip Skinner's dislike for him was immediate, unreasoned, instinctive, and it condemned him to a daily hell, constantly stoked by the prefect's sneering disdain. He never understood it, this being picked on all the time, because it made no difference how hard he tried – the brickbats continued unceasingly. Matters came to a head one day when Skinner was yet again bawling Matt out.

'Time and time I tell you to pull your bloody finger out, you little prick and you still don't listen. Why, for fucks sake? Why in the fuck don't you listen to what I say, Stevens?'

He was foolish enough to answer back.

"'Cause I'm like you, I can't hear properly.'

Everyone knew that Skinner was deaf in one ear. You could see it from the way he always turned his good ear a bit when you spoke to him, but no one dared mention it, not even his friends. Not even when Snip didn't hear the whistle in the first XV rugby match against Selbourne and ran off to score a try when all the others were standing watching him from the other side of the field.

Matt couldn't have picked a sharper barb. Not only that, but in back-chatting he was disregarding one of his own cardinal rules, and it was also a very silly thing to do to a person with ginger hair, a red rag to a bull. With a roar, and a single furious lunge, the prefect seized the boy and took the scabbard of his cadet officer's sword to Matt's backside, bending the steel in the process. That was from beating with the flat of the scabbard, that was what raised the broad welts, but it was the edge when Snip turned it, that flayed him, splitting the taught skin like a ripe tomato. For days afterwards his underpants stuck to the seeping mass whenever he sat down so that he was reminded of it particularly painfully whenever he got up. He stood most of the time. He slept on his stomach. He lived in a place deep inside himself and became especially quiet, almost invisible. What terrified him most, more than anything in his life ever again, was being beaten again – on top of the blue-black lines and the three scabbing slashes in the flesh.

Things improved after that first year. Matt and Paul remained the closest of friends – St. Andrew's saving grace – but Matt never complained or even talked about the treatment he had endured, to Paul or anyone else. Not speaking about it, on the other hand, didn't mean he didn't think about it. He did, but not in any reasoning way, and never by choice, only by association. When the thought of it did come it was like hot oil sliding down the back of his throat spreading into his chest, scalding him inside.

Instinctively, he refused to surrender to the easy nostrum – the one called hate that ran with the devil, spewing it out on others. Perhaps it was his sensibilities that saved him, something of his mother in him that refused to allow another cog in the ghastly wheel that ground out the barbarity year in and year out, generation after generation. Astonishingly, in spite of the school's lofty academic claims, the fagging, the beating and the rest were just lore, accepted custom. The thought that brutalised children often become perpetrators themselves hadn't occurred, the whole of the intelligence on the matter being summed up in the oft heard, 'well, it didn't seem to do me much harm' justifying phrase trotted-out in self-serving, often indignant defence of the monstrous practice. It was a defence that could instantly identify people like Snip Skinner as he spoke the words and then turned his head for the good ear to catch a reply.

Small victories appeared. Unlikely ones. Matt and Paul weren't the only ones in Upper who had come from Transvaal schools, not the only ones tagged with the label that read 'unsuitable material – played soccer at prep instead of rugby'. Rugby was God in Upper, and Cricket sat on His right hand. Perhaps this was why the Albany contingent was so heavily represented: they tended to be long on rugby and cricket, albeit a little short on intellect. If you didn't play rugby, then you played hockey; and if you played hockey in Upper, then you were worshipping at the feet of a false god – an idol. It guaranteed excommunication. Upper nearly always won the inter-house rugby and cricket trophies, and always came last, it had to be last, in hockey. Being last said it wasn't a proper sport at all – a girls' sport, something they played at D.S.G., the girls' school round the corner, an irrelevance.

There were quite a few good hockey players in Upper by the time Matt arrived in his Matric year, he himself being one of the three untouchables in the house who had committed the ultimate heresy by getting school colours. Upper struggled through to the final of the inter-house competition where they met Merriman – a team stuffed with first team players. Matt, in a stroke of ingenuity, abandoned his left-back position halfway through the match (which they were losing), went up to centre-half and loosed the forwards in a sudden goal scoring frenzy. They won in the end, by five goals to three and pressing for more. The win tasted very, very sweet. By this time, the old goat of a house master, Mr. Windgold, had been replaced by a cold-eyed younger version, Mr. Aerial, whose grudging congratulations to the hockey team in front of the house next morning at breakfast was true music to Matt's ears. It was rumoured that Aerial had watched the final from behind a hedge so he wouldn't be seen! True or false, it was a piece of gossip the hockey boys inhaled with glee.

Paul wasn't at all as sports oriented as Matt. He just tried his best and took what came as a result quite cheerfully. What he could do well, however, was draw. Paul's particular love was linear perspective and he spent all his spare time sketching the clock tower, the chapel, and eventually virtually every building within the school grounds. Inevitably, Matt got bored watching him, and picking up a pencil, amused himself – and Paul – by doing exaggerated caricatures of some of the masters. He had a knack, and it turned into a harmless but rather satisfying way of gently mocking their more glaring idiosyncrasies, although his drawing of Mr. Aerial's shiny dome of a head which became a wincing hockey ball about to be thwacked at goal, was a gnaw at the bone of contention Matt had with his house master who'd given him six – the maximum punishment allowed – for breaking a curfew he hadn't been told about.

Worse than the beating was the curt accusation.

'You're lying to save your skin, Stevens.'

It rankled, and it was also quite untrue; so when Mr. Aerial instituted an in-house squash ladder some weeks later and fancifully placed himself on top, Matt espied a rare chance. Good at ball games anyway, he also started a self-imposed and very discreet training program taking time in seeking out and playing some of the best players from other houses, sharpening his sword. By the time he presented his challenge to Mr. Aerial – and as casually as he could – his victim's goose was well and truly cooked. Paul had done his best, too, as second in Matt's corner, as prime motivator, aiding and abetting in every twist of the plot. On the afternoon of the match, at ten to four, the two boys had set out from Upper: Matt, solemn in his whites, trying to feel confident, but horribly dry in the mouth and wondering to himself deep down – and not for the first time - whether he could do this, whether he could pull it off. His legs didn't feel good: weak – too weak. Paul; his legs in grey longs – way short of being nearly long enough, incidentally, white shirt and disgracefully mangled school tie bobbed along beside Matt shadow boxing the air, making sharp little hisses as he flung out his punches, weaving dramatically – tripping occasionally, certainly, but putting on a memorable display nevertheless; building atmosphere – a fighting atmosphere. The boys made an unlikely, incongruous pair as they walked and weaved and bobbed past the chapel, across the road, through the gate to the swimming bath. At the steps up to the side of the pool Paul stopped his antics, gripped Matt's arm and started his pep talk. As they walked down the side of the swimming bath towards the squash courts – the battlefield, Paul harangued his champion:

'Stiffen the sinews, summon up the blood,
Disguise fair nature with hard-favour'd rage:
Then lend the eye a terrible aspect ...'

Paul's pitched intensity strangled the words

'Now set the teeth, and stretch the nostril wide;
Hold hard the breath, and bend upon every spirit
To his full height! ... The game's afoot:
Follow your spirit; and, upon this charge
Cry – God for Matt! Go fuck Aerial and Saint Andrews!'

Matt had given a snorting guffaw at the venomous parody from their English set work – a shrill battle cry Paul had delivered with clenched fist – but his friend had just ploughed on, started at the beginning again, drilling the stirring inflaming words into Matt's brain. In a way it had worked, had stiffened the sinews, had summoned the blood, and even if Mr. Aerial hadn't tamely surrendered like the Governor of Harfleur, it had been enough. A match-fit Matt had run the sweating, egghead man ragged moving him relentlessly from one side of the court to the other, wearing him down remorselessly, controlling the court.

Paul made a leg. He'd doffed his imaginary plumed hat and bowed a deep, extravagant courtier's bow.

'The French herald, Montjoy, Sire.' he'd explained, his eyes glittering, his squeaky voice ready to bubble over.

'The day is yours!'

It bubbled over. The shrieks of delight had turned Mr. Aerial's glistening dome briefly as he was walking away from the courts, making his way home. He could see the two boys in the distance: Stevens sitting on the grass and his friend, whatsisname, Rennat, capering around him in what could only be a victory dance. He grunted, giving a small twist of his lips in begrudging acknowledgement. It had been cleverly done, no doubt about it ... the little shit: not his preferred type at all, he thought, and something of a misfit in some respects, but perhaps the Stevens boy might, just might amount to something after all.

The Machiavellian win was a tasty dish eaten cold, but it was also a novel and important departure. Instead of burying humiliation as he'd had to do all his life, Matt had been able to do something positive about it albeit unconventionally – and he felt astonishingly good as a result. That oil still came down the back of his throat sometimes, but it didn't burn any more. And there wasn't any need to boast about it either – except to Paul of course – but that horrible, depressing feeling of always being some sort of victim had gone. It was replaced by confidence and a faint aura of happiness that brightened his eye and firmed his step. All this was the foundation stone of an independence that he would be exercising much sooner than he had expected.

14

In the years Matt had spent in Grahamstown he had seen very little of his father who was either working all the time or away travelling on business. Jake's career had rocketed meteorically. His director's chair at Brathrow Steel (South Africa) had been followed by invitations to sit in others, the more so when the success of the new company was noted in the city. He travelled to London more and more frequently now, and had quietly purchased a flat in Knightsbridge. It was located in a discreet cul-de-sac where he now opened the door as he heard Ashleigh's taxi putt puttering outside. It had taken some persuasion for her to make the trip, but the prospect of a new flat to look at – and perhaps furnish – had proved an irresistible lure, as he knew it would. He paid and tipped the cab driver while she collected her belongings from the back seat and then hastened to pick up the small suitcase while Ashleigh stood back and looked around the tiny street in delight.

'It's quite delicious, Jake – those darling little flats with the window boxes everywhere – God, what an oasis you've found. You clever old stick!' She leant over and planted a solid kiss on the side of his cheek.

'Wait until you see inside,' chortled Jake as he ushered her towards the open door.

Carpeting aside, the flat was absolutely bare – apart from Jake's briefcase on the floor which he dived a hand into and extracted a bottle of Veuve Cliquot with a magician's flourish.

'Voila!'

Two long glasses followed but there was nowhere to put them.

'You hold these for a second.'

Jake wrestled and popped the cork, and then filled the two

flutes with the foaming liquid.

'To your new flat,' Ashleigh raised her glass. 'Chin, chin.'

'Cheers! Thanks – but better come and see it first.'

Carrying their glasses with them, they started to tour the rooms.

'There are three floors and a basement thrown in for good measure,' Jake began to explain. 'The ground floor has an extension out the back so there's plenty of room. We've got a kitchen, pantry, living room, dining room, cloakroom on your left as you came in, and a courtyard garden which I'll show you later.' Their footsteps echoed in the empty rooms and Ashleigh was silent as her eyes roved around the moulded ceilings, taking in proportions and detail. She shook her head lightly and almost whispered. 'What a wonderful find.'

They slowly mounted the stairs, looking up as they climbed.

'Two en suite bedrooms here and a hidey hole which I dare say I will use as a study if allowed.'

They walked into the first bedroom and over to the window facing onto the mall.

'There's even a small bistro at the entrance onto the main road – run by a pucka Frenchman, so the food is bound to be good.' Jake looked around. 'This will be my bedroom, I suppose, and I'll want that fireplace opened up if possible. Man, I've always wanted a bedroom with a fireplace, but there's precious little call for one in sunny S.A., of course.'

When their tour was complete, Jake and Ashleigh wandered down the little street to the bistro and asked for a table. There was one free in an hour so they booked it and then explored a little further into the main road where a pub called The Wheatsheaf beckoned them in. It was jampacked, but they managed to find a spot at the end of the bar and ordered their drinks.

'Are you going to do it up for me, then? Jake quizzed her,

toying with his whisky and ice, clinking it back and forth in the glass. Ashleigh made a funny little noise in her throat and raised her eyebrows to the heavens.

'God knows I'd love to fix it up and decorate it, but I just couldn't if your family come and live here, Jake, it'd be too close to the bone for my taste, much too close. You know you really should reconsider and let Ash do it for you.'

Jake shook his head firmly and closed his hand over hers.

'This flat is mine alone, Ashleigh – no one else in the world knows about it. Just you, the registry office, and me' he added with a smile, 'and that's the way it's going to stay – forever. It's going to be my bolthole, my refuge, my safe harbour, call it what you will. The same as your cottage is to you – hey, what did you call it? Your fort – that's right, your fort' He paused to light a cigar which took a few moments to get going.

'And it's you I want for the job.'

He leant back on the bar stool, wreathed in blue smoke.

'You're still doing your private nursing I suppose,' he continued, 'have you got much on at the present?'

Ashleigh shook her head.

'Nothing if I don't want it – the agency only looks for posts if I tell them to.'

Jake nodded and continued, 'I'll tell you what then – I'll double your salary and pay for a hotel room nearby – board included if you'll stay here in London for three months and do out the flat from top to bottom. Are you on?' She regarded him with a steady stare – so he continued, 'with an expense account … say you'll do it!'

She gave him a sudden broad grin. 'Of course I'll do it, silly pumpkin, but I think you'll find it'll take more like six months than three – and I'll need a fortnight off, plus minus, in the middle somewhere. I've got to be back in Stock for Alice's holidays.

That's a must do.' Jake clapped his hands once. 'Done deal! Now let's see if they've still got that table for us down the road – I'm starving. My stomach thinks my throat's been cut.'

The Café Marcel was discreetly commended to the public by way of a thin blue neon tube that inscribed the name in neat script over a scalloped white awning with indigo trim. The lower half of the little bay window beneath the awning was covered with velvet fabric run on rings of pale, burnished brass. Above the brass, the cottage panes exuded a gentle old ivory glow. Jake pushed the door open and a bell tinkled cheerfully above his head, matching his mood. The proprietor, having noted his new customer's address, made effusive welcome – the man could become a regular, after all – and steered them to a quiet corner where he could personally attend to their needs. These were swiftly met through inspired recitation of several of the specials in a heavily French accented tongue punctuated with extravagant Gallic gestures. Ashleigh was surprised to see Jake perusing the wine list with a knowledgeable air, and as Marcel departed to the kitchens, needled him lightly.

'Quite the afficianado nowadays I see.'

He glanced up at her and nodded. 'You wouldn't believe the number of business lunches I go to these days, Ashleigh, so I thought I better get to know my European wines a bit better. Of course, once I started reading I was hooked!' He leant forward in his enthusiasm. 'That cellar or basement in the flat is huge ... so I'm planning to lay down a lot of wine – bloody oceans of it. You'll have to go and see one of the Masters of Wine in the city for me – old Simon Littlewood, I would suggest. He'll introduce you to all the mysteries of the temperature and humidity. It's also the opportunity for a little commerce,' Jake smiled his Cheshire cat smile. 'In five years or so I expect I can start selling at a nice profit – not to mention drinking at home for very little money what would cost me a fortune to go out and buy.'

They spent the rest of the evening in nattering about the flat, batting ideas back and forth, but Jake saw that she was tired after the long day. He ordered a taxi straight after dessert, and with the promise of a noon appointment on the morrow, sent her yawning off to her hotel.

Ashleigh sat at her dresser in the Adelphi Hotel room taking off her make up – peering into the mirror, working carefully around her face and eyes with the piece of cotton wool. Her mind, however, was elsewhere. Jake had given her carte blanche as far as expense was concerned – provided she okayed it with him beforehand, and that was stressed – but the pots of money were no great surprise as she had gathered from his conversations over time that he had accumulated great wealth in a very short space of time. The time that had been the worst was just after his boys had been killed in that dreadful motor accident. He'd come on very strong then about leaving his wife and their getting married right away. She'd been privately shocked at the vehemence; his ready dismissal of his wife and remaining son who was, as far as she could gather, still at school. There was a cold calculation in him then that may have served well in business, but was unattractive in a person. She'd shied away from him and he'd left her cottage for London in a fury, only to telephone later in the week – full of profuse apology and ready to make any sort of amends. She had seen him about twice a year since, but had kept him at a long arms length, and this designing of the flat that he had proposed meant taking a closer sort of order that she was a little uneasy with. How long do you go on for old times sake, for Christ's sake? Bugger, bugger, bugger – if only Ash hadn't messed up with that massive overspend on the place in Chelsea, and if only she hadn't mentioned it to Jake! Don't you be doing that my girl, he'd said when he heard about it, businessman bully down to his black boots, you do that and I'll be all over you like a rash. Whereas in the old days she'd have been bursting out with, God, I can hardly wait! Now she just thought – in your dreams, friend, in your dreams. The money wouldn't harm, but that didn't mean everything by a long chalk. Ash was out and that was a pity, just keeping a healthy distance would be the thing, and that would have been so much easier with him around, not to mention Ash's brilliant ideas. Still, if it couldn't be, just too bad. But the truth of it was she couldn't bloody-well resist the challenge – she just couldn't. She'd treat this like any other sort of job ... yes, just a job. Ashleigh stared into the mirror, looking through the reflection of her own unsmiling face. She had almost convinced herself.

During lunch the next day she plied him with magazines she'd bought that morning, showing pictures of interiors of homes and getting him to point out ones that appealed to him and ones that didn't, trying to pinpoint his likes and dislikes – his taste.

'This is your home, Jake, not mine, so there's little point in doing just what appeals to me,' she'd explained. He'd demurred.

'But I admire your cottage so much! The colours, the way it's put together. You should see our Johannesburg home – stuffed and stuffy. Ball and claw, silver and oils – that's it! I wanted to do something unique here – different, and I need your imagination for that. That's why you're here.'

They had argued back and forth – quite amiably – for a while until Ashleigh had called a halt. 'Okay, I think I've got the picture, and I'll tell you what I'll do. While they're doing the structural work I want you to give me one day a week to take you to see whatever I have in mind for fixtures and fittings. Agreed?'

He had agreed – and then regretted it immediately. What she showed him had left him alarmed and aghast: pale angular Danish furniture, Mackintosh's dark forbidding chairs, Liberty's Art Nouveau Cymric silver, Moore's strange sketches of the underground during the Blitz, Impressionist paintings by the score and rolls and rolls of sumptuously rich Beardsley fabrics, thick with colour. She had found pictures of Tutankhamun's burial treasures and mask and then taken him to see Holman Hunt's paintings bringing ancient Egypt alive in fanciful, imagined tableau. There were Guagin's dusky Polynesian ladies and Barbara Hepworth's strange angular sculptures. His senses and properties had been subjected to a shock attack from every quarter, but once the initial alarm was over, he found that he even began to look forward to finding out what exactly she was going to throw at him next.

'Don't panic, Jake' she had placated him, 'I'm not going to fill your precious home with a mishmash of all sorts, but your eye was desperately in need of some enlightenment – come on, admit it! Neither is it your fault that all you ever look at is the inside of a boardroom or a restaurant, but you're most unlikely to find anything original or exciting there I promise you. It's all one big exercise just to show you that there's more to life than you'll find in a second rate print of Flatford Mill.'

He even found himself slipping into shops and galleries when he had spare moments during the day, and browsing through books on art, fashion and style to educate himself further. Ashleigh was delighted with the spark she had fired and was content to let his fuse of discovery fizzle on alone. Adept at looking after herself, and left largely to her own devices, she indulged her love of music, theatre and the ballet, whilst Jake was there to squire her to eateries and restaurants – if the mood so took her and he happened to be in town.

The workmen were soon out of the flat and the cellar ready for stocking. All the paraphernalia necessary for temperature and humidity control was installed. Simon had been, to her mind, an absolute sweetie, but she also supposed that the appointment as

Jake's purchasing agent might have also had something to do with his extraordinary attention to detail. The quarry-tiled floor was flanked on three sides with honeycomb banks of terracotta sleeves that ran from knee height to the ceiling. As with some libraries, a sturdy wooden ladder was fixed to a running rail fronting the sleeves, giving ease of access to every corner of the oblong cellar. The capacity, so Jake bragged, was twenty-six thousand bottles and five thousand or so bottles of young Bordeaux and Burgundy wines were soon housed to begin their maturation. On the opposite side, Simon had put in a mixture of whites and reds – some forty strong – for immediate needs.

The long narrow kitchen pleased Ashleigh's eye – galley kitchens, by her reckoning, being the easiest by far to work – and there was plenty of natural light filtering in through the two windows looking out onto the courtyard. She designed long work surfaces covered in pale elm with simple cupboards above and below. Cooking was by gas over stainless steel and with the pale tile flooring the whole effect was chic and ultra modern. Jake's bedroom was also a homage to modernity with elm fitted cupboards; the Brinton's wheaten wool fitted carpet; and hung flush on three walls, vast, abstract, unframed paintings with swirls of blue, green and white oils ladled thick onto the canvases. The bed that lay in the room provided astonishing contract. 'Good God!' Jake had exploded when a gleeful Ashleigh introduced him to the room. Sat central and gleaming like some eastern potentate's throne, was an ancient, sleigh-shaped bed fashioned from hammered copper and brass and covered with linen bedclothes that faithfully mimicked the swirling colours and lines of the paintings.

'You see why I had to prepare you, Jake – it's pretty way out, isn't it?'

He had slowly walked around the bed with thumb and

forefinger rasping his jaw and then knelt on one knee to peer at the embossed designs on the head and footboards.

'Where on earth did you find such a thing?' he asked.

Ashleigh walked over to the bed and sat down near the foot. 'Well, believe it or not, I had the whole concept of the room in my mind before I started looking. It saves an awful lot of time and indecision! The paintings were commissioned and done by a Slade student: you know – the usual – long on talent but short of cash, and I had the bed linen bought before he had primed a single canvas. The colours in the paintings were to complement the linen and not vice versa, as you'd imagine. The bed ...' she paused and patted it, 'well, that is a bit special. It's from Zanzibar and belonged to some decadent Sultan, I suspect. The lucky fellow probably pleasured all the girls from his harem right here.' She giggled, got up and moved to the headboard. 'The real tricky bit was organising the lighting for the dear boy's – sorry, the Sultan of Knightsbridge's reading in bed. I was determined that the bed would be the only thing on the floor so I've had a tame electrician run a wire under the carpet for you, and ... voila!' She had pressed something on the headboard and soft, hidden lights shone down on the pillows.

'I thought you might need something exotic like this living round here.'

'Meaning what?'

'Jake, dear, your flat is within spitting distance of Harrods. This is prime rich-bitch shopping territory. You know – Sloane Square types. You're bound to catch one or two if you trawl.'

After he'd left, Ashleigh reflected that he had seemed as pleased with the progress as she was. The cellar, kitchen and master bedroom were more or less complete now and she'd wanted his endorsement before moving on to other parts of the house when he was back in Africa. That last comment of hers was a bit crass, but she hadn't wanted him getting any ideas again. The past was definitely the past. In any event ... it was time for a break. Alice would be arriving from Ireland for her school holiday and she had begun to fret about her garden in Stock. She had been away for getting on for three months now and was homesick for her cottage after the city.

15

Alice's trip from Bansha in Tipperary to Stock in Essex was a hybrid journey compounded of road, rail and the ferry over from Rosslare to Fishguard. A sixteen year old was young to travel alone, but her rather dreamy mother, Rebecca, put great faith in the resilience of youth and Alice's fund of common sense. Indeed, Rebecca had reflected, Alice was a great deal more likely to make sense of all the train and bus connections that she ever would.

Alice loved her English holidays, as she called them. She knew that her Aunt Ashleigh and her father had been very close as siblings. The innumerable black and white pictures of them together as children in those dog-eared albums under the piano just said it. She dumped her bags in the narrow hallway and walked through to the kitchen where Ashleigh was fussing around making coffee, looking for the sugar.

'Great stuff, I could just do with a cuppa!'

There was just a hint of an Irish lilt in a not too overly cultured accent that spoke of a good upbringing and decent schools. Ashleigh turned to look at her niece in appraisement, leaning back on the dresser with her hands clasped around a steaming cup. The obligatory jeans, with fashionable flares and coloured patches on the knee covering slim legs on the slight frame that was a family legacy. Less of a child now, thought Ashleigh, as her eyes – as always – were drawn to the thick auburn halo surrounding the elfin face and the dancing green eyes. She had suddenly shot up – so for the first time, they were of a height, and Ashleigh realised her niece was going to become a very striking woman.

'What are you staring at, Aunt Ash?' Alice demanded.

'Well, I was just thinking how pretty you are now that you've grown up.'

'Yes, the rest's okay,' answered Alice, 'but the front's desperate! No decent tits yet.' She pulled up her jersey and thrust out her chest to show the two little jutting hillocks.

'You're lucky, Aunt Ash, you've got lovely boobs. Not too big either – just grand.'

Ashleigh laughed at Alice's outspokenness and forever coming out with the most scandalous remarks – she was always such a tonic.

'They'll grow, don't worry.' Ashleigh started to reassure her.

'Oh, but I do worry, Aunt Ash – I do, I don't want to be like some frigging beanpole all my life. I've tried a mail order cream, massaging them, everything – but no luck: and me being Irish and with no luck – it's just not fair! I've even thought of converting so I can pray to Mary – she's a woman, she'd understand.' Alice pulled down her jersey sharply in mock anger and then burst out laughing.

'So it's boys now instead of horses, is it?' Ashleigh inquired.

'Oh no, Aunt Ash, I've had a couple of them with their hands hovering at the dances, but I'm still honest Irish virgo intracto or whatever you call it.'

'Intacto.'

'Intacto then. I can't honestly say I've got any great enthusiasm for the boys yet. I'll stick to my horses and dogs for a while.' She munched on a biscuit enthusiastically.

'But I do like romantic novels with all the slushy stuff.' She waved an arm around chewing frantically – 'you know, lots of heroines being rescued by knights on horseback – that sort of thing, I can relate to that – and the pale Paddies can't possibly compete with that now can they?'

They spent the rest of the afternoon catching up, chatting about Alice's Irish family that Rebecca had married into and what was happening with the boys and the farm. Ashleigh was pleased to have news of her erstwhile sister-in-law, who was an awful correspondent. An overcast afternoon promised rain from a blue-grey lowering sky and they lit the fire early at about four o'clock. Ashleigh brought in scones from the kitchen and they ate them hot, the honey and melting butter spilling off the sides.

'Nothing wrong with your appetite then,' Ashleigh noted approvingly. 'You're right,' said Alice licking her fingers enthusiastically. 'Mam says I must have a worm to feed inside of me, but I don't get fat and ugly so it's great really. And I do love food as you can see. If I don't become a vet I think I'll be a chef at a fancy restaurant and eat all the profits!'

'Are you still keen on the vetting idea?' asked Ashleigh carefully.

'Oh, yes Aunt Ash, I get amaaazing exam marks and that's all I need. Am I right?'

'Probably – where will you apply?'

'Dublin, I suppose, does it matter?' Alice fixed the innocent query on her face.

Ashleigh got to her feet from the floor where they had been sitting in front of the flames and walked over to the drinks tray. She poured herself a pink gin and then lit a cigarette, thinking hard.

'You know your father was at Corpus Christi?' Alice nodded, 'Yes, and Uncle Ash at Queen's, but I didn't even know there was a veterinary school at Cambridge.'

'There is,' Ashleigh drew on her cigarette elatedly, 'a small one – I'd be just a stone's throwaway, and there's Newmarket for your horses round the corner. Who knows, you might even find one of your knights in shining armour there as well.'

'Pah!!' said Alice, 'and anyway, I bet it's very expensive, isn't it?'

Ashleigh flicked the ash off her cigarette, carrying an amused smile on her face. She sat down on the old settee opposite Alice.

She'd made up her mind.

'You needn't worry about the expense; Rebecca and I can carry that without too much effort. And if you're accepted – and that means startlingly good A level results – I'll stand you the keep of your precious hunter while you're there.' A broad grin stretched over Alice's face as she jumped up and threw herself at Ashleigh giving her a huge hug.

'Do you mean it? My Fred could come with me?............ Fa-a-antastic, bloody fantastic, I'll work extra hard, I will – I promise.' The young girl gave a shriek of delight and twirled around the room with her arms windmilling. 'Steady, steady, you're not halfway there yet!' Ashleigh caught and restrained her in half-hearted fashion as the two embraced, giggling like two schoolgirls, teetering and almost falling over the piano stool. 'I'll tell you what, you go down to see old Mrs. Rogers tomorrow like you planned, and then we can go up to Cambridge on Thursday for a recce. I also want to buy you some new clothes – and we can see if we're able to manage a punt up the river without falling in. Are you game?'

Alice was up early and out of the house before Ashleigh had even stirred. Her first holiday with her Aunt Ash had been when she was six years old, and it had been at Mrs. Roger's establishment that she had first sat on a pony. Tucked into a valley behind the village, the little yard boasted a Thelwellian collection of about a dozen ponies housed in rickety wooden stables and grazed on quiet, undulating paddocks amidst venerable oaks. Here, the mild-mannered and soft-spoken Mrs. Hermione Rogers had taught generations of children to ride and introduced them to muck and that bastion of English equestrianism, the Pony Club. Alice had spent hours every day down in the valley – riding, grooming, mucking out stables and cleaning tack. Year after year the patient old ponies had endured children updowning on their backs learning to trot, and borne them on rides through woodland tracks that they could have done blindfolded. In winter their coats grew long and shaggy and the kids plodded through the mud in their Wellingtons, slower now – wrapped in anoraks against the cold and the damp. But this was a bright morning and Alice skipped over the gate and ran up to the stables where she could see the red splash of Hermione's coat in the yard.

Hermione turned as she heard the foxhunting holler and regarded the flying form coming up towards her. They all come back, she thought to herself, but welcome as they all were, Alice had been something of a favourite. Not only because of her natural and fearless talent on the back of a pony, but also because of the irreverent Irish air she brought to the stables. A real Colleen with the red hair and the emerald eyes! The world needed more like her. Quite typically, Alice threw herself into the feeding as they prattled and gossiped away and the ponies munched in their mangers. She had brought two bunches of carrots with her from Ashleigh's garden, and the lion's share went to tiny old Tuppence. He'd been her first guiding light in the old days when she was still on leading rein – plodding patiently around the arena, and she like an eejit in a riding hat half a size too big that kept falling over her eyes.

16

Hope was at Jan Smuts airport to meet Jake off the plane. This had been the longest spell away from home – about four months – and she had grown lonely at home. Matt, her dear Matt, was away at Varsity, in Pietermaritzburg doing a degree in Economics, which he had stumbled into as a vague sort of choice, Jake having said no to Marine Biology. News from Tartary, or to be precise from 'Maritzburg, was that he found life at that small University pleasantly undemanding, with plenty of time to indulge in the traditional undergraduate pastimes of drinking at the Imperial Hotel bar – the Imp, as everyone called it evidently – playing sport – in his case squash – and getting to know some of the girls from Women's Res and the Nurses Home in town next to Addenbrooks Hospital.

'How is the boy getting on at 'Maritzburg?' Jake had inquired as they made their way from the airport back to the northern suburbs.

'Well enough, I think,' answered Hope. 'He's evidently made some friends in Res, and is playing for the University second squash team already. He thinks he might even get the odd game for the first team this year.' 'What about his work, how's that going?' Jake grimaced as a taxi cut in front of him sharply forcing him to brake. 'Bloody idiot.' Hope lurched forward putting her hand out towards the dashboard to steady herself. It was a couple of seconds before she spoke.

'All right, I suppose, he doesn't talk about work that much. They had initiation first and I don't think he cared for that overmuch.'

Jake grunted. 'Well, just as long as he passes his exams I don't much care what he does.'

Hope gave an almost imperceptible shake of her head and wondered at him – and not for the first time. It was almost as if Jake blamed Matt personally for the death of her two sons. Ever since the accident he'd had this awful angry bitterness. Perhaps he thought that fate had taken away his favourite sons and left him with a poor substitute. But it was hardly Matt's fault if Jake hadn't taken any time to get to know him, perhaps even like him – many other people did, just not his father. She felt the stone sitting heavy in her heart, and to rid herself of it, changed the subject, trying to chat cheerfully about what she had achieved in the garden. Her time alone had given her plenty of time for that. Jake listened with half an ear and then interrupted her flow of small talk.

'I've been thinking about the house at Plett ... I think we should sell it and build something a lot better. Somewhere we can have guests to stay. What do you think?' Hope knew instantly that this was to do with business. Oh Lord, the last thing she wanted in life was her holidays cluttered up with people, very likely Jake's business cronies, and responsible for their entertainment. She ventured timidly, 'Oh Jake, do we really need people staying when we're on holiday?' She could see irritation crease his brow.

'Hope, you won't be bothered by guests at all! We'll build completely separate quarters for them – a large guest wing with their own living rooms, garages, the lot. Pretty well their own establishment, if you like.' He continued, offering Hope the sop he had prepared. 'It'll be fun for you too – perhaps you'd like to plan some rockeries, herb gardens, indoor courtyards, that sort of thing. We're not short of money these days, you know.' She was silent for a while and then turned to him with a bright smile.

'Well, perhaps you're right – it could be fun.'

Jake cheered up visibly and began to look forward to a whisky and soda at home. That was something else he wanted to change as well before long. He wanted a grander house in Johannesburg: something to reflect his wealth – otherwise what was the point of it.

Hope had become very wary of disagreeing with Jake ever since he had battered her. He had never done it since, thank God, but whenever she saw his anger clouds building, her palms started sweating and she panicked. She would do anything, absolutely anything, to avoid a repeat of that night and always hurried to acquiesce and defuse any threatening potential problem.

Two days later, Hope was bumping down the coast in an ancient Dakota en route to Plettenberg Bay. The air hostess was soon asking them to fasten their seat belts for the landing, and as the plane flew low over the airfield she saw the little herd boys running out and chasing the single donkey and motley band of bush cattle off the dusty airstrip. It seemed to take an age for the creaking aircraft to come round again and lower itself to earth. She braced herself as they bounced gently once and then settled, waiting for the bone-jarring reverse thrust of the engines.

Jake had given her strict instructions about scouting sites for their new house – Jake's new house, Hope reflected ruefully. She had been more than content with their old house, which, sadly, she now had to put on the market. He wanted a view to outshine anyone else's, which thankfully let out Millionaire's row – what she thought of as those often hideous and always expensive houses now being built right on Robberg beach the other side of the Beacon Island Hotel. She had a week here before he would fly down. There were evidently more important business matters to deal with in Johannesburg before he was free to join her. It seemed strange to be in a hire car going across the Piesang River Bridge on the way into Plett from the airport, and stranger still to be in the house all by herself. It had always been filled with children before, and this was the last time she would be here she supposed. After she had unpacked her small suitcase she let herself out of the house and walked down the hill to see if Gideon was about. The cottage was empty but she found the key in its usual place behind the stone in the wall and let herself in. The warm interior wrapped itself around her as she walked into the living room over familiar yellowwood boards. She had just put the kettle on the stove in the kitchen when she heard Gideon whistling his usual tune as he racked his fishing rod under the roof over the veranda. She walked back to the front door, poked her head around the corner.

'Surprise!!'

Gideon turned with a crinkled smile as he recognised her voice.

'Hope!! How wonderful to see you – what on earth are you doing in Plett at this time of year?'

Hope skipped the two steps to him like a schoolgirl, gave him a heartfelt hug and a kiss on his whiskered cheek.

'Oh, you'll never believe it, Jake sent me down house hunting, or site-hunting I suppose it really is. He wants to build a new ... huuuge house.' Hope said this with eyes raised heavenward and her arms widespread, all of which Gideon took to mean that she didn't think too much of the idea. The kettle started whistling from the kitchen and they walked through, chatting, to make tea together whilst they caught up with news.

'How's that boy getting on at Varsity?' Hope brightened at the mention of Matt. 'Having a great time, I gather, but I don't think he has a clue about what he really wants to do.'

Gideon picked up the tea tray and started to walk back to the stoep, talking over his shoulder as he went.

'I can't see him sticking with Economics, you know, but there's plenty of time yet. Knowing that boy as I think I do, I think he'll recognise it when he sees it ... but whatever "it" is, heaven only knows.'

Gideon sat down heavily in the wicker chair and motioned Hope to its pair standing opposite.

'He'll surprise us pleasantly, that one ... I'm sure of it.' Hope leant forward to take her mug of tea and sugar it.

'How on earth did you know he was doing Economics?'

Gideon leant back in his chair and fished for his pipe in his pocket. 'Oh, he writes to me from time to time, which is a blessing for an old salt like me'self.' Hope gave him a broad smile and steepled her hands under her chin. 'Oh, I'm so pleased he has done that, Gideon! You don't know how much ... you know his years at St. Andrews weren't the happiest. It must have been a huge encouragement for him to hear from you. He really loves you, you know ... and all this. Hope's hand went back to include the cottage and she thought to herself – Gideon, if you only knew, if only I could tell you. Gideon packed his pipe furiously to cover his discomfort, struck a match and drew on the pipe intently.

'Well, he's a wonderful kid, Hope – the feeling is somewhat mutual.' His pipe bellowed clouds, making tactical smoke – something he'd made his old destroyer do on occasion. Gideon waved the dead match furiously, putting it out another half-a-dozen times before swiftly changing the subject to cover what remained of his delighted embarrassment. 'You staying for supper?'

Hope laughed at the obvious ploy and answered in mock seriousness, 'I thought you'd never ask: all I've got to go back to is a tin of sardines and some baked beans.'

'We can't have that,' crowed Gideon, entering into the spirit of the moment. He jumped up from his chair. 'I'll make you another one of my famous curries – what say?'

They ate out on the stoep on a truly balmy evening with the sound of the waves filtering through the surrounding bush. Hope, with the aid of a bottle of red wine, relaxed for the first time since her husband had come home – free of the loneliness that had plagued her for so long now. Gideon walked her home just after midnight and kissed her gently on the cheek at her front door.

'Wonderful to see you again, Hope. I suppose you'll be busy at the estate agents tomorrow; but why not come out to the Fountains shack with me on Wednesday – we can go in the afternoon, stay overnight and come back after breakfast in the morning?'

Hope drew back and regarded him seriously, knowing that she should refuse, but yearning for just a hint of happiness in a life that seemed to have gone all wrong. She made up her mind. 'I'll come, Gideon ... why shouldn't I?' She turned the key in the Yale lock, slipped through the door and was gone.

She was up very early the following morning keeping appointments that Jake had organised for her from Johannesburg. After an exhausting traipse around what seemed an endless number of estate agents and about a dozen empty stands, her mind was buzzing and her feet aching to get out of shoes that suddenly seemed too small. Lordie, just to get them off, have a cup of coffee and relax! Manoeuvring the little red hire car into the space behind the house at four o'clock, Hope yanked up the hand brake and made her way gingerly down the stepped path to her front door. Once inside she put the kettle on, thankful that she had remembered to get a pint of milk from Monks between appointments that morning. She had promised to ring Jake at the office before five and wanted to collect her thoughts before making the call. There were only two plots on offer that fitted the bill. Both were horrendously expensive, but views of that magnitude didn't come cheaply here. The first one was above the main road that wound its lazy way down past the school towards the Why Not tearoom. The slope was fearful but the view was breathtaking

– out over the Beacon Island Hotel on the rocks way below, and to the right, and far away, the peninsula of Robberg stretching out into the sea. The other, surprisingly enough, was almost next door to their present house, only a little further back and higher up on the hill. The extra elevation, however, made all the difference. In addition to their present view straight out to sea, the vista was enlarged dramatically, taking in the Lookout rocks below, the whole of Lookout beach up to the mouth of the lagoon and way, way beyond this as the sands curled gently and ever smaller into infinity. As a backdrop was the Tsitsikamma mountain range, an enchanted indigo blue in the evenings and sometimes capped with snow in winter.

Well, I know which one I'd choose, thought Hope, as she got up from the sofa. She padded barefoot towards the telephone in the lobby to make the call to her husband.

17

The next day dawned brilliant and clear and Hope gave herself the rare privilege of a lie-in before taking a long bath, washing her hair and shaving her legs carefully. She chose a light cotton dress with simple shoulder straps and overprinted with daisies. It matched her bright mood. Gideon had rung the previous evening to say that he would organise all the provisions and pick her up at the house after lunch – at about two. Hope thought herself quite ridiculous, she felt like a school-girl going on her first date, but it was a scrumptious feeling, she decided, and she hummed a little tune from her childhood as she walked around the outside of the house, looking at her flower-beds and deciding what slips she could take for the garden at the new house. Thank goodness so many of her herbs were in pots. They'd be so welcome.

Gideon was on time, and she went to pick up her beach bag from the tall chair next to the front door as she heard his old bakkie coming down the little cul-de-sac to the house. Gideon gave a cheerful 'hello, Hope!' as he nipped out and opened the passenger door for her.

'My, but you're looking very pretty today!'

Hope nodded her thanks sweetly and smiled. Lord, she thought, as she sat down on the sagging passenger seat, how very different this all was from Jake's enormous American cars.

'I should get that seat fixed, I'm sorry,' Gideon apologised as he got in. 'Trouble is, it's so damn seldom that anyone sits in the thing that I forget.' 'Where's your rod, Gideon?' asked Hope as she twisted in the seat to look into the back of the bakkie where his rucksack was stowed.

'I'm not fishing today, Hope; it's low tide at four so I'm going to collect mussels for our dinner. You do like mussels, don't you?'

'That's wonderful, I adore mussels.'

With the tide running out fast, Gideon said that they would be able to walk along the sand at the water's edge for most of the way from The Gap to the heel of the spit running out to the Island. They walked through The Gap and down on the other side and were soon on the inlet beach without a soul in sight. Hope wrenched off her shoes and gave a sigh of intense pleasure as she felt the sand squidging between her toes. She walked ahead of Gideon with her head thrown back and her eyes shut tight, feeling the heat of the sun of her face.

She looks so good here, thought Gideon, as he watched her surrender her cares and walk free. What an unbelievable contrast to the nervous creature she had become these last few years. Something had eroded her confidence, and he suspected it was Jake who was responsible. He had known them both a long time now, and Jake had seemed so much more approachable in those first years, a much nicer person. Now there was all this wealth, but they seemed to be paying such a terrible price for it. The two of them had to climb up onto the rocks as the beach ran out, and a little further on, they paused on the outcrop called Aaskop, which looked over the stretch of sand running out to the Island. The cove ran across their line of sight to the Island and they sat for a while, watching a school of porpoises surfing the waves. Once they started walking again it was only another ten minutes before they were at the Fountains shack, a tiny wooden croft tucked snugly up against the base of the mountain that reared up behind. Gideon had brought two sleeping bags in a draw-string poke which Hope rolled out onto the rough bunks, and Gideon scrabbled around in the depths of his rucksack before producing a length of flat iron with a curved and sharpened tip and a hessian sack.

'I'll be off then,' he announced. 'I should be able to find some decent mussels just around the corner – it won't take long.' Hope unpacked the remaining rucksack which Gideon had piggy-backed on his own, finding clothes on the top and the provisions below, tightly jammed into a battered and rather deep copper pot. Three-quarters of an hour later she saw Gideon trudging back with what was obviously a weighted sack over his shoulder and dragging a pale and gnarled piece of driftwood behind him in the sand. He grinned at Hope as he came within earshot and shouted across to her in a theatrical accent.

'Shiver me timbers, me 'earty, I've got a king's ransom in mussels, I 'ave!' Hope giggled, suddenly feeling very girlish. 'Got our supper have you, Captain?'

Whilst Gideon had been around the corner garnering his illegal mussels, Hope had searched out the fountain that gave the shack its name. The water, from somewhere deep inside of Robberg, discharged itself gently into a tiny pool right in the beach sand behind some rocks adjacent to the shack. Hope marvelled at the soft, almost creamy texture and taste of it as she knelt drinking from cupped hands. It took three trips from the fountain to collect enough water for their needs and they then spent the remaining daylight hour collecting more driftwood. Gideon explained that he wouldn't light his fire until he was sure everyone was off Robberg.

'It's illegal to light fires anywhere on Robberg, Hope, but there's no risk to anything I promise you: we'll make it on the beach – there's no wind.'

At dusk he opened the demijohn of wine he'd laid in a shaded rock pool nearby and they sat sipping it out of battered tin mugs watching the light slip away and the evening star blinking low in the western sky. Hope had seldom felt happier. Her eyes were drawn to the fire where Gideon was making their supper. The old copper pot sat perched in the bright red wood coals as he bearded the mussels and then chopped a single fat onion. Taking the demijohn, he poured about a pint of the white wine into the scalding hot pot followed by the onion rings and a large bunch of parsley. The pot hissed and bubbled and Gideon quickly threw in the mussels, filling it to the brim as the steam belched from the top and the aroma of grape and herb assaulted their senses. A few minutes later, Gideon was ladling the black mussels into two deep tin bowls and they sat to eat.

'Oh, Lordie, these are too delicious for words!' exclaimed Hope.

'That's the trick,' said Gideon as he nodded his head, 'cooking them in wine vapour. You've just got to make sure the pot is good and hot before you start.'

They mopped up the juices with broken-off pieces of a rough homemade brown loaf and washed it all down with more wine from the demijohn. Taking the pot from the fire, Gideon threw on more driftwood and watched as the flames rose from the coals making lights and shadows flicker on their faces like an old-time movie. Gideon sat on his haunches, pulled out his pipe and packed it slowly and thoughtfully from his tin of Navy Cut. Behind the crackle and spit from the fire the sound of the sea murmured like a lullaby. At length he lit the bowl and then cast the match on the fire. With the experience of all the years of living in solitude behind him, Gideon knew the value of this moment, but he didn't know how to begin to say what he had to say. He cleared his throat nervously and looked into the pair of suddenly solemn blue eyes gazing back into his. 'Hope, you're not very happy, are you?' His heart twisted in his chest as he saw those eyes fill with tears and glisten in the firelight. She looked away from him into the darkness, shameful of her easy tears and waited until she could trust her voice not to break.

'At the moment, Gideon, I'm as happy as I could ever be. This is like the sort of dreams I had as a child.' She drew her breath in deep and then let it go in a long tremulous sigh as sobs tried to catch it.

'The trouble is, that's what it is, "a dream".' She looked across to him now with hopelessness etched onto her face. He rose quickly and went to her side putting his arms around her protectively as she dropped her head gratefully onto his chest. His voice was gruff now.

'No, it needn't be, Hope, it needn't be.' He gathered his courage and held her even tighter.

'I love you, Hope, you know that, I'm sure. I've loved you ever since that first time.' 'You must come to me now; I can't bear you being unhappy any longer. It's time ... it's time.' Her reply was muffled in his shirt. He stood and swung her up into his arms, carrying her like a child back to the shack. There, in the dark, on the rough bunk, they made slow, searching love to one another, rediscovering a world that had been lost to them both for so long. It was a love-making that filled the deep, empty caverns of their souls and Hope's tears became tears of bliss and no longer those of an unbearable pain. She reached out to him to fill her being and to take away the terrible, long ache in her, and when her body rose to meet his she knew that this was right after all.

Gideon slipped out of the bunk just before dawn, carefully taking her blonde head from his shoulder, trying not to wake her. He drew on his corduroy trousers, and bare-chested, went out to pump and then light the little primus stove and put on a billy-can of water. Next, he went down to check that the fire on the beach had burnt down to ash, and scrupulously buried every trace deep in the sand. By the time he returned, the water was boiling and he made two cups of strong coffee with condensed milk and took them to their bunk. He sat gingerly beside her sleeping form and watched her face in the thin early light, loving her deeply. He had waited a lifetime for today.

He thought of the first time they had been together. It was just before the end of the war and they had met and been drawn together inexorably, like two magnets. He had been on secondment from the Royal Navy at the time, still not totally recovered from his injuries at sea. He hadn't known her husband then – he had still been up north in Africa and then Italy. Gideon supposed there had been many love affairs like theirs during the war, but he had never been able to put down the candle he carried for her all these years. Later, after some years, she had asked him about it. Wasn't he ever going to get married and settle down, for heaven's sake, were her words. He hadn't the heart then to upset her and tell her the truth, and had ended up muttering some platitude about not finding the right girl yet. The truth was that he had already found the right girl – but she had a husband and two young children. Hope's third son followed soon after, and Gideon had put his feelings on hold to settle for friendship, and at least being close to her, albeit in a different way. One thing he couldn't ever help was the way his eyes were compelled to follow her around any room. He leant over now to stroke her cheek with the back of his hand. At his touch her eyes flew open and he was treated to the most brilliant smile – a radiance that turned his knees to water. He watched her stretch slowly like a panther and then she curled in towards him putting her head on his lap.

'Your coffee's here.' Gideon gave her the tin cup and she sat up, leaning against his flank, and sipped cautiously at the steaming brew.

'I've got something to tell you.' She turned her head and gave him a soft kiss on his shoulder.

'But you've got to promise not to be too cross with me.' She moved her body away from him and turned so she could look directly at him.

'There is no easy way to say this, so I'll just come out and say it. Gideon, Matt is your son.'

She saw his eyes narrow a fraction and felt his gaze transfix her. He put down his cup, took hers from nerveless fingers and put it beside his, turned and gripped her above the elbows.

'Tell me!' He shook her. Hope was suddenly scared and felt tears welling up inside her. Gideon's grip was like iron bands imprisoning her arms. Gideon saw the fear flit across her face.

'Don't be scared, darling Hope, no one is every going to hurt you again; but please ... for God's sake tell me ... please tell me!' Hope's left hand crossed to grip his forearm.

'I was already pregnant with him when Jake came back from the war! Thank goodness he was a small baby and I just said he was premature but he's your child Gideon ... you've only got to look at the boy to know it's the truth. Jake stamps his children, Sam and Teddy were carbon copies, the same build and hair ... and even that same energy ... Matt is totally different.' Slowly, Gideon relaxed his grip and ran his one hand through his hair, his mind racing and totally perplexed.

'I just can't believe it ... why ... why on earth didn't you tell me? If he's my son ... ah ... then all this time, and I could have ...' His voice drifted into silence as he looked down at his hands and just shook his head. He was close to tears now and Hope's heart went out to him. She took his wrist and put his hand in hers, gripping it, willing him to listen.

'That's always been the most difficult thing for me, carrying this secret for year after year after year. Oh, I've wished I could tell you a thousand times, especially seeing you together like father and son and knowing all the time that you were. My heart broke over and over again.' Her voice cracked and she buried her face against Gideon's chest, weeping uncontrollably, completely undone. Gideon wrapped his arms around her looking unseeingly at the old wooden walls, not hearing anything except the words ringing in his head – my son, my son. They stayed there until she quietened, and then longer – nearly motionless until the unbidden and joyous thought jolted him.

'Hope, my love, we have a family!' She pulled back and smiled at him through swimming eyes.

'We do – we do.'

They walked back on the same route and once they were on the beach under The Gap, Gideon suddenly let go of her hand, shrugged off the rucksack, and then tore off along the sand like some frenetic madman. Just as suddenly he stopped, raised his clenched hands and head and bellowed his primal triumph to the skies. He punched the sky with his fists and roared again.

18

Blissfully unaware of the fateful changes in his mother's life, Matt coasted gently towards the end of his first year at University. He could hardly admit it – to himself or anyone else – but he was just plain bored for a lot of the time. Sam and Teddy would have snapped him out of it, they'd have known what to do, sure they would. At least he could take the picture of them out of his wallet these days without the coffins bumping anymore, but that had taken months. Durbs, the bustling port city of Durban was the only place of real interest, but the birds and the beaches were fifty miles away down the road: 'Maritzburg was just too far away, buried deep and distant in its hot bowl of earth; and somnolent, like a lazy provincial cousin. It made you lazy just living in the place. There were lectures to attend, of course, but even more obligatory, for first-year students especially, were the drinking sessions at the Imp, the local watering hole; a hotel with a rather imposing stepped entrance faced square onto the bricked Victorian façade of the main police station in Loop Street. Few of the students, and certainly very few of the first-year students, owned cars, so in his first weeks, Matt often found himself in one of the several small groups of young men that made their way on foot downtown to the Imp after dinner in Res. The road from the University gates to the edge of town wound past the garage, over the Umsimdusi River Bridge and past the hospital with its view over the cemetery; a view, it occurred to Matt, which provided the hospital patients with good incentive not to forget their medicines. The walk was long enough to work up a good thirst for the beer and the camaraderie and there were immense, delicious, steaming sausages with lashings of hot mustard to be had from the bar. More fuel for more willing thirsts. Beer was followed later in the evening by spirits – usually vodka – taken neat as a chaser. First came the salt held in the fold between thumb and finger thrown straight down the throat. Then vodka, in a gulp, to wash the salt down, and finally a ferocious bite onto a wedge of lemon to blunt the searing edge of the spirit. Then more beer ... and so on, for a lot of them quite literally ad nauseam, and there was plenty of the nauseam; plenty of the vomit, plenty of the puke and the kotching and hurling cats and tigers – hurling stripy tigers even – and when it was bad, on your knees in the bog talking to the Big White Telephone. The Imp closed at eleven o'clock, and soon after the bell and cry for last orders, the hotel entrance would disgorge the drunken students onto the street in their dribs and drabs. There were the shouts, the coarse laughter, and the lewd varsity songs and barracking the cops if there were any around the station entrance opposite. And if the cops didn't come after them like they were supposed to, it was off at a slow meander down to the Pie Cart in the car park behind City Hall, where for two and sixpence you could get a plate of bacon and eggs, baked beans, four quarters of toast piled on the side and a cup of tea. Unique to the Pie Cart, and most important of all, was their ferocious chopped chillies, onion and tomato mix, a concoction that Matt loved ladling onto his plate. Frequent fights round the Pie Cart spiced up proceedings no end, town and gown enmities being no different here to anywhere else.

Billy Huston latched on to Matt quite early. He'd thought it a hell of a joke when he'd heard Matt speaking to a group of seniors trying to get a 'forfeit' out of him during initiation week, especially his telling them in his fuck you voice to go and try elsewhere. Matt had had it up to here with being shouted at and told what to do. Snor Nel, his Permanent Force corporal in charge of bungalow G20 A at the Air Force Gymnasium was going to be the last in a long line but, Matt had to admit to himself, the man had been a real operator.

'Kyk OP, roof, Kyk OP!' Look UP you animal, Look UP he'd scream at his rubbish as he called them all, the bristling moustache two inches away from your face, and going on about the small-change on the parade-ground having all been picked up already. It sounded much better in Afrikaans, though – ridiculously lyrical even. 'Roof,' bawling at Matt or whoever, 'Kyk OP, al die tikies op hierdie parade-grond is KLAAR opgetel.'

'Kyk OP!' mutter, mutter and Snor marching around, jerk, jerk, jerk as if he'd got his pace-stick stuffed up his jacksie.

Nobody really minded Snor too much and a year of National Service hadn't done Matt any harm either, but Billy Huston was another matter. Billy was dead serious about drinking to get dead drunk. He went at it like he smoked his Texans, tap tap on the match box and another one in and lit and a heavy drag, and the Castle just the same, one after the other drunk straight from the bottle. Matt just couldn't keep up and when he said it one evening and that he wasn't coming down to the Imp either, you'd have thought he'd cut Billy to the quick. What Billy had said about it he never found out, but he had got some funny looks from some of the other students. Billy was Rhodesian so Matt called it the defeat of the Matabele, glad to see Billy disappear off in one of the other groups of drinkers.

There were other species of student, of course, like the sports fanatics he'd already had so much experience of. These were easy to sort. Matt tipped them into the same old school file with its same old label. The Politicos – another species – were new and different and just as longhaired and scruffy as dad said they'd be. Bloody bleeding-heart varsity liberals he'd called them and had warned Matt to stay away. What his dad hadn't mentioned was that they attracted women in their droves. Of a certain type, anyway. Pale wispy attenuated women that hung on politico arms for life, gazing crook-necked up at their heroes with a dependent vacuous admiration that could only mean that there was a lot of screwing going on. Hardly tempting because Matt knew his convictions – if you could even call them that – would sink without trace in the pink froth of varsity politics. Apartheid was the thing here. Group Areas was the thing. Dutchmen and their awful, complicated machination of Separate Development was the thing. All things to hate, and hating Dutchmen seemed the most important. But hardly sport, Matt thought, because the Nat Government had set themselves up like wooden figures at a village fete shy. Like black-eyed peas in a pod every Nat politician looked exactly the same as the next. Like the Politburo on the Kremlin wall watching the May Day Parade. Black Calvanist suits and hats that were a bit too small – tub-thumping on about Die Swart Gevaar and fearing only God. A painting reminded Matt of them, a painting he'd seen in a calendar of an Iowa couple standing in front their bleak clapboard cottage. The farmer in dungarees over a poor-white shirt with a pitchfork held in his right hand upright like a weapon, guardian of a cold morality and the po-faced daughter stood next to him. Both of them ... just there. And the expressions! Unforgiving. The American and the local variety, Die Boere, all farmers united in worship of a God you just knew was one of the Wrathful, Vengeful kind.

His dad didn't like Nats because a whole lot of them had been interned during the war for supporting the Nazis and blowing up Post Offices. But dad had a certain begrudging respect for them.

'They're like an old VW Beetle,' he'd said to Matt once, 'ugly as sin but reliable for all that. Slow, and they take all the knocks. But they get you there in the end, hey, even if it's not where you wanted to go in the first place.'

'You,' he said, pointing his head at Matt, 'you're wet still, and you think all these blacks out there are like Elias and Torrance, or perhaps even Watch?' And that was when he'd given him Something to Value to read, the first time he'd seen dad with a book in his hand ever.

Dad was right about Elias and Torrance who lived in the shade of the benign suburban umbrella that was Hillcrest. Here at University it was called - Paternalism, and no threat, a political dirt word, and no one talked about having x numbers of servants at home which everyone did. But he wasn't totally wet behind the ears either. He'd seen the cops at work – and for that read Dutchman at work – when he was running away from his Aunt Edith's place on his bike that time. The cop van with the usual rectangular box on the back had stopped up ahead just as he turned into Fricker Road so he'd braked and pulled over on the verge watching, thinking perhaps, they'd been sent to fetch him. No. A white cop in blue uniform got out on the driver's side and a black cop in khakis from the other side opposite. Just casual and they weren't looking at him. Two other black cops in khaki uniform shorts were let out the door in the back of the van and the three black cops with their knobkerries and sticks in hand sauntered over the road while the white cop leant against the front wing of the van and lit a cigarette with one of those lighters that snaps when you close it. Two black cops waited either side of stone gates of the property next to Mrs. Cowley's place while the third cop disappeared up the drive. Nothing for a minute and then some banging and shouting and a police whistle, then slap, slap, slap, somebody motoring down the drive running and out of the gates comes this black in just his vest and shorts, his shoes not even tied and does an ace sideways two-wheel drift on the sand drive when he sees the van. He sets off at right angles down the verge going like hell but the one black cop is after him – shit, so quick, and comes up almost level and whacks him on the head with a stick really hard, one-two-three whacks and down he goes like a sack of potatoes bouncing and covering his head screaming, legs going mad like pistons. Same with the next black who runs out and sees what's potting and gives up, but he gets thrashed anyway just the same. That's when Matt realised why the Dutchmen call them houtkops, not 'cause they've got wood in their heads but because their skulls are so thick. Hoo boy, he'd have been dead even with one of those smacks on the head.

The two pushed, shoved and beaten to the back of the van and the white cop still hasn't even finished his cigarette and the blacks collapse all over again when the white cop kicks them in the guts and shouts at them in kaffir. Then they're shovelled into the back of the van and the two cops with the sticks get in after them and the front doors slam shut and the van takes off, but slowly like the old VW Beetle dad talked about, not firing on all cylinders until it gets into second, then lurching, a fart of black smoke, then the engine finally catches properly and they're away.

Elias and Torrance might have been safe inside the boundaries of Hillcrest, but weren't outside, and not even a step outside the gates without a passbook. They were forever getting picked up by the cops, caught chatting with their friends in the street and mum was forever bailing them or paying fines. They'd get hammered like those other two blacks for sure, and that's when Matt started hating the Dutchman and All His Works.

In spite of it all Matt couldn't ever remember hearing a word of complaint or seeing a resentful look. Even Watch, their huge Zulu night-watch boy – still unquestionably an honest-to-God real savage – seemed only to radiate strength and dignity, the shadow on the blinds and the slow sound of his measured tread a wonderful comfort to Matt if he woke deep in the night in thrall of some nightmare. Watch, who had not one word of English, wore huge painted wooden plugs in his ears and was the proud proprietor of a wondrous collection of exotic, ochrous wives who appeared from time to time from some other world, wrapped in beaded blankets, moving slow and scratching deep into clayed beehive hairdos with knitting needles. Stabbing the lice baasie, Maggie used to say to Matt because she was cross with Watch. She scowled and clicked her tongue disapprovingly. Maggie hadn't been feeling well for ages and was sure the big Zulu had somehow put a spell on her.

And that was the sum of it.

Paternalism and no threat with the cops keeping it like that and nobody minding too much. Except that he did. His mum talked about faction fights, whole tribes of blacks fighting and killing one another with assegais, knobkerries, pangas and sticks. But faraway: perhaps the blacks did that in the sticks, down in the Illovo in Natal but not near his Illovo in Johannesburg where they lived.

All that changed late at about eight o'clock one Sunday evening when Matt was looking for his football and caught a whiff of dagga as he walked past Elias and Torrance's room next to the garage. A strange cloying smell so Matt thought he'd go and knock on the door and ask if they'd seen his ball. Perhaps he could find out what that funny smell was at the same time. Elias opened the door, and when he saw who it was, moved his body to block the doorway. But not quick enough.

'Baasie?'

'Elias, have you seen my ba …?'

Matt stopped. There sat on an upturned tomato box at the far end of the room was a black he didn't know at all, glaring at him with such naked malevolence that Matt took a hasty involuntary step backwards. Rubber lips, the lower with a horrendous scarred tuck and eyes of pure evil. Pitch-black at the centre and surrounded by whites that looked as if he had been dipped in liquid sulphur, shot through with blood. Matt fled, his ball forgotten. The cops came later and took Yellow Eyes away because of the dagga and no passbook. Matt thought about those eyes when he read about the Mau Mau in Something of Value and thought about them again when they had to memorise Roy Campbell's The Zulu Girl at school. He still knew it off-by-heart:

When in the sun the hot red acres smoulder,
Down where the sweating gang its labour plies,
A girl flings down her hoe, and from her shoulder
Unslings her child tormented by the flies.

She takes him to a ring of shadow pooled
By thorn-trees: purpled with the blood of ticks,
While her sharp nails, in slow caresses ruled,
Prowl through his hair with sharp electric clicks,

His sleepy mouth plugged by the heavy nipple,
Tugs like a puppy, grunting as he feeds:
Through his frail nerves her own deep languors ripple
Like a broad river sighing through its reeds

Yet in that drowsy stream his flesh imbibes
An old unquenched unsmotherable heat –
The curbed ferocity of beaten tribes,
The sullen dignity of their defeat.

Her body looms above him like a hill
Within whose shade a village lies at rest,
Or the first cloud so terrible and still
That bears the coming harvest in its breast.

The nine Kaffir wars, Blood River and the Battle of Ulundi

were the beating of the tribes and the black baby suckled on the milk of the old unquenched unsmotherable heat had grown up into Yellow Eyes. All that stood between the here and now and the coming harvest, Matt reckoned, was the Dutchman, his armies, and the Mirage fighters he'd sometimes guarded at night during National Service.

Matt kept his opinions to himself because they were all far too subjective, all of it was knee-jerk stuff, naïve probably, what Gideon called risible, what the politicos would label as 'Reactionary' – with a big R, and if it was heard, would doubtless lead to a rumour that he was a campus Special Branch spy. Total bloody confusion.

And while the politicos would all be reading Paton, all he could think of was the two old Kenyan birds in the Something of Value book; Sally and whatsername, the lean one who lit matches on her backside and could shoot the eye out of a gnat. That .22 pistol of hers hung on its .45 frame. The big Wog Mau Mau bursting in on them to hack them to pieces and the two women shooting seven sorts of shit out of them. The Dobermans fighting, the cross-eyed cook nailed in the hall and the other houseboy locking himself in the bathroom. The women shooting him through the door, then them blowing the lock and finishing him with one to the back of the head. Matt couldn't get enough of it because the Mau Mau were like Yellow Eyes, he was sure of it.

Confusion; and, as he wryly acknowledged to himself, just as dad had intended.

So ... if getting a long coat, letting his hair grow and joining NUSAS wasn't going to get him peace of mind, a half decent opinion or, more importantly, a girlfriend; what was?

He tried taking out some of the girls from Women's Res, but most of them were already playing the long game – looking for potential husbands with salaries to substitute future children, their lives as housewives and as large a black staff as was necessary to make that pampered life they aspired to as indolent as possible. They sought their men – prey? victims? in the years above him, the second and final-year students, and these prim little girls – what a disappointment; too cliquey, too giggly, with far too much of the coquette in them altogether. Poor Billy Huston had been nailed. Wasn't that a bloody revelation. Hoo Shit. Caught hook, line and short and curlies by some little Blondie from Benoni who'd got him to give up his Castle and Texans for luurv! You could see Billy was as obsessive about her as he'd been about his drinking and Matt hoped he was getting something for his trouble. He doubted it. Some of his friends gave it straight, said the Women's Res girls were cock-teasers the bunch of them, and that the nurses in town were far more fun anyway ... and laid out more. Two good incentives. He was trying to wangle some introductions when he was invited to a digs party in a house up near the railway station.

Kit Salinger certainly didn't look his type. He was pouring himself some punch with an old soup-ladle when she materialised next to him, sweeping long hair over to one side with a practiced flick of the hand. Sideways on, he thought briefly, she had a nice profile with a lovely cleanly drawn jaw line and high cheekbones under rims of heavy glasses. As she turned towards him he could see that the long brunette hair looked vaguely out of control. It was really long, almost down to a waist which could have been any size covered as it was by a denim smock with bizarre appliquéd green and purple flowers. The jeans were pale and patched and flared with frayed edges but they couldn't completely hide the long shapely legs and bare feet.

'Can I have some of that?' she asked, giving him a quick smile that showed perfectly even white teeth.

'Sure ... sure.' Matt gave her his glass, looking around for another for himself.

'The perfect gent, I see.' She raised her eyebrows and smiled at him again. 'What are you doing at this crummy party anyway?' He looked at her and for some reason answered, 'I think I've been waiting to meet some one like you.'

He hadn't meant to say that at all, it was such a terrible pick-up line, but he had said it with such earnestness that the girl forgave him and took him outside to sit on the garden wall away from the heaving music. They talked and drank quietly for hours until late into the evening. Matt found himself opening up to her completely. He talked about his parents – more about his father whom he didn't understand than his mother, about his school, his home, Gideon – about everything in fact. She was a good listener, and when the flow of words had dried up and he was thinking that he didn't know a thing about her yet, she carefully took off her glasses, did that sweep thing with her hair and kissed him deep with an oddly thrilling engagement of feeling, and for a very long, long time. When they came up for air she put her glasses back on whispering solemnly, 'my, my, I think you need some serious looking after. And phew.' She tapped at her throat and felt for his hand. 'You've taken my breath away as they say. Come and dance.' They went inside hand-in-hand and slow-danced until way past midnight into the careless small hours. The slits in her smock weren't pockets after all, and Mama Cass sang about California dreaming and a church found along the way.

It wasn't a matter so much of who Kit was, it was a matter of what Kit was. She was an artist.

'Don't come and see me at the faculty,' she'd said matter-of-factly, 'you won't like the people there at all, and they probably won't like you either. Come and see me at my digs.' Her digs were nearby – near the railway station, so he'd bought a second-hand bicycle so he could get down to see her. That was virtually every day. He loved her art. He loved even watching her draw: the long sweeping lines on huge pads of white cartridge paper that brought images alive. He implored her to teach him.

On that first afternoon when she gave him her first impromptu lesson, she had watched as his hand skittered across the paper drawing the still life arrangement of bottles and fruit in a bowl on her desk. He had a wonderfully accurate eye, she thought.

'You've drawn before, haven't you?' Matt glanced at her quickly and demurred with a half shake of his head.

'Just for fun really, the animals at home, that sort of thing, but I've never had any tuition or anything.' Kit looked at the sketch, tapping her teeth absentmindedly with a pencil – animals, she thought, let's try that. Matt sat up in the chair, and with his hands on his hips, straightened and stretched his back. Kit put her pencil down and moved behind him and started to massage his neck.

'My landlady, old Mrs. Short, has got an old dog out the back. He more or less lives in the kitchen garden. You should try drawing him. If we ask first, I'm sure she wouldn't mind.'

Mrs. Short was quite agreeable to the idea of this nice-looking young man sketching old Socks, so Matt spent the Sunday morning in the company of the old black and white pointer in the back garden whilst Kit tried some ambitious cooking on the two ring plate in her room.

'Lunch is nearly ready,' she called through the window. 'Do you want to come in and have a beer first?' She could see Matt sitting on the grass with his back against the stone wall.

'Sure,' he answered and swung himself up onto his feet and started to walk towards the kitchen door. Kit was opening a Castle for him as he came into the room.

'Bottle or glass?' Matt took the bottle, 'bottle will be fine; what are you cooking up there? It smalls delicious – even from the garden.' Bottle in hand he peered into the bubbling pot.

'Lamb curry,' she answered. 'I've just got to chop some tomato, onion and green pepper and we'll be ready.' She moved over towards the small chopping block on the pine table. 'How did the drawing go?' Matt tossed the sketchbook onto her bed near the bay window. 'Okay I think, I'm a bit rusty, but it sort of came back after a while.'

Kit finished making the sambals and wiped her hands on a dishcloth.

'That's the advantage of wearing glasses.'

'What is?'

'No tears when you're dicing onions!' There were clouds of steam as the top came off the pot of rice and she quickly strained the contents through a sieve over the little ceramic butler sink.

'And this is the disadvantage!' Matt looked across at the laughing Kit who looked like a myopic owl – the two thick, round lenses completely misted by the steam. They dragged their chairs out and sat to eat.

'Watch out for the whole spices,' she warned as Matt spooned the curry over his rice, 'and there are also a couple of bay leaves in there somewhere.' He attacked the food with gusto and enthused over the marrowbones and the yellow potato wedges that seemed to have drawn in all the sweetest spices. She was pleased when Matt asked for seconds and flattered when he quizzed her about her cooking.

'Where did you learn to cook curry like that?' They were clearing the table together.

'Well,' she said, 'if you've been in Natal any length of time, like I have, you learn to eat it first and to love it later – thereafter it becomes pure addiction!' She laughed and he loved the little bell sound of it. 'I get my spices from the Indian market and the bay leaves are fresh from the kitchen garden. There's a bay tree in a pot just next to the rain water tank.'

She put the kettle on to boil for their coffee. 'I've bought the Sunday Times for you. I want to have a look at what you've done.' Matt sat himself in her big squashy armchair with the paper and she flicked through the sketchbook to find his drawings. There were half a dozen or so, and they were a great deal better than competent. The ones that really caught her eye were a series of four that he had done of the old dog loping across the lawn. There was an extraordinary impression of movement – of a glimpse in time, of suspended animation. She knew it was difficult enough to draw animals well, but capturing them in motion demands a special ability. The most extraordinary thing was the way this had been done with such economy. Just the right line here and there had lent the drawings life. There was another, worked in greater detail, of Socks sleeping in the sun with his head between his front paws, the eyelids folded close and the old, speckled muzzle in complete repose. She wasn't quite sure how he had done it but the drawing suggested more than was actually there. He wasn't just asleep – he was fast, fast asleep. She turned the page to find a depiction of Socks sitting down and scratching his ear. From the angle of the head and the languid body posture she could even tell that it was one of those long, slow scratches that some dogs effect behind the ear when there is nothing really much better to do.

'This is terrible,' she announced. There was a rustle of the paper and Matt's head appeared around the edge. 'You don't like them very much? I'm sorry, I'm sure they're very amateurish.'

Kit shook her head vehemently. 'What's terrible is that you have a wonderful talent – a wonderful God-given talent and here you are wasting your time doing bloody Economics! I can't draw like this – few people can. So why in the hell are you wasting time doing something you couldn't care less about?'

Kit took Matt's sketches to her Professor at the faculty for a second opinion and she backed up Kit's initial conviction that there was a raw talent in his work that would be criminal to ignore. Matt took little convincing and dropped his Economics course with a huge feeling of relief. Unable to see his own talent, and shy about professing it, he kept his drawing to himself. The exception, of course, was Kit, who encouraged him at every turn. He knew he couldn't tell his father. He'd blow a gasket – lecture him about wasting his hard earned money, tell him that art wasn't a career, etcetera, etcetera. 'I can hear him now, Kit,' he told her rather hopelessly.

'Well, bugger him then!' Kit responded, 'work out your own plan. You don't have to please your father all the time. Do something for yourself. You always tell me he's so difficult – why on earth do you feel you have to do everything for his benefit?' Matt slumped on the bed and put his head between his hands. She's absolutely right, he thought to himself in surprise, feeling a little hurt at the truth. And it was the truth, he realised. Why do I feel I have to perform for him like some damn circus seal? Trying to get him to like me I suppose, and it's too late for that, he reflected glumly. Face it, he's not going to like me whatever I achieve, whatever I do.

After a long silence he raised his head to meet Kit's anxious eyes. She felt a wrenching ache in her heart as she saw that her bolt of truth had hit home. There was such sadness in his eyes that she could have wept for him. Instead, she put on her most cheerful voice. 'Ag, give us a smile – just remember, God's a frog, my love.' Matt managed a brave smile at her try. She folded his head into her chest and stood rocking him gently for a long time. Kit knew that Matt wouldn't be seeking his father's approval again, knowing also that in his heart of hearts he'd still crave it. The man didn't know what he was missing. A wave of raw anger for this anonymous puppeteer, this cold father, washed over her.

She had to do something. Kneeling at his feet she tugged at his belt opening the buckle.

19

Alice kept her word. She'd worked hard for her slew of A levels, applied to Girton College and been accepted to read for Veterinary Medicine. It's a peculiarity of the Cambridge system that prospective students don't apply to their faculty of choice for admission – it's the colleges that determine who gets in and who doesn't, sometimes making it necessary to trail cap in hand, from college to college, from interview to interview, just to get that all important foot in the door. Newnham and Girton were the only two women's colleges, but with her outstanding A levels, bright open character and cheerful good looks, Alice could quite likely have had her pick.

Ashleigh had taken her up by car one cool autumn day in September, wanting to settle her in, but Alice was desperate to find good stabling for Fred before seeing to herself. Typical, thought Ashleigh fondly as they pulled into the fourth yard they'd tried that morning. This looked far more professional than the last three offerings they'd found in the latest issue of Horse and Hound. The yard was attached to a small country house off the Madingley road near the Vet school and obviously belonged to a well-to-do hunting family. There was one spare box on offer in stables that looked very sound, solidly built in lapped timber with a good overhang at the front – proof against wet weather. Three substantial looking Thoroughbreds came trotting over from the far side of the adjoining field to see who had arrived whilst Alice chatted away merrily with the daughter of the house, a pleasant looking blonde girl in jodhpurs, sleeveless green anorak with hair scraped back into a neat and tidy little ponytail. Ashleigh walked over to the three inquisitive horses with her eye taking in the pleasing proportions of the square-built Georgian house. The horses sniffed and mouthed at her open hand and she apologised to the three faces for not bringing apples. The two girls joined her, Alice beaming in delight.

'Aunt Ash, this is Sarah – she hunts as well, so things couldn't be more perfect. Sarah, which one's Domino?' The blonde girl pointed at the only chestnut. 'Careful, he nips, especially if you've forgotten to bring him a carrot.'

'Domino is Sarah's hunter, Aunt Ash.' Alice gave by way of explanation. The two girls chatted on about horses whilst they patted the horses' necks and stroked the long noses.

Alice was visibly relieved as they made their way back towards Cambridge in the Morgan.

'They even bed their horses on straw, which is great,' she enthused, 'I can't stand shavings … so when do you think I can tell William to book the float? I suppose anytime now, but he'll have to tell me when Fred's going to arrive so I can be there when he gets off the float … It'll all be so strange for him you know … And how long do you think he'll be on the float, Aunt Ash? – Do you think horses get sea-sick?' Alice's mind was working faster than she could speak, but Ashleigh revelled in the pure, undiluted enthusiasm, just plain delighting in the fact that Alice would be walking the same grounds that her brother Giles, Alice's father, had walked all those years ago. In that short life she knew he had been happiest here.

As the Morgan growled over Magdalene Bridge, Alice spied a group of four youngsters traipsing along the pavement in front of them. All had rucksacks with red and white flags stitched on. She pointed to draw Ashleigh's attention. 'Patriotic lot, aren't they? That's the Danish flag, isn't it?' Ashleigh wasn't sure but she knew her history. 'Perhaps they've come to see the place they occupied for two hundred years,' she commented, nattering on about the Danish occupation while they made their way through the streets to Girton.

Alice's college had started life in a private house in Hitchin in 1869, but had transferred to its more permanent but out of the way site just three years later. Ashleigh's first thought as she gazed at the part-castellated, part-spired Victorian pile was of how cold it would be. And that was in spite of all the chimneys and chimney pots that rose high above the spiked frieze and tiled roofs. She gave an involuntary shiver as she remembered the November when she had come up to see Giles, and had just about died of cold. The freezing winter winds here blew relentlessly out of the flat of the Fens – probably straight from Siberia as far as she was concerned.

She'll need a bicycle too, thought Ashleigh. It really was quite far out, and she'd want to get over to see Fred from time to time, but not every day thank goodness. Before they'd left the stables she'd arranged with Sarah that the family groom would also see to Fred's riding-out every morning during the hunting season. That way, she reasoned, Alice could get on with her studies without the extra chore of riding every day. There wouldn't be time anyway, what with lectures and perhaps sport. She helped Alice unpack in her set: two bedrooms and a sitting room that she would be sharing with another girl on the ground floor along a passage near the Stanley Library. The other girl came in as they were finishing up and introduced herself smartly in a cultivated, plumy voice.

'Prunella Rathbone – how do you do,' she shook hands – like a plumber.

'Everyone calls me Pru.'

Ashleigh sized her up rapidly. A large, big-boned girl with clean, thick blonde hair in a pageboy cut: brimming with self-confidence and surprisingly quick in her movements for such a large frame. She'll do just fine, thought Ashleigh, whose whole life had been run on the basis of quick decision after a rapid first impression.

'Pru, I'm taking Alice to my hotel, the Blue Boar, for dinner before I go off tomorrow and leave her to the fates. Would you like to come along and join us?'

'You bet, thanks awfully.' Pru bounced up and down with her large, friendly breasts jiggling about alarmingly under the cord jersey. Ashleigh hid her smile. She was put in mind of two energetic puppies trying to escape from underneath a blanket. Getting three in the Morgan was a bit difficult, but Pru was so ecstatic about travelling in a sports car that nobody minded. Ashleigh insisted they all have a three-course dinner. She had few expectations of greatness from the college kitchens in the months ahead: bread-and-butter pudding came to mind. Indulging her penchant for wine, Ashleigh ordered a Chablis – always a favourite – to start, and a Cos d'Estournel for the main course. She knew the St. Estephe claret would be pretty robust with plenty of tannin, but she'd ordered it for sentimental reasons. Two years ago she'd been in the Médoc and seen the series of eccentric Chinese-style chais that Monsieur Estournel had built in the middle part of the last century, and she related to the girls the story of how when a passer-by had asked what palace this was, one of the workers had replied, 'C'est le parc á'bœuf de Monsieur Estournel.'

'They call us rosbiffs don't they?' Alice giggled, 'you are spoiling us, Aunt Ash.'

'And I shall get quite tiddly if I have any more,' announced Pru who kept saying that she was having a thoroughly good time, a thoroughly, thoroughly good time.

After dinner they all went window-shopping past bookshops and haberdashers, their windows brimming with scarves, coats, crests and colours of all the different colleges.

'It's hard to believe I'm actually here at last,' said Alice, 'I have to keep pinching myself.'

To Alice's delight she had discovered during dinner that Pru was taking Medicine so they would, by and large, be doing the same course through the first three years. The exception would be Anatomy – Alice would be dissecting pickled greyhounds whilst Prunella would be eating her lunch sandwiches over a cold human cadaver.

Girton College had certainly started off doing the right thing by putting these two together, thought Ashleigh as she worked the Morgan through the gears on the road back to Stock. They seemed to get on like a house on fire. She didn't think she needed to worry overmuch about Alice getting homesick now – she could rest easy – especially with the huge heater she had ordered for her that same morning before she left.

'Well, there you are, Giles,' she spoke out loud addressing the pale shade that always hovered in the back of her mind, 'I've done my best to settle her in for you, and you would be so proud of her.' The tears prickled at the back of her eyes. A bugger bugger tragedy that they had been denied one another. She would have given anything just to see them together, even for a day – especially today. She wiped her eyes – angry at fate. As the miles slipped by under the Morgan's wheels, her mind turned to the cottage and the autumn tasks that waited for her. Especially in the garden: bulbs to be lifted, leaves to be raked and composted, and the wood to be bought-in and stacked next to the kitchen door for winter. She hated the cold, but there was the prospect of her yearly winter break to cheer her up. Somewhere warm, of course. If Alice wasn't doing anything over Christmas, they could go to Africa together – find some exotic place perhaps. The thought cheered her up considerably. After she had a couple of weeks to settle in, Ashleigh resolved to give Alice a ring and see.

20

Hope was trying to get all her ducks in a row. She had waited apprehensively for Matt to answer the phone. He had been out when she had phoned that morning, but one of the Res students had promised to leave a message that she would be ringing back again at seven o'clock, and that it was urgent.

'Hello, Mum, is that you? What's up?'

Hope gripped the receiver a little harder and took a deep breath ...

At the end of a very one-sided conversation, Matt slowly replaced the receiver in its cradle and stood for a full minute without taking his hand away. His mind was a whirl. He shook his head very slowly, not believing what he had heard. Mum going to leave dad? It was difficult to remember everything she'd said now. Something about being apart for long spells and then growing apart, but the thing that really perplexed and worried him was that she had said that she was so unhappy with him. For how long? Why? – Perhaps why wasn't too difficult to work out, but he'd never really thought about her happiness or unhappiness before: she had just always been ... there. For the first time in his life he had been made to think about her as a person rather than just mum, and the thought of her being unhappy worried him deeply, profoundly.

'Christ's sake, for Christ's sake,' he muttered to himself and half in a daze, retrieved his bicycle downstairs, and without remembering to tuck his trouser bottoms into his socks started the journey out of the University gates and down the hill towards town. As he parked the bike inside the gate to her digs he prayed silently that Kit would be in and was hugely relieved when he saw the light on in her room. Kit took one look at his ashen face and blank look and quickly crossed the room from her easel where she had been tidying up a painting.

'What on earth's wrong? You look terrible!'

Matt went past her, across the room and sat down heavily on the bed as if suddenly his legs were having difficulty supporting him. He ran a hand distractedly through his blonde hair and started to tell her what had happened – as best as he could remember anyway. He finished and then paused.

'My Dad's not been told yet. Oh my God, he's going to hit the roof!' At the thought of it, another wave of chill concern for his mother washed over him.

Matt was right. Jake did hit the roof, but only after the realisation had eventually filtered in to him that his wife was actually serious. Knowing he was due to fly down in two days time, Hope had phoned him an hour and a half after she had spoken to Matt. She thought he was likely to be home from the club by then, and sure enough, he had picked up the phone on the second ring. She had worked out a strategy with Gideon over countless cups of coffee in the cottage on the day after their trip to the Fountains shack, but had been adamant about two things in particular. The first was that Jake shouldn't know anything about their relationship until much later: she was terrified that there'd be violence if he knew, and the second was that Matt shouldn't be told of his true parentage until much later, until things had settled down. It would be too much all at once. Gideon had argued that unless Matt was told the whole story, he would hold the separation and then the divorce against him, but Hope had held firm. Gideon had never seen her so determined. It was only the occasional tremble in her voice and the whiteness of her knuckles on the coffee cup handle that told him that this was taking a huge measure of control and a great deal of courage. She had booked herself on a flight home the next morning, having made the booking in the mid-afternoon before the two phone calls. Gideon was horrified. She meant to confront Jake at home, away from any help, but her mind was evidently set. They ate a subdued, early dinner, both acutely aware of tomorrow and went to bed early to lie with their arms locked around one another, two bodies seamless as one, trying to both give and draw a comfort they knew wasn't there. Not yet anyway.

Jake had been waiting in the arrivals hall at Jan Smuts airport, his heavy black eyebrows hooding dark angry eyes and his mouth drawn into a thin forbidding line. He hurled her baggage into the boot of the car, slammed the door as he got in and started on her straight away.

'And what the hell is this all about?' He changed from first to second gear with a wrench on the gear stick. Hope opened her mouth to begin to reply when he continued, 'and what the hell do you think that is going to do to Matt when he hears?' He was attacking her at her weakest point, but it was the opening that Hope had prayed for.

'I've told him already, Jake, he knows.'

Her husband did a lightning double take at her words, forcing himself to concentrate on the road as they rounded a bend. He was at a loss for words for a few seconds and then spoke to her in a voice laced with vitriol.

'You heartless bitch, how could you do that to our son? You always mollycoddle him and tell me you love him so much, and now you give him this!' Hope had mentally prepared herself for all the verbal battering – and worse if it came. She just prayed she could see it through.

'Why, for Christ's sake? I've given you everything you could possibly wish for; homes, children, success, more money that you can spend, and now you want to go!'

Not everything I could wish for, she said to herself, but gave no answer.

He snatched his head round and glared at her silence.

'What else can there be ... another man? ... what?' From his disparaging tone, Jake didn't take the possibility seriously and Hope breathed an inner sigh of relief. The most important hurdle was over. Keeping her tone as level as she could, Hope started on her prepared explanations, putting as much of the blame on herself as was safe, and trying carefully not to censure him. She blamed all the time apart, the void left by the death of their sons, anything ... except him. He softened a little as the litany progressed and Hope could see the thought forming in his head – she'll get over it, it's nothing, and this is when she leant over and held his arm so he would look at her. She put all the conviction into the next words that she could muster.

'Jake, I'm so sorry, but I don't love you any more, and I'm leaving ... for good.'

The words hung like heavy melodrama in the charged atmosphere.

'Doris knows I'm coming,' she continued, 'please drop me there, I don't want to come home.' His mouth twisted in distaste. 'For God's sake, do they have to know?' They travelled a little further in silence and at length he said in rather irked fashion, 'what are you going to do about money then?' Always the practical man, thought Hope. 'I've still got some money my parents left me in savings,' she replied, 'I'll be alright for the time being.' They had reached the entrance to the Cleaver's drive at the end of which Hope expected to find Doris, undoubtedly waiting in a fever of curiosity ever since her phone call last night.

'Just drop me at the top of the drive, Jake. I can at least spare you some embarrassment.' He had given her a dismissive grunt but dropped her there nevertheless, and helped her with the bags out of the boot.

'You'd better ring me when you come to your senses, Hope.'

I've just done that, thought Hope as she took the first few wobbly steps down the sand drive. Doris was waiting anxiously on the front lawn as Hope appeared around the corner. As soon as she caught sight of her, Doris fluttered her hands and ran towards her on tottering high heels, the carefully permed silver-blonde locks bobbing up and down. Doris was one of the high social, high fashion queens of Johannesburg, but Hope had known her for years also as her most fiercely protective friend.

'You poor, poor thing.' Doris commiserated, her anxious eyes scanning Hope's washed out face.

'Here, let me take those.' Doris turned towards the low-slung, ranch-style house behind her and let out an imperative screech, 'Eunice!!' Doris' black maid appeared at the front door and hurried over to the two women standing on the lawn.

'Eunice, the madam is staying here for a while, she's been through a terrible shock, a terrible shock.' There was more fluttering of manicured hands, 'so we must look after her well, Eunice ... especially well, you see?' Hope was suddenly enormously grateful for the helping hands and when all strength left her abruptly again she had to grab at Doris' arm for support.

The hot bath, or hot tub as Doris would have it, had a marvellously recuperative effect. Doris had thrown in an excess of bath salts and as Hope lay back luxuriating in the heat and the smell of sandalwood, the tension in her back, arms and legs slowly dissipated and dissolved, and with it went the tired aches and pains, even some of the despair. Her things had already been unpacked in the spare room and there was tea brewing in a sweet little pot on the bedside table. Lapsang Souchong, she thought, from the perfumed aroma in the faint curls of vapour coming from the spout. Doris popped her head around the door.

'Are you all right then, my dear? Come down to the drawing room when you're ready, I'll be in there.'

Hope had her tea and then dressed, putting on a pair of navy blue slacks and a pastel lambs-wool cardigan over a tight broderie anglaise blouse. She brushed her blonde hair, still damp from the bathroom, put on an Alice-band and a dash of make-up – something – anything to try and bring a little colour into her cheeks. She knew she wasn't looking her best, which was confirmed by Doris gentling her into a comfy chair like an invalid aunt. 'What about a nice gin and tonic?' Without waiting for a reply, Doris unstoppered one of the decanters and poured stiff tots into two crystal glasses. Hope glanced around the room, familiar to her over the years, but still exquisite. Doris' taste – and pocket – ran to deep-pile Aubusson carpets and highly polished French furniture with gilt embellishments, the whole house exuding a delightfully restrained extravagance. The gin arrived with the tonic fizzing at the brim. Doris sank into the settee opposite Hope, took a hefty swig of her glass and then looked across, a benign but anticipatory gleam in her eyes.

'What's my little Tittlemouse been up to?'

Doris fixed a cigarette into an impossibly long holder and lit it, waiting for her friend to reply. Hope scratched at the cut glass crystal with her finger absentmindedly as she trotted out more or less the same story she had told Jake: the time he spent away, the estrangement, the disenchantment. As she went on, Hope could see the quizzical, disbelieving look beginning to creep over Doris' face, the eyebrows arching ever higher. The explanation slowed, faltered and then stopped. Doris looked directly at her and then, giving a little quirky smile that came and went in a flash, jumped up and went over to pour herself another drink.

'Darling, darling, darling ...' Doris spoke over her shoulder in exasperated diminuendo as she scrabbled in the ice bucket. 'No one, I repeat no one, gives up two perfectly good homes ... and all that lovely new money,' the cubes of ice chinked into Doris' glass, 'because they are ... disenchanted!!!' The last word came out in an explosion of breath. Doris walked back to the settee wagging her finger at Hope as if she'd been a naughty child. She sat down and crossed her legs expertly. 'Everyone knows Jake has been making an absolute fortune. The directorships, the consultancies, the whatever.' Doris twirled her cigarette around making circles of smoke. 'Clarence says the financial papers are absolutely awash with glowing descriptions of his commercial genius. "Local boy makes good" and all that twaddle.' She had a sip of her drink and grimaced, looking down into the glass. 'God, I've made it a bit strong!' She looked up at Hope with a gentle smile and kindness in her voice. 'Look ... this is me, Doris, remember? I've been your best friend for more years than I care to remember, Hope, and I think you're in some awful sort of a muddle. I know you're far, far too nice and gentle a person to leave Jake if it wasn't for a really good reason, so come on and tell me. You know I can keep a secret, you'll at least grant me that! Whatever you say in this room, stays in this room, I promise.'

Hope gave up the charade and poured out the whole story. It seemed that once she had started, she just couldn't stop. And with it came the tears and the deep racking sobs. She confessed all the anguish she had concealed over the years, the lies to others and the lies to herself, the beating he had given her, and always, the overriding guilt that had hung over her life exacting its daily penance of misery and regret. Doris listened in silence for perhaps an hour, just filling Hope's glass from time to time.

Afternoon had run into early evening, but instead of asking Eunice to come in and light the fire, Doris drew the thick curtains herself and then knelt and put a match to the fir cones lying under the logs. The flare and crackle of the cones drew their attention for a minute until Doris turned to Hope, seeing lights of the fire dancing in teary eyes, her friend's face quite broken.

'My poor darling, you're quite the little dark horse, aren't you?' Doris pulled Hope into her arms and hugged her, patting her shoulder gently. Hope rested her head for a while with her eyes closed. She was absolutely empty, there was nothing left in her. Doris disengaged herself and went over to open the drawing room door.

'Eunice,' she called through to the kitchen, 'could you serve dinner in fifteen minutes? Thank you, dear.' She moved briskly over to the drinks table. 'A drop of sherry before dinner I think, I'm quite gin and tonicked out!' She poured the little glasses and gave one to Hope, who would have drunk arsenic without flinching at that moment. Doris did a little theatrical pirouette, spilling some of the sherry from the glass, her eyes glittering little buttons of glee.

'You know I've wondered about you, Hope, there's always been something of the doomed Shakespearian heroine in you, a sadness in your eyes sometimes. I'd see it for a second and then it would be gone and I'd think I'd been mistaken, but I hadn't been had I? Clarence calls you Ophelia – do you know that? But he's got private nicknames for everyone so don't feel offended.' Doris gave a little titter. 'He calls Jake the Prince of Darkness! Oh, and don't worry, Clarence is staying at his club tonight. I told him you'd be here and there was some sort of crisis, but he won't whisper a dickey bird.'

They sat for dinner with Elijah, Doris' black manservant gliding to and fro behind them like a wraith, serving the piping hot tomato soup with expert white-gloved hands. The Cleavers always did things in style, and Elijah's uniform was no exception: starched white trousers and tunic top, a red sash and fez with a black, fluffy tassel.

'Jake won't give up easily you know, especially as he doesn't know the whole story. He'll think you've had a mid-life crisis or something. But you won't go back, will you?' Doris looked across at Hope and then shook her hand in violent negation. 'No, you couldn't could you, your bridges are well and truly burnt.' She popped a piece of buttered Melba toast into her mouth. 'And even if they weren't, heaven's sakes, it's taken you a lifetime to get this far, you simply can't turn back now.'

21

Matt hadn't a clue what was happening. He'd tried to ring back three or four times on the day following his mum's call, but there was just no answer. He hadn't dared ring his father because she still had to break the news to him. Presumably she'd done so by now, but he couldn't be sure: he wasn't even sure if she was back in Johannesburg. His mind went round and round in circles: a dog chasing its own tail and getting nowhere. They would both have to know what he was doing, or to be precise what he was no longer doing in 'Maritzburg and he hadn't told either of them that he'd stopped going to lectures or what he was proposing to do next. He thought of ringing Gideon but dismissed it. This was too private. All he could do was walk, or cycle, or play furious games of squash – anything to occupy his anxiety-ridden brain.

His father rang on the fourth evening and it was a shock to hear his gruff voice on the phone. Jake went straight to the point.

'Matt, your mother has walked out on me ... I gather you know already. Dr. Aitken says it's probably some sort of mid-life crisis – happens quite often evidently. She's not well,' Jake's teeth sucking tone suggested massive disapproval. 'But I don't want you to worry about it too much, she's bound to come to her senses sooner or later. It's just so damn unfair on everyone, and I don't want it to interfere with your studies. That's why I'm ringing you.'

Matt cut in, 'Do you know where she is, Dad? Is she at home? Can I speak to her?' He heard the exasperation in his father's answer. 'No, she's not at home! I thought she was staying with the Cleavers – you know, Doris and Clarence, but she's not there anymore. Gone to stay with yet some other friends I gather. But I'll let you know. You okay for money?' Matt's mind came back to the mundane. 'Yes, Dad, fine.'

'Good, I'll keep in touch, just concentrate on those studies.' There was a click and then nothing.

He was no further forward, had no clue where she was. He had an idea. The girl at directory enquiries answered in a bored, flat Afrikaans accent, but was efficient enough in tracing the Cleaver's Sandown address and telephone number. He recognised Doris' precise voice immediately.

'Matt, is that you?' Your mother has tried to ring you several times, dearest, but she's not here at present. Have you got pen and paper?' Matt cradled the receiver between his shoulder and cheek to steady his scrap of paper and write down the number. He repeated the number back to Doris. 'You'll ring her straightaway, dear? I know she's in at present. You will? Good, well bye-bye then.'

He dialled the number and waited impatiently while it rang and rang. A female voice he didn't recognise answered. 'Is Mrs. Stevens there?' Matt asked. The reply was cool.

'May I ask who is calling, please?'

'It's her son, Matt, I've been given this number.' He searched in his pocket for the slip of paper as he spoke.

'Just hold on a minute,' came the reply and then his mother was there.

'Matt, I couldn't seem to get hold of you, darling! Did you get the message I'd called? Whoever it was seemed a bit dim – not the brightest crayon in the box. Have you spoken to your father yet?'

Matt nodded unconsciously. 'Mum, he called a few minutes ago, he says you're sick, Dr. Aitken ...' Hope interrupted quickly. 'Matt, he's going to say those sort of things, but believe me, there's absolutely nothing wrong, with my health or my mental state. It's going to be tough on you, I know, but believe me, it's for the best.' Matt could feel the thin backbone of steel in his mother's words, and because it sounded so astonishingly resolute, and so unlike her, he suddenly believed that this was all really going to happen. He was silent.

'Matt, are you there?'

'Yes, Mum, I'm here.' Matt had been doing some quick mental juggling, trying to decide whether he should tell her. He decided to – but he'd run out of coins for the pay phone. 'Mum, can you ring me back, I've run out of change.'

When she rang back, he told her about everything, everything that he'd been afraid of telling for the last two months. The thrill he found in doing something he honestly loved – his drawing – and the progression from pencil to pen, and the new worlds of charcoal and pastels that he'd never tried before. Hope had known about Kit, the new girlfriend, but not that she was an artist. She listened in amazement at the enthusiasm that poured over the wire, and her heart began to lift.

'You mean you want to do this as a career?'

'Mum, Kit has shown some of my stuff to her Professor at the faculty, and she - this Prof Hollis - says I've got real ability.' Matt knew this was no time to be modest.

'You won't believe it, Mum, but I've even landed a commission doing sketches for a book on Jack Russells – you know the little dogs? And the author is delighted with the stuff I've done – delighted. Mum, I … really … want … to do this.' Matt's conviction was overwhelming. Hope had never heard him speak of anything in his life with this degree of passion, not even his fishing, and her answer to him wholly instinctive.

'Darling, if you feel like that about it you must do it … and I'll give you all the help I can. I'm not sure if that's going to be worth very much at the moment, but I'll support you as best I'm able, I promise. What are your plans, are you going to do an Arts degree or what? Some sort of training surely.'

Matt took a big breath. 'Mum, I want to travel and see a bit of the world. I've got to see the art I'm reading about in the flesh, in the original, on the canvas. Perhaps I can study in someone's studio – learn from them, but I don't want to go to some college. Would you mind very much? I wasn't sure you'd think it such a good idea.'

Hope did have one good idea, and as the thought crossed her mind she pounced on it.

'Why don't you give Gideon a ring and see if you can go down and spend a couple of weeks at his cottage in Plett? He's dying to see you again and you can mull things over with him – perhaps he'll have some useful advice. He's even got relatives in England: that might be a great help.' Matt needed no persuading.

'Ace, Mum, that's a great idea, I'm sure I've got his number somewhere; but what about you Mum, are you sure you're going to be all right?' Hope was moved by his obvious concern but quick to give him reassurance. 'Matt, I'll be fine, just ring me every couple of days at this number, give Gideon my love, and please don't give this number to your father under any circumstances. I've got lawyers to see and your father needs time to cool down. I really don't want to speak to him just now.'

Kit watched Matt pack with sad eyes. They had been living together in her digs ever since he had decamped from Res, and she was going to miss him terribly. She wished it was mutual, but he couldn't disguise his anticipation for what lay ahead. He loved her yes, but only after a fashion, and nothing like her feelings for him, which had grown and grown, and now threatened to consume her entirely. She had conspired with him, and watched him take his life by the scruff of the neck and shake it until it rattled. It took guts and what he proposed would take more of the same: but she was sure of one thing, completely sure. He had the talent. If he'd given even the slightest hint that he wanted her, she would have dropped everything and gone with him, but he hadn't. She wasn't sure it would have been the right thing anyway. She suspected there were material rites-of-passage ahead for him, but that knowledge didn't dilute the pain. It made it worse. As is the way with some women, she had given her body to him more completely than ever as the schism of parting came nearer, day by day, minute by minute. And now it was here, and he'd be gone, probably forever.

He finished zipping up the suitcase and turned.

'The taxi's here.' She buried her head in the crook of his neck and the searing pain rose high in her chest choking her throat.

22

Hope felt singularly calm. After a short stay with Clarence's sister in Parktown, Doris had secreted her away in a small one-roomed flat of theirs in Rosebank which Clarence used for visiting overseas clients, and it was here that Hope started to live her simple, somewhat lonely, but more fulfilling new life. The confession, the disclosure of her whole life to Doris had been wonderfully cathartic. Guilt had been peeled away layer after layer, eventually baring a small kernel of soul at the core. In the new and unfamiliar light her spirit had first stirred, and then slowly and tentatively started to grow. Hope husbanded her scant resources carefully, shopping frugally but eating healthily nevertheless. She read a good deal and kept in daily contact with Gideon by phone, making sure she was in when he rang at seven every evening.

'What am I going to tell him?' Gideon was on the phone sounding nervous as a kitten. 'He's arriving by bus in Port Elizabeth. I'll be picking him up there tomorrow morning and what if all these awkward questions come up – they're bound to.' Hope listened with amused and tolerant affection as Gideon rattled on. The solitary life he'd led certainly hadn't prepared him for this avalanche of complications and entanglements; a host of new-sprung feelings stirring deep within and their offspring bubbling to the surface in the most disconcerting fashion.

'Don't you worry,' she reassured him, 'it's just a fortnight before he flies to the U.K., so be yourself, your lovely, quiet charming self that I love so much and everything will be fine … Gideon, it's not going to be an inquisition, he's just going to need lots of advice and I'm quite sure you're the best one to give it.'

Gideon sighed over the phone. 'Oh, I do so wish you were

here!' He paused, 'but I dare say you're right … I'm so thrilled he's coming, just so damn nervous that's all.'

And no less so when he espied the fair-haired young man alighting from the bus on the following day. My God, he's grown, thought Gideon. Matt saw the familiar old bakkie – gave an enthusiastic wave and went to look for his luggage. A suitcase, a small portfolio and a rucksack which Matt swung over one shoulder as he walked towards Gideon.

'Matt, great to see you!' Gideon gave the proffered hand a firm shake and then helped with loading his luggage onto the back of the bakkie.

'I'd better put the canvas on, if I can find it, or else that folio of yours will end up flying off somewhere down the road. The canvas was located behind the passenger seat and they were soon on their way with the nose of the bakkie pointed west.

'Have you had any breakfast?' asked Gideon, 'you look a bit worn out.'

Matt ruffled his hair brusquely and squinted up at the sun.

'I'm knackered. No, I've had nothing to eat yet and could do with a bite I suppose, but I'm not really all that hungry.' Gideon glanced over at him. 'Do you want to wait until we get home?' Matt nodded and then cast around with his eyes looking for a way of explaining himself.

'I've had so much on my mind, and then leaving Kit – she was my girlfriend in 'Maritzburg – well, that just finished me off completely.' He shifted in the old seat to try and get more comfortable. 'Jeez, Gideon, these seats are worse than those on the bus!' Gideon smiled mirthlessly. 'All that University life has made you soft, I can see it!' They laughed. Gideon had to stop himself from staring at him … his son, it felt unsafe even whispering the thought – in case he heard.

'No, Matt, I haven't had the seats fixed. We don't do many

long trips, me and the old bakkie – I just come up to see my horses run now and again. The trip to P.E. is the equivalent of the Great Trek for us local yokels. But tell me about University, what have you been up to?' Matt groaned and then smiled ruefully.

'I don't really know where to begin. There I am trying to pluck up the courage to tell my Mum and Dad that I want to do something so totally different, worrying about that, and then Mum rings me out of the blue a few weeks ago with this bombshell. You know about it, I suppose?' Gideon suddenly felt like a betrayer, a Judas, as if he alone was accountable. He cleared his throat loudly and looked at the road ahead purposefully.

'Yes, your mother told me she's … um … left – has in fact left your father.' It came out so awkwardly. The look of curiosity on Matt's face convinced him he'd made a hash of it, that the young man could see right through him, but Matt continued. 'The funny thing is I don't think I've ever heard her sound happier. Not "ha-ha" happier, just something in her voice.' He looked out of the side window and then shook his head, shedding the thought. 'Anyway, I've spoken to her often and I'm not quite as worried as I was at first.'

'And your Dad?' Gideon prompted. Matt opened his eyes a little wider and cocked his head. 'My Dad? My Dad is livid! You should have heard him on the phone, Mum's sick in the head, do I need money and can I just get on with my studies while he sorts out things at home!' His short laugh was humourless. 'And if you think my Dad's heartbroken, you're mistaken – inconvenienced more like it!'

Gideon could hear the frustration and anger mounting in his voice. There was a moment's silence in the bakkie, just the squeak from the clutch pedal as Gideon shifted gear up the incline. When Matt spoke again his voice was level and controlled. 'I don't think I can give my father what he wants of me, Gideon: in fact I've just proved to him what he's always suspected, that I would turn out to be a massive disappointment. He won't understand what I'm doing, won't even want to understand, so I'm just going to see him in Jo'burg to tell him I've dropped out, and then I'm off overseas. If he ever wants to find me after that, he'll just have to come looking.'

'And where should he look?' Gideon asked. Matt's humour returned. 'Ag, I've got stuff to show you at the cottage, then I'll tell you my plans. I'm not going to tell you everything now, that would spoil it. Tell me about the fishing so long.'

Gideon had nothing to tell him about his own fishing. He'd done very little. Standing alone on the rocks had given him too much time to think and he'd exchanged his rod for his walking boots, trudging along the Tsitsikamma coast line looking for otters, his favourite. He had spotted one family, four of them, bouncing along a thin strip of beach between rocks and the sea like animated commas. The daily hiking had kept his mind occupied until he could make his phone call at seven each evening. As the little bakkie started the run down to the bay from the Crags, Matt wound down the window to catch his first glimpse of the sea, as he had as a child, and caught instead that most evocative aroma of all, the compounded essence of brine and coastal bush. He drew a deep breath. 'Gee, I've missed this place, Gideon – it's like home to me.' Gideon smiled a contented smile and thought that now, in a sense it was – or would be one day when the drama of their lives had finally unwound.

Gideon cooked an old fashioned breakfast for lunch: fried eggs with bacon, sausage, tomato and onion. The smell of the bacon signalled the restitution of Matt's appetite. He was ravenous and hurried into the kitchen to find Gideon trying to keep a rather old and bent saucepan in the right position while he basted two eggs in bacon fat.

'That's the trick to getting them looking perfect, Matt, basting them so all the flecks of sizzled bacon lie on the eggs.' He pointed with the spatula. 'See how great they look ...' Matt grinned, 'like Humpty Dumpties with freckles, you mean?'

Doing a little pa-pa pum pum pum to some imaginary operetta, Gideon scooped the eggs out onto slices of toast, heaped on the bacon, sausage and the rest from the oven warming-drawer and triumphantly led Matt out onto the stoep. They fell to, and when Matt eventually flopped back in the wicker chair he knew he had eaten too much, and too fast.

'I'll get the coffee,' said Gideon as he gathered up the plates and set off for the kitchen.

'No, wait, I'll do that,' called Matt, but Gideon turned with a smile.

'Just stay where you are, young man – you just treat this as your home for the next fortnight. Relax ... ontspan. I'll ask if I want help, don't worry. Put your feet up ... I'll be back in a tick.'

They had a leisurely cup of brewed coffee, absolute heaven after all that University instant coffee Matt assured him, and then it was time to look at the drawings. Matt brought his portfolio out onto the stoep and undid the ribbon ties.

'Kit started this folio for me about six weeks ago, and as you can see it's mainly animalier work. ... That's old Socks, the dog at Kit's digs, and the tortoiseshell cat from next door, and then a few I did of some cattle in a barn. We did a field trip one afternoon.' Like all those who had looked through the portfolio before him, Gideon could instantly recognise the high quality of the work. Matt's hand and eye seemed to be able to capture the quintessence of movement, and with remarkable thrift. Even the stationary cows in the gloom of the old wooden barn seemed to have just swung around to face him that instant, the stalky hay still protruding from the corners of their mouths. Any worries about what Matt was embarking on disappeared from Gideon's mind and he felt the secret swell of a father's pride.

'Tell me,' he asked, 'do you work from photographs? How on earth do you catch their movement so perfectly?' Matt's lips pursed as he shook his head. 'The funny thing is, photos don't do it for me, I find it very difficult to draw from pics.' He leant forward earnestly and the wicker chair squeaked in complaint. 'I have to draw from life, I have to see the movement myself before I can draw it. I've found that it's the exact type of movement – its character – that gives every animal a big part of its personality – well, not personality … individuality perhaps. Take old Socks, he's got a peculiar type of rolling gait and he's a bit pigeon-toed. That's what makes him Socks and not any other old pointer. My job is to work those things into the drawing if I can.'

The phone rang in the living room and rather unwillingly Gideon pushed himself off the chair and went to answer it. Matt was idly wondering what he could find to draw over the next few days when he heard the murmurs of conversation coming through the window cease and the receiver go down.

Gideon was pleased. 'You'll never guess, that was Mack Flood. He's got his boat Katonkel down here and we're going looking for tunny tomorrow!' Gideon rubbed his hands together briskly with evident relish. 'I've heard there were some in the bay – where else but in Tony's barber shop!'

'Tony's reduced to flogging tunny from his barber shop is he, Gideon?'

Gideon barked a laugh then stretched contentedly and yawned, 'We'd better get an early night if we've got to be up at sparrowfart – and if I know Mack, it'll be a long, long day.'

They were on the beach at eight, standing on bare feet on either side of Katonkel as the ski-boat wallowed in the shallow surf off Middle Beach. Both had their hands on the gunwales just in front of the burbling twin thirty-five horsepower Evinrude outboard motors, keeping the prow pointed directly out to sea, waiting for the right moment. The moment came and as Mack yelled 'Go!!' he thrust the stick forward and the two of them vaulted forward into the charging boat. The blue glass-fibre boat skipped through three or four waves before slamming into the next, burying the nose and throwing the two of them violently forward as they hung on for dear life. The screaming engines cavitated for a split second and then they were through, drenched by the cascading salt waters.

They hunted all morning, scanning the horizon for diving birds, the Malgas that might tell them where the schools of fish were near the surface, chased there by the predatory tunny. Mack was also on his radio constantly, calling up other boats that were out, seeing if they had had any luck or seen anything. At a height of five foot eight inches and weighing (mainly around his midriff) perhaps some one hundred and ninety pounds, their skipper was almost easier to jump over than walk around. Gideon had told him that Mack appeared never to have heard of vitamins, or fruit, or any other of the benefits of healthy living. His diet, for all the time Gideon had known him, had seemed to consist of a never-ending procession of steak, hamburgers and chips, all washed down with beer or copious quantities of Mainstay cane and coke. Mack's incongruously thin legs supported a beachball of a body clad in a short, faded blue shirt hung loose over voluminous khaki shorts. The shorts were secured by means of a thin black belt wound round his girth like the circumference of a considerable circle. His active little head sported thin, reddish-blonde hair and intelligent little blue eyes that darted constantly about. There was a shout as Mack threw down the radio handset, quickly lit a cigarette from his crumpled pack of Lucky Strike, and then gunned the engines.

'That fucking, bloody Dutchman, Fanie Swart is into the tunny off Lookout,' he shouted over his shoulder, and Gideon and Matt hung on again as the engines howled and the boat rose up onto the plane and skittered and slapped over the waves towards the Lookout rocks. They spotted the cruising ski-boat, no doubt that of the maligned Meneer Swart, about half a mile off the front of the Lookout rocks. There were birds everywhere, disappearing one after the other, plummeting like chalked arrows into the sea. Mack slowed the boat and they deployed the boat rods, dropping the big, brightly coloured feather lures into the water, running them out behind the wake. They set the butts of the four rods in the stainless-steel sleeves mounted in front of the growling engines, and Mack tested the drags on the reels quickly before hurrying back to the wheel and turning towards the thick of the mêlée of wheeling and diving birds. As the boat moved forward slowly at trolling speed, Matt saw them. He half rose from the pedestal chair and stabbed with his finger.

'There!!' The hair on his forearms and neck prickled as he watched the echelon of dorsal fins crest in the water, coming in at a forty-five degree angle astern. As the tunny struck, the first two rods on the port side dipped violently with the ratchets screaming and the line stripping off. Matt and Gideon lurched towards the two rods – suddenly Mack was yelling behind them.

'Leave, wait, wait.' The boat had slowed fractionally and Mack nursed the stick forward, keeping the remaining two lures aloft for the two seconds needed for the third and fourth strikes to starboard. All hell broke loose as the engines were stopped and the three men grabbed rods and fought with the tunny, the air filled with grunts and shouts, swearing and coaxing. They desperately tried to avoid crossing their lines as the tunny thrust down and weaved below them. There was a rattle as Mack grabbed the gaff and expertly hooked his fish and drew its wildly flapping torpedo shape over the side and into the well of the boat where it landed with a thud and then continued its useless, frantic struggle. Mack dropped his rod and quickly reeled in the last, and by now empty rod. He stood between the two men gaff in hand, both cajoling and cursing in a filthy but fluent mixture of English and Afrikaans. Matt's fish came aboard accompanied by a whoop and a roar.

'You fucking beauty, jou lekker ding!' Mack slipped the gaff and knelt down to give the fish a resounding smack of appreciation and delight. He beamed up at Matt.

'Twenty pounds, my china! ... at least, fok my boetie , tonight we hit the blue top I'm telling you!' They both looked over to Gideon who had called urgently. 'Mack, give us a hand, there's not too much line left here!' Mack stepped over and peered at the reel.

'I'll fucking smack that brother of mine – somer 'n snot klap! Every time he borrows the boat he leaves some sort of cock-up. Last time stinking fucking bait left in the hold – vrot chokka and redbait – now it's line he's lost and doesn't replace. Always pissing on my battery that oke – always! I'll kill him!'

He moved up to the wheel and pressed the electric starter button. The engines whined and then rumbled into life. 'Look, Gideon, I'm going to try and back towards him, it might give you some extra line, boet.' There was a thunk as he engaged reverse, and curls of blue smoke from the ports wafted around the sides of the engines as the boat slowly began to edge backwards. Gideon battled on while Mack kept up a running diatribe against his brother. 'What sort of arsehole brings redbait onto a ski-boat anyway? Red-bait's for rock fishing, man ... the stupid pampoen has got bloody rocks in his head!'

What Gideon eventually landed was a monster that later weighed in at twenty-eight pounds. Mack was in his seventh heaven as they turned for home. He stuck a red pennant on the end of an old telescopic car aerial that he had welded to the windscreen in front of the wheel and then drew it out with a flourish. 'Bobby's gonna be watching us through the binoculars on the front stoep. This is my little tunny flag. Once she sees that up, boet, she goes and checks on the blue top!' He roared with laughter and they sped for home, less bumpy now as they were running with the swells. Mack circled Katonkel twice outside the breakers waiting for a decent wave and then rode it in at speed, the ski-boat sliding out of the surf right up onto the beach, the engines kicking up their heels as they hit the sand.

There was work to do. They ran the trailer down to the prow of the boat and then pulled Katonkel up onto it with cable from the winch mounted on the front of Mack's Land Rover. Matt washed down the decks whilst Mack and Gideon off-loaded the rods, haversacks and other paraphernalia. There were masses of interested onlookers, especially when the bathers and walkers saw the tunny being lifted out of the boat. Once they were finished cleaning up, all three fishermen crowded into the cab of the Land Rover. Mack started up the old workhorse and pulling Katonkel behind them on the trailer, they crawled slowly up the hill to the Fisheries in Main Street where Mack disappeared to sell off the two bigger fish. Ten minutes later he was back, jumping into the driving seat and banging the door shut. He leant forward to stuff his wallet into a back pocket, beaming at them both.

'Helps pay for the petrol – I tell you this trolling business chews up the petrol hey! The small one we'll cut up for steaks, there's plenty for all of us.' He paused with his fingers on the keys, ready to start, and looked across at them – pure mischief glinting in the blue eyes. 'You guys, it's time for some blue top.' He laughed happily, started the Land Rover and pulled out into the late afternoon traffic.

Mack's Spanish-style house on top of the hill was surprisingly neat and tidy, and so was Bobby, a cheerful, chubby little lady who opened the front door as she heard Mack toot-tooting in the drive. There were several people already gathered round a roaring, crackling fire in the inbuilt braai on the stoep, but Mack fixed both Gideon and Matt with their drinks before he moved to his friends to tell of their successful day. 'They're all his local ski-boat buddies,' Gideon confided, 'even the redoubtable Fanie Swart will be here shortly. Rivals and buddies, all rolled into one. And don't take all that stuff about his brother Ian too seriously either, it's just that Ian fishes for pleasure and for Mack it's a sober religion – sorry, wrong word – a serious religion.'

Matt took a couple of deep, thirsty swallows from his bottle of Castle. 'That tastes so good! What a day we've had, Gideon. Absolutely fantastic – I'm going to sleep like a log tonight. And what the hell is blue top, by the way?'

Gideon grinned, 'it's the colour of the screw caps on Mainstay bottles.'

Matt shook his head. A lazy smile crept onto his face and he took another swig.

Gideon nodded at the picture of tired contentment. This break will do him good, he thought, it'll do us both good. He excused himself and moved across to Bobby who was busy bringing out the meat and rolls for the braai. 'Bobby, can I use your phone?' It was nearly seven o'clock and Hope would be waiting for his call. There was much to tell her.

23

The miniscule trout-fly landed in the centre of the shadowed eddy swirling languidly under the overhanging tree. Jake grunted in satisfaction. He really was getting the hang of this fly fishing lark. His eye followed the sinuous track of his floating line back to his new Hardy rod which he now lowered as he started to slowly retrieve the line, pull after gentle pull. There had been little activity today, in spite of his host's confident predictions earlier that morning. He glanced to his right at the tall figure some thirty yards down stream, and watched as John Cunningham flicked his fly expertly onto the river. Ever since he had moved to England, he had been a frequent weekend visitor here at the Hall, John's beautiful Georgian country home in the Cotswolds. How long was it now, he thought, probably all of six months since he'd relocated from Johannesburg to London. Jake lifted the fly from the water and cast a fraction higher upstream, watching the fly settle on the glassy water and then drift down towards the self-same eddy. Hope had almost done him a favour, running off like that: and then Matt, that stupid, ungrateful boy of his, throwing away his University education, wasting all that money. He remembered the phone call from London that had come almost as a lifeline amidst all the interminable discussions and meetings with the lawyers about the divorce. The offer had been impressive, but it needed to be, it meant giving up his house, his holiday home, his clubs, directorships, work, friends – the lot; his whole life in South Africa in fact. He was much fêted then as something of a phenomenon of the time, a golden boy of the financial world, and was being headhunted assiduously because of it. The financial scribes had written of his Midas touch at length; of his ability, time and time again, to turn failing companies around and to promote year end profit figures from poor to average or from average to outstanding. Jake could interpret company accounts like a soothsayer reads her cards, divining flaws and strengths instantly, and would set about sacking, replacing or trimming staff without a second thought if he deemed it in any way necessary or advantageous to the bottom line. That was his lodestar – the bottom line, the profit margin. He was ruthless, he knew that – took perverse pride in it in fact, and was even mildly flattered when a furious manager he had sacked turned and swore at him, calling him a cruel swine, a heartless bastard. Why couldn't people understand, business was business. His prime responsibility was to the shareholders and he'd never heard them complain, quite the contrary.

He saw John had reeled in and was bent over packing his gear into his fishing bags. Yes, John's offer had been impressive. Appointment as Financial Director of the Group was all very well, and the package would put him amongst the super-wealthy, but Jake was after more. He knew his own worth and was supremely self-confident to boot, confident enough to fly to London and negotiate a thumping salary and a substantial number of shares in Brathrow Steel U.K., a hefty stake in his own future. He pointed out to the board that he was in large measure responsible for the astonishing results achieved by the South African subsidiary since start-up, and had in his capacity as director, succeeded in turning around three other companies that had appointed him to their board. It was a virtuoso performance in the impressive boardroom of the London company headquarters and a dazzling demonstration of self-belief, all backed by an impressive amount of substantiating paper work. The board were convinced, and had remained so since as Jake had bent his considerable financial intellect and unbelievable energies to the new task: that of streamlining and reforming Brathrow's entire operation. He spent the first six weeks of his tenure travelling to Cardiff, Manchester and Glasgow – to the company branches there, doing inspections and tours, meeting senior managers, studying accounts and asking questions, always asking questions. Then had come the sweeping changes that encompassed both head office and all the far-flung subsidiaries. Jake had conducted the operation like a synchronised military campaign; pruning, consolidating, streamlining and generally cutting the fat from the carcass of the company. Mindful of the future, he promoted ambitious young men to key positions ensuring that each and every one of them understood that their future prospects lay firmly in his hands. They were instructed to provide detailed and completely confidential reports on designated performance parameters to him monthly so he could monitor profit constantly and minutely. Jake's fingers settled lightly on the Brathrow pulse. As his tendrils spread into the fabric of the organisation, Jake soon came to be recognised as the eminence grise, the power behind the throne that John Cunningham continued to grace with his distinctively facile and apparently benevolent air. Jake knew only too well that the genial Cunningham façade was merely a well-tailored smoke screen that effectively concealed an astute and razor-sharp business brain. After all, he'd had the good sense to employ him as his right-hand man, hadn't he? But Jake wondered whether John's acumen extended to being aware enough to watch his own back. Jake smiled – a secret, sly slash on his face as he watched the bobbing tweed hat on his host's head progress up the slope towards him.

'Could have sworn we'd have some better luck this morning, old man.' John grounded the butt of his trout rod, puffing from the exertion of the little climb. 'The whirly bird will be here at half past twelve, so I suppose we'd better pack it in and get back to don the old glad rags.' He waited while Jake collected his tackle.

'Be nice to have a G n' T while we wait, what?'

The affectations of the English spoken by the upper classes still amused and mystified Jake, but he was nevertheless taking considerable pains to change his accent away from the flat South African tones and colonial tag that came with it. He had decided that the rather non-specific BBC type accent, most often heard from their news presenters would suit him best. It would fit in any and everywhere; and Jake aimed to fit in.

As they walked up the river bank, the uncompromising symmetrical splendour of the Cunningham's Georgian home, Hyde Hall, came into view across manicured grassed lawns that lay prone before it like some tightly woven brilliant green carpet. The contrast with the pale, mellow Cotswold stone walls was striking, the more so with the brilliant mirrored sunlight reflections thrown from the perfectly proportioned windows, a bank of huge elm trees providing the perfect sylvan backdrop. Jack felt the same stab of envy he always experienced here, confronted as he was at every turn by the trappings of great wealth. It was a sensation that he welcomed, serving as it did to burnish his ambition and stoke the fires of his venal appetites.

'Your mare's running in quite an important race today, isn't she, John?'

'You're damn right she is!' answered the older man. 'It's a Grade II ... she stands a chance too, providing they don't dawdle at the start and then sprint for the finish.'

Jake's interest wasn't feigned. He was absolutely consumed and fascinated by horse racing. As with much else in England, his introduction to the sport had been via his business colleague, patron and now host, a man whose family and roots had been entwined with the racing turf, the sport of kings, for four generations. Hyde Hall was replete with paintings, silver cups, trophies, photographs and mementoes that singly and collectively attested to the sport and the passion that the Cunningham family had indulged in for over one hundred and fifty years.

The flagged side entrance echoed to their steps and then to the clatter and rattle of rods and haversacks being racked and hung amidst the other paraphernalia of country living. Green Wellington boots, tennis rackets, walking sticks, several Barbour jackets, furled umbrellas and long woollen scarves. The wall opposite carried the saddles and bridles of yesteryear – little used these days, as John had explained, saying jocularly that he had long since reached the age of discretion and incipient arthritis.

'Used to hunt twice a week in my time, with the Heythrop. A fine huntsman Wallace, best in all England. I'll confess it makes me a bit sad to see the old stable block so empty and forlorn, but they are all gone now, my hunters – kid's ponies too of course. I miss it you know.' He gazed at the saddles, lost in wistful reminiscence for a moment. 'Ah well,' he turned and stumped through to the massive tiled entrance hall, talking as he went. 'I'll see you down here in half an hour or so, Jake, I better see how the old ball and chain is getting on. These women – never on time y'know!' As he mounted the flight of stairs to the first floor he paused with his hand on the oak balustrade and bawled to no one that Jake could see, 'Jane!! Drinks in the drawing room in fifteen minutes, shake a leg will you?' Jake heard a muffled and indistinct reply coming from somewhere in the general direction of the kitchen as he followed John up the majestic broad staircase.

Jake bathed and then dressed with care. The lightweight three-piece tweed suit had been exquisitely tailored in London with the greatest attention to detail. The discreetly checked cloth in country earth brown and oak leaf green was the finest; and the trousers that he now drew on were cut to lend the impression of a better length of leg. He tucked in the cream linen shirt, fastened the cuffs with square cut gold cufflinks, and then sat to put his shoes on over plain woollen socks. He'd worn the brogues around his London home every evening for the last week, breaking them in, scuffing the soles to ensure that he wouldn't slip on racing turf and taking the brand-newness out of them. The tie was diagonally striped and he tied it on carefully, the old fashioned way, with small knot and slight flare beneath, eschewing the more fashionable Windsor variety. The waistcoat fitted like a glove and he quickly did up all the horn buttons with the intentional exception of the last and lowest. Moving to the en-suite bathroom, Jake stood in front of the vanity mirror, combed his greying black hair neatly back into submission, and then donned the jacket in the bedroom, shooting the cuffs and then turning half left and then right to see that it sat well behind. He slid his long, slim wallet into the inside breast pocket cut into the old gold silk lining and then checked again in the long dressing mirror, ensuring that the cut and line wasn't in any way disturbed. Two monogrammed linen handkerchiefs, one for the hip pocket and the other almost completely thrust home in the breast pocket, just a fraction showing. He picked up his binocular case from the dresser, remembering how difficult it had been to find this and the old shooting stick. He had wanted to avoid the nouveau riche label at all costs and had eventually found what he was looking for in an unlikely Kensington pawnshop. The binoculars and case weren't anywhere near new, but the Zeiss glasses had been carefully maintained, and the long leather case had just the right patina to convince anyone who cared to look that the owner had been racing for years. There were even two small badges hanging off the strap where it joined the case. One read Ascot 1953 and the other Cheltenham 1956. Jake had torn them off, taking care to leave the one gold and one blue string intact. The garrulous old pawnbroker had told him that the shooting stick had come from the same source, and turning it over in his hands, Jake could see that it showed an equal measure of the distinction that comes with repeated use and diligent care.

Grasping the stick, Jake let himself out of the bedroom and made his way downstairs, through the hall and into the drawing room.

'Ah, there you are, Jake … hmm … looking very dapper too if I may say so. What's your poison? Pink Plymouth as I recall.' John Cunningham was now obviously in very good spirits, looking forward to the day's racing and watching his good mare run. Jane Cunningham arrived in the drawing room looking like a flustered blue turkey and clad in a short silk twin-set ensemble that her ample curves threatened to escape from at any minute.

'John darling, I can't find my binoculars anywhere!'

John whirled around with a large pacific smile. 'Darling they're with mine! Didn't I tell you? Look, you're all of a bother … have an Amontillado, it'll settle your nerves.' Jane patted her hair nervously and gave Jake a weak apologetic smile while her husband poured the sherry into a diminutive Waterford crystal glass.

'Jake you'll have to forgive me, I always get into such a tizz-wizz before a big race and Caraway is such a super, super mare, I couldn't bear it if anything happened to her!' John tush-tushed Jane with a dismissive but not unfriendly wave of one hand whilst offering her the charged sherry glass with the other. Jane took two little sips from the brim and then appeared to relax suddenly. John cocked his head at the faint chattering sound of the approaching helicopter.

'Drink up chaps, methinks our chariot approaches.'

24

The blue and white corporate helicopter carrying Jake and the Cunninghams from Gloucestershire to the Newmarket races flew directly over Fen Ditton, a small hamlet nestling on the banks of the river Cam just outside Cambridge. Alice squinted up at the slapping noise of the helicopter rotor blades way above her as she carried yet another cardboard box into Fen Ditton Hall.

Moving her things over from Girton was a pain but she was absolutely thrilled with their find. Paul Rennat, her student of Architecture friend and his diminutive wife Sue had asked her if she would move in with them – to share the rent, and she had jumped at the opportunity. They had what Sue had grandly decided to call 'The Hall' all to themselves; in fact a separate annexe; a humbler side addition to the large, brick built, 17th century Manor House, Fen Ditton Hall, with its high-thrown Dutch gables that dominated an overgrown, high-walled and delightfully mysterious garden next door. It was literally only a stone's throw away from the Hall's petite front garden to the river, and took only the shortest of walks to reach the village which offered the choice of two pubs: The Ancient Shepherd just up the lane nearby, and only a little further on and right on the banks of the Cam, a much-favoured student haunt, The Plough. The green front door of the Hall led into a small quarry-tiled lobby with kitchen to the left and to the right, a huge drawing room complete with bay window and vast inglenook fireplace quite big enough to park a Mini in. Alice's room led off halfway up the narrow carpeted stairs from the lobby, the stairs culminating in a small landing, with bathroom off, and Paul and Sue's bigger bedroom.

Alice's first three years completing pre-clinical courses and her

B.A. degree had revolved around lectures and pracs – practicals – on the Downing site, an ugly and somewhat gloomy collection of buildings near Pembroke College. How typical, an amused Alice had thought, three years of studying Science and what does Cambridge do? Award an Arts degree! Pru had gone down and would be continuing with her Medicine at Newcastle – Alice missed her dreadfully and kept wondering what Pru would think of Newcastle after Cambridge. She remembered their rather drunken toast at a Drones' cocktail party last June after the exams, 'to life after Cambridge – if there is one!' It was enough in their tipsy state to reduce them to fits of hysterical giggles but there was a tacit acknowledgement there. Both knew that the chink of their glasses as they made the toast also sounded the death-knell of their time together in Camelot.

Ashleigh had been right in her first appraisal – the two girls had become inseparable. The amount of freedom that Cambridge offers, to do whatever one has a mind to really, is virtually unbounded – from the most banal to the most esoteric, and the two girls had explored their new world with all the zest and naïveté of convent initiates. What with lectures, pracs, societies and sport it was difficult to make the time for everything and even poor Fred, Alice's hunter, with little to do and becoming crotchety, had been sent back to Ireland. As opposed to everything else, which was so novel and exhilarating, Alice thought that the hunting around Cambridge was too boring for words – it suffered in comparison with that in her beloved Ireland. She had been out first with Mrs. Gingell's Harrier pack, and then with the Cambridgeshire foxhounds. Both packs hunted the flat clay country of East Anglia and Alice soon tired of the interminable, circuitous meanderings around the end of ploughed fields. She missed the charged excitement of galloping over the green fields and banks of her native Tipperary.

'It's like a follow-my-leader type of bloody procession!' Alice had exploded to Pru after her second day out with the Harriers. 'All I've done, all day, is follow some old bat's farting cob through seas of sticky yellow clay. Just look at me, I look like some sort of champion Welsh bog snorkeler.'

Pru giggled. Alice struggled to undo her stock pin; finally wrenching it out, undoing the stock and then downing the sherry her roommate had poured her. Pru watched in amusement as her friend's Celtic temperament flashed in the emerald eyes and she waited for the exasperation to wash out into her more habitual good humour. It's going to take a while longer, Pru reflected, as she could see Alice's thoughts gathering pace again while she refilled the sherry glass. Her amusement turned onto astonishment as Alice downed the second glass as well. 'Steady on!' Pru exclaimed, 'you're getting your knickers in a real knot here, you know!' Alice threw her muddy riding gloves onto the table half-heartedly. 'Aunt Ash is going to be so furious with me, I know it. She's paid all this money to have Fred here for me and now I've got to tell her that he's got to go back ... back home. Oh, Pru, he hates it! It was all I could do to hold him and stop him going wham bash into the horse in front of him. Grabbing hold of the bit, boring down, almost yanking my arms out of their bloody sockets: he's never like this at home – all he wants is a damn good blow-out and he hasn't even had a good pipe-opener since he's arrived. Just fed-up to the back of his great big teeth, that's what he is ... fed-up, and I don't blame him a bit, 'cause so am I, flipping fed-up!'

So Fred had gone back to Ireland and Alice had watched the big horsebox leave with tears in her eyes, at least secure in the knowledge that he would be so much more content and happier at home: and to her great relief Ashleigh hadn't been angry at all when she'd phoned and explained it all carefully. Instead, Ashleigh had suggested she go out and buy herself a little scooter so she could get around more easily.

'Oh no, I can't!' Alice had protested.

'What nonsense, poppet,' Ashleigh insisted, 'just listen to me: it'll be a great deal cheaper than paying for Fred's board for another God knows how many years, and I do want to do something for you after all. It's the prerogative of a doting aunt!'

Alice thought scooters were really pathetic, so she bought a second-hand 250cc Triumph motorbike instead which was great fun – had a bit of zip, and could also carry Pru's generous frame without the suspension collapsing. Most significantly, it also meant that they could set the alarm clock fifteen minutes later in the mornings and still be on time for lectures.

With Pru gone, Alice did not want to stay on in Girton – it wouldn't be the same, and all the girls she'd gone up with three years ago had also disappeared. All of a sudden she had felt rather lonely and the offer to share digs with Paul and Sue was so wonderfully opportune. And Paul had been so helpful, carting her boxes, books and suitcases over from Girton in his Citroën. Alice hadn't been in one before and was fascinated by the pump-me-up and let-me-down suspension and the sort of wave-cum-glide ride she got from the funny looking, futuristic car. Paul was a Jesus College man, and in a city full of men, stood out as one of the most strikingly good looking of them all. Alice put him at a touch over six foot, a height that was crowned by a generous head of black hair that fell wide to his shoulders in gentle waves of liquid jet. He sported a neatly trimmed beard, and a thin moustache in the style that Errol Flynn had sometimes favoured some twenty years before, and it leant him that same raffish, debonair look that the legendary film star had habitually used to bemuse his women. Unlike Mr. Flynn, who was by reputation quite a cruel and callous man, Alice recognised Paul as one of the kindest and gentlest souls on God's earth. He also affected a flamboyant and highly individual manner of dress, one that favoured an almost theatrical style, with black cloaks and navy blue coats with large winged lapels and gold crested buttons. The dark clothes would customarily be relieved by the flash of a vibrant single or multi-coloured scarf at the throat, and if occasion demanded, complemented by a waistcoat drawn from an exotic collection of peacock coloured finery. He had ever been a source of complete fascination for Pru who would always beg or inveigle an invitation whenever Paul invited Alice for tea in his Chapel Court rooms in College. This was still in the twilight of Paul's bachelorhood before he married Sue some months later in high summer, and Pru would sit gazing at him in dreamy adoration whilst she absent-mindedly sipped at her Earl Grey tea.

'It's obscene, Pru!' Alice would teasingly admonish her roommate back in their set in Girton with their shoes off and feet up in front of the comforting gas fire.

'Oh, I know Alice, I know – pure lust and wantonness, especially the lust, but a cat can look at a king, can't she? I know I can't have him – he's much too gorgeous and rich a dish for plain old Pru, but I do love dreaming about my Lancelot. If I could just be Guinevere for a day … or preferably a night …' her voice had trailed off in smiling fantasy as she gazed up at the ceiling wistfully.

'Really, Pru!' Alice had giggled at her friend in feigned censure, yawned and then also settled back into the armchair in comfortable companionship and after a moment felt her eyelids heavy and starting to close.

Paul and Sue had been married in Jesus College Chapel where once the nuns of Saint Rhadegund had prayed until Henry VII gave licence to Bishop Alcock of Ely to dissolve their nunnery. Two days before the wedding, Sue had been reading aloud to Alice about it from a book on the history of the College, which Paul had picked up at the second-hand bookstall in the market, whilst Alice knelt at the hem of her wedding dress with a mouthful of pins – trying to get it straight. Sue had decided at the last minute on shoes with a higher heel and the dress now needed letting down.

'How long ago was this?' mumbled Alice trying not to drop any of the pins. Sue had turned a page of the book with a hand which was also trying to keep hold of a half eaten peanut butter slice.

'Let's see – nearly five hundred years ago according to this – 1496 in fact, fascinating if you like history … God, I could do with a drink and a cigarette!' Sue had thrown the book on the bed, finished off the slice and then carefully licked her fingers clean one by one.

'Won't be much longer,' said Alice, whose back had started aching terribly, 'then you can take it off and stitch it. Sue had groaned. 'Then I'll definitely need a drink.'

Alice had been thrilled to be asked to be Sue's bridesmaid, it was one of the things that had made her feel less foreign in England – that and some of the wonderful people she had met. Pru would be a close friend for life, and there was Ashleigh close by in Stock, and now this super house in Fen Ditton sharing with Paul and Sue. There was every prospect they would be together for the next three years and this delighted her. Paul and Sue had brought up some spare and rather good furniture and pictures from Paul's parents' house in Sevenoaks in Kent, and once these were combined with Paul's faintly bohemian touch, the whole place began to take on an ineffable air of relaxed and colourful contentment. The atmosphere in the Hall reminded Alice in some ways of her Tipperary home – informal, relaxed and agreeable. Sue's rather fey manner and refusal to take life or herself too seriously was an added wonderfully refreshing change from some of the rather intense and introspective students that Alice had met in her three years at Girton. Paul simply adored his wife and they made a couple of quite astonishing contrasts. Paul's tall dark piratical good looks and Sue's tiny elfin face and reed-slim body sheathed, as often as not, in narrow calf-length skirts and knitted tops that clung to her waif like body. She seemed so dreadfully frail, and indeed Paul always treated her like some most delicate piece of priceless porcelain. In spite of the apparent fragility – and this baffled Alice completely – Sue could work her way diligently through one huge meal after another – meals that would have kept a fistful of deprived orphans content for a week. In time, as she came to know her well, Alice came to think that all food went to feed Sue's backbone, because under that brittle mien lurked a vitality and vigour that astonished Alice and served Sue well in keeping any of life's crueller surprises at arm's length. Alice saw that Paul's considerate, loving manner towards Sue was requited by a fierce determination of hers to protect his gentle soul from any harm or hurt.

Paul had gone back in the Citroën for the last of Alice's boxes from Girton and the two girls sat amongst Alice's boxes and luggage in the drawing room at the Hall. On a whim, Alice asked Sue the age-old question of how she knew he was 'the one'. Sue paused in lighting a cigarette with the lighter halfway to the tip, and taking the cigarette from her mouth, gazed past Alice into the middle distance through the bay window.

'Looks apart,' she said, 'because I know you're not asking about that, I suppose that something inside of me recognised him straight away – in fact the second I spoke to him I knew, or inside of me knew, that I had to be with him – forever, and he felt the same. Instant karma if you like.' She put the cigarette to her mouth and then withdrew it again, a small frown of deliberation on her brow, and paused again before speaking. 'I know that I'm more when I'm with him and I know that I'm less when we are apart … it's so difficult to explain properly, but when it happens to you, you'll recognise it I promise.'

'I do hope you're right,' said Alice wistfully, fully caught up in the romance of Sue's words. She stood and moved towards the kitchen. 'I'm going to make some tea to keep me going, Sue, do you want a cup? I thought we could go down to the pub when Paul gets back and I can buy you both a drink to say thank you for all the help.'

'And we can drink to true love.' Sue added. They laughed happily together.

Alice stood tapping her fingers idly on the melamine dresser waiting for the kettle to boil and thinking about Sue's words. There had only been one boyfriend in the last three years – Clive; big, tall, freckly Clive – one of the students up at the Vet school, but he'd qualified already which meant that he'd been ensconced in a Yorkshire practice for over a year now. There had been a few letters back and forth, but a lukewarm romance had finally fizzled out into silence. More companion than lover, thought Alice. She envied Sue having something magical happen like that. She'd even read about it in The Godfather and memorised the phrase from Mario Puzi's book when Michael had first seen Apollonia in Sicily, the coup de foudre – the thunderbolt. Alice sighed and her eyes softened as she mouthed the words to herself. She was brought back by the kettle threatening to whistle and spooned tea leaves into the pot, affectionately in mind of her mother's voice as she did so: one for you, one for me and one for the pot. There would be a minute or two before the tea set, so she turned up the volume on the little radio above the sink, hoping to catch the weather report after the news and sport. She'd catch it all right; they were still giving the racing results from Newmarket.

25

Jake stood in the parade ring with the Cunnighams watching the bay mare being walked around in the company of a dozen other Thoroughbreds. John was deep in earnest discussion with the trainer and diminutive jockey clad in his crimson and black quartered silks. Giving advice about the pace no doubt, thought Jake, remembering his host's remarks earlier in the day on the way back from the river. Jake had been obliged to learn a considerable amount about racing; about sprinters and stayers and the importance of bloodlines. About horses that acted on the firm and those that didn't, about mudlarks, about short heads, necks and distances and a thousand other phrases and terms that made up a language that on occasions was almost unintelligible to outsiders. It was a language moulded over centuries of semi-isolation, away from the main stream of life, and steeped in all the idiosyncrasy of the notion that owning the fastest three-year-old colt in England over a mile-and-a-half some time early in June was just about the most important thing in life.

The jockeys were beginning to mount up and John's trainer gave Caraway's pilot a quick leg-up, shooting him into the saddle in a single fluid shimmer of crimson. As the jockey found his stirrups and took up the bridle, the mare felt his presence and jig-trotted away at a half pass, bending her neck to the bit like a broad bow of burnished mahogany, eager to go and impatient at the restraint.

Jake felt a clap on his back. 'C'mon old man, we better get off and see them down to the start. Hope you've got a couple of quid on, she looks a real picture today.' They hastened up to the box and watched as the horses cantered past, some languidly and some hard held with their necks arched and heads tucked so tight that it contrived a prancing, almost hobbyhorse like action. One almost burst away from his jockey with head held high and hindquarters bunching and stabbing at the turf in a frenzy of action and energy. 'He'll have run his race before he gets to the start,' commented John from behind his binoculars and then turned to follow Caraway's more measured progress down the green track towards the starting gates. The horses settled around the back of the starting gates, circling at the walk while the handlers started loading them into the stalls.

Jake could see a lone figure with a flag some way in front of the stalls. As he raised it the gates opened and the horses burst forth as one. 'They're off,' the commentator intoned and started to take up his commentary, sounding to Jake for all the world like an auctioneer in full flight, the words all run together in a babble of sound pouring from the loudspeakers. He battled to keep his binoculars steady enough to pick out Caraway's jockey's colours but the field was tightly bunched at the turn and he had to rely on John's terse, staccato asides.

'She's handy ... Christ no, she's going to get bunched in ... switch her you fool ... yes she's clear.' John put down his binoculars as the horses hit the two-furlong marker and began to bawl his horse home. Caraway was in third place some way adrift, but with clear light ahead started to eat up the deficit hand over fist, and with a furlong to go, was suddenly on the leading horse's quarters. Jake saw the jockey crouched over the withers riding her out for all he was worth with sawing hands and scrabbling heels and was suddenly caught up in the thrill of it, screaming like a banshee as the leading horse suddenly found it in him to stretch out a fraction further. The two horses were locked together, stride for stride, as they flew over the finish with the roar of the crowd beating all around.

'She's got it!' John crowed with his bunched fists held high, 'by a nose ... she's got it!' He turned to hug his wife, lifting her clear off the ground. Jane gave a delighted shriek and tried to catch her feathered hat which went toppling to the ground. Jake picked it up and then turned to wring an ecstatic John's hand and clap him on the shoulder.

In spite of the obligatory photo, John proved to be right and Jake watched as the Cunninghams led their mare to the winner's enclosure with press cameras clicking furiously all around. Caraway, the heroine of the hour, stood with her flanks heaving and almost black from sweat that evaporated in steamy whisps about her, careless of the smacks of acclaim on her neck and the flying plaudits from the ecstatic connections. Jake took in the scene with his dark, gleaming eyes agog. He inhaled the intoxicating sounds and scents of success – the shouts, the sweet, sweated smell of wet leather and horse, the adulation and desperately, desperately wanted part of this: this winner takes all, this fêting of the victor, the glory of the champion. He shook with the knowledge of the depth of his desire and ambition as he also did later, watching John and Jane Cunningham receive their trophy amidst the enthusiastic cheers and applause from the crowd.

They dined at the Rutland Arms, the coaching inn in Newmarket High Street with the cobblestones and high-arched side entrance still waiting for the landaus and phaetons of yesteryear. Jake's hosts were in mighty form. It was the best win they had had for years and put Caraway in line for some of racing's richest prizes. Bottles of Veuve Cliquot, the widow's champagne, were disappearing at the rate of knots as John's and Jane's friends and acquaintances kept arriving at the table to offer their congratulations. Each and every one was inveigled to stay for a drink as the story of the race was retold a thousand times, and to Jake the lustre of it just grew and grew. The pace only slackened as John called for brandy and cigars after dessert. Jane had pleaded exhaustion after the excitement of the day and happily disappeared upstairs to a no doubt very welcome bed whilst the men drew back in their chairs and sniffed and cut the large Havanas.

'So you've really caught the racing bug, Jake?' John smiled across at Jake, exuding bonhomie from every pore and reached for a matchbox on the table, his cigar clamped firmly between bared teeth. Jake nodded and smiled as if in guilty and rueful collusion. 'I'm certainly going to give it a try, John. What do you think the first step should be – for a novice like myself?' Jake had no intention of giving John any sort of hint of his true goal, one that he had thought out very carefully. There was the Derby of course, but that Holy Grail seemed too reaching an ambition and Jake was, above all, a practical man. It would suffice him to win one of the Classics, which broadened his chances of success quite considerably. All were designated for three-year-olds, the One Thousand Guineas and the Two Thousand Guineas over a mile-and-a-quarter for fillies and colts respectively early in the season, the Oaks and the Derby, again for fillies and colts over a mile-and-a-half in June, and then finally the St. Leger over a mile-and-three-quarters run up in lonely Doncaster. Any one of these would spell success under his terms and Jake wouldn't be paying much attention to breeding prospects for the future. He wouldn't be buying horses where pedigree weighed heavier than stake winnings in the line. He wasn't a meritocrat for nothing. Unlike some owners, Jake had no intentions of founding a breeding dynasty. He had no children to hand it on to, none that mattered anyway, and he knew that breeding bloodstock successfully sometimes took generations of application and effort. He wasn't going to dilute his efforts; it had to be the straight arrow approach, single minded and decisive, allowing him to concentrate all his energies and resources. He would pursue his goal like he ran Brathrow Steel and his other business interests – with ruthless single-mindedness and God help anyone who stood in his way.

John was rabbiting on about different bloodstock agents and how he could effect introductions for him. Jake pretended to listen attentively whilst he sucked on his cigar, but he had already picked out which three agents he would appoint, a decision based on assiduous inquiry as to who had bought which horses for whom over the last five years – in other words, on their success rates. The appointments were going to be made in the following week, but Jake's budgets and strategy were already set. Bold, novel, costly measures he knew would be raising quite a few eyebrows, much like those of bloodstock agent Colin Jorbett on the following Wednesday when his secretary, Bronwyn, told him that this Mr. Stevens had appeared ten minutes early for his nine o'clock appointment and just walked straight into his office.

'Without so much as a by your leave!' she complained with a piqued look on her doll's face. 'The cheek of it!' He had only just arrived himself, having hurried his short, tubby torso in from the street moments before. His frizzy, ginger hair bobbed as he leant over to snatch the morning post from Bronwyn's hand before hastening towards his office door.

He noted the immaculate, pinstriped navy blue suit and the bleak appraisal in the dark eyes that bored at him steadily during his opening pleasantries. A real cold fish this one. The thought ran through his mind as he called to Bronwyn for coffee and then sat in the chair behind his large desk.

'Well, how can I help you, Mr. Stevens?' Jake crossed his legs and shifted to make himself more comfortable.

'Mr. Jorbett, I'll be buying horses, and you come recommended to me.'

Colin Jorbett's self-effacing little smile and duck of the freckled head were expunged by his client's dismissive wave of the hand. 'I don't care a damn about Joe Soap's recommendations by the way. It's only your track record that counts – your track record over the last five years in fact. You bought that Oaks winner for Lawrence Stilman and you've been involved in one way or another with the purchase of eight other Classic runners over the past five years, and that, Mr. Jorbett,' Jake leant forward emphasising his words, 'is why I pick you: I want that Classic winner – with my name on it.' He slowly leant back, still mesmerising the agent with his hypnotic gaze and extraordinary sense of purpose. 'Your budget for the sales this year is two hundred thousand pounds, and you will use these funds to buy at least two, but not more than four horses to go to a trainer that I'll be telling you about later. You will inform me of names and all relevant particulars of all the horses you propose bidding on on my behalf no more than twenty-four hours after publication of the relevant catalogue or private viewing, and every horse you propose bidding on will be examined prior to purchase by a veterinary surgeon of my choosing. Are these terms acceptable to you, Mr. Jorbett? Do we have an understanding?' Colin Jorbett's mouth hung a little slack as he tried to digest the barrage that had been thrown at him. His head gave a convulsive nod.

'Good,' said Jake rising from his chair and placing a large manila envelope on the desk in front of the bemused agent. 'What we've agreed to this morning is spelled out there in the form of a legal contract between us which you must sign and have witnessed, notarised and stamped and then returned to my offices today by messenger before five o'clock this afternoon. There is also a letter from my bank, which will establish my financial bona fides. You will see, Mr. Jorbett,' and at this point Jake placed both his hands flat on the desk, towering above the unfortunate agent, 'there is the matter of secrecy – of confidentiality if you like, that is also subject to provisions of the contract, and it's something I take very seriously ... and so should you.' The dark eyes took on a menacing cast. 'If you mention me by name or by association to anyone at all, and this comes to my knowledge, I will sever all contact with you immediately and seek both personal and legal remedy. All you may mention, because we both know you will be asked, is that you are buying on behalf of a consortium. You'll also find details of that consortium in the document – names, addresses and so on.' Jake stood up straight, dropping his intimidating manner like a snake shedding a skin. He smiled down at Colin Jorbett, the agent almost cowering in his chair under the unexpected verbal assault, and his voice took on a silky, coercive tone. 'Of course, it'll never come to that – what with the fine reputation you enjoy in the industry Mr. Jorbett, nice house in the Fulham Road, wife, two kids and the fat mortgage you have – you'd never risk all that for some indiscretion, now would you?'

The smile didn't waver as Jake picked up his briefcase and exited the office without another word, leaving the bloodstock agent alone with his astonishment and the ominous buff envelope.

What Colin Jorbett wasn't to know was that virtually the same scene was repeated in the offices of two other agents in the next forty-eight hours. The same sum of money, virtually the same contract, the same swearing to secrecy, and the same threats, both overt and implied. Only the names of the agents and consortiums differed. By close of business on Friday, all three signed and sealed documents were locked away in Jake's office safe and he could begin the next phase whilst his agents went to work scouting for hoofed talent, each in ignorance of the other. The anonymity would be more difficult to maintain with the trainers he wanted for his horses – too many ears everywhere – so he decided to rely on the impersonality of the consortium word – that, and the natural antagonism between competing yards. He assigned one trainer to each agent, making fairly low key but personal visits to all three, all of whom had been subjected to the same minute scrutiny as had the agents, and all of whom had produced Classic winners or contenders in the recent past. They all agreed to take horses, the more readily when Jake had mentioned the name of one agent to each and implied that his purchasing power was very substantial. Two of the trainers were in Newmarket and one in Lambourn in Berkshire, and the veterinary practices used by all three were also visited – not only for the purposes of introduction, but for unusual and very specific instruction.

Jake believed in crosschecking. He had an extensive army of informers inside Brathrow Steel – his moles – bookkeepers, secretaries and foremen, all of whom reported to him secretly on designated private lines, and they had already yielded vital information. The young managers he had appointed in the initial reconstruction of the firm had performed brilliantly – with one exception. By the time he had called in the head of the Cardiff operation and summarily fired him, Jake had known that young Seymour had been falsifying figures in his monthly reports to him, and had two tickets booked to Bolivia where he was planning to abscond to with his mistress à la Butch and Sundance. As Seymour left Jake's office after the most corrosive dressing-down and wondering how on earth he had been discovered, two police officers from the fraud division had quietly cautioned him, cuffed him and led him away.

There were no vehicles in the car park at The Chequers, a pub at the entrance to a village called Kentford on the Bury St. Edmonds road just outside Newmarket. Jake marked the fact as he swung the black Jaguar Mark 10 off the road and parked it. Inside the swing doors he found the landlord polishing glasses behind the bar and ordered a pint of Adnams before sauntering over to the far corner where the old man was waiting. He knew a considerable amount about this particular old man. Harry Jarvis had been a top-flight jockey in his time – retired now, but there was still the quick mind signalled by the canny eyes that trailed Jake as he approached the table. Jake couldn't see one spare ounce on the gaunt, bow-backed frame: a frame that was close wrapped in a thin brown coat with a piece of orange bailer twine securing it around the waist. Harry's index finger went to the faded check of the flat hat in terse acknowledgement.

'Guv'ner.'

Jake nodded in reply and pulled out a chair to sit. He didn't think pleasantries would get him very far with this old pigeon.

'I'll come straight to the point, Mr. Jarvis. I wonder if you would care to perform a service for me? For a fee of course.' Harry took a sip of his half pint and looked Jake evenly in the eye.

"Pends wot it is, doanit? Doan waner po-lees knockin darn me front door, do I? Donnow you from a bar a soap do I?' Jake smiled at the native suspicion of the man and placed one of his business cards on the table. Harry looked at it as if the embossed card had suddenly brought a bad smell to his pinched nostrils.

'Wot's it all abaht anyroads?' Jake filled him in with the details quite briefly, explaining that he wanted him on the gallops watching his horses, but anonymously, covertly, seeing them at work, timing them, gauging them and then reporting back to him regularly. He would require Harry to seek out contacts in their yards, among the lads, but very, very cautiously, and never, ever letting on that one horse was of more interest than the other.

'I'll 'ave to be a betting man, woan I?' remarked Harry. "At'll be the best way if I'm not gonna be spikuous like, woan it?' Jake nodded – it would be a good modus operandi and cause no suspicion.

'You gonna make it werf me warl then?' Harry asked with a

hint of aggression in his voice, 'I've gotta find some 'commadation in tarn durin the week – not gonna be cheap y'know, an you gotta stake me – and sumfink for me trouble.' Harry leant forward to light a Woodbine in the cupped hands of a man who lived most of his life in a windy outdoors. He squinted up at Jake through the smoke as he killed the flame with a shake of the hand, waiting for a reply. Jake reached into the inside pocket of his suit jacket and drew out a long white envelope which he slid across the table towards Harry. The old man lifted the open flap and saw the stack of ten-pound notes within. There was no change in his expression, or his eyes. Jake watched him carefully and approved of the deadpan poker face. Harry would do.

26

Paul shuffled through his post, pausing at the unfamiliar stamp on the airmail envelope. It was addressed to him at his parent's address in Sevenoaks and had been redirected to the Hall in his father's handwriting.

'Sue,' he called through the kitchen, 'guess what, there's a letter from Matt, Matt Stevens, the South African chap I was at school with in Grahamstown, in the Cape.' Sue came through into the drawing room, drying a plate as she walked. Paul was reading the letter intently. 'According to this he's travelling around Europe first, and is due in England some time about now. He's going to spend a week or so with people in London and then wants to come up and see us. Fantastic! I haven't seen him since we came back from Africa. He's given me a contact number, the London people, so I can give them a ring now and find out when he's arriving. Great!' Paul jumped up from the chair and hurried through to the phone in the lobby with an amused Sue following in the wake of his billowing coat.

As Paul dialled the number, Matt was sitting with Gideon's cousin Ruth and her husband Mannie in their Chelsea flat, talking about his travels. He'd flown directly from Jan Smuts airport to Rome for three days and then hopped on a bus, first to Florence and then to the bridges and malodorous waterways of Venice. He had lost his heart to Italy: falling completely in love with the ether of decayed opulence that oozed from every pore of the ancient buildings, seduced by the extraordinary colours. The unfamiliar smudged pinks and myriad shades of umber, ochre and sienna had streamed through his eyes setting the palette of his senses alight. And he'd never seen so many greys: landscapes of grey earth, grey tree stems, grey olives and grey grass. Even the blue skies had a hint of pearl-grey vaulted over grey-green rivers. He had been so right in wanting to come here, just mortified that he had no one to share in the spectacular discoveries he made every minute of every day. By late afternoon each day his poor feet had ached from tramping around museum after museum, gallery after gallery, his brain boggled and overwhelmed by the sight of paintings, tapestries and sculptures created by the great artists and their legendary masters – the Popes and the Medici princes. Before he knew it, Matt's ten days in Italy had gone and he had regretfully turned west towards France. But he would be back, he knew it. The boot that hung off the belly of Europe no longer just meant Vespas and spaghetti: now it was Venice and Siena, Verrocchio and del Sarto.

If Italy had earth, then Paris had elegance, and it was here that Matt had found the art of Toulouse-Lautrec with paintings and lithographs like Le Paddock and Le Jockey: paintings of men and horses that excited him hugely because they spoke to him of energy and radiated the same vitality that he tried so hard to achieve in his own drawings. Like Lautrec did so brilliantly, he tried in his own way to deliver the essence of what he saw – almost by suggestion, but he was now so aware of colour – and it was with sudden dismay that he thought of his own pencil sketches packed flat in the bottom of his suitcase. Apart from two attempts with pastels, there wasn't a speck of colour anywhere and any pride he may have had in them dissolved in the knowledge that his work so far was merely a tentative first step, an amateur's initiation. It was very humbling, very sobering, but his mind was nevertheless awash, not only with the hues and tints of Tuscany, but also the brilliance he had seen in the Jeu de Paume and the Paris salons. And not only Lautrec, but Degas too – and the other Impressionists and Post-Impressionists who could work such wizardry with colour. In spite of his misgivings about his own work, Matt was filled with a bursting enthusiasm to try his hand, and he had to learn, somehow, just how to translate what he could see in his mind onto canvas, and in colour. A huge mountain to climb: he consoled himself with one of his family's dictums that anything could be achieved if you put your mind to it, but then the thought sounded so suspiciously like his father talking that he took refuge in an innocuous fatalism instead: it was or it wasn't meant to be. Thinking of his father put him in his mind of their meeting in the bar of the Johannesburg Country Club the day before the Alitalia flight whisked him off to Rome. All very predictable.

The cold words.

' I suppose you want me to finance this bird-brained idea of yours, do you?'

The ice stare.

'No, Dad,' he'd answered slowly, 'I've just come to tell you what I'll be doing and that you don't need to worry about my 'Varsity fees any more.'

Then the dig.

'Why on Earth I've been left with an idiot for a son, God only knows.'

He'd met his father's eyes level and delivered even measure for once.

'You know, Dad, you're not my idea of a perfect father either.'

Not as good as Mountjoy shouting the day was his ... not even close.

Curiously unsatisfying. In a hurt against hurt contest like this who could ever win anyway?

It meant bugger all.

The phone rang and Matt tucked in his legs as Mannie squeezed past him to go and answer it.

'Matt, it's for you, Paul someone or other, I didn't catch the surname.'

Matt bounced out of the chair like a rocket. He'd really prayed that his letter would find its way to Paul one way or the other. Mannie and Ruth could hear Matt chatting away and laughing on the phone. They exchanged smiles, it was never easy being on your own in a foreign country and the young man would find it so much easier now with a friend of his own age.

The late autumn landscapes that flashed past the carriage windows had all the earth tones that Matt remembered from Italy, but the reds and yellows of the English countryside had been squeezed in a juicer, drained of their warmth and vitality. He checked his watch. The train was due in Cambridge in five minutes so he started to get his luggage down from the rack.

He hardly recognised Paul – there was all this hair, and the clothes too: both were a far cry from the school regulation uniform and short back-and-sides he'd last seen him in. He looked again – not even a very far cry, Paul was right out of earshot! What hadn't changed was the honest enthusiasm of Paul's greeting and wringing handshake ... and a bear hug, my goodness ... so nice.

'You're as brown as a button,' Paul complained, 'lucky bugger.' They walked down the longest platform in England. 'That's still something I miss terribly in England, the damn sun. He's a very occasional visitor here.' They fell into animated conversation, granting the intervening years very little except that there was much to catch up on on both sides. Matt caught glimpses of some of the colleges as the Citroën weaved through the city. As they swept around the roundabout at the end of Jesus Lane, Paul pointed at a mass of solid buildings behind heavy railings. 'That's my college - the back end of Jesus, if you'll excuse the expression.' It seemed only a few minutes later that they arrived in Fen Ditton, past The Ancient Shepherds and Paul was toot-tooting the horn to tell Sue they were home.

They found her in the kitchen busy preparing a roast, and Paul effected quick introductions. Sue dried her hands to shake Matt's and then shooed them both out.

'Why don't you two go down to the pub for a pint while I get on with things here?' She checked the time on her watch. 'This will take an hour or so, so be back at seven and we can all have a civilised sherry before dinner. Sorry it's not South African, Matt, but Paul will tell you I'm a fino fan. It's my one extravagance and my luck that Paul says it suits me.' She dimpled at her husband. Paul wanted to show Matt The Plough so they went down in the Citroën and took their pints of beer onto the pub lawns and watched as two college eights glided past on the silvery flat calm of the river. Matt was entranced by the measured harmony as the rowers glided forward on their seats, sweeping the oars up, and then the synchronous slap as the blades entered the water and were hauled for power – shooting the bow forward. It had all the fascination of a metronome. He turned with an apology as he realised Paul was talking to him.

'Sorry, I was a dwaal, what did you say?' Paul snorted a laugh. 'God, I haven't heard that word in a while; I was just wondering what your plans are now that you've dropped out of University?' Matt felt an immediate reluctance to tell Paul – not because of any secretiveness, it was purely an innate modesty, especially after what he'd just seen abroad. His puny sketches were hardly earth shattering, and, after all, Paul was doing Architecture – real drawing. His self-confidence fell another notch. Well, he's probably my best friend, thought Matt, and I'll have to tell him sometime I suppose; and so, taking a deep breath, he hesitatingly started to explain it all.

Paul listened to what Matt had to say with unfeigned

astonishment. 'An artist, I don't believe it!' But then he snapped his fingers as he remembered. 'Of course! Now I think about it – those funny caricatures you did of all the masters in Grahamstown. I was always drawing buildings and you were always drawing people.' Then he'd asked Matt the same question as his mother had. 'Are you going to take some sort of course?' Matt shook his head. 'No, perhaps I can find someone to study under, but at the moment I'm just going to try and find a part time job, you know – to keep myself alive, food and lodging.' Paul clapped his hands delightedly. 'Absolutely classic – the starving artist in the garret! We'll just have to fix you up with something here. It's just too good to miss. Sue's going to be thrilled; she just loves a bit of romance! Look no further, my friend, you've come to just the right spot!' Paul chuckled and rubbed his hands delightedly. 'Drink up – Sue will kill me if the roast is spoiled and she wants to have that sherry beforehand. Boys don't have all the fun in our household.' As they turned back to the pub Paul clapped Matt on the shoulder. 'Don't worry, Matt, we'll have you fixed up in no time.'

Paul was on a mission. In the car on the way back from the station, Matt had explained what was happening in his mother's and father's life back in South Africa, and Paul's concern had grown apace. It was the natural concern of anyone whose own childhood had been nurtured under the umbrella of loving parents and Paul could hardly conceive of his life without it. The Matt of now was no different in mind or spirit to the Matt he had known at school, except what was hinted at then was glaringly and, literally, painfully obvious now. He could scarcely credit Matt's father – what a bastard, he thought. He'd often thought of the almost unnatural happiness that had crept into his own life since he had first met Sue, a happiness that now spilled over into a resolve. They would do something together to try and right the wrong. They would share some of their good fortune and make it count in someone else's life – and who better than Matt. If fate had conspired to bring him here right at this moment, he was glad of it.

Sue's roast turned out perfectly as had the Yorkshire puds. 'We usually survive on meat loaf and potatoes, so this is a bit of a treat,' she remarked, 'and thanks to you we have this wonderful wine.' Matt had brought them two bottles of good claret from France and the nutty red wine was the perfect accompaniment in washing down the first real home-cooked roast he'd had for some time.

Sue was content to listen to the two of them do most of the talking. It was nice to hear Paul reminisce, and after a couple of glasses of the claret his South African friend unbent a little too. Definite opinions, but nice manners and gentle ways – not that she knew quite what to expect from a colonial – but she could see why Paul thought so highly of him. Good looking too, a pity Alice wasn't here, she thought, but she'd be back from Stock tomorrow morning and could meet him then. She had organised a bed of sorts on the drawing room floor with a spare foam mattress, sheets, blankets and pillows, and when Matt started yawning repeatedly, she had made Paul call it a day. They'd have coffee and a yak up in their bedroom before bed anyway.

Sue was taking off her make-up as Paul opened the upstairs bedroom door, carrying in a galleried wooden tray with coffee cups, sugar bowl and a china milk jug in the shape of a cow. There might well have been chips here and there, and none of the pieces matched, but these were all little treasures bought for a song at junk and bric-à-brac shops over the past year, marking unofficial anniversaries. Tokens of the day they had first met, the night of the first kiss, and a memory of Paul's byronesque proposal one night in a summer-scented rose garden. The nightly ritual served as a delightful aide memoire to them both.

'Matt seems very nice,' Sue commented as she tidied up a little on her dressing table and lit a cigarette to have with her coffee. Paul's eyes looked troubled as he stirred his cup thoughtfully. 'Yes, he is, Sue, but he's told me a little of what's going on at home and none of it sounds very pleasant, I'm afraid.' The quizzical lift of Sue's eyebrows bade him continue. 'His father sounds a really nasty piece of work and his mother's evidently walked out on him. She's living in a flat somewhere in Johannesburg, on her own, and Matt's very worried about her. His father is absolutely livid with him for dropping out, and from what I gather, they don't even speak anymore!' He shook his head, horrified at the thought of such devastation. 'I thought we could help, I really think we should.' Sue walked over to her husband and rested her forearms on his shoulders, locking the fingers of her two hands at the nape of his neck. The elfin face that looked into his held a serene look of compassion – not so much for his friend, but her for husband. She could hear Paul's mother's voice, telling her about the fledglings that Paul used to bring to her as a child. 'Paul's just like that,' his mother had explained: but Sue had known it all along and she loved that in him. She smiled up at him now. 'So what's to be done then, my love?'

27

The Cambridge streets were still empty of traffic as Alice accelerated down Jesus Lane, the rough noise of the motorbike engine reverberating between the high college walls on one side and the terraced houses opposite. In spite of the cold, she rather enjoyed travelling in the early hours of the morning, always making good time and seeing the dawn slowly creeping up over the dormant countryside. She was almost home now, and began to look forward to a hot cup of coffee to thaw the chill from her bones. The weekend in Stock with her Aunt Ash had been so cosy. They'd taken long walks in the countryside amidst the falling leaves, admiring all the shades of autumn and returning to a cheerful fire in the cottage hearth and thick soups burbling in the pot. Ashleigh always spoilt her so, thought Alice, but it was still so wonderful having a home from home nearby.

She killed the engine of the Triumph outside the Hall and straightened her back before putting her gloved hands up to the helmet and dragging it off to the accompaniment of an explosion of exhaled air. It was always such a relief to get the thing off but the cold hit her face sharply and made her hurry towards the sanctuary of the Hall, fishing for the front door keys in her jacket pocket. Alice put the kettle on in the kitchen before hanging up the helmet and scarf in the lobby and getting out of her thick leather jacket and chaps. She made her coffee quickly, and delicious warmth seeped into her fingers as she wrapped them gratefully around the cup. As she walked through into the drawing room to seek out the thin rays of sun she knew would be slanting in through the east window, she did a double take at the body stretched out on the mattress on the floor, fast asleep on his stomach. It was definitely a him. An attractively shaped back tanned into a honey colour was topped by a head of thick blonde hair that curled in gently at the nape of the neck. The sheet and blanket lay at his waist and she instinctively wanted to pull it up against the cold. God, he'll freeze, she thought, and just as she leant forward to do so, he turned his head towards her and opened his eyes. The eyes that looked into hers were clear and untroubled until he registered the stranger there – then they widened and he whipped the remainder of his body around, half sitting and pulling the bedclothes with him.

'Sorry, who are you?'

'Jesus!' said Alice, 'who am I? ... I live here, who the hell are you?'

'I'm sorry,' he apologised again, and then leant back on the flats of his hands, smiling at her. 'You must be Alice.' The front bit was even nicer than the back, thought Alice. She took a sip of her coffee.

'I suppose you'd be wanting some coffee. You'd be a friend of Paul's?'

He rubbed his head in childish fashion and gave her a rueful nod. 'That's yes, and yes, I would love some.' She turned back to the lobby and kitchen wondering about the flat accent – foreign for sure, probably Australian with that nice tan. She hadn't, she thought quickly, ever actually seen a body she liked very much in the flesh, outside of a magazine. All the Irish and English ones she'd glimpsed or had whole sight of had been either too podgy or too scraggly, and so terribly pale. She sang Procol Harum's words as she hunted for the new tin of coffee.

So it was that later,
As the miller told his tale,
That her face, at first just ghostly,
Turned a whiter shade of pale

Alice giggled and then scolded herself fiercely – for God's sake Alice Baker, take hold of yourself, you're ... it slipped out – beyond the pale. She couldn't stop now, and by the time she came back into the drawing room with two cups of coffee she was in danger of losing most of the contents to a minor attack of hysterics. She'd heard Paul coming downstairs and he was sitting in the old Victorian nursing chair facing Matt's makeshift bed.

'Coffee for you both, I presumed you'd want a cup, Paul?' she giggled again furiously and the cups clattered and wobbled dangerously.

'Alice, what on earth has got into you?' Paul asked as he got up and went to help her, taking the cups from her outspread arms. Alice gasped her thanks – in his dressing gown and straight from his bed, Paul's wild hair made him look like a maniac magician. He peered down into the cup.

'Did you put in one spoon or two?'

'Sorry, is it a bit weak ... a bit pale?' Alice was now just about incapable, the tears beginning to roll over the lids of her eyes and the poorly suppressed giggles escaping in torrents from a tortured chest. It was infectious and both of them couldn't help the broad smiles that grew at the sight of an Alice who had now collapsed on the settee, all pretence of control lost in whoops and gales of laughter that filled the room. Paul shook his head in quizzical bemusement as they waited for the storm to pass.

'What the hell was all that about?'

Alice finally caught her breath and stammered out. 'You wouldn't understand,' and was promptly seized by another fit of paroxysmal shrieks. By the time normality prevailed all the coffee was cold and Alice staggered off for a remake, clutching her painful chest.

'Crazy kid,' commented Paul, lighting a cigarette. He whirled it around his head. 'Mad Irish,' as if that would explain everything.

It wasn't a very auspicious beginning, but Alice had certainly caught Matt's attention.

Within the week Paul had organised Matt with digs down the road with old Mrs. Featherstone, a Beryl Cook look-alike who was pleased to let Matt have a room at the back of her cottage.

'A nice little supplement to me pension, dearie,' she'd explained, 'and I'd be happy to do you a proper breakfast, like, if you need it – can't 'ave a nice young man like you fading away, now can we?' The room was a converted outhouse with a peculiar L shape which worked out surprisingly well, with the bed in the toe of the L, and the long thin section being home to a stable door entrance, coat rack, a sink unit below a long window, and pine table and two chairs more or less at the foot of the slatted, timber framed bed. As far as work was concerned, The Ancient Shepherds turned out to be conveniently short of staff and were happy to take on Matt for the lunch and evening shift three times a week for bar and waitering duties. It wasn't much money, but it was a start, and would help with his rent while still leaving time for painting. But it was Sue who'd had the best idea of all. Matt's room was just that – a room, albeit a long thin one, with a toilet round the back, and there wasn't going to be space for much else, and certainly he couldn't paint there. 'Not unless you're doing miniatures, Matt!' Sue laughed and then turned to Paul as the idea struck her. 'Why not ask that American potter in the barn if he's got some spare room somewhere?'

The American introduced himself as Stuart Granger. 'Easy name to remember if you like the movies,' he drawled. The wooden barn was a rather tumbledown affair that lay directly between the Hall and the field that ran down to the banks of the Cam. Stuart took Paul and Matt through the side door into the one corner that housed his wheel and the rather modern looking kiln stood up on bricks at each corner. The remainder of the barn was filled with a collection of dusty farm machinery including a trailer, fertiliser spreader and an old tractor with a bird's nest in the exhaust.

'The farmer who rents this section to me is something of a philanthropist, I reckon,' said Stuart when Paul tentatively asked about any space for Matt. 'I just pay some sort of token rent and there is a loft which he doesn't use at all, so why not ask?'

'Can we look?' asked Matt keenly. He had a good feel about the place already.

'Sure thing,' answered the American in his easy-going manner, 'the steps up are on the other side – to tell you the truth, I'd be happy to have the company. It can get mighty lonely out here on your own sometimes. My family live in Cambridge you see, so I hardly get to speak to any folks from one day to the next.' The steps on the outside of the barn led up to an open landing lying within the end of the A-shaped gable. The wooden gable was recessed so the landing was under the roof, and centrally placed large double doors were flanked by what looked like mediaeval loopholes. The right hand side door of the pair opened under squeaky protest as Stuart led the way in. It took a few seconds for Matt's eyes to adapt from the sharp autumn brightness of outside. The hayloft ran half the length of the barn, some twenty-five or thirty feet away into a stygian darkness that was only slightly relieved by Stuart snapping a light switch behind them. This brought the feeblest of yellow glows from a single bare light bulb hanging from the rafters on a two-foot wire. Matt unbolted the remaining door to let more light in and they explored further.

'What do you think, Paul?' he asked. Paul was looking up into the rafters.

'I think it's just the thing, Matt, but it's going to need a bit of work. Let's see if Stuart's landlord is amenable – and if he is, we can start straightaway. Winter's coming, so it's light and heat that we've got to sort out – especially heat. Africa thins the blood, and unless your constitution has been raised on a diet of dumpling stews and plum duff, you're going to suffer – believe me, I know! When we first came back to England I nearly died. Chilblains and depression – what an unholy, fucking alliance.'

Matt looked alarmed at the prospect, the more so because Paul had used the f word, which he very rarely did. Winter was obviously something to be taken seriously here.

'That bad?' he queried.

Paul smiled. 'Only if you allow it – but don't worry, Matt, you'll acclimatise, we'll have your veins stuffed with goo as thick as that claret you brought us in no time. Anyway, a Civil Defence coat will keep out the worst of it, that and some gloves, and for Christ's sake get thick socks and decent shoes. Once you get chilblains it's like marriage – till death do us part. But we've got power here which is a good start, and Sue's got to go down to Sevenoaks this weekend. There are some bits and pieces in the storeroom at home that are going to come in very useful.'

'I suppose I'd better do something about my room at Mrs. Featherstone's as well. Get a heater or something.'

'Get Alice to keep you warm,' replied Paul with a glint in his eye, 'much more economical than a heater!' The idea alone warmed Matt, he had been thinking about her a great deal lately.

Matt was in his lodgings on the following evening when he heard a tat-tat-tat on the door. It was Alice. 'Is the famous artist in?' she asked from behind the door. 'He's-a een,' Matt replied, letting her in, 'but thees ees notta Sistine-a chapel.' He was whitewashing the pitted bare bricks and waved the big brush at the wall. 'I don't think whitewash is supposed to be for inside but it's cheap and cheerful.' He put down the brush and waved her towards a chair. 'The first place that I can call my own, you see, so I've got to make something of it – tiny as it is.'

'Tiny?' laughed Alice, 'it's minute, you'll have to go outside just to change your mind, Matt.'

The image that had floated in front of his eyes was of Gideon's cottage in Plett with its rustic uneven walls and yellowwood floors. No yellowwood in Cambridge, he thought wryly, but there were old quarry tiles on the floor, and with some elbow grease he'd hoped they would clean up nicely. Anything to make it more of a home. With his mother in some flat in Johannesburg and his father God knows where, he had no real home anywhere now, just this little scrap of a place.

Alice, being Alice, had soon scrounged a brush off Mrs. Featherstone and was attacking the wall with gusto, chatting away about what it was like up at the Vet school and the enormous amount of work they were expected to do in fourth year. They finished the walls just before nine o'clock and as Matt washed out the brushes in the sink, Alice suggested they go down to The Plough for a drink.

'And I don't suppose you've had anything to eat, have you?'

Matt admitted that he hadn't. Alice put on her quizzical look, seasoned with a pinch of long-suffering care.

'Perhaps they do pies or something, Matt, although it's getting a bit late to expect anything.' The faintly proprietary air wasn't at all unwelcome; he was getting sick of coping magnificently.

Alice and Sue had agreed that there was something about Matt that brought out the mothering instinct in both of them. That and something else, Alice said silently to herself at the time, something else that bothered her. The sight of him brought a curious tightening in her chest, and she found herself thinking about him at strange times – like yesterday in the middle of a lecture, when there was simply no trigger in what the lecturer had been droning on about. No reason at all why that picture of him should suddenly materialise in front of her. She had decided it was just idle day-dreaming and putting her chin in her hands had tried to concentrate extra hard on what old Fanshaw was saying. It hadn't worked. Okay, she had admitted to herself, she fancied him, but what was the harm in that? Well, the harm in it, as she knew very well, was the extent of it. She fancied him a lot and she knew so little about him: it was barely a week since she had come across that sleeping body early in the morning, the remembering of which, half-naked like that, made her eyes widen and brought a sharp moue to her lips. And there it was, there was the clench under her heart again! Why couldn't she think of him as half-clothed instead of half-naked? Eejit! It was like the half-empty or half-full wine glass: it depended on your point of view, and hers was making her feel very vulnerable – not a feeling she was comfortable with, not to mention the difficulty in keeping a regular train of thought when her mind kept peeling off at some stupid tangent. Damn, damn. The end of the lecture was signalled by the noise of books shutting and people moving about, and Alice made up her mind. She was going to find out more about him, if he would let her, but Alice's self-confidence would hardly entertain the idea if she didn't interest him! And anyway, she had a notion that she did.

Matt was hugely grateful to Paul and Sue – overwhelmed. They'd both pulled out all the stops for him. Paul had secured the barn loft for him at a nominal rent on the understanding that they would convert it to a studio at their own expense, and Sue had appeared back from Sevenoaks with simply loads of stuff in the Citroën, including a wood burning stove that could be fuelled all Winter from the copse behind the barn. Paul fitted the flue through the roof in the centre of the loft while Matt and Sue tacked yard after yard of calico sheeting to the rafters, completely draping the interior, lightening it, and making the studio considerably more cheerful. Two banks of neon tubes running either side of the flue further improved the illumination. Matt had initially been dismayed at the sight of the jam-packed Citroën.

'All this stuff must have cost a fortune, Paul. You must let me know how much I owe and I'll pay it back somehow, I promise.'

'Rubbish.' Paul had dismissed it, 'all this stuff was just gathering dust at home, doing absolutely nothing and ready to just rust or rot away. But if you really want to do something for us,' – he paused and smiled at Matt's pensive face, 'you can paint us a picture when you're ready. There you go,' he clapped Matt on the back, 'your first commission.'

Alice tried to see Matt on most evenings he wasn't working at the pub, and at weekends. The trouble was, she was at the Vet school all day and there was so much studying to do, just to keep up. She was astonished at the rate at which her files and textbooks kept multiplying. If she hadn't gone over to his room by eight o'clock in the evening, like now, she'd hear the sound of a handful of gravel on the window facing the garden. He was there, hands bunched in the anorak pockets and looking up at her.

'You okay then?' She nodded and answered. 'Should I let my hair down or are you coming in for coffee?' She skipped down the stairs to open the front door for him and then went to fill the kettle in the kitchen. She was at the sink when she felt Matt's arms around her waist and the gentlest of kisses on her neck below her ear. Desperate! The downy hairs on her arms prickled and a pleasant shudder passed over her like a squall on calm water. She put the kettle on and turned to his smiling face.

'Listen, Liss, there's an auction on tomorrow and lot fifty seven is a whole stack of artists' materials, including – guess what – two easels. It's all I need now, and then I'm ready to start.' Matt did a couple of exaggerated brush strokes in the air. He was obviously thrilled with the idea of starting, but not as thrilled as

Alice was with her first kiss. She caught his hand and looked up into the bright eyes.

'Just do that again for me,' she tapped her lips, 'here.'

28

He was feeling guilty. He hadn't written to his mother since he'd stayed those few days with Mannie and Ruth in London, and they certainly deserved a thank you letter as well. Thinking of the pleasant little Chelsea flat and their kindness simply reminded Matt that he should also write to Gideon. To date, he'd just sent him the two postcards, one from Florence and one from Paris – but he had made that promise – the only one that Gideon had ever extracted from him, funnily enough; and not for himself either, it was a promise to write to his mother once a week. Time for a marathon session then! Matt sat at the table at the foot of his bed, opened up the pad of airmail paper, wrote his address in the top right corner and dated it.

The first of the two air letters arrived in Gideon's Plettenberg Bay post-box a week later. The second came two days later, redirected from the flat in Rosebank. Gideon called as he hurried from the stoep into the cottage living room.

'Hope, there's a letter from Matt.'

She was sitting reading in the comfier of the two living room settees with her bare feet curled up underneath her and jumped up at the sound of his voice.

'Give, give, give!' she demanded, hand outstretched, but Gideon held it above head height.

'It's for me! You had your letter from London, remember? It's my turn.'

Hope pouted in chagrin. 'Well, you've got to read it aloud then.'

Gideon tore the envelope open and started to read the letter to her.

Hope had stayed in the Rosebank flat until the divorce had come through. To her huge relief, Jake hadn't even come to court – she had been dreading seeing him. The thought of it had been the fuel for some harrowing nightmares. His expensive Johannesburg lawyers, Finkelstein, Finn and Hartzenbaum (rather like a nice vase with two ugly handles, she'd commented to Gideon) had explained that Mr. Stevens had now relocated abroad. The use of his surname had helped enormously somehow. It put a distance between them and made her wonder about her surname too. Perhaps she could think about reverting to her maiden name. They hadn't said where he'd gone to, but Hope presumed it was London, the further the better – six thousand miles was good.

She hadn't asked for any alimony or maintenance or whatever they called it either. Her lawyers and Doris had protested vigorously, and at length, but she had seemed adamant. All she'd asked for was the furniture and paintings that had come as bequests from her parents and a lump sum that equated to the value of their Johannesburg home. Her parents' money had paid the whole deposit after all, and the beautiful garden had been largely the result of her own care, love and diligence. She wanted something for that – that much was her due. Men, especially these lawyers, didn't seem to understand gardens – didn't understand that they were living, breathing, temperamental things. Giving up her house was one thing – a wrench, but giving up her garden was the real heartache. Jake could have the proceeds from the sale of the house in Plett. He was welcome to that, and it had been sold already, thank goodness, Gideon had told her as much and that the new owners had already set about with extensive alterations. That pleased her: the less it looked like the place it was, the fewer the bad memories, and the fewer the sad ones too – she still thought about Sam and Teddy first thing every morning as she woke: but best of all, Jake would never sit on the hill glowering down on them – that would have been too much. Relocated to London – she'd whispered the words to herself over and over again, and the Plett house sold, the serpent out of Eden – thank God, she thanked Him a thousand times – fervently.

Her modest demands had been acceded to by Jake's lawyers with alacrity – in case she changed her mind no doubt, Doris commented acidly, but Hope desperately wanted the whole thing over with as soon as possible. Living without Gideon was living in limbo, but she had sworn she wouldn't go to him until the divorce was final. There was enough money from her settlement to see her through for a good while and for a small Trust for Matt when he turned twenty-one. In the meantime she could send him a little money from time to time, when she had an address to send it to of course. Even with the monthly cheque to Mrs. Marais in Knysna to try and help out a bit with those poor fatherless, dear little twins, she still could come to Gideon with her pocket and pride intact. Jake could stew in his millions for all she cared – seeing him on the other side of heaven or hell would be far too soon. The strength of her feelings quite alarmed her sometimes. Even Doris said that she was more of a Mighty than a Tittlemouse these days!

She adored the cottage – and living there with Gideon. More of a croft really, but crowded with happy memories and the time to begin nurturing a higgledy-piggledy garden that had her content for hours. Gideon had remarked that if it was true that the hours spent fishing and gardening weren't counted in a life span, they would probably both live forever. This had been what kept her going – the single thought that one day she'd be able to live here quietly within his strength. Getting here, living that life, holding him tight, tight against her, and then taking him joyfully into her, gave her a measure of fulfilment and contentment she could only have ever dreamed of before. And what they did in bed! – When she thought of it she'd just grin at him in that mischievous way, take his hand in hers and scratch his palm with her middle finger and he'd know – he'd know. This new little lewd eroticism of hers – an electric shock delight to them both.

Gideon had huge respect for her bravery through all the lonely days of the divorce and the separation. He'd so desperately wanted her to come down to him earlier, but understood what her dignity and pride had demanded, and had to admit, finally, that she had been right. By the time the Dakota carrying her had landed on the little airfield behind Robberg all the alarums and excursions (as he thought of them) were over and they had been able to get on with their new life without looking over their shoulders – free of the menace of Jake's shadow. Her happiness was paramount to him and he delighted in seeing her so content. It helped that she knew the cottage so well and he'd given her carte blanche – encouraged her to alter whatever she liked – or what she didn't like more accurately, but she'd wanted little change, just a few new curtains and linens for the beds. She teased him that it was the cottage she'd fallen in love with and not him, but in truth she loved the atmosphere just as it was, just as it had always been. There wasn't a day in Johannesburg she hadn't thought longingly about it, she told him, missing even the waxbills and fire finches that came to feed on the lawn.

The garden, however, was quite different. This was her forte, and she had cleared out about half of the pots on the stoep the minute she had arrived and stuffed them with petunias, busy Lizzies and pansies. They were now thriving in the spring warmth and Gideon was thrilled with the unaccustomed medley of colours among his old faithfuls. There was less evidence of the huge amount of work that she had put into the beds, but he had seen all the new shrubs she had planted – mostly indigenous plants, at least half a dozen varieties of proteas, leucospermums –

pincushions as they were vulgarly but accurately called – and the smaller ericas tucked in here and there amongst the rocks.

'Well, that's all my news for now.' Gideon was finishing reading Matt's three page letter aloud to Hope. 'You've got my new address; so let me know how the fishing is going. I miss it! Much love, Matt.' Gideon handed the letter across to her.

'He's done some little sketches of the cottage and the barn that's going to be his studio. Well done, Matt!' Gideon gave his knee an enthusiastic smack. 'I'll get some coffee for us,' he paused ... 'thank goodness for young Paul, I remember Matt telling me about him one evening before he left, hoping he could contact him. Thank goodness he did, what a good Samaritan that lad is.'

Hope was still re-reading the letter when Gideon came back with the coffee, picking up any snippets she may have missed first time round. She looked up at him as she took the cup.

'He's settled, Gideon, we can tell him!'

Gideon smiled – a mock scared grimace made lie of by the easy assurance evident in his eyes. His face relaxed and he nodded. 'We've got to do it sometime, darling, but who is going to write the letter? We could phone, I suppose, if we had a number ... but there is a great deal to explain, isn't there?' He pulled the pipe from his pocket – his thinking signal – and started to pack it – pondering.

'Perhaps it's too important to leave to a letter, Hope, perhaps we had better go over and see him – what do you think?'

Hope ran the options round her mind as she had done a thousand times before, but they had never discussed it together – purposely – waiting for Matt to get settled. That had been her condition and Gideon had been considerate enough, and sensitive enough, to leave the subject well alone until she decided it was time. She suspected that avoiding mines at sea had been much easier for Gideon than the ones he was encountering now. Affording to go and see Matt wasn't a problem either, because in spite of all her efforts to juggle expediency with pride and money with dignity, she had found Gideon quite untroubled by money matters. She had explained to him very early on, and quite determinedly, how she had no intention of becoming a burden to him and had then produced her savings book and little calculations and workings showing what interest would be forthcoming every month.

'I thought I could also work, Gideon – try and find a job if it would help ... I see they're offering a job at the PNA,' she had added nervously, made apprehensive by his silence and the little smile that had hovered around the edge of his mouth, but finally he had taken her hands in his and given them a gentle reassuring squeeze before answering.

'Hope, all these years I've been single before I retired, were spent working very hard, and there was nothing to spend all the money on. In fact I became very good at making money, and now I find I have more than you and I could ever spend – in several lifetimes – and my tastes haven't changed one bit. I still prefer my simple life in my simple cottage, and even the old bakkie was all I needed until now.'

Hope's letter from Matt arrived two days later, filled with the same enthusiasm and another series of little illustrative sketches. Having talked everything over at length together, they decided on a compromise – part disclosure now – by letter, and a visit for the really difficult bit. Truth by stealth, Gideon called it. And so Hope's reply was couched in the most general terms – but gave him the bare bones of it, nevertheless – that the divorce had been made final, and that she was staying with Gideon at the cottage. Let that sink in first, she thought; then we'll see – see what he makes of that. She also mentioned that the two of them were planning a trip to England in the near future and would dearly like to come up to Cambridge to see him. Would he mind? That's the critical bit, thought Hope, as she added a postscript asking him to open a bank account with Barclays and send her the branch name and account number. The added thought that Matt would never have to go on bended knee to Jake for anything pleased her considerably.

She walked up to the village post-box hand-in-hand with Gideon and slipped the envelope into its gape. The simple act gave her a queer mixture of feelings. There was apprehension, anticipation – even a tinge of fear, but predominant was a chilly comprehension that a certain train of events had been set in motion – quite irrevocably.

29

It took all of those first winter months for Matt to develop any sort of distinct style. He liked painting with acrylics best – they dried quickly, not like oils that took all that time to set. Being young meant being impatient, of course, but it was also true that his natural inclination leant towards obsessive, quick, instinctive brushwork. Luckily, Matt's eye and the natural ability that Gideon had spotted all those years ago meant that he could afford this, so there was often very little need to rework anything inside a completed painting. Instead, if he was dissatisfied with a result, he'd discard and start again from scratch and try a different approach. It was make-or-break painting and one that led to some good pictures, but more usually to monumental swearing rows with himself when brushes and paintings were hurled around the studio in intense frustration.

The artist in him understood why watercolour was the preferred medium in England – so ideal for capturing the blanched character of the countryside he saw all around him – but that wasn't how he wanted to paint. He always, always hankered after the rich colours, the strong line and the impression of energy and movement – sometimes he dreamt of dancing harlequins. Matt was fortunate in that his intrinsic talent in describing movement translated so well from pencil to brush, but the frustration came because he had so much to learn about colour – the behaviour of one colour next to another – of colours applied thickly or thinly, or overlayed, and which shades and tones appealed to his eye and characterised his subject matter best. He remained subjective – intensely so.

His first efforts were, he thought, very two-dimensional. He struggled to find the way to give depth with paint in the same way he had so successfully with shading in pen and pencil, and experimented endlessly through the Winter in his loft, using anglepoise lamps on simple still life subjects, learning how to paint the deep shadows and brilliant highlights that the lamps contrived. A long dead, thick old oak branch that he'd dragged in from the copse had been his favourite throughout and he must have painted it a dozen times. Gradually his efforts bore fruit and his best result had been achieved by brushing a glaze gently over thick impasto. The resulting contrast between light and shade areas in the fissured bark, his chiaroscuro, at last produced the impression of depth he'd been seeking. The treatment, however, remained rough and vigorous, a distinctive hallmark of all his work.

Matt thought that the exactitude so cherished by the photorealists was pure anathema. He explained as much to Alice as he stood cleaning his brushes in the loft one spring evening early in April.

'I don't know why they bother – if that amount of accuracy is what they want, why not just be a good photographer? They'd get a better job done at half the price and a third of the effort. It's beyond me.'

Alice smiled at the vehemence. It pleased her to see him so enthusiastic about his work, and with such strong opinions. She admired strength and it showed in his work too, which even now after just six months had an uncompromising feeling of power about it.

'What is art?' she asked mischievously, 'or rather, what do you think art is?'

Matt shot his answer straight back.

'Degas ... Edgar Degas had it ... he said something like,' Matt screwed his eyes shut, trying to remember, 'that's it – "one sees what one wants to see, and this falsehood constitutes art."' He nodded in agreement with the words. 'That's what I try and paint, the feeling of it, or how I feel about it, or how I see it if you want ... it's a bit selfish I suppose,' he conceded, 'and probably doesn't relate to the real world – you know, producing pictures that Joe public will want to buy, and to be honest, Liss, that's the bit I'm afraid of – I don't know yet if what I want to do is what other people are ever going to pay good money for.'

Alice digested Matt's intricate but candid answer.

'Well, I'm other people and I believe in you, and if you do that horse picture you promised me, I'll tell you soon enough if I like it!' Matt looked across at her from where he stood next to the easel and smiled.

'You and your horses!' he rattled his brushes upside down into a glass jar. 'I've done some preliminary sketches, but I've got problems,' he looked rueful, 'I've got nothing from life and they're rather inert, and another thing ... colour. I've got to see some horses in the flesh to organise my palette, to see what I can use for coat colour. Then I'll have some idea of what to block-in with.' Alice had seen him work often enough to know about blocking-in – the initial stages of a painting when Matt laid down tone in his pictures in translucent glazes. She thought of Sarah, where Fred had been stabled up on the Madingley road near the Vet school. 'I'll give Sarah a ring if you like – it's where I kept my Fred. They've got three horses up there that will make perfect subjects. Two bays and her horse, Domino, a chestnut, so you can play around with colours to your heart's content ... but no playing around with Sarah, mind – I don't want my exotic boyfriend pinched by some blonde, even if she is a friend of mind.' Matt laughed, there was precious little chance of anyone even catching his eye when Alice was around. He told her so and the compliment bought a contented smile.

'Tell me when are your mother and her fancy man arriving in Cambridge.'

Matt winced at the description of Gideon as a 'fancy man' – that's the very last thing he was. It nevertheless reminded him that he was going to find it strange seeing them together, even if the relationship was platonic – and that, he realised, wasn't likely. This was something he had in common with all other men: the thought of someone else sleeping with his mother was faintly repugnant, even if it was Gideon. He loved them both, but in separate pigeonholes in his mind, not together, and the thought of them being together was going to take a little getting used to. He explained this to Alice, apologising for the fuzzy logic as he did so.

'Don't fass yourself,' she replied, 'nobody believes the Queen of England gets wind either – she's probably just as grateful for a decent fart to ease it as the rest of us: now when are they coming up?'

Matt laughed at the irreverent remark and then ran his fingers through his blonde hair, thinking back to his mother's letter. 'The twenty-first – that's two weeks from today as far as I remember.' Alice pulled up the blanket on the old settee, tucking it in around her. In spite of the wood stove it was chilly, Spring still a whore's promise of summer. Matt fed another log into the stove and stirred the coals to wake them up. He loved his studio with its view over the paddock onto the river – and the place had a more comfortable lived-in look now, with paintings stacked against the walls and all the general paraphernalia of art scattered around. He was happier still when Alice was there, often as not as she was now, tucked up on the settee hard by the stove. If they weren't nattering, she'd be reading, with her nose buried in a novel or one of her textbooks, but it was really her presence that gave him this wonderful contentment. Difficult to explain, but exactly what he wanted.

'Do you know how long they'll be here for?' asked Alice.

'Just ten days or so, I gather,' Matt answered. 'They haven't asked me to arrange accommodation so I presume that's all being done for them by the travel agent.' He paused. 'Perhaps Paul wouldn't mind showing them around Cambridge – being in Architecture makes him the ideal candidate for the job. I'm sure I can bribe him with the offer of a slap-up meal.'

Alice stopped him with a copper's hand gesture.

'Better make it Paul and Sue, you know how she loves her food, Matt.'

The day arrived. Gideon had phoned from London the day before saying they would be coming up to Cambridge in a hire car, were booked into the Blue Boar and how about dinner?

'Can I bring Alice?' Matt had asked, hoping for some moral support.

'Your girlfriend – of course – see you in the foyer at about seven?'

Matt wasn't sure how he would feel about everything so he gripped Alice's hand a little more firmly than usual as they crossed the hotel threshold at seven on the dot.

'Gideon enjoys punctuality,' – the politeness of princes he was about to say when he spotted Gideon's silver mane and beard at the reception desk. Bringing Alice had been a very good idea indeed, and she, knowing about Matt's misgivings, went out of her way to smooth everyone's path. It wasn't difficult as Gideon and Hope were much taken with the slim girl's sparkling personality. Matt was even faintly jealous of the attention they gave her, but it did give him a much needed breather as onlooker. Gideon was a revelation in his formal tie and blazer, his beard and hair neatly barbered to perfection, lending an air of distinction he could hardly credit. It was difficult to imagine this was the same 'old man' he'd tramped around Robberg with year after year. He saw that they often held hands, which was something he'd never seen her do with his father in all the years, and it warmed him greatly, as did the brimming looks they gave one another from time to time – quick looks that were somehow conspiratorial in a delightful, simple way. All his doubts disappeared and he began to relax and join in the animated conversation with enthusiasm. His mother, he realised, looked stunning in what even he could recognise as a couturier cocktail dress, and she was obviously happy – the small furrow of worry that habitually sat between her eyes had gone. He was astounded, and so happy for them both. It made him happy just looking at them.

Alice was telling them about the long vac in June and their plans to spend it with her family in Bansha.

'It's not the Riviera, but my family are sick and tired of hearing about my foreign painter boyfriend. They want to see the apparition for themselves, and my mother says all artists are starving so she's dying to get the chance to fatten him up! It's a great advantage he's not English, by the way, they were terrified I'd go off with some posh bloke and never go back to Ireland. This way they've got no idea of what's coming, so I've got the advantage for once!' They laughed together in as relaxed an atmosphere as Matt could ever remember in his family – his new family, he corrected himself. The distinctly better one. He couldn't wait for Paul and Sue to meet them. He had something to be proud of after all.

'You never told me your mother was such a looker, Matt. She's bloody beautiful – and Gideon is a real cracker!' Matt basked for a second before answering.

'Quite honestly, I've never seen my mother so happy in my entire life – it's great!' If his Aunt Edith had seen the first mask Matt wore, so Alice was the first to see the opposite – the reverse, the shedding of one. A missing part of a jigsaw had been found, and it effected a strange transformation in her Matt's life, bolstering his self-assurance and, she suspected, his sense of self-worth, something that would affect their relationship quite radically in the weeks ahead. For the moment, however, they could all enjoy having Hope and Gideon as tourists in their city. Sue had invited them all for dinner at the Hall on the following evening and Paul had been coerced without much difficulty for 'the history bit' as Matt put it. Paul conducted Gideon, Hope and Matt on a tour around the colleges with that special emphasis on Jesus, knowing as he did, practically when every stone and brick had been laid. A pub lunch at the Pickerel opposite Magdalene and, for dessert, an expert punt round the Backs which was a welcome opportunity to rest aching feet and feast eyes on the beautiful lawns and daffodils waving gently from the river bank. Alice had arranged to meet them for an evening drink at The Plough in Fen Ditton before dinner.

'It's much the same as any other pub, Gideon,' Paul had commented as they walked in, 'just that the lavatory graffiti here is more likely to be in Latin or Greek ... or Urdu.'

Sue's dinner was a collaborative affair. She cooked her second roast of the year whilst Alice was responsible for the lemon meringue dessert, which, due to time constraints and self-confessed rank cowardice, had come ready-made from Matt's landlady, Mrs. Featherstone. The Hall dining table looked quite spectacular with an antique lace embroidered sheet as table-cloth, candles in bottles in two family groups, (two short, one taller and one tallest in each group) and Paul's eclectic collection of polished antique glasses catching and reflecting the flickering ivory yellow flames at each place setting. Sue had gathered narcissi and daffodils into two vases at either end of the table, and matched the colours with barber pole paper serviettes curled onto side plates and tied with single strands of soft straw. Everyone had dressed up, and Hope looked over to the window seat where the three men stood chatting and laughing at something Matt was saying. Gideon, dapper and distinguished in his dinner jacket; Paul, quite beautiful she thought, in a pitch-black frock coat with kaleidoscopic waistcoat and huge, red velvet bow tie, and then Matt. Her eyes lingered fondly on her son. His blonde hair was now long enough to be caught in a neat ponytail and secured with an ethnic bead band at the nape of his neck. A hint of the African sun remained in his honeyed colouring looking quite astonishingly healthy against the pure white of a rough linen shirt. She'd caught his initial reticence last night before dinner at the Blue Boar, but fleeting, and soon lost as they'd all been in Alice's stories about her Irish family. What a delightful girl she was, just so bright and bubbly and the two of them so well matched. She had seen too many unequal relationships – unequal in love that is, to ever believe that they worked. This one might.

'Did you see any of Matt's paintings today, Mrs. Stevens?' Alice was asking.

'No, we've been sightseeing all of today,' Hope replied, 'we're coming over tomorrow morning again to look at the studio and then Paul says we should go racing in Newmarket – you're coming, I believe?'

Alice nodded enthusiastically, the light flaring in her green eyes, 'I've had enough of lectures stuffing my brain this week, and I haven't been racing since the Curragh, oh ages ago. It'll be a great craic – I can't wait.' Hope remembered something from Matt's letters. 'Matt says you're a great horsewoman; is that what you're going to specialise in when you're qualified?'

Alice turned quickly to see that the men were out of earshot.

'To tell the truth Mrs. Stevens, it's Matt I want to specialise in when I qualify!'

She grabbed Hope's arm quickly with a gleeful laugh. 'Oh Mrs. Stevens, I think he's wonderful, and I suppose you must think I'm a brazen hussy – that's what they call them in books isn't it? – But I'm not at all, I promise. We're just made for each other you see, even if he's not as sure of it now as he will be.'

Alice looked at Hope with a smile and imploring eyes, 'you're not going to tell him what I said now are you Mrs. Stevens ... pretty please!' Hope just burst out laughing at the impudence but recognised also a shattering undoubted sincerity. She could hardly utter her next words for the giggles that kept tripping out.

'No, I won't ... I promise.' She covered her smiling mouth with a hand as they both turned to look at Matt.

30

The weather for Newmarket promised to be good. Matt was listening to the news and weather report on the radio when he heard the sound of their car crunching on the gravel outside. His eyes did a flick around to check that everything in the studio was neat and tidy. For the umpteenth time. He hurried out and down the steps on the side of the barn, still firmly in the grip of a thousand insecurities about his painting. What if they didn't like what they saw, or worse, were diplomatically polite about it? The only completed painting was the one for Paul and Sue – an interior study of the drawing room at the Hall in the early morning with the light streaming in through the east window. He'd painted both of them: Paul in his red moiré silk dressing gown, his electric hair wild, sat engrossed in the morning paper; the smoke from his cigarette a lazy blue wisp climbing into slanted sunbeams. And Sue, caught putting a tray with two steaming cups of coffee down on the table leaning and looking over towards what Paul was reading. There was something of the Degas ballerina in her right foot – planted, but angled and the left stretched away, the toe just touching on the floorboards. His other paintings were either works in progress or studies he'd done during the winter as he'd experimented with colour, form and dimension. Forgetting about the sketches in his letters, Matt thought that his mother had never seen any of his work – just his childhood scribbles, and that the last thing that Gideon had seen was his pencil work from Pietermaritzburg when he was with Kit. All that seemed light years away now.

They said nothing at all, apart from the occasional hm and hmm as he explained the sequence of paintings: first the old oak branch painted from every conceivable angle, stage-lit with his lamps.

Then the cartoons for Paul and Sue's picture, and finally the completed painting. At least they know them both, he thought as they looked at it – and the room too, since last night anyway. He started to move over to show them the preliminaries he'd done up at the stables with Sarah's horses, all the work with shapes and colours for Alice's promised painting, but they stopped him, engrossed in Paul and Sue's picture. It was a big painting, four foot by three and a half, unframed, and sitting on one of the easels. Gideon leant forward, his elbow cocked, a finger tracing in the air over part of the background.

'Look at the masonry frieze around the inglenook, wonderfully well done, and the two of them; you've got them to a tee. It's a lovely moment you've caught. Have they seen it?'

'No, they haven't,' answered Matt, 'they gave me a commission to pay them back for all the stuff they brought up from Sevenoaks for the studio – but it's their wedding anniversary in July so this is going to be a present for them. I'll do their commission some other time when the idea for it arrives. The idea for this one came when I saw them, exactly like that, one Sunday morning, and I knew straightaway it was what I wanted to paint.'

Gideon turned to him. 'Your painting is so very different to your drawing, Matt. The drawings you showed me in Plett were also very animate – but this!' He drew himself up, put hands on hips and shook his head, 'this is totally different: so powerful a treatment and so private a moment.' Matt glowed inside. This was the Gideon he knew, seeing straight through the painting – right down to the essence of what his art meant to him.

There was a holler outside from the bottom of the stairs. Paul, Sue and Alice – ready for Newmarket. The youngsters all climbed into Paul's Citroën and set off with Gideon and Hope following in their blue Ford hire car. Their approach to Newmarket town was signalled by glimpses of paddocks behind tall trees lining a long, very straight road. They had been discussing what they had seen in the studio and Gideon was commenting. 'Well, you won't have too many worries about Matt in the future, will you, darling? He won't even have to settle down with a redhead veterinarian for support if he chooses not to (Hope had told him about Alice's startling declaration). The talent is so obvious and his style is unique. I've certainly never seen anything like it, and I've collected quite a few paintings in my time.' Hope was reassured by Gideon's informed enthusiasm. She had loved the painting he'd shown them – she thought it was brilliant, but realised she wasn't in any way knowledgeable enough to pronounce on his abilities. And of course she was hugely biased – what mother didn't think her son wonderful.

'I don't mind if he does decide to settle down with Alice, I've decided Gideon. You must admit she's right for him – her whole pizzaz – everything about her … I just have a good feeling about those two.'

Gideon stroked his beard and smiled to himself – matchmaking must be something women were born to, he thought, and followed the Citroën going left at the roundabout. There were police signs out now and much more traffic, so the racecourse would be nearby.

'If Alice can make our Matt just half as happy as you make me, Hope, then he'll wallow in contentment forever.' Hope's face shone at the compliment and she rubbed his forearm affectionately. But what he said, sentimental as it was, was nevertheless quite true. Doris had remarked on it when they'd stayed overnight in Johannesburg en route to London. Hope had been dying to confide in someone about her newfound happiness – and the good sex – God it was fantastic. Now she really knew the meaning of the word reborn, it was a rebirth, and the new confidence she had in her body was so damn exciting. As she told

Doris she was mildly shocked at her own words, describing how they had done it in all sorts of unlikely places and then blushed, giggled and stammered a little as she raced on, explaining the unlikely appetite for erotica that she had developed.

'It's as if my body and mind are de-determined to make up for lost time Doris – and there's e-even s-some sort of race between the two of them to see how they can outdo each other!' Doris had shrieked with delight. 'You lucky fish, Hope, I'm so jealous! Clarence is strictly mizz pozziz – good old missionary position. He only does me doggy if he's had a Valium and his back's not bothering him!'

Gideon and Clarence were having a studious whisky together in the lounge when they heard the gales of laughter coming in from the lawn. Clarence had snorted. 'Thick as thieves those two, wonder what on earth they're finding so funny.'

'Have you decided when you're going to tell him?'

Gideon asked the question as they swung into a parking space beside a gleaming Jaguar. As he yanked up the brake, Gideon cast a jaundiced eye at the kitsch silver horse mounted on the bonnet next door – affectation was high on his list of cardinal sins. Probably have a personalised bloody number plate too, he muttered to himself and he scooted around to open Hope's door for her. She swung her legs out prettily, the perk for being a gent.

Hope stood and took Gideon's arm, 'Tomorrow,' she announced, 'I'll tell him tomorrow morning. If you pack the bags at the hotel, I'll take the car out to Fen Ditton.'

'Are you sure you'll be okay?' Gideon asked, a tinge of concern in his voice.

'It's high time he knew, my darling,' she answered, 'high time.'

The racing was the craic Alice had predicted, but no one saw anything of Matt for the whole afternoon. He joined them after the sixth race and Alice could see he was all-agog about something.

'This place is a gold mine – too fantastic. I've got at least three paintings in my head already. He dragged the little sketchbook from his jacket pocket. 'Look!' There were about a dozen little pencil sketches; horses, jockeys, tic-tac men, bookies, punters, grooms, grandstands – a wealth of material – something had plainly touched a chord.

'Did anyone win anything?' he asked as Alice showed the little vignettes to Hope.

'Yes,' answered Alice with a grin, 'I betted on all the sound principles of form and conformation and your Mum betted on horses with nice sounding names and lucky numbers – and guess who won!' There was a chorus of laughter.

Hope returned the sketchbook to Matt in the car park.

'Matt,' she said, taking him aside, 'darling, I know it's Sunday tomorrow, but can I come out early and discuss something with you? – It's important.' Her face gave nothing away.

'Sure, Mum,' he answered, 'can I have a clue? Nothing too awful, I hope.'

Matt's antennae were twitching.

'No, it'll be fine,' said Hope with a lot more conviction than she felt.

'About nine o'clock okay, after breakfast?' They left Matt, sketchbook in hand, looking quizzically at the retreating back end of the car. 'What's up?' Alice asked as she came over and took his hand.

'I don't quite know,' he answered slowly, 'Mum has something she wants to discuss with me evidently – something important she says, but I can't think what. Anyway, she didn't seem unhappy about it, so whatever it is, it can't be too radical.' No cigar, Matt, no cigar.

He thought little more about it as all four of them got into a hectic darts match that evening at The Ancient Shepherds. They'd drunk enough to get really silly on the walk back home, waltzing down the lane in exaggerated one, two-threes, finally stumbling happily into the Hall where Paul went looking for a bottle of port that had come as a gift from his father and which was probably by now 'getting very lonesome' as he put it. Sue made coffee and by the time a second pot and the port bottle were empty it was after one o'clock.

Matt's alarm clock went off at eight. The port and knowing it was Sunday made it difficult getting out of bed. The table at the end of his bed worked just as well as the mantelpiece at Plett for his alarm clock. Hope arrived alone in the car just before nine and suggested a walk down to the river; she thought it would be easier sideways on. There was some activity in the barn, so Matt made a little detour to introduce Stuart to his mother. The American was sitting at his wheel, moulding one of his delicate oriental style bowls, and took pride in showing them a set that had come out of the kiln on the previous day. Hope made noises to show her approval but her mind was elsewhere, spinning like that pottery wheel in fact, intent on what she was going to say. She had a preamble, and as they took their slow steps forward, picking their way through the paddock towards the water, she started her story – about what had happened in 1944, the year before he was born. At least she'd had some practice, telling Gideon first and then Doris later in Johannesburg and she'd had a great deal of time to think about what she was going to say and how, but that didn't make things any easier. This was so important. Her son, walking loose-limbed beside her, was silent, just listening and occasionally pulling up long pieces of grass, turning them, and absent-mindedly chewing at the soft green-white stalks.

'So you see, darling, this isn't the first time Gideon and I have been together – we had an affair – a very intense affair, just before your father came back from the war – from Italy.' Hope stopped and turned to look at her son, 'and that's the thing, Matt, that's the real problem, your Dad isn't really your Dad – I was already pregnant when your father returned. Gideon is your real father.' Matt looked as if he'd been pole-axed. The good jaw that he had hung half open with the stalk of grass hanging ridiculously loose. What he'd just heard was just too great for any sort of organised response – he couldn't take it in – all he could vaguely see was his mother's terribly concerned face looking at him, biting her lip, waiting for a response that he couldn't give. The first conscious feeling he would remember later was that it felt as though everyone else had been to a party that he'd never been invited to. His mother was pressing something into his hand.

'It's a letter from Gideon, I don't know what's in it exactly, but we're going up to Cromer on the Norfolk coast today for a week, to give you time to think it all through. I'll give you a ring on Paul's number at the Hall next Sunday morning … to see if you want to see us.' Hope's eyes filled with tears. 'Just remember, whatever happens, I love you, my baby.' She took his forearm and reaching up, kissed him gently on the cheek, turned and walked away towards the Hall. Matt put a nerveless hand up to where she'd kissed his cheek. She hadn't called him that for years.

31

While Matt sat on the riverbank reading the letter from Gideon, the author was in the foyer of the Blue Boar waiting for Hope. He'd paid the bill and packed and the suitcases were now neatly stacked in reception. Their route to Cromer on the North Norfolk coast would take them through Newmarket, down an almost empty and gusty High Street. There was just one old man in a cloth cap and brown coat scurrying along, his thin frame bent forward against the wind.

It was Harry. Jake had been well pleased with his Newmarket mole – as pleased as Harry was with his new found source of income. As soon as Harry was settled in his modest digs off the High Street, he set about resurrecting his old racing contacts and these had in turn led to new ones, including some in the two yards that were of particular interest. There had been a few questions about his new role as a betting man – where did he get the money from and so on – but he bet small, drank sparingly and was soon accepted and absorbed into the fabric of the busy racing world. His weekly telephoned reports to Jake sitting in his London home were a mixture of anecdote, gossip and fact – and included reports on any races his two-year-olds had run – like yesterday, delivered in his rough, smoker's voice.

'Ee's a really good 'orse, Guv'ner – 'is pilot gives 'im a shake up onner furlong marker, an inna cupla strides ee's clear. Wins as easy as ee likes … your filly Deneuve wiv Armstrong gotta abscess in 'er near fore. Vet sez ee's finking of an X-ray coz it's near – wotzee call it – the pe'al bone – the bone in 'er 'oof. Wants watchin' Guv'ner, like me ole Guv'ner sez, no foot – no 'orse … An' your filly, wiv Bailey, Guv'ner, the grey, you can get rid of 'er, coz 'er lad sez she's bloody lazy an' gutless. Like me firs'

274

missis, all looks an' no bottle. Not gonna win no races fer ya, is she?'

Jake had to concentrate particularly hard to decipher the London patter intermixed with the racing jargon. He replaced the receiver when Harry had finished his report and looked for Philip Mitchell's telephone number in his directory. The young partner in the Newmarket veterinary practice, the one he knew looked after Bailey and Armstrong's yards, had only protested briefly when Jake had asked him some weeks ago for his home telephone number.

Mitchell's wife answered the phone and Jake, never one for pleasantries, barked at her, 'Stevens here, tell your husband I'd like to speak to him, would you?' He heard the phone clatter down on a table, the diminishing footsteps, a faint call, and then approaching heavier ones. The phone was picked up.

'What's this with my filly, Deneuve, Mitchell?' Jake demanded, impatient for a response, drumming his fingers as he waited. There was a moment's silence as the vet constructed a reply with his disorganised, off-duty weekend mind.

'I don't know if Mr. Armstrong has spoken to you about the abscess in her foot, Mr. Stevens, but it's near the pedal bone, and I was thinking, perhaps we should take an X-ray in the next few days.'

'Do it tomorrow, Mitchell' came Jake's reply, 'without fail, and ring me with the results immediately.'

The purring noise in the vet's ear signalled disconnection. Mitchell's tubby face was suffused with crimson. He was livid and bawled into the mouthpiece, 'I'm not your fucking skivvy, you know!' The phone was banged down violently and the furious vet determined to do the job first thing in the morning – take as many X-ray views he could think of, and charge the absolute maximum, plus some. 'That'll teach the bastard!' he muttered, knowing full well that it wouldn't, and stomped off to complain about it to his wife.

It was just as well for him that Philip Mitchell was as thorough as he could be with the X-rays, and that he syringed out and forced a radio opaque material into the mouth of the abscess. It showed the full extent of the problem, and with the faint shadowing on the pedal bone around it visible on the X-rays, confirmed an osteomyelitis – an infection in the bone. He telephoned Jake to report, and ask permission for an operation under general anaesthesia. Horses sometimes died under anaesthesia, and he wanted to know if Deneuve was insured – she was not; and anyway, as Jake curtly informed him, if there was any insuring to be done, then the practice could do it.

Jake was now rather knowledgeable about matters veterinary in racehorses. The knowledge had been gleaned by the laborious reading of hundreds of back copies of the Equine Veterinary Journal, Adams' Lameness in Horses, and the American text and reference book, Equine Medicine and Surgery. This new grasp of veterinary medicine and the snippets gleaned from Harry's eyes and ears weren't the only insights Jake had into his precious two-year-olds. Every ten days, blood was drawn from each horse and sent to the laboratory for what was called a general equine profile. This included all red and white cell parameters and estimations of the levels of enzymes originating in liver, kidney, heart and muscle. This served as an early warning system for the detection of disease and also helped in determining, say after a viral infection, when horses could safely be returned to work. Jake also had all his youngsters' knees X-rayed before they started work – to check if the growth points had closed. He knew all about what could happen for want of a nail.

Deneuve's foot abscess was a real setback. The operation went without a hitch but it involved curetting out the diseased bone and then flushing and packing with antibiotics. Mitchell gave a good prognosis: he expected her to make a full recovery, but the sole would have to grow back, and it would grow only at the rate of half an inch every fortnight. That meant she'd be out of work for months, and she'd had such a brilliant start, making her debut in a four furlong Sandown maiden in April. It was an educational outing and she had started at 7 to 1 with the jockey being told not to touch her. She'd started slowly and then run on strongly into second place, a good enough showing for her to be made favourite for her next two races and she won both, easing up at the finish. Both the two-year-olds in Lambourn were mediocre and together with the lazy grey in Bailey's yard, would be sold – offloaded. The black colt in Armstrong's yard however – Peppermint – was a class act, the one Harry had reported on so enthusiastically, and had shown talent from the word go. In spite of running green in his first race at Epsom, he'd run third – only a head and a neck away from the best. Now he'd won as he liked, and Jake had also a glowing report from the trainer who rated him highly saying he was lightning-quick and - Jake just loved the description – simply thrived on work. In fact, Armstrong had a super-reliable old handicapper to test his two-year-olds at home and Peppermint had thrashed him, giving plenty away in weight, which amounted to an astonishing amount in weight for age.

The last of Jake's horses was the bright bay colt in Bailey's yard. Carlo looked the typical sturdy sprinter, with a washerwoman's backside and short cannon bones that (according to the trainer) were simply made for galloping. He'd roared out of the stalls on his first outing and left the others for dead. Bailey hadn't any line on the form yet, but the time was good, and he assured Jake he could tweak him for even more pace with 'a few more sweats' as he put it. All in all, Jake was well satisfied with his start and looked forward to the forthcoming races with impatient anticipation, to what Admiral Rous had called 'the glorious uncertainty of the Turf.'

32

'Well, Coward wasn't being very accurate about Norfolk, was he?' Gideon was casting a lazy eye over the gently undulating countryside surrounding the little car as they coasted towards Norwich. 'What do you mean?' asked Hope as she popped a mint into her mouth and turned a quizzical head towards him.

'Well, isn't that what Noel Coward said?' Gideon mimicked the pernickety, precise tones of the man, '"flat – very flat, Norfolk", or something like that – it was supposed to be a monumental put-down.'

Gideon and Hope's journey towards their ultimate destination – Cromer, on the north-east Norfolk coast – had taken them on through Newmarket and Thetford Forest and thence towards Norwich where they had decided they would spend the day as tourists once again. The guidebook informed that the city sat solidly astride the river Wensum at the northern border of the Broads and boasted a fine Norman Cathedral capped by a magnificent soaring spire. To one side, and on a hill, they'd later see the brutish mass of an immense castle glowering down in constant disapproval at the locals – who never look up as they walk, and the tourists – who always do. Gideon parked the blue Ford, and after a pub lunch overlooking the river, took one of the pleasure-boat cruises from the jetty below onto the Broads, a waterway maze of mere, marsh and river and much-favoured holiday and weekend haunt for the English. Hope knew, that as a race, the English loved 'messing around in boats', but she was astounded at the extent of it. Every conceivable size of yacht, motorboat and barge pottered up and down on the water, and dotted here and there were fishermen on the banks, intent on the water; and all, studiously minding their own business. Hope thought that they looked as they were intentionally rather solitary, but in Gideon – and her son – she felt that she knew two dyed-in-the-wool fishermen rather well, and that she understood that insular feeling quite a bit. She pointed at one of the fishermen briefly as their boat passed by, (giving him what she thought was probably an annoying amount of wake) 'Gideon, did you ever fish when you were in England?'

'A little, a long time ago,' answered Gideon, taking the pipe from his mouth and scratching his beard with the stem 'but I've been spoilt at home, darling, I'm afraid I couldn't come back to sit-on-your-arse fishing like these chaps are doing, not if you paid me. I've just got to be on the rocks. God, look at that!' He pointed with the pipe towards a yacht, which appeared to be sailing quite briskly through a sea of corn, two fields away. 'Quite extraordinary! I suppose it's because the watercourse meanders so here.'

There were quaint little windmills here and there and the afternoon jaunt in warmer than usual spring sunshine induced a pleasant lethargy. They lapsed into a companiable silence, just sitting holding hands and watching water, time and the greener than green countryside slowly slipping by.

Leaving the city behind them in the rear view mirror, it was a short trip north-east to the little market town of Aylsham where they booked into a bed and breakfast tucked up behind the old town water-pump, an ornate curiosity plonked down right on the middle of a T-junction and sporting its own diminutive, thatched roof. Hope had looked up Blickling Hall in her guidebook and they had decided they'd make a little detour. It had a big write-up – even provided loos for wheelchair people, so they thought it probably quite a grand place, certainly worth a visit, and conveniently only a few miles outside Aylsham. The Spring weather continued its beneficent mood and the following sunny morning found them walking down between two vast yew hedges flanking the gravelled entrance to the weathered, soaring red brick of Blickling. The gardens and huge lake at the back of the Hall were quite magnificent to Hope's eyes but by the time they had taken in both house and grounds, her feet were throbbing. 'Imagine that,' she said to Gideon as they sat for coffee, 'Ann Boleyn once lived here. It reminds me of Mrs. Arkwright, my History teacher at school teaching us about Henry VIII's wives. Divorced, beheaded, died, divorced beheaded, survived.' Hope ticked them off on her fingers as she recited the couplet. She turned to Gideon, 'and what will my fate be, my liege?' Gideon chortled and took her hand. 'Well, we'll just have to see what sort of wife you make.' He caught her eye, serious now 'but don't worry Hope, you're a survivor, definitely a survivor.'

Hope thought of Matt in the same instant. Gideon could see the thought strike across her eyes as just the faintest glimpse of a shadow. Matt wasn't ever far from their thoughts and he was the reason they were 'doing' so much, to stay busy and to keep their minds off that phone call at the end of the week.

'Hope, you're thinking about him, aren't you?' She nodded silently and looked away as a small crush of apprehension rose up into her chest. It was a great deal to ask her son to understand, and now, more than any other time in his life, she needed that sensitivity that had so often worked against him, for once to work for him. But she also knew it was still just one big lottery as to how he would eventually work things out in his mind. She dreaded any antagonism, although she knew that some measure of it was a distinct possibility, perhaps even her due – after all, it was a huge burden to lay on him, and just straight out of the blue like that too.

'It'll be fine, Hope,' Gideon reassured her as he saw the mill of her mind at work, stirring her fears, 'I know the boy, he'll work it through, and the letter I wrote him will help, I'm sure of it.'

From Aylsham it was only a hop and a skip to Cromer – an archetypal seaside town with a pier and hotels facing a stony beach washed by diminutive waves. They walked the elevated promenade looking out over the Channel, seeing just the odd ship move across their line of sight. It was so very different from Plett, thought Hope, but so like the seaside postcards and English book illustrations of her youth. She wondered aloud if they were all really so alike, the Bournemouths and the Brightons that she had read about so often. 'I don't know, to tell the truth,' answered Gideon, 'I haven't been, but I do know that Churchill and his family used to holiday here in Cromer, so there must be some attractions somewhere here. What's certainly true is that this' – he waved at the sea, 'doesn't hold a candle to the West Country. The coastline round Devon that I saw during the war was unbelievably beautiful – a sort of a pirate's paradise with coves, cliffs and secret sands – and I do mean sands, not these cobblestones! Perhaps there are better spots further around the coast.'

And there were. The next morning they travelled up and round the coast, past Sherringham and into Overstrand, where low lying land and sand beaches encourage vast flourishing acreages of sedges and meadow plants. Past Stiffkey, where they found an uncommon little shop specialising in the most unusual old lamps at the most astonishing new prices, and finally into Blakeney, dribbling down through tiny uneven streets and onto a foreshore-cum-jetty where the main occupation appeared to be in the hands of scores of children catching crabs with pieces of bacon. It was all very quaint, somewhat isolated, quiet and very much to their liking. It didn't take long to find an old pub called The Anchor nearby that offered a few rooms for board, and to eat, a local speciality – huge, shiny, black Brancaster mussels, served in a creamy white sauce brimming with garlic. They walked the beaches covering mile after mile of seashore, striding on sands that covered the ancient, arcane timbers of Woodhenge, a circle of prehistoric stakes that the tides would only uncover some twenty years later to baffle the professors and pundits alike.

Unusually for people on holiday, they both lost weight, became fitter and thrived on the regime of exercise, fresh air and good food. Over the remainder of the week they learned to worry less and made love more. It became a special time, with reality held at arm's length for a while, a spell only broken when the landlord asked Gideon after dinner on the Saturday evening if they would be staying on or not.

'I'll have an answer for you tomorrow,' he answered, and there it was suddenly. When the landlord had gone, Hope gave Gideon a quick, small smile.

'What is it that people say, darling? Reality bites ... I think we are about to find out.'

33

The Blue Boar
Cambridge

Sunday

Dearest Matt,

By the time you read this, your mother will have told you the news. Astonishing, isn't it? It even feels quite extraordinary for me to write the words down for the first time, but the hard fact remains, you are my son and you have been since you were born, and you will be for all your and my tomorrows. I will be your children's grandfather and your children's children's great grandfather no matter what. The reality is immutable. You cannot change it, your mother cannot change it, and neither can I – nor would I wish to.

How we view the facts – our perceptions – is quite another matter. I had no idea of the truth until your mother told me at the Fountains shack just a few months ago, and from that point of view, we have both been in the same blind boat for all these years. It might well beg the question of why the deception? But you must try and put yourself in your mother's shoes. It's quite true that your mother and I had an affair towards the end of the war, and some might say that that was quite wrong, but I cannot agree. It wasn't ever wrong for me: you see your mother has been the great love of my life. I met her and instantly fell hopelessly in love. When your 'father' came back from the war in Italy some months later, your mother and I had a terrible time. And society was so different then – divorce was almost unheard of, and a deep disgrace. Most important of all were your two brothers, both still very young, and your mother and I both decided that they had done nothing to deserve a broken family. If you ever think that this deception has all been a waste of years, then reflect on what it has meant to your brothers, or half brothers I suppose. They have been wrenched away cruelly I know, but all their childhood and young adult lives were played out with the shelter of a secure family, and that is worth a great deal – in my book anyway.

Perhaps if your existence on this earth was the result of a 'fling' – a wartime one off, then you may have felt differently about it – but it wasn't. Your mother has always been everything to me because, as you know, I never married. Yes, I had girlfriends after your mother and I decided not to pursue things, but all were very pale imitations of the real thing. I never let on to her the real impact of her just being on this earth – and what it meant to me. More than anything in this world, I want to marry your mother. It would legitimise you of course, but that's just red tape as far as I am concerned. What it would do would be to make each and every dream of mine come true and bind us all into what we should be, and what I have always wanted – a family.

It's also true that you and I have always had a wonderful relationship, and it's largely been due to your mother's efforts in placing us near that we have drawn close. It's been a terrible, bittersweet pain for her all these years, she tells me, but it's been something very special to me, and I suspect to you. Most parents have children that, with luck, later become friends. With us it's just the other way around.

This letter is really to tell you how I feel and isn't designed to preach or to tell you how you should feel. That's going to be a matter for you to work through and work out. Just remember that whatever your mother has done has been selflessly done – there has been little in it for her all these years. She desperately needs a break and a chance at some happiness. I will do my absolute level best to make that happen, but in some part anyway, it will also depend on how you view things and whether you are going to apportion blame to her. Whether you like it or not you have always been her favourite child, and what you think now that the truth is out, will matter to her dreadfully. I trust you, and in this one great thing I must trust you utterly. We love you, and with this letter I am putting all our futures in your hands.

I am excessively proud to sign myself as

Your Dad

Matt must have read the letter ten times, and least half of those ten times were on the same river bank where his mother had left him open-mouthed and speechless. Alice had eventually come looking for him after Stuart mentioned that he'd seen the two of them in the studio before they went down to the river. She'd heard the blue Escort drive away but there was no sign of her Matt and she knew anyway, intuitively, that something was afoot.

She spied his form sitting on the bank reading what appeared to be some letter or document.

'Not worth chucking yourself into the river for, I hope?' she called as she neared the intent figure. He turned around as if waking from a dream.

'Liss, you won't believe this … it's … it's unbelievable … bloody unbelievable! My Dad's not my Dad, Gideon's my Dad!' He gazed out into the river seeing nothing at all. 'Here,' he offered the letter which Alice took rather tentatively and then started to read. She read it through twice. 'Jesus! You certainly are an interesting fellow, Matt, and your family twice so! – Better than a novel – God what a bombshell! I'm amazed, but it's fantastically good news' she paused momentarily 'isn't it?' When Matt didn't answer she went on, 'well, your ex-father now being well and truly ex isn't such a great loss then is it – surely?' Matt just shook his head violently in negation.

'That's not the point, is it, Liss? The point is I've tried God knows how hard to please my father all of my life, up until recently that is, and to absolutely no effect, and now I discover I've been busting my gut to please somebody who, hey man, is nothing more than a bloody unpleasant stranger. What a bloody waste!' He let out a frustrated roar and buried his head in his hands.

'Matt, you're surely not going to blame your Mother for this, are you?'

Alice looked across at him with concern wrinkling her brow.

'Oh, God no,' he lifted his head and replied, 'I don't blame her at all, not at all, I couldn't, I love her to bits, and anyway, Gideon has explained it all so well. I've just wasted so much of me on him ... that man!' Matt exhaled deeply in a sigh – his frustration evident. God's a frog – Kit's phrase popped unbidden into his mind. He smiled to himself and thanked her silently. It was over – finally over. 'You know what, Liss, it really doesn't matter any more, I've just got to let it go, and one thing I know for sure is that the bugger sure doesn't lose any sleep over me!' He got to his feet, hauled Alice up and gave her a bone-cracking hug that left her breathless.

'C'mon, let's go and give Paul and Sue the news – get it over with, and then we'll find somewhere to celebrate tonight. What about the Tickel Arms? I could do with getting out of this place for a while.' They linked arms and turned for home.

Gideon never said I told you so afterwards. He had agonised in seeing Hope bent over the telephone, nodding sharply every now and again and gnawing furiously on the corner of a fingernail, something he'd never seen her do before. Then she'd slowly relaxed the tight frame, released the guiltless finger from her mouth and turned to look up at him, her face beaming. 'It's okay,' she'd mouthed silently to him as she'd continued to listen. Then it was, 'yes, darling, we're leaving early this afternoon so we'll be with you this evening,' a further nod, and then, 'yes, I love you too – we both do,' this with an emphasis that bounced her up and down like an over-excited kid.

Hope had shown even more of the child as she pounded a little tattoo on the dashboard of the Escort in a mock frenzy as they left Newmarket, the last hurdle before reaching Fen Ditton.

'I can't wait!! Can't you go any faster Gideon? I'm frantic!'

He'd smiled tolerantly, changed up, and floored the accelerator until they were hurtling along. The joke over, he'd changed down again and resumed the same brisk pace. 'This is quite quick enough, Hope, believe me! We'll be there in less than an hour, I promise.'

As the Escort grumbled over the gravel outside the Hall, Hope lent over and punched a pah-puppa-pah-pah on the hooter.

The reunion, or more properly the first real union of the family was both a heart-wrenching and heart-warming affair. Alice, standing ten paces back, put two clenched fists to her cheeks and just cried at it. Everyone did.

Gideon had confirmed his booking at the Blue Boar that morning so they all dined at the hotel: and he had something to announce, which he did over dessert and a specially ordered bottle of Château d'Yquem.

'Matt, Alice,' he took Hope's hand, brought it up onto the table, folding it into his other. 'We two ... are to be married,' it came out in a gush, 'and I can't tell you how happy that is going to make me! It'll just be a registry office affair but we both want you two to be present, so it's got to be in Cambridge.' The intendeds were instantly engulfed in kisses, wringing handshakes and backslaps and the one bottle of d'Yquem quickly became two.

'I'll be able to sign my paintings "M. Lidman"' Matt teased, and when Hope asked about his painting, Matt was able to tell them that he had made huge strides.

'Newmarket last week and this new, wonderful thing, this new life that you've given me – I don't know what to call it, has just put me on an amazing roll. I've planned four big paintings – I mean at least as big as the one of Paul and Sue that you've seen – all racing scenes, and I've been going at them hammer and tongs – painting right through the night sometimes. The only thing that's held me up is running out of paint and having to rush off to town to buy more!'

Alice pitched in, 'Matt is doing them all at the same time, can you believe, and the pace is fantastic. I can't wait to see them finished.' Gideon sat back in his chair, thinking, while everyone chatted on around him. At length he chipped in, 'Matt, can I have a look at them as they are now, your new pictures, and borrow your completed one? We'll have spare time while we organise the wedding with the registry office, so perhaps I can try and do some marketing for you. What do you say? And there's one other thing,' he went on before Matt's open mouth could answer, 'I've decided to give you something. It's something associated with your work, something Alice knows lots about, and something that's lots of fun.' There was an expectant silence around the table.

'Well, tell us then!' Alice piped up. Gideon drew his pipe from his jacket and started to pack it, a mischievous smile lurking at the corners of his mouth. 'A racehorse – I'm buying you a racehorse!' A clamorous hubbub crowded the table with everyone trying to speak at the same time. Alice shushed everyone, 'Gideon, it'll cost you an absolute fortune to keep a horse in training in this country!' Gideon waved his pipe, 'I'm aware of that, Alice, but don't you worry about it, I'm not short of a shilling. And I'm not going to be buying any old sort of rubbish either; it'll be something that will win for you. We can't have Lidman colours on some useless old hack, now can we?'

34

Bubbles was doing her best to please the man lying spread-eagled beneath her. Her naked, generous body lay coiled over him, a manicured hand and her painted mouth drawing his erection up like a rank weed. As he quickened, Jake's hand swept down onto her peroxided curls, holding her tight, forcing her down. The girl had never had it so good – not the sex, but everything that went with it. Summarily plucked out of the Brathrow's typing pool, he'd fired her from the company, and – joy of joys – then proceeded to set her up in a flat in Knightsbridge. And more joy – there wasn't even a wife to worry about. Divorced, yes, but single (she had hopes) and rich as Croesus by all accounts, it was perfect. True, she found him dreadfully serious, a stickler for punctuality and brutally demanding in bed sometimes – lots of kinky rumpy-pumpy she called it, but the generous expense accounts and allowances more than made up for all that.

Bubbles thought that her nickname alluded to her character rather than to the frothy contents of her head. She felt it almost a duty to be happy; that light, bright cheerful thing that everyone seemed to like, forever nattering on about something or other. Giving Jake his orals was one of the few occasions when she was quiet – and, little did she know it, could please him doubly. She'd shut up for a start and he could take his pleasure without the bloody chatter for once. He could concentrate on his fantasy: he could do it now, the voyeur in him picturing his black horse thundering forwards, clods of earth flying about, straining heads see-sawing, clawing towards the finish. As he neared his climax his loins started to buck like the black horse's jockey driving the horse on, riding the finish, the roar from the stands joined his own, swirling in his head.

The illusion wasn't without substance. Peppermint had franked his form even further by winning again – emphatically – in the autumn at Phoenix Park. Crucially, it was his first race over six furlongs and he'd won easily, by three lengths, giving weight all around. It was a raise in class too, and the second placer, The Confederate, went on to run second again by only a length a fortnight later. The horse that beat him was non other than Mandalay, already the racing scribes' early favourite for next year's Derby. Suddenly there was enormous interest in the black horse, with everyone starting to sniff around Armstrong's yard. Jake had seen enough, and gave instruction that Peppermint wasn't to run again until he was a three-year-old. 'Pack him away in cotton wool,' he'd said, and Sam Armstrong had agreed. The trainer had long held the opinion that the black horse was the best he'd had through his hands in twenty years and he already had a small fortune on before the Phoenix Park race, when he'd appeared at the very shy 100 to 8 in the Derby lists. There was every likelihood of a tremendous betting coup and reports were circulated that the horse's wind was now suspect and he was tailing off in his work. It was all bunkum, but Jake enjoyed the trainer's subterfuge, even if he had no real interest in the betting himself. He had put a thousand pounds on, but merely as an amusement, whereas for Harry, who was also convinced of the sting, and who'd splurged an equal amount, it was a very serious matter, a lifetime's savings in fact.

Deneuve's foot problems mended slowly, annoyingly slowly, and the ever irritable Jake was resigned to trying her out again only in the following year as a three-year-old. There were still questions to be answered about her stamina and whilst the form on her three races was good, it wasn't phenomenal. Furthermore, Armstrong, who had a strong line on her through Peppermint and his old handicapper, rated her as better than good but less than brilliant. It would just have to wait. 'You just never know how they're going to mature and train-on Mr. Stevens,' he'd cautioned and left Jake to mutter and grumble about it to himself.

The real disappointment was Carlo, the bay colt in Bailey's yard. He'd promised so much, and had looked an absolute picture once the flesh had been sweated off his Herculean frame. The trouble, seemingly, was that he now just wouldn't run – not fast anyway. Philip Mitchell, the vet, had been in to examine him half a dozen times and Jake pestered him ceaselessly for some sort of answer. 'Well, what's the matter with my bloody horse then Mitchell?' he'd asked, 'you're the professional – I need some sort of answer, man!' And so Mitchell had started going over every conceivable option and examining every single system. It was patently and painfully obvious watching the horse on the gallops. He ran with a stiff, crabby action, ears laid back simply loathing the work. Bailey asked for the whip, and even spurs, but all it produced was a furious windmilling of the tail and no speed. 'What about his blood results,' Jake asked. There was nothing there. 'If anything they've improved, Mr. Stevens,' the vet whined a plaintive reply, 'his CPK levels – muscle enzyme levels – were low, very low in fact. Now at least they're up where they should be for a horse in training. The rest, all his red and white cell counts and his other enzyme levels are all dead normal. Everything's within the normal range.' There'd been just silence on the other end of the phone. 'And there's nothing on X-ray either,' the vet continued, 'I thought he might have some sort of foot problem with that dodgy action, but there's nothing, and I've looked at everything, believe me! Nerve blocks weren't going to be any use because he isn't lame at the trot, so I've X-rayed everything, absolutely everything. Pedal bones, naviculars, pasterns, knees, stifles and hocks, the lot. He's been over to the Equine Research Station and they've X-rayed his pelvis and spine under anaesthetic. Still nothing! We've scoped him and done ECG's, the lot. There isn't a stone we haven't turned Mr. Stevens, I promise you!' The frustration in the voice was very evident. 'Perhaps you can have a word with Mr. Bailey and see what he says about it all.'

The trainer was more forthright. 'Sell him, Mr. Stevens, it's a waste of a box keeping him here. He's not a genuine horse – he's a slug – just not interested in racing at all. The vets have been through him with a fine-tooth comb and there's nothing. I've even had him shod with pads and put him on the softest going I could find and he still crawls along like a London cab looking for a fare. You'd be better advised ...' Jake cut it, 'but what about that win of his, Bailey?' the trainer had made an annoyed sound, a sharp exhalation of air, 'A flash in the pan I reckon. Look, Mr. Stevens, the only horse that got near him that day snapped his cannon bone a fortnight later, and the rest – back in the ruck, haven't amounted to anything since, so there's no form to speak of. He was probably just the best of a bad bunch on the day.'

Jake made his decision. 'Very well, sell him then. I'll send you another couple of youngsters next year. See if you can do better with those.' The trainer put the phone down and shook his head. He was irked. The man made it sound as if it was his damn fault that the stupid horse wouldn't run. He rummaged in his coat pockets for his packet of Senior Service, drew one out and tapped the end of if thoughtfully on the box before lighting it, thinking about the horse. No, he convinced himself, they had tried everything. It was right that he'd just have to go, and the sooner the better; there were plenty of others in the yard that had at least earned some attention.

Jake also instructed Harry to put his feelers out about Carlo, and the consensus in the yard amongst the lads had been that he amounted to a no-hoper.

'The more 'ee has of everyfink Guv'ner, the more 'eez goin backward-like. The betta 'ee looks the worse 'ee works, the more 'ee works the less 'ee wants it. I seen 'im work last week Guv'ner, an' it's pitiful – scrabblin' an scratchin' along somefink terrible. Vets 'az bin all over 'im 'cording to the 'ead lad an' carn find nuffink.'

The decision left Jake with just two horses to carry his hopes, and realistically it was only Peppermint who was a real Classic contender. Deneuve was still an outside chance for him, but he was aware of Armstrong's perception that she was just short of the highest class. Peppermint it was then, and the horse gave glorious, glorious lie to the adage that black horses weren't genuine. He had quite unbelievable speed, and he ran to his potential every single time.

'I could hardly ask for better,' Jake muttered to himself, turning the horse in his mind like some fabulous rare coin.

'Oh good, darling,' piped Bubbles, giving his limp and shrinking penis an affectionate little pat, 'you enjoyed that?'

35

Alice and Matt's trip to Bansha was cancelled. They'd aimed to go over for the long vac, which would have been fabulous, but the Newmarket practice where Alice had been angling for a spell 'seeing practice' had rung suddenly, saying they would take her for a month – mid-July to mid-August over the holidays. It was a Vet school requirement: all students were required to spend time in different types of practice, helping out, learning and watching real vets at work, and then writing up case notes. The Newmarket practices were top class in the equine field and, as Alice explained over the phone to her disappointed mother, 'it's just not the sort of chance I can afford to give a miss, Mum.' Her mother's voice held a plaintive edge, 'but when are we going to meet this mystery man of yours, dear?' 'For Christmas, Mum, I promise,' Alice answered soothingly, 'he'll keep till then, to be sure!' She could feel the Irish lilt and vernacular creeping back into her voice as she spoke.

It wasn't all Alice could feel. There was now a growing urgency in her relationship with Matt. There had always been something in the way before. Initially there was all the uncertainty of his starting up as an artist, the finding of his feet, and she had felt his initial lack of assurance quite acutely – empathised and understood it fully. But he'd just gone at it with a will, and it had been the event of a lifetime, watching his talent unfold, take wings and fly. He had been so very reticent and unsure of himself at first, right up to the time Gideon had seen his work and loved it. The man was obviously extremely astute and so knowledgeable about almost everything, and his undiluted enthusiasm had convinced her Matt of his worth. The whole Newmarket series of paintings – the four – had burst out of him like the eruption of a volcano. Thanks to Gideon, they now reposed in a very smart dealer's gallery in London – already sold en bloc for a quite staggering two thousand eight hundred pounds – and there only for the remainder of the week before the purchaser was due to take them to grace his dining room walls. Then there'd been her studies, and Matt's waitering at The Ancient Shepherds at odd times that had also contrived to give them less time than they would have liked together. And she burned for him. But it was a flame coloured with more than a hint of trepidation. This because Alice was still a virgin. In this day and age, that was a novelty: she knew this, and was certainly no prude. It was quite simply that she had never felt the inclination to sleep with anyone she'd met before, and so she just hadn't. Now it was quite the opposite, and the thought of it hovered in her subconscious constantly, sometimes like an annoying itch she couldn't quite reach to scratch, but more often – especially when she looked at him working in his studio and her imagination ran riot – like heat coursing down into her body filling her with plain, honest-to-god, want. She felt weak afterwards, her limbs drained and her body soft as liquid chocolate inside. Worse still, Matt was also being scourged. The way he kissed, the way they kissed, hot and hungry, and the hardness of that body pressed ever insistently on hers. So welcome, so wanted. The glaze in his eyes when they were hot together, and his searching mouth, and the smell of him. Desperate! It was driving her frantic.

From what he'd told her about his University girlfriend – the artist – she'd gathered that it had been quite an intense relationship. And they'd obviously lived together for a while too. Well, at least one of us has some experience, thought Alice, as she climbed the steps up to the studio.

Everyone had gone: Gideon and Hope had flown off suddenly because Gideon's older brother had suffered a stroke, Paul and Sue down to Sevenoaks and Stuart to Heathrow and then Connecticut to see his family. Quite artlessly she'd asked him yesterday whether he'd ever painted a nude.

'No, I haven't actually,' Matt had answered, raising his eyebrows, a little smile appearing at the corners of his mouth.

'Well, Matt, if you're going to, I think it should be me.' They'd looked at one another in silence, Alice hearing her heart tripping in her chest and suddenly needing to swallow. This morning she'd just put on a short, summery slip – no bra, no pants – and then run to the steps up to the studio.

'Anyone in?' she'd called at the studio door at the top of the steps, knowing full well he was there. Matt appeared from the back of the studio wiping his hands on a cloth.

'All set, I'm just not sure what pose ... there's a chair there ...' He stopped, his hands still, Alice had shrugged off the two shoulder straps and the slip lay at her feet like a pool.

'God, Liss, you're beautiful ...' the compliment was instinctive to his lips. Alice was so. The fine sculpted face, now serious, held the wide spaced, deep-emerald eyes. Her auburn hair lay thick and shiny, with rich curls turning on the gentle slope of her shoulders. Matt's frank look took in the perfection of her high breasts, and swept down over the flat stomach to the deep auburn vee. One of a pair of long, long legs – the left, was leant against the other in a small pose. 'You like?' she asked, looking at him intently, earnestly, something indecipherable swirling deep in her eyes.

'Yes, yes,' Matt recovered with a start, and he was instantly solicitous – professional, 'just sit on the chair ... here, wait, let me put this throw on it first and then we can do a three-quarter view.' As he cast the throw and it landed draping the simple wooden chair, Alice took a half step backward and tripped on a corner of material. Matt caught her forearm and in that instant she slid into him. As his arms instinctively went about her he felt a soft kiss on his neck in the hollow and she licked him there, just the once, but slow, lascivious and hungry. It was the erotic event of his life. He gasped, stepped back and without a word, began to tear his clothes off, his eyes still feasting on her. Her eyes sought him, all of him, and as she saw it, felt this thing he could do to her, this response to him, the liquefying inside. There was no stab of pain as he entered her – the horses and the hunting had seen to all that a long time ago – only the exquisite pleasure of a coupling in the pure, white heat of passion. Alice had ached for him to possess her for so long that the fact of it consumed her utterly. She strained her body at his, willing him further, her eyes cast up unseeingly at the rafters above hung with their pale calico mantles. Body and soul she took him into her and then, as the peak of her passion drew close, her eyes fluttered shut, the elfin mouth began to open, her breaths hitting harder now and building quicker.

36

'So your boyfriend is an artist and his father's just bought him a racehorse?'

Philip Mitchell's words and quick glance at Alice seated beside him in the Land Rover carried a heavy measure of disbelief – scorn even.

'What does an artist want with a racehorse, young lady?'

Alice heard the note of disdain. She bridled inside for a second and then decided to lay it on a bit thick. 'He paints racehorses, racing scenes – that sort of thing, Mr. Mitchell. His work is in all the big galleries in London – have you not heard of him?' She contrived to make her enquiry sound excessively polite, but it was, nevertheless, a well-disguised barb aimed at his unmistakably provincial mind. There was just an annoyed and dismissive shake of the head from the vet by way of answer. God, they're an intense lot, thought Alice. She'd have to think again about equine practice if they were all like this. It was serious work, she knew, but that was hardly any reason for them to run around like a bunch of pocket Napoleons all day. All three of them in the practice took themselves so damn seriously – all the time! Not a smile between them – it was positively suffocating, not to mention the intimidation as she walked through the door on the first day. 'This is the lady that wants to be an equine vet' had been the derogatory introductory line then, and ever since, to all the trainers, in every yard. The only day she'd really enjoyed had been when they had sent her off to the Equine Research Station down the road to tour round the place. Colin Eastwood, the head of Biochemistry, had taken one look at the long legs, conducted her personally around the labs and then whistled her off to a local pub where they'd spent the afternoon drinking bitter and discussing his latest research projects. No misogynist hoity-toity attitude there!

'Where's this horse then?'

Mitchell's abrupt question broke into her thoughts.

'He's at a yard in Royston,' answered Alice, 'Cy Francis' yard.'

'Cyril Francis,' Mitchell rolled the name around his tongue. 'Cy Francis – should be Sly Francis!' He chuckled grimly at his own joke. 'We used to work for him years ago, but he's very small time – and old fashioned. Full of his own lotions and potions.' Mitchell's hands fluttered briefly above the steering wheel. 'We parted company, thank goodness. I can't stand these old types – won't take instruction and tight as hell with money.' He stopped the Land Rover at the red traffic lights in the High Street.

'Has the odd winner though.'

He jammed the gear stick forward as the lights changed and accelerated away.

'Tell you what, it's lunchtime and I've got a yearling to look at out that way this afternoon. Let's go and look at this wonderful horse of yours – sorry, your boyfriend's. What's this horse's name then?'

'Quixote,' Alice offered, 'Don Quixote.'

'Rings a vague sort of bell … and you say he's had a win?'

'Yes, over four furlongs in April.'

The grunt Alice got in reply was non-committal and dismissive.

The small yard in Royston was a little ramshackle, she had to admit. She saw that some of the wood slats on the stable doors could do with replacement, but it was nevertheless neat as a pin. Cy Francis and her Aunt Ash would have agreed – a place for everything and everything in its place. A dapper little man with a roly-poly walk came rollicking towards them, appraised of their presence by the click clacking of footsteps on the cobbled yard.

His clothes, like his yard, could have done with replacement. All so old and obviously threadbare, with the faded brown jacket leather-patched at the elbows and the trousers cross-stitched at the knee. Between the knot of the scrawny tie and the Adam's apple Alice could spy the gleam of the brass stud attaching collar to shirt. The last time she'd seen one of those was as a child on her grandfather's dress shirt as he donned his tails, God knows how long ago. The Adam's apple worked now.

'What's Mr. High and Mighty Mitchell want in my yard then?'

His eyes then lit on Alice and he instantly swept off the flat hat, giving her a second of his full and polite attention. 'Begging your pardon, Miss.'

'Long time no see, Cy' drawled Mitchell by way of a greeting.

'Out of sight is out of mind, Mr. Mitchell, and I've not minded.'

The vet frowned at the somewhat obscure remark, trying to discern if he'd been slighted. He decided not. 'We've come to have a gander at this lady's horse, Cy, or rather this lady's artist friend's horse.' Alice's mouth tightened at the heavy-handed innuendo and she took a step forward. 'Mr. Francis, it's my boyfriend's horse, Don Quixote, the one his father, Mr. Lidman bought for him a couple of weeks ago.' Cy Francis' eyebrows lifted quickly and then he turned on his heels with an invitation to follow. The horse was in the box closest to the office with his head in the corner pulling at a hay net. The trainer collected a head collar from the office and talking quietly to the animal, drew it on and then gentled him around and out onto the cobbles.

'Good God, it's Carlo!' Mitchell blurted out.

Alice turned and looked at Mitchell in astonishment. He rounded on the trainer.

'Cy, this horse is from Bailey's yard, isn't he?' The trainer nodded.

'Now I remember!' Mitchell waggled a finger. The lads couldn't get their tongue round "Don Quixote", so they just called him Carlo – the first Spanish name they could think of!'

He guffawed and then started a loud, braying belly laugh until tears of merriment were squeezing out of the corners of his eyes. Still laughing, he turned to Alice.

'Young lady, you tell you dauber boyfriend, you tell your painter, tell him that his father has just bought him the biggest piece of four-legged rubbish available.' He stabbed a finger at the unfortunate butt of his remarks.

'He's useless, absolutely useless. The last unfortunate owner spent a fortune on him – blood-tests, X-rays, ECGs, the lot.' He paused to wipe the tears away. 'I'm sorry, but this horse can hardly put one foot in front of the next ... bad luck.' He glanced at his watch, 'see – I'm going round the corner to check on this yearling. You have a shufti at your horse with Cy here' – another bolt of laughter threatened to explode out of him – 'and I'll come and fetch you in three-quarters of an hour.'

Alice stared at the retreating figure, the snorts and snickers trailing him out of the yard. As his words came to her again she felt the heat of embarrassment climb onto her face, burning her cheeks. There was a light pressure on her shoulder. It was Cy.

'Now don't you worry about Mr. Mitchell, young lady. I'll just put the horse away and we'll have a cup of tea in my office.' Alice was tearful but the kindness of the old trainer deflected the worst.

'That Mr. Lidman, your young Mr. Lidman's father, he's a nice man, and no fool either, believe you me.' He poured Alice's tea for her, offering sugar and milk. 'Knows a fair amount about horses too. Are you a veterinary student then – going round with that Mr. Mitchell?' Alice nodded. 'Well perhaps you can help in finding the key to that horse.' He settled back into an old squeaking chair behind his desk and supped at his tea noisily. 'You see, Mr. Lidman got me to go down to Lambourn to see old Chester Morley – 'cause Chester is a mate of mine from way back. He's a trainer like me'self and he knew all about Single Sanction.' Alice looked totally bemused. 'Did Mr. Lidman not tell you about any of this?'

'No,' said Alice, 'Gideon – aah Mr. Lidman – had to fly off suddenly, a family member is in hospital with a stroke.' 'Well, that explains it,' Cy was content with the explanation. 'I dare say you know that this Don Quixote or Carlo or whatever his name is won a race earlier in the year.' Alice nodded, on track with this part of the story anyway. 'And that he came out of the stalls – you'll excuse the expression – like shit off a shovel and won as easily as he liked.'

Cy peered into the teapot to see if there was another cup's worth. He poured quickly and settled once again into his complaining chair. 'Now there were seven runners in that nursery. Your horse,' he pointed with his teaspoon, 'and six others. Five of the six haven't done a thing since, but the other one, the one that got closest to your Don Quixote, Carlo, was Single Sanction. Trouble is, the silly bloody horse broke his leg a week later and had to be put down. Now, as I said, Chester used to train him and told me some very interesting stuff when I went to see him – after a few pints that is. So interesting in fact that Mr. Lidman and me'self thought we definitely ought to buy this horse of yours. Chester was in tears by the end of the evening – eight pints to the good mind you – but he trained a very quick sprinter called Dunedin a few years back and reckoned Single Sanction even faster. He was very upset when the colt was beaten first time out, he told me he couldn't understand it. Of course when the horse broke his leg it was the finish, and he's refused to speak to anyone about the horse since.'

Cy drew a cigarette out of a box, lit it and squinted through the smoke at Alice ... 'until his old friend Cy came along that is, with his sympathetic ear and eight pints of best bitter.'

They both heard the banging of the Land Rover door and saw the hastening figure of the vet making his way to the office. Cy leant forward, close to Alice – 'see what you can find out about the horse from this fellow Mitchell – I've never liked him at all and it would be a rare treat to see him eat his words.'

37

Alice only had to wait two days. Mitchell had mentioned that he had an afternoon wedding to attend on the Friday, and soon after he deposited her at the surgery at noon she made her way to the bank of filing cabinets where the practice records were held. The receptionist made it very easy.

'Oh, you mean that horse at Bailey's yard that Mr. Mitchell did all that work on? I remember it well ... the bill was huge and Mr. Mitchell was always complaining about the owner being on his back for no good reason. It's under some business name or other ... what was it now?' She paused giving the grey files on her left a fierce interrogatory look through horn-rimmed spectacles. Alice held her breath and mentally crossed her fingers. 'Thaat's it ... Steel Syndicate One, they're the owners,' she jerked out a lower file on it's slides, 'some London address, from what I remember.' The practiced fingers walked themselves rapidly forward and then stopped. 'Yes, here it is.' Out came a bulging manila folder, which she handed to Alice with a flourish. 'Have fun, and just put it back in order when you're finished, will you dear?'

Alice bolted herself in the ladies toilet, opened the folder and started to read. Most of the entries related to a bay colt, Carlo, and rather fewer to a grey filly, Sancerre. The vet's scribbled entries were difficult to decipher and there was a lot of shorthand. Vaccinations, masses of 'Visit B/S to lab clot EDTA' – that would be blood samples sent to the lab and then notes about X-rays – a great number of them she saw, then 'refer ERS G/A Rad spine pelvis NAD!' That'll be a referral to the Equine Research Station Alice surmised, general anaesthetic and spine and pelvis X-ray. NAD – no abnormality detected. The sheaf of papers at the back of the file was all the lab reports from the blood samples. Every one of them was headed General Equine Profile so the comparisons were easy. Frighteningly normal – except for the one thing. The CPK levels in the first weeks. Alice flicked back and checked again. There it was – April 2nd 14 units per litre, April 12th 21 units per litre, April 24th 23 units per litre. The lab comment next to each of these was a bald low. Then suddenly they rose steeply through the June, going up by leaps and bounds to a maximum of 200 units per litre in the last sample taken on June 23rd. As she sat on the toilet seat, frowning at the reports, something that Colin Eastwood had said to her at the pub that afternoon flashed through her mind. She started and sat bolt upright. I wonder, thought Alice, I just bloody wonder!

Nobody seemed to mind when she asked for the afternoon off to go down to the Equine Research Station again. Colin was sitting in his brightly lit oblong office trying to get a recalcitrant pipe alight when Alice knocked at the open door with her most winning smile in place. 'Could I speak to the oracle for a minute?' The biochemist's eyes slid up and down as he snapped his old Zippo lighter shut and waved her in. Obviously a legs man, thought Alice. He was a tall, slim man of about forty: sandy haired, freckle faced and possessed of an enormous, electric energy. Clad now in his lab coat, open at the front with the collar up, he whizzed past her to call for two cups of coffee and then breezed back in a cloud of blue smoke, sucking furiously at the pipe's battered stem.

'What can ho-hum Science do for a hey-hey lovely lady then?' He'd revealed himself at the pub as an unabashed flirt, but it hadn't bothered Alice because it was all conducted in the lightest of manner and with no obvious expectations of success. It was just his manner, she realised, but she would have just hated to be his wife all the same.

'Tell me about that fabulous idea of yours,' she began, 'of each horse acting as its own control.' Colin Eastwood's washed, blue eyes flashed his enthusiasm at her as he embarked on his hobbyhorse. 'We've got all the data ready for publication, my dear, so it's more than an idea – it's fact, and it's going to revolutionise equine biochemistry, make it extremely precise. Your colleagues at that practice you're working in, they think it's all pie in the sky. But publication's going to make them think again.' He grabbed a file from the shelf above the desk. 'Look at these various enzyme levels in different breeds – see,' he spread the graphs out, 'the normal range differs quite markedly comparing, say, Shires with Thoroughbreds. So there's a between-breed difference.' The biochemist flipped over several pages to another set of graphs. 'And look here. Within a single breed – obviously we've taken the Thoroughbred – there are age and state of training differences.'

'What about CPK then?' Alice interjected. 'A good example,' he flipped two pages, 'look here,' he stabbed a finger at a graph, 'CPK levels in two-year-old racehorses are, in general, different from those of three-year-olds – that's the within-breed age difference. But it gets even more complicated now!' he chortled, warming to the theme, 'because CPK – a muscle enzyme, as you know – reacts radically to the state of training. Relatively low at the start, it rises rapidly with training, so a high CPK figure can be quite abnormal for a youngster starting training yet quite a normal characteristic just a few months later.' He slammed the file shut. 'You see, Alice, the more you tell me about a horse, the more I can tell you about a horse. So when you get into practice, remember to fill in all the information on the lab request form. When we ask for breed, age, sex and state of training, it's for a damn good reason.' Alice gave a pantomimed applause with what she hoped were star-struck eyes.

'Colin, but what if I tell you about a horse, a Thoroughbred, a two-year-old Thoroughbred in fact, that wins a race with a CPK of 21 units a litre and can hardly move a month later when his CPK is 200?' There was absolute silence in the room as the biochemist slowly drew the pipe from his mouth, staring at her hard.

'So you really listened didn't you, young lady?' He knocked the pipe out in a large wooden ashtray on the desk. He nodded, smiling, 'yes, that's it,' then continued ruefully, 'I really should be careful of letting on about my current research ideas to all and sundry.' The bowl of the pipe was being filled again spiritedly. 'The best idea of all, as I see you've twigged, young Alice, is to let each animal function as his own control. To plot each horse's individual biochemistry early on to establish normals for that horse and then relate all subsequent results back to his own. Biochemistry is a function of genetics. Your DNA programs your biochemistry – as simple as that.'

Another cloud of smoke arose from the gurgling pipe and the file was flopped open once again. 'If we presume your two-year-old that wins a race is fit, then that would put him on an equal plane with horses having a CPK up here,' he pointed at the graph and scrabbled on the desk for a calculator, 'and you say his CPK was 200 at last testing?'

Alice nodded. The scientist punched the calculator a few times, 'Well, that's the equivalent of most other horses in his age group having a CPK of 1166 ... Grossly abnormal – for him! I'd say – on the verge of – what do you vets call it?'

'TYING-UP' Alice shrieked, 'HE'S TYING-UP!!'

She jumped up and gave the bemused scientist a healthy smack of a kiss on his cheek. 'Thanks a MILLION! I gotta go.' She grabbed her bag from the desk. 'And please, don't mention this to anyone – especially not to the practice. You've saved my life!'

The astonished man watched the flying figure hurtling away down the corridor and slowly brought his hand up to his cheek.

'Hmm,' he murmured to himself, 'smashing legs … but saving her life … I think not.'

38

The bright bay horse stood four square in his box tearing hungrily at his hay net.

'He's come on a treat in the last week, Miss Alice,' Cy remarked. 'I've put young Christy onto him.' The young lad working energetically on the horse's flank with brush and curry comb paused a second and nodded greeting at the threesome before returning to his task, hissing through his teeth each time the brush contacted the glowing coat. As he worked down behind the ribs the horse snorted and lashed backwards with a hind leg. Christy didn't miss a beat.

'Full of himself,' commented the trainer. 'Come to the office, we'll have a chat.' Matt's eyes lingered on the horse as Alice took his hand and they followed Cy the few steps to the office. It was his first view of his horse, and the painter's eye had taken in the substantial form and formidable hindquarters with delight. The coat was every bit as lustrous a deep coppery colour as the old Victorian pennies he'd polished up with Brasso as a child, and the huge, liquid eyes had regarded him steadily for a second when he'd first called his name.

Cy had nodded his head in the direction of the stable as he'd pulled his chair out in the office and sat. 'That Christy has got a way with horses.' He lit a cigarette and then leant forward with elbows on knees.

'Tell me what you've got on this horse then.'

Alice gathered her thoughts quickly. She knew from Philip Mitchell's comments that Cy was one of the old school, and she was determined to put the results of her scientific sleuth work in the simplest way possible. To do otherwise would be counter-productive – it could even engender a degree of antagonism, and that was the very last thing she wanted.

'Mr. Francis, you've been in the racing game since before I was born probably, so you'll know all about horses tying-up – or with Monday Morning disease.' The trainer didn't answer; he just waved the two fingers holding his cigarette which Alice took as office to continue.

'Well, it causes muscle damage which releases muscle enzymes into the blood stream – and we can measure those in the blood by taking a sample and having the lab analyse it. And what I've discovered about Carlo – Matt and I are going with the stable name by the way – is that because of some quirk of nature, his muscle enzyme levels are normally way, way below those of other horses. Now, when vets think a horse is tying-up they usually take a sample and look for a big increase in muscle enzyme levels, but when Carlo's blood has been tested, his muscle enzyme levels have just come out on the high end of the normal range. But Carlo's not normal, so for him they've been way too high. I think he's on the verge of tying-up all the time, which I think is why he moves so stiffly whenever he's worked. My veterinary books also tell me that heavy muscled horses are more susceptible to the condition – and Carlo's certainly that!'

Alice paused to draw breath and then went on, ticking points off on her fingers. 'They also say that tying-up often shows in horses as they start work, and Mitchell's notes say he was quite sound at the walk and being trotted-out in hand – this stiffness only showed at work. And why do you think they X-rayed his back and pelvis at the Equine Research Station? – 'Cause they saw back-pain, and tying-up affects loin and lower back muscles more than any others!' She ended the litany with a triumphant note and then, remembering her earlier resolve, quickly dropped her voice.

'What do you think, Mr. Francis?'

The trainer's eyes were two glittering needlepoints in a face that had now taken on a feral cast. 'You might just be right,' he answered slowly, his mind whirling round and weighing what he had heard. He took a sudden, stabbing, intense draw on his cigarette. "Course I've seen horses tied-up before, but we didn't have all this blood testing hoo-ha in those days. We just had ways of dealing with it – did it and got on with it. It worked with some and not with others. Simple as that.' He stubbed out the cigarette.

'You're also saying that the vet has missed it 'cause he's been relying on blood samples to tell him and the blood samples have lied to him.' The glee that crept into the voice was unmistakable.

'In a way, yes,' answered Alice. It wasn't true, precisely – but close enough.

The tidy little man jumped up from his chair and started to pace up and down. 'That means we've been doing the right thing so far then: all he's had is some roadwork – walk and trot, with Christy – trying to get him to settle. He was mighty excitable when he arrived, like a lot of the others that come here from the big yards. No individual attention you see – not like they get here anyway. But I'll have him out in a little catching paddock I've got at the back here for a few hours each day – make sure he doesn't seize up and then he can have some bicarb in his food every day – and Guinness – quarts and quarts of the black stuff. Nothing better as a tonic, I swear. What do you want to do from your side?'

Alice was prepared and fished in her pocket. 'Let's take a sample and see where his CPK – sorry, muscle enzyme levels – are now, and then an injection of Vitamin E and Selenium every week for a month starting today. That's supposed to be the thing. Plus of course the sodium bicarb – that's good for neutralising the acid in his bloodstream.'

Alice giggled as they made their way to the feed-room where Cy said they'd find Christy. 'I think I'd like to be a horse in your yard, Mr. Francis – Guinness every day sounds wonderful!'

As they entered the feed-room Christy was standing in front of a giant half barrel of oak, mixing a steaming concoction within with a Hiawathan wooden paddle. An old water boiler hissing vapour at its seams stood to one side. 'Best rolled oats and bran,' Cy gestured towards the barrel. Christy evened the top of the sweating mixture and then covered it reverently with Hessian feed sacks. 'Now we let it steep until it cools a bit – the smell and taste by then is quite grand. You'll hear my fellas knocking at their doors for it in a minute.' He poked Christy on the shoulder. 'New orders for Carlo, lad: a quarter pound of bicarb in his food split morning and evening and a quart bottle of the black stuff in the evening as well. You'd better nip round to the Lone Star and see if they've got some.'

As they left the feed-room the yard was filled with buoyant expectant heads, and cocked ears turned towards them. Carlo stood stock still as if waiting for the command to charge the enemy. He snickered as Matt offered him a handful of dry oats taken from the feed-room. The mobile lips hoovered the offering up and then licked the flat of his hand clean, enjoying the salty taste.

39

Hyde Hall
Upper Booting
Gloucestershire

Mr. and Mrs. John Cunningham cordially request the pleasure of

the company of

Mr. Jake Stevens and partner

at a Dinner Dance to be held at 8.00 pm on Saturday 31st August

at Hyde Hall

to mark the occasion of John's Sixtieth Birthday

Dress: Black / White tie   *R.S.V.P.*

THE SPORTING LIFE   Monday 2nd September

If punters were astronomers they'd all be out tonight looking at the new star that has risen in the racing firmament. Don Quixote is the name of the super-nova who has burst on us. This bright bay colt with his Superman build charged out of the gates on Saturday in the five furlong Autumn Breeders Stakes at Newmarket and handed a comprehensive thrashing to the much fancied Confederate, recent impressive winner of the Richmond Stakes at Goodwood and stout second runner behind Derby co-favourite Mandalay. Don Quixote's only previous run was out of the Newmarket yard of Peter Bailey in the spring, when he spread-eagled a lack-lustre field of also-rans with ease. Reports filtered back to us that he had failed to train on thereafter, but a change of owner and yard has appeared to do the trick. He now runs out of Cy Francis' Royston yard and the change of scenery has put the spark back into his Hailey's comet of a horse who streaked home by an impressive two lengths on Saturday. This tipster has marked him down as a good Guineas candidate as he's built for speed and is by respected miler Espanol out of the sharp sprinting mare Windmill. We'll be hearing from this superstar again so remember this is where you heard it first.

Jim Jackman your 'Man on the Spot'

THE SUNDAY TIMES
Sunday 3rd November

Arts review

Semper ex Africa aliquid nova!

Viewers at last week's celebration exhibition of Sporting Art at the Pinksman Gallery in Knightsbridge came in for a treat of some proportion. David Hornby's charmingly discreet employment of line and form has seldom been seen to better advantage than in his series depicting the wildfowl of our marshlands. One of our favourites, dare I say, for several decades now, David's more recent work contrives to invest his milieu with an ethereal texture that is quite the quintessence of those secret waters. I particularly liked his treatment of the lowly mallards skimming the evening waters of the Bolden reservoir. It's one of his larger canvasses but the sheer size has in no way intimidated David. His draughtsmanship is as sure as ever and his familiar competence in the management of colours remains, as always, a treat to the eye. I am certain that a good proportion on what was on view will be gracing the senior London boardrooms within the near future.

My readers will know that I am seldom at a loss for words, but let me say that young Matthew Lidman's treatment of the contemporary racing scene left me speechless. I was unaware of how yawningly tedious the interminable grind of wooden equestrian portraiture has become in recent years, but these bold, rough, unframed canvasses have breathed new life into a genre become jaded of late. One hopes that the commissions from racing's pre-eminent grandees that will undoubtedly come the way of this most exhilarating South African artist will leave his untainted brush free to flourish. The weight of his hand lies one hair's breadth below impasto, imparting a compelling virility that draws the eye and captivates: all the more so, because the hues, tints and colours are quite foreign. It's Tuscany and Provence in Albion. How quite astonishing to have these earthy imports fleshing out the intent expressions and rough garb of the Lad and Trainer in the Feed-room. Frankly, none of this would be possible without the elusive quality that makes Lidman's work quite singular. Facile to describe as the deliberate abrogation of the conventional mores regarding pigment, line and perspective, let me rather merely say that it thoroughly defies definition through anything I can pen. One must see them for one's self. His paintings are a voyeur's delight – one becomes an intrigued bystander for twinklings of time – witness to vignettes simply shot through with brio. **Himself full of himself** is breathtaking. The extravagantly muscled horse stands in his stable, dominant as any petty overseer of old. His patient lad attends to his grooming near the gleaming flank and the ticklish attention is rewarded by the threat of a kick in the coiled hind leg and an irascible glint from a choleric eye. The exhibition – which in its entirety is utterly commendable – lasts until the end of this week.

Madelaine Smyth

40

'Oh my God, he's got that quite dreadful Bubbles woman with him again!'

Jane Cunningham whispered the words into her husband's ear as they stood at the entrance to Hyde Hall welcoming their guests to the dinner dance. John's eyes flicked over to where Jake and the offending article stood waiting their turn behind two other couples. What is offensive to a woman in another woman is often not abhorrent to men at all, and matters far less – particularly if she effectively manages to constantly and obviously exude all the more crass signals of sex. That Bubbles was somewhat coarse hadn't escaped John Cunningham. But he only saw that her usual lavish, sigmoid curves had been accentuated even further by the night's close fitting, sequined evening dress. He had a moment's frisson at the prospect of pressing himself onto those soft shapes during the dancing.

He nodded at his wife giving his sotto voce rejoinder. 'Quite appalling dear, I agree, quite appalling.'

The evening for three hundred guests was a resounding success. Hyde Hall had been dusted off, turned out to look its gleaming best, and a vast candy-striped marquee, pennants aloft, did good duty as dining room and dance floor combined. The caterers plied mountains of exquisite food, wine and champagne constantly and even the microphones behaved, carrying the host's gracious wit to the farthest corners as he answered the toast. John and Jane Cunningham led off the dancing to exuberant applause and the fuelled assembly were soon all foxtrotting or gyrating in genteel manner to orchestrated versions of pop hits.

Bubbles wasn't initially keen on following her instructions at all, but Jake had been frighteningly insistent, and now with John's lean and gracious form held close to her by a compelling arm in the small of her back, it suddenly didn't seem so bad after all. She smiled up at him dazzlingly as the ballad ended. 'John, be a darling and come and help me with my zip thingy – it's got caught and I've got to go to the loo.' He followed her like a lamb, across the lawns, up the staircase in the Hall and into the en-suite bathroom. Bubbles locked the door and then slid to her knees, starting to undo the buttons of his fly.

'What if Jake …'

'Jake doesn't mind,' Bubbles purred.

'Well … Oh all right.' John's mind was now firmly between his legs – all logical thought banished by a galvanising, thrilling expectation.

She set to with a practised expertise.

It was John James Cunningham J.P. O.B.E. and Chairman of the Board's least expected and best present for years.

41

Jake didn't read his Sporting Life until the evening he returned to his flat on the evening of Monday 2nd. He threw the paper down in front of a perplexed Bubbles.

'Shit!!! Fucking hell.' He snatched the phone, dialled furiously and then glowered at the phone whilst he waited for an answer.

'Harry, get down to Royston wherever that is ... it's where? ... Good, you get down there pronto and find out what the fuck is going on with Don Quixote ... CARLO, YOU IDIOT, CARLO ... Yes the bloody horse you told me was effing useless. He's now beating the shit out of all sorts. CO BLOODY FAVOURITE FOR THE GUINEAS, HARRY – JOINT BLOODY FAVOURITE, FOR CHRIST'S SAKE!!!!' The receiver was crashed down.

'What's the matter, baby?' Bubbles enquired timidly. She'd never seen him this cross – ever!!

'WHAT'S THE MATTER? IDIOTS ARE WHAT'S THE MATTER, BLOODY IDIOTS.' He turned his boiling eyes at her and she flinched involuntarily under the onslaught.

'Go home,' he waved her away like some pesky fly. 'Go home and leave me alone ... I've got some thinking to do.'

Teetering on her high, white heels, Bubbles grabbed her small suitcase and bag and made for the door with as big a step as the short tight skirt would allow.

It was only a minute or two to get out of the mall and she was lucky to catch a prowling cab. She climbed in and sunk back gratefully on the seat, glad to get out of the poisonous atmosphere. Her thoughts drifted back to the weekend and she smiled to herself as she thought of her host's obvious pleasure and deep gratitude for her ministrations.

'John!' – her smile softened as she murmured to herself quietly, 'now there's a gentleman that knows how to treat a lady.'

42

Alice kept her promise to her mother and took Matt home to Ireland for Christmas (and joy of joys, Pru would be coming over too). His considerable success as an artist had allowed Matt some financial leeway, so in celebration, and on impulse, he'd bought something totally impractical out of the smalls in the paper: a second hand, green MGB GT. They christened the car Spud – for no particular reason, except that it was Irish and appealed, and had packed-up and set-off across country – aiming for Wales, with the miniscule boot and back seat stuffed with a mixture of cases, haversacks, coats, clothes (still on hangers), Fred's bridle and saddle, sketch-books, pens, pencils, brushes and paints.

'You'd better pray for good weather for the crossing tomorrow, Matt.' Alice had warned him cheerfully, 'otherwise we'll be knee deep in kid's vomit. Once one of them starts it's like a trigger reaction – the whole lot start hurling their darling little guts out all over the place.'

He made a face. 'Sounds dreadful, but I've got reasonable sea legs I think,' and because they had time, he told her the story about catching tunny with Gideon and the amazing Mack Flood. Plett seemed an awful long way away, but he did sometimes, like now in frozen December, yearn wistfully after the sun and the miles and miles of golden sands – even Piet's kaapie accent. 'Ja, baasie, next time it's a geelstert, my baasie'' – when the Ja came out as Jar, the voice coming out of the past as a wistful reminder of another world. And Robberg ... always Robberg. He would take her there one day.

Fortunately, the crossing to Rosslare was calm and they were spared the worst that seasickness could threaten. Bumping off the ferry they had picked their way slowly through Wexford,

Waterford and Cahir, travelling due west towards Tipperary until, on the outskirts of Bansha, Alice made him turn left towards the Glen of Aherlow. The farm entrance looked like little more than a track cut into a hedge, but behind the hedge a gently sloping vista led the eye over green fields and down to where the sturdy half-timbered walls of a farmhouse lay nestling under thatch. Beyond the farmhouse the valley bottomed out, rising up again distantly towards peaks covered with winter snow. It was picture book perfect and Matt stopped the car on the track and got out to look.

'How could you ever bear to leave this, Liss? It's quite beautiful.' He looked around taking it in. 'This is when I wish I was a landscape artist. Imagine being able to do true justice to something like this!'

'What you see isn't always what you get,' answered Alice enigmatically. 'Come,' she said, climbing back into the car, 'I'm dying to see them – and Pru should have arrived by now. What's more, I can almost smell my mother's cooking from here and I'm famished!'

The family that Matt was thrown into fitted well with the mind picture he'd painted from Alice's descriptions. Her stepfather, William, was a tall, thickset, jolly man with a ruddy, weather-beaten exterior, and rough hands that wrung Matt's painfully as they were introduced.

'The mysterious painter at last! Welcome!'

He turned his shock of curly, red hair and shouted towards the house, 'Rebecca! Alice and her man are here!'

He grabbed his stepdaughter and enveloped her in a bear hug.

'Your mother's in a state with all of you arriving at long last!'

The slamming of doors heralded Alice's mother's emergence from the house. A slight figure, she was the precise mould from which her daughter had been cast, with the same rich coils of auburn hair that bobbed as she ran calling a shrill and delighted

'Aliiice!'

Two carrot-top bolts in blue overalls arrived simultaneously thudding into the combined figures of mother and daughter, enveloping them – the younger brothers Noel and Tom. There were more shrieks as Alice spied Pru's generous shape gallumping towards her, and the hugs turned into a circus carousel.

'Come on everyone,' boomed William, 'inside for a jar!' He turned to Matt, clapping him on the shoulder, and drew him toward the house.

'Can't tell you how I've missed that daughter of mine, young fella, can't tell you.'

Matt was a bemused outsider looking in, at least for the next few hours, as the family squeezed every bit of news they could out of Alice. It had taken him back somewhat; in fact he was astonished. So very, very different to the cooler emotions of the handshake and the peck that had been the hallmarks of his – by comparison anyway – rather cool and restrained family. He was envious, straight envious, and it explained, better than anything else could have, the font of Alice's outgoing character.

Pru was next in line, monopolising Alice's attention during dinner around a vast kitchen table, while William wanted to hear all about Matt from Matt – and especially about the horse.

'I can't believe it,' he remarked jocularly. 'Here we are – been breeding horses on the side for generations for all the glory of a selling-plate winner, and there you are, first time round, and you've got a bloody good Guineas prospect!' He thumped the table enthusiastically. 'If he runs, we'll be there, guaranteed. Old Jack and the farm will just have to look after one another for a change.' He quaffed the remainder of his beer. 'Another jar – a drop of the hard stuff?'

Matt woke with a monumental, thudding hangover that

threatened to beat through the back of his eyes. He'd never binged like that with adults, and William had kept on pouring him whiskies, one after the other. The noise that woke him – the knock on the bedroom door – was repeated and Matt croaked a weak 'come in.'

Alice appeared with a tray, cup, saucer and a pot of tea. She sat on the bed smiling at him with crinkled eyes.

'Welcome to Ireland – how do you feel?' He groaned as he sat up, 'you haven't got a couple of aspirin have you? I've got a terrible head.'

'Your eyes look terrible, Matt – poor thing!' There was limited sympathy in the voice.

'You should see them from my side, it's a massacre,' he answered, a comment which widened her smile and brought the balm of her cool hand to his pounding head.

'What time is it?'

'Ten o'clock. Everyone's been up and about for hours! I'll make you some breakfast if you like?'

Matt scrunched up his eyes to look at her, the bright light from the window behind bringing further stabs of pain to his eyes. 'That'll be great, just remind me never to try and match your father in the drinking stakes again.'

'My Dad's renowned for it. He's got the longest, hollowest leg in Tipperary – and up at six this morning, can you believe, whistling some damn cheerful tune, making Mum tea and then off to market at seven thirty! Anyway, stir your bones, I'll do you some bacon and eggs and we'll go down to meet Jack.'

Jack was the sole hired labourer on the farm. All the rest of the work, Alice explained, was done by William, Noel and Tom whilst Rebecca cooked gargantuan meals, kept house and managed her chickens and a considerable vegetable patch located in a sheltered walled-garden behind the kitchen. Matt supposed Jack was sixty if he was a day – a small, dark, crooked gnome of a man, lame on one leg and with a beak of a nose sprouting from behind two bright, beady eyes. He cocked his head up at Matt.

'Tith a pletha tupee thore.'

'Jack, put your teeth in!' Alice hissed.

Jack scrabbled unconcernedly in his jacket pocket and turned his head briefly to slot in his teeth.

'Dat's better, 'tis a pleasure to meet ya … When your man says dere's an Hafrican painter comin, I taught we'd be havin a great big black fella giving the bairn a licka paint, but I spoze it's an hartist is as what you are.' Grinning broadly, Matt nodded acknowledgement as Jack leant on his cane and turned to Alice.

'And I tink it's not before time you were coming home for a spell, Miss Halice. You know, your poor harse tinks you've forgotten aboat 'im entirely! I've gat 'im clipped oat fir you coz I'm sure yer'll be wanting to take 'im oat wid der Scarteen and I've prevailed' – Jack invested the word with meaning – 'over your kid brudder to do some work wid de harse since ever we hnew you wiz coming home!'

Alice grabbed Jack and gave his stubbly cheek a kiss.

'Ah, thanks Jack!'

The wizened little man protested furiously, 'ah, away wid yer gerl – don't be fassin me now!' but the smile and the rush of colour on the old cheeks gave him away.

Hunting was high on Alice's agenda, either with the Tipps, as in Tipperary, or with the Scarteen black-and-tans, smaller darker versions, descended from the Kerry beagle and still a private pack, kept in the Ryan family since the year dot. Matt was keen to gather material and on a day with Tipps, was thrown in with Charlie Parker, the terrier man, who followed the hunt by way of foot and peremptory demands on car followers for a lift. He was an etiolated, rather intense man radiating immense energy with a spade in one hand and a brace of Jack Russells carried in a bag strung from the shoulder. He had few words but on the brow of a hill he'd turned to Matt.

'See them?'

He couldn't. Parker pointed to his right, deep in the dale beneath them.

'See those sheep, they're moving too quickly, that's where they are,' and he plunged away to commandeer yet another car for a lift in exchange for directions. Matt just had to hurry along as best he could – nobody waited. At the bottom of the hill they found the tail end of the field looping past a Land Rover with the back open and a groaning man in hunting regalia lying spread-eagled within. He was obviously in some considerable pain after a fall – his loose, mud-streaked horse having been caught up by a helpful follower and now placidly cropping grass on the verge. 'Physician, heal thyself!' someone in the field shouted, much to the amusement of the others. Parker nodded towards the unfortunate man. 'The local doctor.'

The small field were a colourful lot, Matt saw, including what he was later told was a cleric, a cheery, rotund barrel of a man with a splendid top hat and rimless, round, pebble-stone glasses who looked if he had just jumped out of an Alken print. Having seen a two-wheeler horse-drawn milk-float disappear into the farmyard as they went by, Matt was astonished to see the same squib of a horse, still blinkered, arrive not ten minutes later to join the field, with the milk-float driver, a boy certainly no older than fifteen, now sitting astride! And still in cap, jacket and breeches! Hunting in Ireland, Matt perceived, was decidedly part of the fabric of the place and a very democratic affair. The pace was phenomenal, as were some of the banks, riders leaning hard back as the horses scrambled down, down, with barely enough time to gather their haunches and launch themselves over the water ditches lurking inevitably at the base. Just as Matt thought he was completely out of puff and the stitch in his side would pierce him through, they were onto the hounds milling around an earth. Charlie loosed his Jack Russells who were into the earth like rats up a drainpipe and within a minute the clods began to fly as Parker started to dig.

Matt turned as he heard twigs cracking behind him – Fred's big feet. The big horse's eye had a comfortable look as he stopped, blowing hard, and then craned his neck sideways, reaching for leaves on a handy branch. Alice's eyes were electric.

'What a run! Fred's going like a bomb, Matt, like an absolute bomb! And jump! He's got an almighty lepp on him today.' The horse continued to munch the leaves, unconcerned with the flattery. 'How's it going with Charlie?' she asked.

Charlie Parker, Matt was to discover, was something of a hunting institution: a legend, a weird eccentric, so Alice told him later, who was reputed to know more about foxes than foxes did themselves. As master earth stopper, and in league with 'God' – the renowned Huntsman and Master of the Heythrop, Ronnie Wallace, this brace of men had evidently transformed the face of foxhunting in middle England completely – or so the story went. Alice quipped that if the two of them had finished with middle England, they could quite easily turn their attentions to Cambridgeshire.

With the hunting, and Christmas in the lap of Alice's family, the time flew, but Matt slowly began to read the meaning behind Alice's comment when they'd arrived. There was more to the country than met the eye. First impressions of a happy-go-lucky country in some sort of time warp didn't tell the whole story. One evening when William had asked him how he got on with Jack, he'd replied that he thought rather well. 'Well, you would wouldn't you,' came the rejoinder, 'you're not English.'

'Not English?'

'Yes, not English. Do you know that Jack very likely doesn't consider my family Irish, even though we've been here more than two hundred years? We're Anglo-Irish, descendants of the English who dominated this country for more than seven hundred years – up until 1922 that is – and that's just yesterday as far as these people are concerned.'

William warmed to this theme as he walked to the drinks tray to recharge his glass. 'They never forget that there was a time here when Catholics weren't allowed to practice their religion, or speak Gaelic – barred even from buying land! All thanks to the bloody English – they'll tell you.'

He sat and lifted his glass to a face carrying a rueful expression. 'So we're here on sufferance by and large, but you won't find people saying that of course. You just try asking Jack one day what he thinks of the English, and see what he says. I guarantee you'll get a response – a good one.'

William was right. When he asked the question, Jack's expression had instantly taken on a cast of undisguised loathing. He'd lent over his cane and spat with a jerk of his head.

'Der bastards still have the six counties in der Nart.'

He'd turned his head up at Matt. "'ave you seen de burnt oat buildings on der way inter Tipperary?'

Matt nodded. 'Well, dey were de barracks and deer deer to remoind us,' he waggled a finger at Matt, 'not dat we're likely to forget mind cher!' Jack gripped on his cane a little harder and lent forward.

'Young fella – did you know me granfaddy went to fight de British in your country in 1900 – two hundred Irish lads wid yer man John McBride. Ya see, de bloody English, 'ave been a blight on der whole of humanity, Nart en Soat, East en West, all over der werld, a heeden race, nhat to be trusted, nhat now and nhat ever.'

There was more – Matt related Jack's sweeping denunciation to

William who jumped on the 'heathen' epithet.

'That's another burden for this benighted country Matt – bloody religion! Catholicism permeates every Celtic pore. The Bishops influence the law of the land, the church controls all the state schools and the parish priest very likely knows what bloody time of day you go to the toilet! There's Mass and the confessional, the two pillars through which the parish priest exercises the dominance of Rome, and believe me, dominance is the right word. It's a not-so-benign repression of a whole people, and it breeds an unholy intolerance of initiative and original thought, and of what they call impurity. That's why peasantry still flourishes here – that and primogeniture – and that's why the church rails so viciously against the sexual revolution it sees in full swing in England. It's the work of the devil, no less, because it seeks to undermine the authority of Rome. Remember, there's no contraception here – just impoverished women giving birth to their thirteenth or fourteenth child, for God's sake! And no divorce – men just leave their families, an "Irish divorce". Homosexuals are criminals, they say – abortion is a crime, they say; and if you stray from the path of their righteousness they will denounce you in church – you'll be "read from the altar" – excommunicated virtually!'

The more Matt learned about Ireland the less he understood it. Certainly he'd been confronted with Catholicism just about as soon as they had driven off the ferry, when he saw the first astonishing religious statuary at the side of the road, later followed by many others: pitted and worn, streaky white tableau of Christ on the cross, Mary and the baby Jesus – subjects that looked alarmingly out of place to him. Through his mother's Methodist eyes, Matt saw them as crass, mawkish idols, more fitting in an Italian grotto than here silhouetted against the emerald-green fields. Even more macabre were the graveyards he'd seen further west on the stony Dingle Peninsula. Dotted here and there on these burial grounds, and above ground, were carved stone sepulchres which, to his infinite horror when he peeked in, contained coffins, stacked one upon the other. He thought of his brothers – it made his skin crawl, and he never did ask the question that begged: were there people inside – and wouldn't they smell as they rotted? It was altogether too ghoulish to pursue. He was happier to remain in a queasy ignorance and try and forget the glimpse as soon as possible. The trouble was it was unforgettable, and it was only after he accepted it and had even drawn a little picture of one in his sketchbook that the bogey was laid to rest.

His sketchbooks were crammed and Matt was beginning to look forward to getting home and translating the elements he had into pictures. He was ruminating over what his treatment of Ireland's soft light would entail when Alice burst in.

'Matt we must go, we've got to go. Cy's phoned … Carlo's been shot.'

43

They found Cy in Carlo's box with the vet peering at the horse's hindquarters.

'You're here at last. Pardon me,' he turned to the vet, 'Mr. Carter, this is young Miss Alice ... Baker isn't it? ... And Mr. Lidman, Matt Lidman ... he's the owner.'

The old vet, who instantly put Alice in mind of a plump Mickey Rooney, turned and peered at them in friendly fashion over his half glass spectacles. He folded them into a breast pocket and waddled over with a hand outstretched.

'Dennis Carter, how do you do.' They shook hands. He replaced his spectacles on his nose and peered over them once again.

'Somebody has had a crack at your horse.'

'How bad is it?' asked Alice, her voice laced with concern.

'Well, it could have been a lot worse.' He turned to the horse and pointed to the shaved area high up on the back of his right hind where a short length of what looked like rubber tubing protruded between the line of sutures.

'Smack into that big muscle mass. I've got the bullet out after a bit of fishing, and as you can see, I've put in a drain, which is due out tomorrow. We've done all the usual – tetanus booster, antibiotics and so forth – and there's no infection, so it's just a matter of waiting for everything to granulate up and he'll be right as rain.' He gestured at Cy.

'Cy here is going to keep the hole open for a few days with some good old-fashioned salt water once the drain is out, then we'll just let is close just as soon as it stops seeping.' He gave the trainer an affectionate clap on the shoulder.

'Cy's forgotten more about horses than I'll ever learn, so you'll be in good hands.' The extravagant praise brought a smiling 'humph!' from Cy who went over the horse's head and gave his neck a couple of pats.

'Don't worry, old fella, we'll look after you.'

'What about racing?' asked Alice, 'will he be able to run again?'

'Surely,' the vet answered, 'he'll just need letting down a bit and some R and R, say eight or ten weeks, and then it's slowly back into work. Cy's given me the low-down on the tying-up story, so I'll be monitoring his CPK every now and again just to check everything's okay. Not much use taking a sample now of course, it's bound to be up a bit with all the muscle damage that bullet's caused.'

'I've laid a charge with the police,' Cy said as they left the stable.

Dennis Carter stopped. 'Yes, they've spoken to me too, and I'll tell you what I told them. But first I'd like a look at the spot where it happened, Cy, if you don't mind.' He turned to Alice.

'Would you mind putting on the kettle in Cy's office so we can have a cup of tea when we get back? There's a dear.'

They were back fifteen minutes later and the stocky vet sank into a chair with a grateful 'whew!' and a 'how's that tea getting on?' When he'd settled comfortably into his chair and had his first sip of tea, he began ...

'Well, I can tell you a bit about your assassin.'

He took another sip and then put the cup of tea aside and folded his arms.

'That bullet – that came from a rook rifle – I know 'cause I've got one myself at home and it's an unusual calibre. It wasn't squashed either – didn't get to bone, thank God – so it was quite pristine. Now Cy knows exactly where the horse was that morning – Christy was just giving him a little hack, and from the trajectory of the bullet – straight in one plane from back to front –

your fellow with the rook rifle was standing in the only bit of cover thereabouts, a little copse backing onto the road, 'cause he'd want to be hidden, wouldn't he? That copse is absolutely level with the ground where your horse was pootling along, which tells me something else. It tells me that whoever it was, was a short man, a very short man in fact, because viewed from the side – in the other plane – the trajectory of the bullet was upwards, slanted.'

'But what if he was prone,' asked Matt, 'lying on the ground when he fired?'

'Nope,' answered Dennis, 'couldn't have been: there's a heavy bracken cover there – too tall – so he couldn't have got in a kneeling shot either.' The vet unfolded his arms and put his hands on his knees.

'So here's your man. He's short, but he's not a lad 'cause a rook rifle is an old type of gun that an old man would have, say one over fifty. And it's a countryman's gun so your short man – over fifty – dresses in countryman's gear, rough worn gear, wears a tweed hat or cap perhaps – and one more thing: this wasn't designed to kill, just to maim and that can only be because the horse is a late-comer, a late threat to other big names for next year's races. So someone's due to take a big loss if this horse of yours runs and wins – a bookie? Not likely, they'll be happy if your horse wins 'cause all the early money was on the others. It's somebody who's put his shirt on one of the others, and most likely someone well connected with one or other of the favourites – someone who had early knowledge of their worth – an inside line.'

'Okay,' Cy interjected, 'a short man but not a lad – in our world that's got to be a jockey. Over fifty – that's got to an ex-jockey. Connected with the two other short priced Guineas and Derby favourites – well, they're both trained in Newmarket: so our ex-jockey lives – say just outside the town if he's a countryman – gambles heavily, and has some sort of connections with those two specific yards.' He looked grimly at the others. 'I'll put some feelers out ... we'll catch the bastard.'

'Do the police know all this?' asked Alice.

'Some of it,' answered Cy, 'but our police here are a bit like God's mills, Miss Alice, they might grind fine, but they're also exceedingly slow! And I'm worried this bugger might have another go when he finds out that Carlo's going to be back in work in time for a crack at the Derby, definitely, and perhaps even the Guineas. Bye the bye, I'm getting a security firm in tomorrow – I can't go on sleeping in his box like I've done for the last three nights, my sciatica is giving me hell!'

44

Harry was pretty sure he hadn't been seen. The horse had staggered and lurched to one side as the bullet struck, and then kicked out twice as if he'd been stung. He hadn't waited to see the rest – just scuttled back through the copse to his old post-office van, thrown the rifle in the back and high-tailed it for Newmarket.

It was an act of desperation. That Mr. Stevens was a mean bugger, a cold and vicious one too Harry reckoned, and when this horse that he'd sold started winning again, the invective and abuse poured on him had been unceasing and unnerving. Harry could usually hold his own, but he was no match for this man, and he knew it. The prospect of losing his new job which he loved, in particular the good money, appalled him. At his age options became fewer and it was likely to be his last and best chance ever. Then there was the thousand quid he'd bet on Peppermint for the Derby. The prospect of losing that chilled him to the marrow of his scrawny bones. He'd played the game of what he could do with his winnings so often now that any threat to those dreams couldn't be allowed, had to be extinguished.

He'd hurried down to Royston in September as per instructions and managed a sneaked view of the horse at work just the once, sandwiched between two others and bowling along as nice as you please. Certainly they'd freed up his action completely and he looked quite a bit bigger now too, quite heavily muscled-up on his hindquarters. Next he'd tried the Lone Star and found himself standing between two others at the bar in the pub, also trying to get information. He'd introduced himself in a mumble to a young racing journalist and soon had the worst of it.

'What am I doing down here? Well, I'll tell you what I'm doing down here, I'm trying to get something for my paper on this "wunderkind" – this horse Don Quixote, but the stable's tied up as tight as a you-know-what. No interviews, nothing!' He'd slammed his empty glass down. 'How a fella's supposed to write about a horse no one will talk about is beyond me!' The barman hadn't been much help either.

'All I can tell you, mate, is that the 'orse is partial to Guinness – drinks quarts of the stuff!' He'd guffawed and turned to another customer.

Harry hadn't wanted to make his inquiries too persistent and become too obvious, so he returned to Newmarket and phoned his report to Jake.

'Can't find out nuffink Guv'ner. I seen the 'orse working an ee's fine – nuffink wrong wiv 'im now.'

Jake's steely voice had come threading down the wire. 'Well, you find a way to change that, do you hear? Otherwise you can kiss your arse and job good bye, Harry.'

There was almost a silence on the phone, just the faintest hum.

'And Harry ... it's the spring meeting at Newmarket I'm talking about – not now, do you understand me?'

Harry had understood, and really didn't want to lose his job – or his money. That was when he thought about the rook rifle in the cupboard at home in Kentford.

He had planned it all silently and carefully, and when all the hullabaloo about the horse's win had died down, Harry went back to Royston. There he had spent an inconspicuous week booked into a remote B&B, travelling up early in the mornings to scout his quarry. Hidden away, he had watched the string and noted the route they took. It varied, but what didn't vary was the first quarter of a mile out, and that's where Harry sought his own spot in the copse – nice and close to a B road that led away from town. All that remained was to oil the rifle, some practice in the woods over the precise distance he reckoned the bullet would have to travel, and picking a date. He would have liked to do it a bit later but the insistent voice from London kept badgering him, threatening him, so he'd gone and done it. His nerves couldn't stand the wait either.

45

P.O. Box 212,
Plettenberg Bay,
Cape Province

31st. March

Dearest Matt,

Many thanks for your letter and news. Your weather sounds quite dreadful and it makes me feel a bit guilty sitting here on the stoep in bright sunshine. The swallows haven't started gathering on the wires yet but I suppose they soon will. The pair in the nest in the corner behind me has raised two sets of youngsters this year and I will miss the chirrup-chirrup when Mum and Dad come swirling in to feed them.

I was so pleased to hear that Carlo will be running in the Guineas after all. What a shameful business, someone shooting him like that – I still can't believe it. I see from my diary that the race is on a Wednesday so I'll be keeping my fingers crossed for you all day. I'm sorry we can't be there, but Gideon's brother's estate is a complete mess. He was still a young man – by our standards anyway – just fifty-three, and Gideon is executor.

We thought we'd come over in June. I'm longing to get married – but we do so much want you to be there – and we have promised, so that's that – and Cambridge it is. Gideon gets so embarrassed when we get introduced to people. He says he's much too old to have a 'girlfriend' and doesn't know what to call me quite. He positively squirms sometimes, poor thing. He's so very proud of you, darling, and will talk to anyone about you for hours – your *painting, your fishing, your Alice – it's absolutely endearing. And he's so excited about Carlo. When he heard about the shooting he went into an apoplectic blue fit. I've never seen him cross before and he just stood there and shook with rage. You know he wouldn't harm a fly, and was quite the horseman in his younger days – so the idea of someone maliciously shooting your Carlo enraged him completely. Do you think they'll ever find the person who did it? Gideon says it's bound to be something to do with money. One of the bookies or a big gambler – remember Sea Cottage? I just hope they catch him, that's all.*

That's about all I can squeeze onto this air letter. Please give all our love to your Alice – I think she's a very special girl. Your time in Ireland with her family sounded quite wonderful. I've never been there – but Gideon says it's an extraordinary place, and he's dying to see what your paintings will say about it.

*With all my love,
Your Mum.*

P.S. I've just heard this minute that Doris and Clarence will be coming over with us. I'm so thrilled – they've always been so very kind to me and are the dearest people ever. Write soon.

46

Alice was looking over her Aunt Ashleigh's shoulder as she peered at one of Matt's set of four pictures of hunting in Ireland. Each was set on its own easel in the attic studio and once again they were substantial paintings – both in size – each about four foot by three – and in execution, all unmistakably franked by the driving, robust treatment that was Matt's hallmark.

'Well, what do you think, Aunt Ash?' Alice prompted.

Recognition flooded through Ashleigh. She turned a pair of widening eyes on her niece and blurted out, 'I've seen his work before!'

'Must have been in the Pinksman Gallery in London,' Alice answered, pleased. 'He exhibited there in November.'

No, not there, thought Ashleigh to herself frantically. It was in the flat, Jake's flat in Knightsbridge, that she'd seen work from this hand. The style was unique, original, and distinctive. She couldn't be mistaken. What had started as an uneasy feeling when she was first introduced to Matt that same morning and begun to hear the extraordinary history of his family, now hardened into galloping alarm as pieces of a perverse jigsaw started to slot into place. When Alice had mentioned her new boyfriend on the telephone to her in Stock it had been Matt Lidman, then this morning in conversation it turned out that his surname had been Stevens, and he was a South African! What if ... her mind started racing and then she stopped herself, and instead, in as cool a voice as she could manage, half whispered to Alice, 'Could you take me outside – I'm feeling a little odd.'

Alice took her arm and walked her carefully past a puzzled Matt and then down the steps to solid ground. They walked on for a few yards before Ashleigh spoke.

'Tell me, Alice, what sort of contact does your Matt have with his father – his ex-father, I mean – Mr. Stevens?'

'None at all from what I know,' said a bewildered Alice. 'Why, for heaven's sake?'

Ashleigh ignored the question and went on, 'You don't know his Christian name, I suppose?' She grimaced as she waited for the answer.

'… Jock or Jake, I think.'

The answer pierced her through and she let out a gust of breath. 'God! Alice, do you know who bought the four paintings? The racecourse ones – of Newmarket?'

Alice shook her head slowly, 'No – Felix, the owner of the gallery, organised the sale. All he said was that they went to some businessman or other who was a racehorse owner and that he wanted them for his dining room We were just so ecstatic about the sale we didn't ask for any details.'

'Jake Stevens bought them Alice, Jake Stevens.'

Alice stopped and turned towards Ashleigh. 'You mean Matt's ex-father? Chrissakes!' She shook her head slowly as the news sank in. 'Matt isn't going to be happy about that, Aunt Ash, not a bit! And how on earth did you see them anyway … do you know him? 'Cause Matt says he's – excuse me – he's a real bastard.'

As she nodded her reply, Ashleigh thought briefly about the unpleasant changes that power and huge wealth had wrought in Jake. 'Yes, I'm afraid I do, and have done for some time. I helped interior decorate his London home ages ago and he showed me the pictures just a couple of months ago. Very proud of them he was too, and he certainly doesn't know Matt painted them. What I mean is, he just said they were evidently by some young South African whom he was so pleased to support. He even had to read the signature on the canvas to remind himself of the name – "Lidman". He can't know about the whole saga, Alice, or about the name change, I'm sure.'

'God, what a weird coincidence. Matt never mentioned anything about him – Mr. Stevens, I mean – being interested in horses in South Africa.'

'Well he's certainly interested now, and it's a thing tycoons do, Alice – own racehorses. He's a real captain of industry these days, and he kept reminding me how I'd once taken him to see a Stubbs portrait of Gimcrack in the Fitzwilliam Museum in Cambridge – oh, that was years ago now – and he was bragging to me about owning a horse that could turn out to be just as famous. Something mint – Spearmint, or …'

'Not Peppermint!!' Alice was aghast.

'Yes, that's it – Peppermint.'

'Oh my God – Oh my God – he's one of our main threats for the Guineas.'

Alice's thoughts were in turmoil. 'You know about Carlo, Aunt Ash, well, this means they're going to race one another – cuckolded father against son – or who he thinks is his son.' Alice's agitation flared up and she whipped round to look up at the studio, the anxiety etched deep into her face.

'It's bound to all come out now, it's bound to!'

47

Ashleigh watched the Guineas on TV at home – crouched anxiously on the front edge of the settee and trying to will Carlo home. It was all something of an anti-climax. Jake's horse, Peppermint, had won going away from Mandalay with Carlo running on steadily in fourth place.

'He'll be thrilled anyway,' she muttered to herself unconvincingly. There was something vaguely disappointing about the expected happening – it would have been such a thrill if Carlo could have pulled it off after all. Imagine somebody shooting the poor horse. She shook her head at the notion. The TV picture suddenly had Jake's smiling face answering questions from a fawning interviewer.

'Talk about the cat who's had the cream,' Ashleigh muttered to herself, sniffed dismissively, and turned off the set.

48

Jake wallowed in his victory. There'd been a sumptuous dinner at the Bedford Lodge with the Cunninghams, the trainer Sam Armstrong and his wife, the Jorbetts, Evelyn Wauchope – Brathrows bank manager from Barclays ... and of course, Bubbles. No expense had been spared, as Jake had known that whatever the outcome, Peppermint would give a good account of himself. The win had just gilded the lily to perfection and gave Jake that wonderfully ineffable, choice cachet that he desired so especially. He knew both he and his horse would be in all tomorrow's papers – both racing and national – on people's lips, in their thoughts, and inscribed in the record books forever. It was glory, it was fame – he had arrived – somebody to be reckoned with, a celebrity. And didn't they all just scrape, bow, bootlick and brown-nose him too beautifully! If he could have crowed out aloud he would have.

'Well, you know what's next, don't you?' Sam Armstrong was bending Jake's ear over the twenty-five year old Duoro Port.

'You tell me, Sam.' It was all first name stuff now, and the toasts had become progressively more bacchanalian as the evening progressed. Even Jane Cunningham was becoming distinctly glassy-eyed and appeared not to notice Bubbles' hand placed firmly in her husband's lap.

'THE BLOODY DERBY!' They bawled it out together and then threw back their heads and laughed uproariously. Sam wagged a tipsy finger at Jake. 'No need to look any further than our old Peppermint then, is there Squire? I mean, bar a freak accident he's got it in the bag, hasn't he? He'll canter home by a country mile – bound to. That Don Quixote – well it's all been a bloody storm in a teacup – completely one-paced, and a sad slow one at that. Not quick enough to catch a bloody cold.' He giggled.

'Seriously though,' Sam lit a large Havana and exhaled. 'Seriously, that horse of yours is bred for the mile and a half and Quixote, well he's all sprinting blood, isn't he?' Jake nodded – the spectre of having sold the horse that beat his own had faded for him as well. A passing well wisher captured the trainer's attention and Jake was left free to ponder and contemplate the extra notch in his swollen ambition. He had read copiously about the Derby. He knew about the Derby lunch before the Epsom meeting with the menu always in black and white – the Earl of Derby's colours. He knew about the ups and downs of a course that had the straight, flat-racing Americans shaking their heads in amazement, and he knew about Tattenham Corner where the suffragette Emily Davidson had thrown herself to her death in front of the King's horse Anmer in 1913.

The race was known world wide and positively stuffed with tradition. Like the Grand National, the Derby attracted bets and office sweepstakes from people who normally never gambled at all, people who hardly knew one end of a horse from the other. The Derby was like Wimbledon and the Boat Race – an institution. In spite of his painstaking efforts and meticulous planning, and even in spite of Harry, Jake knew this could well be the one and only opportunity of a lifetime. If I win, he thought to himself, I must get that South African artist to do his portrait. Jake's mind made a connection and he frowned and turned to Sam Armstrong.

'Sam, have you got the race-card with you?' The trainer fished in his jacket pocket and dragged out the card.

'There you go, Squire.' Jake paged through the card and then ran his finger down the list of runners for the Guineas, stopping at Don Quixote. The owner's name – M. Lidman.

'Tell me, Sam, did you see Quixote's connections in the parade ring?'

'Sure,' beamed the trainer expansively, 'Just old Cy Francis and a slip of a girl – good looking, but couldn't have been more than twenty or so. No one else.'

'Do you know the owner by any chance? She can't be it can she, the owner, I mean?'

'Couldn't tell you, Squire, owners never mean too much to me – not unless they bring horses to my yard that is.' He laughed. Jake's mind searched the coincidence for meaning and found none, but being thorough, worried at it a little longer before shrugging it aside for the time being. He'd make some inquiries. Not the sort of inquiries Harry could have helped with – but then Harry wasn't around to help with inquiries of any sort anymore, thought Jake with some grim satisfaction. He didn't like having loose ends of any sort lying around and for the time being at least, Harry's had been well and truly tied.

His eyes slipped to one side seeing that Jane's chair was empty and that John Cunningham's eyes were drawn deep into Bubbles cleavage as she leant forward to laugh at something he'd said. That little plan, that little strategy, was also coming along very nicely. The girl was playing the part superbly, and soon he'd have all the leverage he wanted – all the leverage that he needed to get rid of the man. Sixty years old now – albeit a good sixty, he had to admit – but a juicy and very public scandal heaped on top of the sum of his years. That should be enough, Jake thought, enough to topple him, persuade him to go. Just right for a Justice of the Peace – a degrading ignominy: he just wanted to make very sure of gathering all the sordid evidence.

All it would need would be a judicious tip dropped in the right quarter and the gluttonous English Fourth Estate would do the rest. Their appetite for the disclosure of what was delightfully called 'moral turpitude' in public figures was formidable. Then his lifeline – a generous offer to buy Cunningham out – to let him go and bury his shame somewhere. Jake had virtually everything in place.

49

Cy Francis had no expectations whatsoever of Carlo winning the Guineas.

'Christy says he's not got the spark back in him yet, Miss Alice,' he explained to her on the phone in the weeks preceding the race. Cy usually asked for and directed his conversations to Alice rather than Matt, mainly because she was the one who understood them – and his comments – best, in the practical sense anyway. Alice had agreed to come down to Royston to see him work.

'He's come on well enough,' Cy commented to her as they stood together in his yard, 'but he stayed lame on that leg for a mite longer than the vet expected. Mr. Carter says the bullet might have got close to the nerve, or hit a blood vessel and given him a haemorrhage we couldn't see from the outside.' Flat cap in hand, Cy ran his fingers through his pale thin hair. 'Christy knows that horse like the back of his hand, Miss Alice, and if he says he's not quite right yet, then I believe him. But I've got this jockey from his Newmarket win here this morning, so we can see what he says after the gallop.'

So they watched Carlo at work, Alice taking delight in watching the brute strength of the horse as he gathered and stretched so very effortlessly, coming rapidly towards them between two flanking stable mates. The pounding of the hooves had grown stronger and stronger, quickly building into an electrifying crescendo, and then the trio flashed past and she was left with the vision of flapping exercise blankets, jockeys, turf and hooves disappearing into the distance. Standing behind her, Matt absorbed the spectacle with his uniquely skilled eyes, capturing and recorded its essence.

'Well, Brian?'

Cy looked up at the jockey as he circled the trio on the blowing horse. The diminutive jockey gave a brief shake of his head as he reached down and loosened the surcingle a notch.

'Better than last time, Mr. Francis, but he's short of a gear still.' Cy nodded in acceptance, turned and took Alice and Matt back to his office.

Over tea and around the old desk he sat and explained his stratagem, first going over the horse's progress since the incident, convincing them that they'd tried everything – left no stone unturned. What it had meant waiting for the drain to stop seeping, the twice daily flushing of the deep hole the bullet had left, the walking exercise, the Faradism sessions with the physiotherapist, Christy's kneading massage; all eloquent measure of everyone's infinite painstaking care and concern.

Cy could see the disappointment mirrored in their faces, but he wasn't finished yet – the important bit was still to come.

'If you agree, I still want to keep him in the Guineas – to have a run, but I'll be giving Brian instruction to take it easy. Not to pull him you understand, the Stewards will have us for that, but just not to light that afterburner he's got lurking inside him somewhere.' Cy had poured himself his habitual second cup, sugared it and commenced stirring slowly and thoughtfully.

'At this level, ninety-five percent, or even ninety-nine percent fit just isn't enough, Miss Alice. He won't beat that Peppermint from Armstrong's yard. That colt is a shoe-in favourite for both the Guineas and the Derby – and with good reason too. He's got all the credentials: the breeding, the form, he's honest and just to make assurance doubly sure, Armstrong has pinched Stinky Yates from Bailey's yard for the ride.

'Stinky Yates!' Alice gave the trainer a disbelieving look.

Cy shook his head begrudgingly. 'Nobody calls him that to his face these days, but he got the nickname as an apprentice years and years go. Stinky's personal hygiene isn't good, Miss Alice. He's only ever had a passing acquaintanceship with a cake of soap all his life. But he's a cruel little bastard is Yates, and if anyone can squeeze or thrash an extra yard out of a horse, he can, of that there's no doubt.' Cy plonked his cup in its saucer with a rattle and lent forward to engage their eyes and drive home his point. 'We won't win this race then because our horse isn't a hundred percent. I know that much as a certainty, but what we can do is get them to drop their guard. If we give Carlo an average run in the Guineas, and they discount him, then perhaps – just perhaps – we can steal a march on Derby day when I know Carlo will be ready. Your horse,' Cy ducked his head at Matt, 'is a speed merchant. Built for it and bred for it, and on paper he shouldn't stand a chance against Peppermint over a mile-and-a-half. But if we can hoodwink the field into running the first uphill section slowly, keep him handy down the hill to Tattenham Corner and then set him alight before the others realise what's happening, then perhaps we can do the impossible.' Cy gave them a wry smile. 'It's going to depend on a whole lot of "ifs", but Armstrong's only got the one entry so he can't put in a frontrunner to set the pace, and as for the others, well, we don't know what they're going to do, do we? It's all going to be a bit in the lap of the Gods. Are you game?'

They were, and then Alice told Cy about Matt's connection with Peppermint's owner.

'Well, that beats cockfighting!' exclaimed Cy, 'and you say he doesn't know anything about it yet?' Matt nodded. Cy paused before going on, 'well, we must keep it that way then, I don't want any attention on Carlo at all. The less everyone and anyone thinks about him, the happier I'll be, and the better our chances.

You two must keep away from the press, you especially, young Mr. Lidman, and definitely no pictures, no photographs in the press. Be as close to invisible as you can, young sir.'

There were some Press inquiries before the Guineas but Alice had deflected these with bland replies that Mr. Lidman was 'out of the country'. The one that came after the Guineas had been run was singular and to the point.

'Tell me young lady,' the flat voice had asked, 'is Don Quixote's owner the young equestrian artist Mr. Lidman, by any chance?'

Alice had her answer prepared, 'No, no, Mr. Lidman is a businessman, and abroad at present, and who can I say called?' The caller disconnected. She wondered if it had been him. The voice may have been South African, but not typically so. It was overlaid with something artificial – almost synthetic, a nothing accent. But Matt was convinced.

'That's him all right – he always does that, just puts down the phone when he's finished. Typical of him.' It transpired later that Cy had fielded the same inquiry on the same day, but the stock answer he'd given had been the same as Alice's.

Over the next two months Alice and Matt scoured the racing press assiduously, seeing little or no mention of Carlo when Derby hopes were under discussion. The French entry Provocateur began to attract some attention, and Mandalay too, excited some interest with reports that he was working impressively at home. The consensus, however, was that it had all the makings of a one horse race unless something extraordinary happened. The only thing that appeared to exercise the scribes at all was the debate as to whether Peppermint could take the St. Leger as well and with it the Triple Crown. Alice discovered to her horror that the race was going to be run slap bang in the middle of her exams, and that having successfully put off her parents and brothers from coming over for the Guineas, there was now simply no holding them back for the Derby.

Matt's parents had written too – they'd be coming to England as promised and were desperately keen not to miss the race either, so there was a great deal of organising of dates and accommodation to do. Then William and Rebecca telephoned in a state because Jackie was now insisting on coming, and he still had to get hold of a passport for his first trip out of Ireland.

'I bet he's never even been out of Tipperary, much less Ireland!' remarked Alice, 'and who the hell is going to look after the farm now?'

'That's the vet in you worrying about all the animals, I dare say,' said Matt as he stood back from a little frowning at the canvas. It was May and he was nearing completion of the fifth and last of his paintings of Ireland. He wanted them finished mainly for Gideon, whose opinion he respected. There was more landscape in these than others he'd done previously and he'd struggled endlessly to get the velvet feel of that air and colour onto canvas. It had taken a great deal of trial and error, but complete, they weren't like any other hunting paintings he'd seen and in both style and content, he was content.

'What do you think?'

Alice got up from the old settee and walked across the studio to the easel. She saw the ragged figure of Charlie Parker pointing deep down into the vale below him. The gaunt face carried the intensity of the man whilst the other hand gripped the spade with all the vigour of a Moses clasping his staff. The two Jack Russells peered intently out of the shoulder bag – ears cocked, eyes following the sighting finger.

'I think it's great, Matt, but I think you should leave Charlie Parker now and take me to bed. With all that's going to happen in the next couple of weeks and all these people arriving soon, I need you to myself for a while – I really do.'

Alice lay on her side in naked contentment – eyes half shut and a moony, beatific smile creasing her mouth. This was almost the best bit – they'd made long, greedy and intensely passionate love and in the afterglow, Matt was now kneading her back and shoulders, massaging slowly and deeply into the muscle. She daren't think too long about where he'd gained his expertise, but it didn't matter too much anyway – it was hers now: what was it they said? Women didn't necessarily want to be their man's first love, but they sure as hell wanted to be their last. His hands stopped and then she felt the tips of his fingers trailing down her back, rising over the two perfect globes, down the hamstrings to her calves where the soft kneading continued. She shivered, gooseflesh everywhere. Her mind drifted lazily about, thinking about Matt – her lover, she liked that word. She'd opened up to him like a parched desert flower at the first drop of rain – she knew that, and knew also that it was pure instinct that had led her on and on. What they had done together couldn't have happened without complete mutual trust – he'd lapped and entered at her every secret place and opened the envelope of her mind to an extent that beggared fantasy.

Trust and desire – lust was probably the better word, but it wasn't one she liked. Lust always seemed to her to be a dirty thing that men had for unsuspecting women in novels. This was a mutual passion. She liked that word too. Passion, trust and desire: that was okay. The bed complained beneath her as he moved up and curled himself into the sickle shape of her back with a sleepy sigh. Alice's mouth flattened and then pursed into a hint of mischief. She waited a few minutes until he was half asleep and then reached behind to scratch him gently with her fingertips – there where the line of golden curls led down from his navel, waiting in benign anticipation for him to stir. First she felt the faint heat of his breath in her neck and unable to wait any longer, went lower with her hand to grasp him – sweet affirmation of her power.

'What do they call it in Africa … what do the Africans call it?'

'Call what?'

'You know … doing this – sleeping together, making love.'

'Jig-jig.'

'Jig-jig!' Alice screeched with delight.

'Christ! … Careful!'

She turned to face him.

'Oh, come on Matt, give me jig-jig. Please give me jig-jig, Matt!'

50

'Can you describe the man, Mrs. Kerrigan?'

'Well I suppose I can, Constable,' answered the heavy, matronly figure standing in front of the policeman, beefy arms akimbo, floral housecoat straining at the seams and rollered hair tied up in a riotous scarf.

'Scrawny little fellow, very ordinary type, smoked all the time, London ... well Cockney accent really. Out of here about five a.m. every morning in his little post-office van – you know, one of them old ones. I know 'cause that's when I'm up to let my cats out. He was always back at about seven-thirty for his breakfast mind you – never missed that – and then he spent most of his time in his room watching TV. Lots of racing in the afternoons – I could hear it from the front parlour.'

Constable Vespers laboriously wrote all the information down in his notebook whilst Mrs. Kerrigan waited impatiently, her expression clearly saying that she had better things to do with her time. 'What's he done then Constable, poaching? Bank robbery?' Her voice rose in ill-concealed sarcasm. 'Can't think a little fella like that could manage anything very criminal.'

The Constable raised a pair of lugubrious eyes from his note pad.

'Madam, we're making inquiries in connection with the shooting of a horse in Royston in January. You may have read about it in the local papers.'

Mrs. Kerrigan instantly dropped her attitude like a clanger and was all outraged concern. 'I did read about it, poor thing. You can't think that that man had anything to do with it, can you? Well, I mean he looked like a racing man, someone who cares about horses, he wouldn't have shot one would he?'

Constable Vespers thought briefly how astonishingly naïve the public were. This was the first decent lead the station had stumbled on in months of inquiries at hotels, boarding houses and bed and breakfasts, but he doubted he'd get a name worth anything and the payment of the room had been made in cash of course. Anyway, it was a start and the post-office van was interesting. Quite distinctive that, and surprising – considering that the fellow had gone out of his way to board ten miles away. His friend Cy Francis had better hear about the van – the Constable knew Cy well from congenial pints taken together in the Lone Star over the years, and knew the trainer was convinced the man responsible for the shooting came from Newmarket. Two not very exciting clues when taken individually: somebody who lives in Newmarket, and a post-office van. But put together – somebody who lives in Newmarket and drives a post-office van – then you had something, and with the good description and the accent – well, well, well – Constable Vespers thought as he snapped his notebook shut, we might just be onto something at last.

The station Sergeant listened to Constable Vespers whilst scratching his beard in thoughtful consideration. 'You really believe all this stuff about trajectory and angle and so forth, Constable?'

'Well, yes Sarge, it's possible. I've been up onto the heath and to the copse where the shot probably came from – and the distance is only thirty feet or so to where the horse was.'

'Real bunch of armchair detectives aren't they, Vespers? Reading too much Dick Francis. Very well, what do you propose we do next – inform the station at Newmarket, I suppose?'

The grey-haired Constable shook his head regretfully at his younger superior. 'Sarge, if we tell Newmarket and they start sniffing around, the stable lads will clam up tighter than my old man's wallet. They loath coppers and they look after their own.'

'Even if one of their own shot one of their precious horses?'

'That'll just spook him if he's there – the word will get round and the villain will scarper right sharpish.'

'So?'

Constable Vespers took off his helmet and wiped his brow with a large handkerchief. He smiled apologetically at his Sergeant. 'Sarge, I know it's a bit unorthodox, but what say we go with Cy Francis' suggestion?'

'And what's that?'

'He sends one of his lads up to Newmarket for a week to see what he can find out in the pubs. They reckon there's a connection with specific yards up there 'cause of the betting angle, and if he finds anything, then we inform Newmarket. It's a long-shot anyway, but this happened on our patch, Sarge, so if it comes off, we could stitch up the collar nice and tight.'

Christy was back in Royston five days later.

'It's a fella called Harry Jarvis, Governor, post-office van an' all. Trouble is he's disappeared – gorn. No one's seen him for weeks and weeks. Van's got a puncture and 'is landlady's crying blue murder for the rent.'

Newmarket police station was informed and the long arm of the law swung into action. The van registration number and licence yielded a Kentford address and it wasn't long before a police car was gliding out of Newmarket, eastwards, past the gallops, then right at the fork onto the Bury road, past Lanwades Hall on the right and on towards the village. The miniscule flint two-up two-down house was fronted by a long, thin path and a flanking garden, rank with bramble and morning glory, nettles and grasses, all untamed and unloved and now running to seed. The blue front door with chips in the paint around the handle and Yale lock remained indifferent to the repeated knocking and calls from the two by now impatient policemen.

'We'd best try the pub, it doesn't look as if he spends much time here anyway.'

The landlord at the Chequers was more forthcoming. 'Harry's never here during the week anymore. Tells me he's got some sort of job in town. Come to think of it, he hasn't been in for quite a while now – not that it should worry me too much, the old bugger doesn't run a slate anymore, not like he used to. Quite flush, our Harry, these days.'

'So he's making good money, then?'

'I should say so. Drinking best bitter, pints instead of halves and smoking bloody Senior Service of all things! Always Woodbines before – hung on his lip like a leech.'

'When did all of this start?'

The landlord stopped polishing the glass and looked up towards the ceiling, searching his memory. 'About a year ago, I think, when he met that fella here.'

'What fella was that then?' The two policemen leant forward like a brace of greyhounds given first sight of a hare.

'Gotta be a city gent, I mean – dressed like that, dark pin-striped suit, candy striped shirt, white collar and tie – the car too, lovely new Jag – as shiny as he was.' The notebooks came out. 'I mean, you don't see many people like that round our neck of the woods. And that's when Harry came up and ordered himself a pint of best, and the Senior Service, and paid me with a brand new ten-pound note. Pleased with himself, pleased as punch – that's why I remember it so well. You could have knocked me down with a feather.'

'Do you reckon you could give us a description of the man – what he looked like? Would you be able to recognise him if you saw him again?'

The landlord pulled himself up as if he'd been affronted. 'Course I can, I always remember people, that's why I'm in this game, and anyway you don't see too many evil looking black haired devils like him in a lifetime. Fair gave me the creeps, those black eyes and the widow's peak.' The flabby shoulders convulsed once involuntarily.

There were two thuds and then on the third try the blue door burst open to the weight of the policeman's shoulder. It was a sorry place, Harry's place, the sort of place you might expect of a solitary old man who had suddenly come good. Filthy throughout – filthy bedding, filthy kitchen, filthy floor, un-swept, un-dusted – cheap, old threadbare furniture, but a brand new, expensive TV, racing literature and a half empty case of Johnnie Walker black label whisky.

'Just the essentials, eh Sarge?'

The Sergeant shook his head. 'Come on, Constable Ingrams, time to move your thin arse, we're evidently looking for a rifle – one for shooting rooks.'

51

They never found any rifle.

'You got it all then, Harry?' was Jake's first question as Harry climbed into the passenger seat of his Mark X with his long parcel. Jake had instructed him to be outside the entrance to Lanwades Hall that afternoon at exactly two in the afternoon.

'It's ore here, Guv'ner.' Harry patted the package.

'And the ammunition?'

'Everyfink Guv'ner, everyfink!'

By early evening Harry was in Brighton with Jake showing him around his new place, a small apartment on the third floor of an anonymous block overlooking the foreshore. Jake opened the doors onto the small balcony and turned to Harry, a thin smile in place.

'Think you could be happy here, Harry?'

Harry's eyes were on the big TV.

'Looks right enuf, Guv'ner. You got 'orses racing down here?'

'Possibly,' Jake replied, ' but your main job at the moment is to keep your head down. Think of it as a holiday, Harry. And no phone calls or postcards to your mates, you hear?'

He fished inside his jacket pocket for the cash envelope.

'This is to tide you over until the end of the month.'

Harry took the envelope. 'You gonna be looking after that rook rifle of mine then, Guv'ner?'

'Yes, Harry,' Jack smiled carefully, 'I'll be looking after the rifle.'

Back In London, Jake parked the Jaguar off Grosvenor Road. Taking the long parcel from the boot he walked towards the river and then out along Vauxhall Bridge. About halfway across the bridge he stopped and, when there was a lull in the early hour traffic, dropped the packaged rook gun and ammunition into the black Thames below.

He'd thought about leaving the gun at the Brighton flat but something told him not to. Perhaps it was the thought that the less that could be proved, if ever Harry was found that is, the more tenuous the link between himself and Harry's work as assassin. Jake just knew he would rest easier with the dissimulation as complete as he could make it, reckoning that if the police were even half competent they'd probably either suspect Harry of the shooting or arrest him for it eventually. But with the rifle, ammunition and Harry out of the way, well, they'd just have to be content with their suspicions for the time being, wouldn't they? That's really why Jake wanted him parked out of the way. He'd move the old man every couple of months: nothing could be simpler, and he was quite sure everyone would forget about the whole business in a year or two anyway. All the loose ends were tied-up, and Jake's organised ice-cold brain was content to put the matter to bed. Once he was back in his Knightsbridge flat, he poured himself a whisky from the decanter, put on a Nat King Cole record and then glanced at his watch as he sat. Fifteen minutes to relax, and he reckoned he'd still be able to get in four hours sleep before leaving for the office.

It would be another three and a half weeks before the police broke into Harry's front parlour and by that time Harry's trail was as cold as his old rook rifle lying in the muddy depths of the Thames.

None of Harry's neighbours remembered him owning a rifle, but as Constable Ingrams wearily explained to his Sergeant, 'he was a loner, Sarge, kept himself strictly to himself and never had anyone into the house – not surprising really, considering the state of it.'

'Nothing at his digs in town, I suppose?'

'A complete blank there – no diary, no notes – nothing.'
'Married ever? A wife perhaps?'
'Died five years ago. That was from the neighbour in Kentford.'
'Children?'
'One, a son who one neighbour remembers as coming up for Christmas every year until the old lady died, but never since. A taxi driver evidently, 'cause she remembered him coming up in his own cab.'
'Well, check registered owners of taxis – start in Newmarket and then try London, the old man is a Cockney after all – and see if you come up with a Jarvis.'

Ingrams' inquiries were fruitful.
'Bingo, Sarge! The son still drives a cab and he lives in Clapham.'
'Good. See if he remembers his old man having a firearm, but don't let on what type. See if he gives it to you.'
The son spoke to Ingrams over the phone in the same abrasive, fractured manner as his father might have.
'Wot's it orl abaat. Me farver gone missing 'azee – an' fir 'ow long? ... a cupla munfs? Carn staan de oal geezer most ova tarm. Proppa mean iffe puts 'is marnd to it ... Wots zat – a gun? – naah, neffa 'ad no gun, me Dad – just an oal rook rifle inna pantry.'
Even with the rifle now missing – a fact which gave Sergeant Evans and Constable Ingrams much occasion for conjection, the tie in with the shooting of the horse was firmly established and they now took the process one step further and started to look for the mystery 'businessman', the one the landlord at the Chequers had remembered so well, the one whose appearance had signalled Harry's change in fortune.
'You know, I wouldn't be surprised if we were dealing with a case that ends up with a high Press profile, Constable,' said

Evans. 'It's all so very juicy: sudden money in the picture, then this Jarvis moves into Newmarket and starts gambling – rumoured to anyway, and we know near as dammit he shot this horse. Now, why and how does this Mr. X fit into the picture? We'd better speak to the bookies in town and find out where Jarvis betted and how much he betted. You go down and ask our publican from Kentford to come in and do an identikit for us and we can show a picture of Mr. X to the bookies at the same time. Getting very interesting this case, Constable, very interesting indeed. Time I had a word with Detective Chief Inspector Willcox I think.'

There wasn't much to be gleaned from the bookies. Harry's betting was pretty lightweight – with just a single, glaring exception: a wager of a thousand pounds on Peppermint to win the Derby. And none of them recognised the picture of Mr. X.

'Well, there's your motive, Sarge,' said Ingrams. 'This horse he shot was reckoned to be a hotshot candidate for the big races. Jarvis was probably scared of him upsetting his big plunge.'

'Wasn't necessarily his money he was betting with, Constable, and why shoot the horse months and months before his bet on the Derby? That's only run in June – the horse was only lightly wounded, and purposely so our Royston colleagues say, in January sometime. No we're missing something here. I still want to find out about Mr. X. Why was he paying Jarvis to bet tiddly little amounts? It doesn't make sense – none at all. There's something we're not seeing here. Tell you what; take that picture around to the trainers and the lads. Cast your net a bit wider Constable, cast it wider.'

The interview took place in Jake's office at Brathrows.

Introducing himself, Detective Chief Inspector James Willcox reached over the desk to shake Jake's hand and nodded briefly before lowering his large frame into the proffered chair. The

Inspector's pallid, rather bovine face didn't fool Jake at all. It was all in the eyes. Two round, pale, unblinking orbs.

'Inspector, how can we help you?' Jake offered.

The Inspector's face came to life as he posed gentle inquiry. 'Tell me Sir, would you know one Harry Jarvis by any chance?'

Jake smiled comfortably at the solemn face. 'Of course I know Harry, Chief Inspector. I've employed him for some time now, up in Newmarket.'

'In what capacity, Sir?'

'Well, to keep some sort of weather eye on my racing stock up there, Inspector – in an unofficial capacity you understand ... I have a lot of money invested. But why the interest in poor Harry, what's he done, the silly old bugger?' Jake sounded amused.

'Well, we're making inquiries into the shooting of a horse in Royston back in January of this year, Sir, and we're anxious to interview Mr. Jarvis in connection with this incident.'

I bet you are, thought Jake. The Inspector made a sudden shift forward in his chair as if he was uncomfortable.

'The trouble is, Mr. Stevens, we don't seem to be able to find Mr. Jarvis ... he seems to have disappeared – disappeared for some time now. You wouldn't know where he is by any chance?'

'No, and why should I, Chief Inspector? Harry used to phone me now and again to report on my horses, but he hasn't done so in fact for, as you say, some time now. But if there was nothing to report he wouldn't phone for long periods quite frequently. I wasn't worried about it – quite the contrary, I took it to mean all was running smoothly – if you'll excuse the pun.'

'Hmm.' The police officer met Jake's steady gaze with one of his own momentarily. He appeared to make up his mind about something.

'You bet on your horses do you Sir?'

Jake leant back in his chair making a move to go with a lopsided shrug.

'A little, Inspector, a little, occasionally, for amusement.'

'You'll not mind me asking Sir, how little is little?'

Jake looked over the Inspector's head, searching his memory lazily. 'Well, it's only ever for big races, Inspector, and I suppose a thousand is about tops for me. As I say, it's only for amusement.'

'That's a little for you, Sir?'

Jake smiled half apologetically. 'I'm afraid it is, Inspector.'

The police officer rose from his chair.

'Sir, would you be able to give me your bookmaker's name and particulars? It's just for routine purposes. There's no offence intended.'

'And none taken, Chief Inspector. Let me see you out – my secretary will furnish you with all the details.'

Well, that will be the end of that, thought Jake as he closed his office door. He knew all about Harry's savings going on the Derby and he was sure the police would too. An excellent motive for the shooting, and one that meant that suspicion was pointed fair and square at the old cockroach. Not that they'd find him in Brighton. And even if they did ... his word against Harry's?

No contest!

'What did you make of our Mr. Stevens, Chief Inspector?'

'Cast iron bollocks if he's criminally involved Sergeant, that much I can tell you. But the man owns the Derby favourite, his secretary told me – oh so very proudly on the way out when I was getting his bookies' details. Horse by the name of Peppermint evidently. One thing is for certain, if our Mr. Stevens' horse wins the Derby, Sergeant, and our Mr. Jarvis fails to collect his winnings, then it's a guinea to a green apple that he's been topped or put out of the way.'

The Inspector started searching in his pockets for something.

'And if that happens, then we put a fine-tooth comb over both Mr. Stevens and the bookmaker who took the bet. I hardly think any bookie is going to go bankrupt over one bet for a thousand quid, so my money is going to be on Stevens – you see it was his horse that beat the Royston horse – what's his name – Don Quixote for the Two Thousand Guineas no less, pretty soon after the shooting too. Stevens is a multi-millionaire evidently, so if he's got all that money, what does he want most ... I'll tell you – prestige, bloody prestige.'

'So you think Stevens put Jarvis up to nobbling his main rival and then shut him up for good afterwards?'

'Exactly, but we don't have any body, do we? For all we know, Mr. Harry bloody Jarvis could be on a beach in Cornwall, but if Stevens' horse wins and if Jarvis doesn't collect, like I say, it's serious.'

'When's the Derby being run?'

Willcox found what he'd been looking for. Extracting a tube of Triple X mints from his trouser pocket, he made offer to his Sergeant, took one for himself, and slid it into the corner of his mouth.

'We can all have our own type of peppermint, can't we, Sergeant?'

The Inspector hooked thumbs into an expansive waistband sucking energetically on his mint.

The Derby? On the seventh of June. Feel like a day at the races?'

52

Matt and Alice's pre-Derby party was still going hammer and tongs at midnight. It had been Matt's idea weeks before when he'd complained to her at length.

'Everyone's so damn, damn, depressingly serious about it, Liss.'

He had made a mournful face and intoned 'The Derby' at Alice in a deep gravelly monotone, and went on in the faintest of mocking tones 'at the end of the day it's just another race after all.'

'Just another race! Matt, that's sacrilege and you know it!'

Matt had laughed delightedly at Alice's outrage.

'It's just that you're another one of these excessively horsy people, Liss, and it's some type of Holy Grail to you all. Most people in the world either haven't ever heard of it, or if they have – couldn't give a monkey's about it.' He had been dodging volleys of cushions by this stage, although Alice's efforts were half-hearted. She had recognised the grain of truth in Matt's comments and so, together, they had decided to celebrate Carlo's run before the event rather than wait for a probably depressing wake afterwards.

The venue was a small country hotel just out of Epsom, which their entourage had taken over completely. The entire Irish contingent: William and Rebecca, Noel and Tom, old Jackie, with his teeth in, thank goodness, Ashleigh down from Stock, and Paul and Sue who'd collected Gideon and Hope from the airport in the big old Citroën.

Called The Hive, (evidently because there was guaranteed to always be at least one queen in residence) the converted, rambling half-timbered home reminded Matt a lot of Alice's Irish home with the same easy character – here exquisitely augmented by the unquestionably creative flair of the flamboyant gay diva who owned and ran the place. Every brass-bound chest, every rococo candelabra, every mahogany table was polished to gleaming brilliance and all lay enveloped in a sea of deep and rich cloth and carpet. The delightful, overwhelming effect was of a unique and all-encompassing luxury – a perception only heightened by the extraordinary use of unlikely colour combinations of mustard, purple, dark blues and greens.

Keith had welcomed them all individually as the cars arrived piecemeal through the afternoon. With the pony tail hair, black satin knee breeches, flowing white shirt, hose and silver buckled pumps, the outlandish proprietor looked like everyone's idea of a Porthos or a D'Artagnan and Jackie's uppers almost dropped out as he saw yet another incarnation of the English devil.

'Gart Almoighty!' he had whispered to William 'And what sort of ting is dat?'

Before William could answer, Keith had taken two steps to grab Jackie's limp and unprotesting hand and pump it enthusiastically.

'My dear fellow,' he'd boomed avuncularly, 'welcome to my home – I do hope your stay is quite blissful.' Taking Jackie's elbow he'd gentled the terrified old man towards the front door with a smirking Irish family following obediently in their wake.

Some of Jackie's indignation and fears were allayed by copious administration of Jamieson's Irish whiskey at the downstairs bar. At six o'clock the Irish group that Alice had scouted and hired arrived and started setting up. With the music in prospect and his stomach starting to grumble, Jackie was content, at last, to be led upstairs to his room for a wash and change for dinner.

Keith had designed and arranged a superlative 'Derby Dinner' at his leaved, twelve seater Georgian dining table. He had taken infinite care, using Matt's racing colours of green and gold quarters (something of both South Africa and Ireland) as the theme – from the central flower-arrangement to the table linen, and even the food itself. Golden pheasant soup with a hint of Chartreuse, asparagus layered over with a thick Béarnaise sauce, hand-written folded menu cards tied with tiny, bright ribbons and a sketch of Carlo's head as frontispiece. The inherent Irish talent for enjoying themselves meant they took over proceedings entirely, and as they did it so artlessly, it was painless, and much to everyone else's delight. William made toast after toast, and it was ten o'clock before they left the table and the lilting cadences of the fiddle started toes tapping. After two insistent calls for encores and one passing of the hat, the band stopped playing at about twelve-thirty and started to pack up. Gideon brought a nightcap over to Hope from the bar, and as she smiled up at him in thanks, the goose walked over her grave. She shuddered as the chill of it caught her shoulders and she looked behind her fearfully – quickly. There were only the lights of a passing car that briefly illuminated the curtained window in the corner.

'Hope?' Gideon looked down at her in concern.

'No, no it was nothing, nothing.'

It was Jake's Jaguar sweeping past, the lights briefly illuminating the white walls jigsawed into the black timbers of The Hive. He saw the artistically scripted sign offering 'Superior Accommodation' and wondered how much longer before he'd be at his hotel. The business meeting for the Brathrow's partners scheduled after work had gone on much longer than he'd anticipated, but now all his thoughts were on the morrow, on the race. Everything he'd worked for in the last year and a half hinged on Peppermint's performance, and his trainer, Armstrong, was supremely confident. Jake had been assured that the colt was right on top of his game, and nothing had happened in the intervening weeks to make him change his mind one whit.

Detective Chief Inspector Willcox and Sergeant Evans were fast asleep in a small, inexpensive hotel four miles away. The Sergeant had asked Willcox what exactly was the point of the foray into the world of racing, of going to the Derby. Willcox had tapped the side of his nose, 'know thine enemy, Evans, know thine enemy – and known associates, I want to see just who's there. He knows my face already, you see, so you've got to be the ferret with your telephoto lens. I'm only here to point you in the right direction.'

He'd smiled, 'and to have a little flutter of course. All in the line of duty, you understand, Sergeant, all in the line of duty.'

At two o'clock in the morning the parched ground of that sovereign one-and-a-half miles of grass received the first drops of rain, the moisture drawn instantly into the Epsom turf, soothing as an unguent on a blistered brow.

53

'They're off aaand racing.' As the loudspeaker laconically announced the start, Alice gave Matt's hand a quick squeeze and took up her binoculars. Carlo bounced out of his stall and his jockey, Brian Hoy, gave him his head. He was drawn on the inside, a perfect position, and the horse's phenomenal acceleration gave him the lead up the hill. The remainder of the field tucked in behind and then slowed fractionally, just barely, bit by bit, as Brian imperceptibly drew Carlo in. It was something he'd practiced and become skilled at under Cy Francis' eye at home. The horse, too, had become accustomed to the manoeuvre, slowly getting to know that he would be asked for something else later. As they came down the hill to Tattenham Corner, Carlo led Mandalay from Peppermint followed by Provocateur. The French horse was last of the leading four with the others in a group of three just a length adrift. As they rounded the Tattenham corner Carlo held his line beautifully, but Mandalay, under some urging, started to drift a little wide. The gap that opened between the two horses in front of him gave Yates the glimpse he had been waiting for. He dived Peppermint into it. Mandalay's jockey had meanwhile switched his whip to his right hand trying to straighten his horse. The answer from Mandalay was to float back towards the rails, but Peppermint's speed had already brought him level with Carlo and then fractionally in front. Yates saw the danger from Mandalay's erratic line but knew that his momentum would in a second put him clear of the inside front runner, Carlo, giving him the space to race between the rails and Mandalay – he'd be through and away.

As Peppermint's black form came upsides, Carlo's flaring nostrils were drawing in great draughts of air, and with it came

Yates' stench, the acrid, sour odour of the jockey's unwashed body. It was so indelibly associated with the raking spurs and whip that had bloodied and scoured him when he was in Bailey's Newmarket yard that rage possessed Carlo's mind completely, and as his head dropped on the next stride, the horse bit to his right – savagely. The immense power of it reflected the welts, the bruising, the blood – but most of all the sharp shocks of pain, repeated time and time again. Stinky Yates shrieked in pain as the six upper incisors sheared through the paper-thin leather of his left boot, through the skin and onto the bones of the foot, crushing them against the sole of the boot. His spine stiffened and then he was falling to the left as the tug and the pain unbalanced him completely. As he fell, Carlo's stifle clipped his head under the helmet, tumbling him half-conscious into the path of the oncoming bunch. All Brian felt on Carlo was the knock as Yates' head contacted Carlo somewhere behind him. At the moment that Carlo bit, his jockey had shifted his eyes to glance quickly over the rails, looking for extra room in case the camber of the course and the drifting horses called for it. Peppermint bled backwards instantly, disappearing from view and Brian now only had Mandalay in front and, unbeknownst to him, Provocateur, who had unleashed a punishing run on the outside and was going like a steam train. The extraordinary course of events and the cruel revenge that Carlo had exacted galvanised the horse. All the suffering, even that inflicted by the bullet and the ensuing surgery, was atoned for and his fuse was well and truly lit.

'Christ, look at him go!' Cy's binoculars thudded against his thin chest. They all saw Brian's characteristic crouch deepen as the jockey sat, clasped his legs and drove forward. Carlo bunched once and then flew, devouring the ground, lengthening and lowering simultaneously. Mandalay was beat and floundering and Carlo was past. Provocateur's run had built up an enormous momentum and the French jockey, scenting victory, was flailing his horse furiously. Carlo clawed him in, stride on stride, still – unbelievably – accelerating even more and driving up level. Provocateur was game for the match and found another notch, lunging almost – Carlo responded and the two horses flew over the line as one. 'Photo, photo!' Cy gasped, elbowing people aside and taking Alice and Matt in his wake.

They had seen Jake in the parade ring before the race but the man was intent on his own affairs, on his own horse, and chatting to his trainer and jockey and exchanging confident banter. Matt did see him take in Carlo's form as he strode past, but it was casual. He obviously didn't expect much from that quarter. The unknown – form-wise, the French horse, had come in for the most interest and inspection. Now, Jake was nowhere to be seen and Matt, Alice and Cy were waiting for their horse to come in. Gideon, Hope and all of Alice's mad Irish clan were hung on the rails behind them chattering back and forth in high, excited voices. Provocateur was the first to come in to a loud cheer from his vociferous French supporters and his jockey turned him into first place and dismounted. Carlo came in next to an enormous cheer and clapping – he was by no means the betting public's favourite but had carried a considerable amount of sentimental money, and the performance on the track that afternoon had earned huge admiration from everyone – with one exception. Jake's eyes lit on his son shaking a beaming Brian Hoy's hand – not understanding anything. He strode up to Matt angrily and pushed the jockey aside.

'What the hell is this? What are you doing here?'

'Waiting to see if my horse has won, that's what.' Matt's even gaze held Jake's seething black stare quite steady.

'YOUR HORSE? What do you mean YOUR horse? This horse

belongs to ...' Jake fished in his scattered brain.

'L i d m a n.' Matt leant towards Jake and enunciated the name precisely. Jake's eyes flickered – signalling his confusion. Matt turned slightly and stretched out his hand towards Gideon and Hope behind them.

'You've met my parents, I think.'

There was a great roar from the crowd and Cy shouted at Matt: 'Dead heat! I can't believe it, it's a dead heat!'

54

Bubbles had John Cunningham's hand tucked into her lap during take-off. The noise from the Boeing's engines softened as the plane levelled off, and the ping from above as the seat belt light went off generated a click and clatter around them. She turned and smiled contentedly and lovingly at him. It had been a terrible few weeks – his wife Jane, prey to a devastating heart attack that had her lingering for five days on the cusp of the abyss, only to succumb on the Saturday – on her birthday of all days. Their marriage had been more one of minds than bodies, and after their children had been born Jane had been content to let him go in that respect. This in no way injured their regard for one another, and John had been mortified at the turn of events – he'd refused even to set foot in the house again. Suddenly he'd resigned from Brathrows and asked her to pack, 'I've got this villa in the Canaries, Bubbles, we'll have the best climate in the world – in fact we'll have the best of everything – please say yes you'll come.' Bubbles had needed no persuasion.

* * *

'Did that jockey go home today, Matron?'
'Yes, Doctor, he's due back in three weeks to have the cast off his foot.'
'And the amnesia?'
'Still doesn't remember a thing about the race, not a thing, but he was lucky to get away with his life really – being trampled like that.'
'Well, I for one hope he at least remembers to wash occasionally. What awful body odour, Matron, quite appalling!'

Matron Pilling shook her head sharply. 'Dreadful!' She wrinkled her nose at the memory. 'Reminded me of my grandchildren's ferrets, Doctor. But, believe me, even they're pure eau de Cologne next to our Mr. Yates.'

* * *

'Seen this, Sergeant?'

Detective Chief Inspector Willcox thrust The Times article in front of his Sergeant's nose and then sat down heavily opposite him, waiting impatiently whilst Evans read it through.

THE TIMES
<u>Saturday 4th June</u>

Lord George Bentinck's shade

Celebration of the dead heat for this year's Derby was good for business in the Lone Star at Royston. There is fierce loyalty here for long time trainer Cy Francis who prepared Don Quixote so brilliantly for his Epsom epic. I'll freely admit that it was the most astonishing display of strategy and raw speed that I have seen in twenty years of reporting on the turf. The shocking incident of the shooting of this brilliant horse prior to the Two Thousand Guineas saddened followers of the sport profoundly and left the Guineas a poorer race, in spite of Don Quixote's gallant fourth place.

It appears that it was only very recently that horse returned to anything like his old form, but who would have imagined that this out-and-out sprinter – because that is what his blood and physique proclaim – would be blessed with stamina as well as speed. Full marks to jockey Brian Hoy, under instruction no doubt, who contrived to hold the field back from the front – a singularly difficult task without having eyes in the back of one's head, and one requiring considerable judgement too, as to what pace is fast enough.

What happened just after Tattenham Corner has provoked considerable speculation; the hot favourite, Peppermint, inexplicably unshipping his unfortunate pilot who was then seriously mauled under the feet of the pursuing horses. One would presume that he was bumped, but Don Quixote (who goes under the stable name of Carlo at home) couldn't be seen to be doing anything but hold his line. It's true that Mandalay was drifting perilously towards the rails, but a view of what really transpired was obscured by the same horse's obstruction of any sort of decent view – even by the cameras, I'm reliably informed. With jockey Yates' amnesia about the entire race; we may never know the full story.

What we do know, what we saw unleashed, was one of the greatest sprints ever seen. The French raider Provocateur had summoned the sneakiest of fliers on the outside (who can ever trust a nation that eat frogs?) and his jockey and connections must have thought they had the race won – but if so – they reckoned without the native speed and guts of our champion. In the end it was a fair result as the Frenchman stuck to his guns manfully enough, but spare a thought for Peppermint's unfortunate owner, the luckless Jake Stevens and his trainer who must have had Lord Bentinck turning in his grave.

At the Goodwood meeting in 1846, George Bentinck sold over a hundred of his horses for a paltry ten thousand pounds to go into politics – including a horse called Surplice. Surplice won the Derby two years later and when Disraeli saw Bentinck the day after, the 25th May, in the library at the Commons he gave 'a sort of superb groan'.

'All my life I have been trying for this, and for what have I sacrificed it!'

Commiseration was pointless.

'You do not know what the Derby is,' he wailed.

'Yes, I do;' answered the Statesmen, 'it is the Blue Ribbon of the turf.'

'It is the Blue Ribbon of the turf,' Bentinck repeated slowly. Surplice went on to win the St. Leger and Bentinck died two weeks later – a 'visitation of God' was the coroner's verdict.

We would earnestly hope that no similar fate awaits Mr. Stevens in the weeks and months ahead for he too sold a Derby winner – or co-winner, none other than our celebrated Don Quixote who dashed his hopes so thoroughly. Cold comfort that the horse was performing abysmally at the time, and strength to whoever found what it took to bring him round. One suspects there may be something to be said for the smaller, old-fashioned yards where horses are treated as individuals, and certainly the landlord at the Lone Star will be looking forward to more wins from their favourite son in the near future.

John Evans
Racing Correspondent

'Well?'

'Didn't take you for a Times man, Sir, more sort of ... Daily Mirror.'

Willcox took the jibe in good humour. 'It's just for the crossword, Sergeant, just for the crossword.'

'Well, I know we're not going to collar him, Sir – not without a body, and not without that Thingammy-mint winning the Derby, and Jarvis not collecting on his bet.'

'No we're not, Sergeant, we're not.'

Willcox leant back in his chair with a satisfied smile.

'But I'll tell you this, Sergeant – reading that,' – he stabbed a finger at the paper, 'makes it quite bearable really, quite bearable.'

* * *

Jake destroyed the Newmarket paintings in his flat on the day the article came out in The Times. Cursing with rage he was energetically stuffing their remains into a black rubbish bag when the phone rang.

It was Harry.

Jake listened impatiently to the litany of woe and then broke in.

'Listen here, Harry, you're not the only one who's lost money here.'

He gripped the receiver tighter.

'And if you'd listened to me carefully, you bloody little cockroach, you'd be picking up your winnings instead of bleating on about being ill and being broke.'

Jake slammed down the receiver.

Harry heard the connection break and slowly put the receiver back in its cradle. He should have expected it, he supposed, from that bloke. But Stevens hadn't even given him the time of day, had he? And no time at all to say what they'd said about his X rays down at the hospital. He didn't give a monkey's toss, did he? His world was in tatters.Harry poured himself a drink of whisky in the kitchen and went over to sit in the sofa facing out through the balcony doors onto the sea. The bottle came with him. He'd called him an idiot, hadn't he? And now a bloody cockroach! Slowly, over the next hour, Harry drank himself into a decision … but he'd have to go shopping first.

55

Jake surfaced into consciousness at 9 a.m. A bit hazy at first; but by teatime he'd worked it out. Something must have happened at the racecourse because the last thing he could remember was walking Peppermint in after his fantastic win in the St. Leger. Five lengths - just brilliant. Then what? because here he was stuck in a hospital bed with a bandaged head and a hammer beating inside it. None of the nurses would say anything except that there had been 'an accident'.

What accident? 'No, Mr. Stevens,' they'd tut-tutted, ' you must just rest, Mr. Stevens, someone will come and speak to you about it later, Mr. Stevens ...' At least they'd given him something for the headache.

Rest be buggered, but as he was still hooked up to monitors and a drip, he supposed he couldn't do much about it ...

Well, he could think about Peppermint.

It hadn't taken too long to recover after the ignominy of the Derby. In fact, some of the racing journalists had said that Yates' fall had been a great pity and undermined the value of resulting tie, thrilling as it was. There had been a clarion of calls for him not to pull out of the St. Leger and opinions were voiced here and there that a win at Doncaster would put the horse in a category of his own – ' the best horse never to have won the Triple Crown.'

The Japanese, too, had come calling, offering an obscene amount of money for the horse. He'd met them in his office at Brathrows, three absurdly young men in identical black suits, and all wearing black-framed glasses. He'd enjoyed the refusal, wondering, as he ushered them out of the door, how on earth their forbears had managed to conquer half of the Far Side of the World without their specs.

Someone had come into the room and was pulling up a chair. D.C.I. Willcox in his very plain clothes.

'How are you feeling, Sir?'

Jake didn't feel like this.

'Not, too good, Inspector; the nurses say I need to rest.'

'I'm flattered you remember me, Sir.' Willcox patted the bed sheets sympathetically, 'and I'm sure you do need the rest, Sir, but I won't be taking too much of your time.'

'Well, perhaps you can tell me what's going on here, Inspector. I've simply no idea why I've ended up in hospital like this looking like a ... mummy. No one will give me the first clue.'

Willcox leant back in his chair and regarded Jake quizzically.

'You've no idea? You've been shot, Sir. With a .22, by your friend Mr. Jarvis ... from Newmarket.'

Jake sat bolt upright.

'Harry? HARRY? Why for heaven's sake!'

The Inspector looked apologetic. 'He claims you got him into all sorts of trouble, Sir, that you got him to shoot that horse in Royston you once owned: Don Quixote, Carlo to some. You remember him, Sir? I'm sure you do.'

'Bullshit,' replied Jake, subsiding back onto his pillows.

The Inspector seemed not to hear.

'Old Harry says you were forever calling him names, too. "Cockroach" was one of the ones that he mentioned. Quite a good one that, Sir, but now that the old boy's got – you'll excuse the racing terminology – a galloping tumour in his lungs he says he doesn't give a shit what happens to him. Says he just wants to put one over on you.'

'And you believe all this?'

The police officer shrugged his shoulders and smiled.

'The papers might, Sir. That's the worry.'

There was silence as Jake digested what had come his way.

Inspector Willcox pulled his chair a little closer to the bed. He beamed at Jake suddenly.

'Many congratulations on the win, Sir.'

'The St. Leger, well yes.'

'That horse, what a performer! You could name your own price with a horse like that couldn't you, Sir? Not to mention what he'd earn for you in stud fees if you decided to keep him. Sky would be the limit. He'd be more of your Royal Mint than your Peppermint now wouldn't he, Sir … a licence to print money you might say.'

Jake gave a weak smile.

'Pity, then.'

'A pity?'

'That your skull is so thick.'

The Inspector leant closer to Jake.

'You see, because of the angle, and your thick skull, and the fact that the bullet just winged you, well, it ended up going straight through Peppermint's left eye.'

'No!!'

'Yes, I'm afraid so, and a thousand pounds of Thoroughbred collapsing THUMP on the ground in an absolute welter of blood and thrashing around. It was a terrible thing to see, they say. Now you can see what I mean, can't you?'

'Errrh?'

Jake struggled upright in his bed again and vomited. Inspector Willcox rose from his chair, drew a large handkerchief from his jacket pocket and wiped the yellow splatter from his hands and sleeves.

'The papers, man, they've got the story and they're after your hide.'

Walking to the door, he paused before taking the handle and turned.

'All of them. To a man.'

* * *

He slipped into the back of the darkened auditorium and waited for his eyes to accommodate. There she was, halfway down on the right with an empty seat to her left.

Matt crept down the centre aisle and slipped in next to Alice as quietly as he could. He tapped his jacket pocket.

'Got them,' he whispered.

Alice gave him a thumbs up.

'Eleventh hour. Brilliant.'

Matt settled back in the seat and tried to concentrate on the commentary to the slides being flashed up on the screen. It was hard going: tables and graphs about enzymes with impossible names. And what were enzyme half-lives?

His mind drifted. There had been the most almighty fuss in the papers about Peppermint being shot up in Doncaster and it hadn't taken a genius to work out that the Press would be onto their backs pronto for more of the story. So escape – and it hadn't been difficult to decide where. A direct flight to Jo'burg and a connecting one to P.E. where Gideon could pick them up. God, he was so lucky to have got the cancellation tickets. He wondered if Piet was still about. Already he could picture them all walking out on Robberg before daybreak together, towards the Point … looking for yellowtail or leervis … or musselcracker, perhaps, at Sterksloop.

The lights came up in the auditorium with a ripple of applause. This was Colin Eastwood, Alice's Newmarket biochemist friend's keynote address at Congress and he'd insisted they come.

Colin nodded his thanks to the audience and caught Alice's eye. Alice pointed at Matt quickly and nodded. Shuffling his papers together, Colin smiled broadly at Matt, then addressed his audience.

'As biochemists, we so often stand accused of living in ivory towers; of living in another world, speaking a different language, a world of laboratories where strange coloured liquids twirl in transparent coils and bubble in test tubes.

And if people ask – and I'm sure this has happened to all of you - and you say you're a biochemist, then they put on that quizzical look and say, "but what do you do?"'

There was laughter as Colin continued.

'In the latter part of the nineteenth century, James Thomson spoke of "The gracious power of sleep's fine alchemy," and, you know, if you try and explain to people what you do – the alchemy – that's exactly what it does, it puts them straight to sleep!

But!' ... Colin pointed a dramatic finger out at his audience, 'I'm here to tell you that it isn't always the case. Sometimes, just sometimes, something marvellous happens and when it does we can all realise that what we do can be very important, vital even, and that we belong in the mainstream of life after all.'

He folded his arms and leant on the lectern comfortably, pausing.

'I want to tell you a story about Alice.'

He wagged his finger in negation. 'And no, not the one in the Looking Glass; this is another story about another Alice, a story about Alice and the horse and a man ... a man who was a Horse Painter.'

Acknowledgements

Page 90-91
The Zulu Girl
Roy Campbell Selected Works Volume 2.
© Jonathan Ball Publishers